SHE

YELLOW DRESS

Also by John R. Cammidge

Abandoned in Berlin
Unplanned

SHE WORE a YELLOW DRESS

JOHN R. CAMMIDGE

Author and Lifelong Birder

gatekeeper press
Where Authors are Family
Columbus, Ohio

This is a work of fiction, based on the experiences of the author and true events involving well-known, historical public figures, natural occurrences and government organisations. All names, characters, incidents, situations and dialogue, and some timelines, have been fictionalised and should not be construed as real or accurate.

She Wore A Yellow Dress

Published by Gatekeeper Press
2167 Stringtown Rd, Suite 109
Columbus, OH 43123-2989
www.GatekeeperPress.com

ISBN (paperback): 9780999855553
eISBN: 9780999855546

Library of Congress Control Number: 2020942490

Disclaimer: This book is an independent work and bears no connection to or affiliation with any other book, song, play, website, trademark or any other product using the words *She Wore a Yellow Dress,* or any variant thereof.

Note from the Author: In most chapters of *She Wore a Yellow Dress* reference is made to a bird that features in the protagonist's life in some way. The bird's relevance may be explained in the text, but the author also provides an ornithological summary of the species at the end of the chapter in case the reader is interested.

"KNOW THYSELF"
Greek Delphic maxim, made famous
by the philosopher Socrates (470–399BC)

Contents

1

The Abandoned Cuckoo

In spite of adversity, I'm determined to make something of myself by perseverance, hard work, intelligence and humanism. I'm British, aged 21, I love birdwatching, I live in Yorkshire and I'm called John. This is my story.

Autumn 1965 arrived when I was living in the city of Hull, preparing to start my third and final year at university. Hull was not the most glamorous of cities, but its people looked like me, dropped the "h" in Hull like me and, again like me, were not well off. I felt at home. My real residence was near York, about 40 miles (65 km) away. The university had allowed me to study for a joint honours degree in Geology and Geography, my two favourite subjects at school. I enjoyed the field work, the sciences dealt with the environment in which I lived and neither subject required a proficiency in mathematics. Maths was my worst topic of study in school. I thought it very abstract, and once I dropped behind in class, I was sure I would never catch up. I was bussed between school and my village each day, and therefore denied any opportunity for additional instruction because it was an eight-mile walk home if I missed the once-a-day school transport.

I wondered how obtaining a degree would influence my career, but at the same time I was uncertain that I would ever graduate because I suspected I lacked the necessary talent. During the summer holidays, I lived at home and worked as a porter in a nearby hospital to earn money. The wages I earned supplemented the grants I received from the local education authority.

Had Britain not introduced free-of-charge higher education a year before I started, I would never have attended university. My student tuition fees were paid by the government and I received a maintenance grant to help with living expenses. At the time, I was one of only approximately 4 percent of school leavers who received an undergraduate education, and although the maintenance grant was means-tested, my mother earned no income and my stepfather consistently refused to provide for me. He was a retired farmer, and no fan of education. He could not understand why my mother kept me at school after the age of 15; he believed that further education was unnecessary, arguing that I should find a job and earn a wage.

Because of my family's financial situation, the living expenses paid to me by the government was the maximum possible. It had been a similar situation at school where I qualified for free school meals. These were outright grants, not loans requiring repayment, and my earned income gave me sufficient funds both to purchase and maintain a vehicle during my last two years at university and also have savings available to participate in student social events.

Attending university helped me to develop my self-confidence, matured my academic abilities and transformed my rural shyness into a capability to relate to others. However, the latter required listeners to understand my strong Yorkshire accent. Had I not continued in education, I would have ended up as either a hospital porter or a farm labourer, but if I could pass the "big bang" undergraduate examinations the following May, it would open up a whole new range of career possibilities for me whose details were as yet unknown.

An earlier threat to my freedom was Britain's requirement that men aged between 18 and 21 serve two years of National Service. Fortunately, my fears were averted when the government ended compulsory call-up for those born after 1st October 1939. It was a near miss, with conscriptions not formally ending until 31st December 1960, just 17 months before I turned 18. Now there was no need for me to find work in an "essential service" to avoid conscription. A job in farming would have qualified, but I found farm work unsatisfying. It involved long hours, and it did not pay well. As a child, I worried about not conforming to military discipline and imagined I would be killed in some distant corner of the British Empire; in the jungles of Malaya fighting the communists, on the banks of the Suez Canal fighting Egyptians, trying to keep the peace in Cyprus or even fighting the Mau-Mau in Kenya.

A more private reason for being delighted that conscription had ended was my bed-wetting habit. I was one of only 5 percent of boys who continued to struggle with nocturnal enuresis after the age of ten. What caused it, I did not know, but the embarrassment that I imagined it would create in the armed forces was terrifying. For no apparent reason, the problem ceased when I was about 15.

My stepfather died during my first year at university, and my mother, several decades his junior, found work as a part-time hospital administrator. She had always wanted to be a nurse, and she had used her Nursing Reserve qualification and 12 years of voluntary service to support her application. The appointment gave her the opportunity to find me employment at local hospitals during university holidays. Her income primarily supported my two younger siblings, but despite our financial limitations, she refused to allow me to end my education. I was the first in my family to go to university, and I heard from others how much she boasted about my academic accomplishments and expected me to end up in a very successful career. We were country folk and you might have classified us as socially dysfunctional.

* * *

My mother was pressured into marriage immediately after I was born, and her spousal relationship was dominated by occasional physical abuse and frequent and intense verbal quarrels. I was tolerated but not welcomed by my stepfather. There were regular arguments at the dinner table, often ending either with food being thrown or my mother being chased around the table by my stepfather. She would quickly usher me and my siblings ahead of her through the back door of the house and have us wait outside until it was safe to re-enter. She accepted this as a way of life and her duty. I learned to make myself scarce during these incidents, as it seemed that I was often the cause of the outbursts, although my mother assured me that my stepfather's behaviour was due to his diabetes, not me.

When I was a child, this was normal family life. We first lived on a remote farm without access to electric power or running water. Oil lamps and Calor Gas cylinders were used to provide lighting, our drinking water came from an outdoor pump, and the toilet was a pit latrine in a dark and smelly outhouse. On cold winter nights we used a chamber pot under the bed rather than venture outside. During my stepfather's diabetes fits, I would be told to hide in my bedroom or run across the road to the farm opposite until the all-clear was given. Once we moved off the moor to live in a small village, electric light and running water were available, but the latrine remained outside until we built a small bathroom. My stepfather's diabetes episodes continued, and the nurse next door gave us refuge whenever violence occurred.

These outbursts were unpredictable and usually lasted less than an hour. My stepfather had been diagnosed with diabetes around the time my mother married him, and he was prescribed insulin to control his blood sugar. Every morning an injection was self-administered, but he had no way of knowing if the amount of insulin he injected corresponded with what was necessary for his planned activities and diet that day. Sometimes he was lucky, but there were many times when he took the wrong dosage and he would either collapse into a coma or become angry and violent. This behaviour always targeted my mother and me. Whatever the situation, there was always a flurry of activity to provide him with cups of hot tea, usually with lots of sugar, and a little time later we would be allowed back into the house.

Friends were not welcomed by my stepfather. He once saw some of my pals returning to the farm to "scrump" (steal) apples, so he took out his double-barrelled, 12-gauge shotgun and fired at them. I do not believe he hit anyone, but I watched as they ran to their bicycles and disappeared, never to return. For school holidays, I was placed with an aunt and uncle living on an isolated farm where I stayed until school resumed. It was under these conditions that I learned to be independent and fend for myself.

I was happiest wandering through fields, exploring woodlands and searching the hedgerows. The birds were my friends, and the peace of the countryside helped suppress my anxieties about the squabbles at home. I loved being outdoors. I found no greater pleasure than disturbing a covey of partridges, causing them to scuttle to safety in the long grass, watching a hovering kestrel waiting to descend on its unsuspecting prey, or fending off the noisy lapwing as it tried to discourage my presence near its nest on the ground by dive-bombing me. It is not surprising that my childhood hobby became birdwatching.

It began at the age of ten, when I ceased egg collecting because the British government decided to make the gathering of wild birds' eggs illegal. Up until then, I freely took eggs from birds' nests, and I usually took all the eggs because the adult birds would typically abandon the remainder anyway, knowing that a human intruder had been present. Also, I needed spares to trade at school. Over the years, this national hobby had severely reduced the bird population, and in hindsight I think the regulation was justified. I would blow out each egg before placing it on cotton wool in a perforated shipping box that had previously been used to transport one-day-old chickens. The process involved piercing both ends of the egg with a pin and carefully puffing into one of the holes until only air was left in the eggshell. The practice was relatively easy for eggs the size of those laid by a hen, such as a partridge, crow and wood pigeon, but it was not unusual for the cleaning process to collapse smaller eggs, such as those produced by a wren, swallow or robin.

The Protection of Birds Act, 1954 was passed to safeguard birds, their nests and their eggs, but it did not apply to game birds. The restrictions annoyed me at first because they took away my only hobby, and I could no longer trade with other egg collectors at school. My last transaction was to swap two small, glossy white eggs marked with purplish squiggles and laid by a yellowhammer, plus one white and mottled red egg from a tree pipit, for a much larger, spotted dark and pale brown egg, laid by a merlin. The merlin is the smallest bird of prey in Britain, and the egg presumably came from a nest in the Yorkshire Dales. I never saw a merlin, just its egg.

Birdwatching was my main activity outside school. My grandfather helped by giving me a pair of used binoculars, and I obtained second-hand bird identification books to learn what I was looking at. I became a member of York Bootham School's Natural History Club in order to discover the best spots for birdwatching and what other birders were reporting. The members of the club catalogued the birds they saw, gave advice on how to recognise the species most commonly seen and supplied maps of local birdwatching sites such as Strensall Common, Castle Howard Lake, Fairburn Ings, Askam Bog and certain locations along the River Derwent, all of which were accessible to me by bicycle.

As my list of observed birds grew, I registered as a junior birdwatcher with the Royal Society for the Protection of Birds (RSPB) and contributed to their Junior Bird Recorders Club. Notes were kept on what I spotted—although, early on, the varieties I recorded were relatively common, such as blackbird, song thrush, chaffinch, robin, blue tit, magpie and jay. In the summertime I added migrant visitors, such as the swallow, house martin, flycatcher and wheatear, and in winter it was the redwing, fieldfare and occasional flock of waxwing. Through my membership of this organisation I learned about the existence of the Spurn Point Bird Observatory, a few miles outside Hull and supposedly Britain's best birding location on the east coast. It was beyond my cycling range, but it became accessible to me once I was 17 and could drive a car. The facility provided overnight accommodation and I was always the youngest birdwatcher present. I never saw any women there, presumably because the Observatory lacked the necessary amenities.

* * *

I spent my 1965 summer holidays working at a hospital providing mental illness, maternity and general hospital services to the public; it was located on the southern outskirts of York, close to the River Ouse. The mental health unit had opened 60 years earlier in defiance of the York Commissioner of Lunacy's refusal to allow poor people admission to the more prestigious York Lunatic Asylum. Other services were added after World War II, using facilities constructed during the war.

My job was to supervise two inmates who had worked with me the previous year. They were physically strong and did everything I instructed, except they were much slower than I expected and frequently needed to be reminded of what it was I had asked them to do. They just kept forgetting. They never spoke, and I used sign language even though neither of them was deaf. Each day, dressed in their dark-coloured shirts and light brown trousers, they waited next to the clock where I checked in. They would stare right through me, giving no indication that they were aware of my presence. Nevertheless, they seemed to welcome the privilege of working outside without psychiatric supervision, and I was conscious of feeling healthy and free.

I never felt unsafe at the hospital, although unexpected incidents did occur. There was one situation that involved a patient who assisted the butcher in the kitchen; it almost caused the end of my employment. At around twelve stone (168 pounds/76 kg), the assistant was physically strong and greeted everyone he saw with a piercing look, a shaking of the head and the words "Good morning". On this particular day, he had apparently greeted me, but I never heard him and so did not respond. Before I knew what was happening, he was running at me brandishing a butcher's knife and screaming that I had insulted him. Fortunately, his colleagues intervened and dragged him away before he caused me serious injury, but it was a frightening experience. I later learned that he was a manic depressive and subject to sudden outbursts of temper and violence. It taught me to be more aware of my surroundings and to expect the unexpected.

My two assistants serviced all the maternity and general wards in the hospital, but they did not have any responsibility for the mental health section. Twice a day, we delivered clean linen and towels to each hospital unit, and we collected dirty bedding that we took to the laundry room. Occasionally there were spills to clean up, and sometimes the nursing staff asked us to scrub and polish floors. Food carts were wheeled into each ward for breakfast, lunch and tea, and later in the day we collected messy food leftovers and took them to the storage yard for consolidation into bins. The slop was taken away as pig feed by a local farmer.

Officially I worked a five-day week, and I usually took my days off on weekdays because I wanted to earn the extra wages paid for working on Saturdays and Sundays. It was during one of these weekdays that I found at home something that changed my life for ever. Up until then, I always did what people told me, believing that doing whatever was asked of me was simpler than making my own decisions.

* * *

While living at home, I was assigned to what was known as "the spare bedroom", or the sleeping space reserved for guests. It was a large room with a window overlooking the farm next door, and my egg collection was perched on top of the wardrobe. The room was also used by my mother as a part-time office, and she had designated the centre drawer of the dressing-table as storage for her private correspondence. This drawer was normally locked, but on this particular morning I noticed papers protruding from its front. Clearly, she had forgotten to secure the drawer and, as I lay in bed, curiosity became the better of me.

I decided not to search the drawer's entire contents, in case of detection, but I thought an examination of the top few papers would limit the risk as I could replace them in the order in which I found them. There was a recent application for a road tax licence, several letters to my mother from her mother, my mother's nursing certificate and, on top of everything, a handwritten, undated letter addressed to someone whose name I did not recognise. It was penned in blue-black ink on pale blue paper, the same brand as my mother used. There was no prefix to the salutation, the name was unfamiliar and the recipient's address was not given. However, it was clearly written to a man because of how the letter began.

"John, our son, graduates next year and needs help with his career. I don't know what to tell him and wonder if he should become an engineer like you."

The letter continued by asking the recipient to contact "John". Since I had not received any communications from an unknown person, I was not sure if the letter was referring to me, but I was immediately suspicious. Maybe I should have stopped reading at this point, but I could not.

I sat on the bed and read the whole letter. Its tone was firm and purposeful, and it went on to say that "John" was not suited to farming, and that nursing was considered a woman's occupation. My mother suggested that it was not wise for "John" to return home after graduation and implored the addressee not to ignore the letter as he had done with previous correspondence. Furthermore, the communication seemed to confirm what my grandfather had told me after a particularly harsh confrontation with my stepfather: That the man with whom I lived was not my real father. Therefore I deduced that I must be the "John" mentioned in the letter.

I replaced the document exactly as I had found it, and I part-closed the dresser drawer while deep in thought. My reaction was a mixture of shock and apprehension. If I had not pried, I would have remained ignorant of my personal situation and not worried about my future, but it was too late now. Apparently I was abandoned by my father at a time when my mother could no longer give me guidance. Suddenly I felt like one of my favourite birds: A young cuckoo, in its hosts' nest, waiting to fly off into a world without support.

The annual appearance of the cuckoo always announces the start of spring and the breeding season for birds, although the cuckoo does not build a nest of its own. Instead, it relies on other birds to incubate and feed its offspring. The female cuckoo lays her egg in a nest built by another species, and the hosts are left to hatch the egg and rear the young cuckoo. I felt that I was exposed to a similar process.

I happened to like the cuckoo. Its two-note song "cu-ckoo" was usually associated with warm weather and masses of colourful flowers appearing during spring. Hedgerows became adorned with the white and pink-tinged flowers of hawthorn and blackthorn, masses of white elderberry buds fought to find sunlight, and the pale pink, wild dog rose petals were stuck like postage stamps on an otherwise green background. These were special times for taking walks in the fields, with the cup-shaped flowers of the yellow cowslip, white and purple clovers, the golden tapestry of meadow buttercups and the vibrant blue forget-me-nots. As for the cuckoo, it was more usual to hear it than to see it. There was a local custom that, if you saw a cuckoo and then spit on a coin, the coin would bring you luck for the rest of the year.

* * *

Physically, I was five foot nine inches (175cm) tall, and of slight build. My weight was a little under 10 stone (140lb/64kg) and did not seem to respond to whatever I ate or drank. I possessed short, stubby arms and small, chubby fingers that in my mid-teens ended my ambition of becoming a professional cricketer. My fine blonde hair suffered from six years of having to be forced back over my scalp using greasy Brylcream, a well-known brand of hair oil. I was now training it to fall in the opposite direction but encountering something of a rebellion. To foil this opposition, I started using my mother's hair lacquer and would spray my hair excessively to flatten its texture, especially after it was washed, and I was having some success. However, because the lacquer turned sticky and matted my hair as it dried, I stopped using it whenever I went out with a girl.

At that time, I had no steady girlfriend. My most recent sweetheart at university dumped me on the shores of the North Sea shortly after my 21st birthday. Do not ask me why. Now I was too busy working and did not have time to renew connections with former school friends, but I hoped to remedy the situation once I returned to Hull.

My eyes were electric blue, striking yet soft, and could hold the gaze of anyone who chose to look at me. At school I knew how to stare intently beneath my long, dark eyelashes at teachers and colleagues if I needed their forgiveness or assistance. The remainder of my shaven face suffered from the remnants of adolescent acne, made more visible by a normally chalky-white complexion. Should I spend time in the sun, my skin would turn a bright pink, but at least it camouflaged the facial blemishes and dispensed with the need to use Clearasil, a popular cleansing cream.

The almost permanent smile on my face was more a mischievous grin than a cheerful expression, and I found it difficult to control. I was often likened to the Cheshire Cat in Lewis Carroll's *Alice in Wonderland.* Worse still, the smile would expose my unattractive, yellow-coloured teeth. Since childhood, I had possessed far more than my fair share of molars and incisors, and as a result many had become crooked and overlapped. Without smiling, my handicap could not be seen, but a grin would often spread spontaneously across my face, despite my efforts to suppress it.

I was not interested in fashion and typically wore clothing you would expect to see on a farm worker. I was brought up dressed in cast-off clothes donated by a friend of a friend of my mother's. Once I had funds of my own through delivering newspapers, I bought the occasional shirt, pullover and pair of trousers, but I usually preferred to buy heavy outdoor gear to keep me warm during my birdwatching excursions. An important exception was the purchase of a dove-grey, long-haired, merino wool cardigan during my first year at university; this was worn only on special occasions. It proved to be a hit with the girls, as they loved stroking its fine, soft hair, and snuggling into its warmth during cold evenings. I also purchased a pair of black, chisel-toe shoes that I wore on Saturday nights at the Student Unions' dances.

My vocal characteristic was a broad Yorkshire accent. It was warm and soft, and unnoticed by me as a child, as nearly everyone spoke that way around York. I certainly never thought of it as a class barrier that might interfere with my career or influence my love life. Originating from the countryside, as I did, it was not unusual to be called a "country bumpkin" and it did not matter to me if people thought I was out of touch with the modern world. They were townspeople whose interests were different from mine.

* * *

Thus, I returned to Hull for my final year in higher education. It involved a move to live in a one-bedroom, rented attic flat in a row of dilapidated terraced houses near the city centre. I resided there with two of my closest colleagues, Richard and

Anton. Richard and I had become friends only a few months earlier, and Anton and I had shared lodgings during our first two years at university. Richard was studying history and came from Nottingham, while Anton was a geography student who had grown up in a suburban area of west London, and both of them helped me with my diction.

While graduation was my top priority, I was also busy trying to improve my awareness of world affairs as a means of socialising more effectively. During school, an understanding of the world outside of Yorkshire was unimportant and I had little access to national news. At university, far more information was available and I was able to research whatever interested me. I became aware of Britain's economic difficulties, the effects of trade unions on the country's economy, how the 1964 general election had returned the Labour Party to power after 13 years of Conservative rule and the discovery of natural gas in the North Sea. I also read about the expansion of the Vietnam War and Lyndon Johnson's re-election as the United States President.

From a leisure perspective, Radio Caroline celebrated its first year of illegal broadcasting in March 1965; *My Fair Lady* won eight Academy Awards during April 1965; Liverpool won the Football Association Cup for the first time in its history on 1st May 1965; the "Early Bird" (Intelsat) satellite began television transmissions between Europe and North America on 2nd May and the Beatles released the film *Help* at the end of July. More seriously, Winston Churchill was buried on 30th January 1965, and Edward Heath became leader of the British Conservative Party on 27th July 1965.

My third year at Hull University was now underway.

The Common Cuckoo: it is a squat, medium-sized bird, 33cm/13 in. in length, with a sleek body, a long tail, a short bill and pointed wings. Its upperparts are blue-grey, and the underbody is dark barred-white. The male makes the distinctive call of "cu-ckoo, cu-ckoo, cu-ckoo", whereas the female "bubbles" (a sound like that made by bathwater gurgling down a plughole). The birds arrive in Britain from Africa during late March/early April and symbolise the arrival of spring. There are about 15,000 breeding pairs in Britain, and they leave in late July/early August. Each season the female lays 12 to 22 eggs, but only one in each host's nest, and usually in those belonging to the same species of bird that reared her. The dunnock (hedge sparrow) and meadow

pipit nests are often used as hosts. Eggs are usually laid at intervals of two days and mimic the colour, size and shape of the eggs of the host bird. Sometimes the female removes the host's eggs, and on other occasions, as soon as it is born, the young cuckoo pushes any other eggs out of the nest.

The European variety of cuckoo is not found in North America. There are three types in the United States, but none is a brood parasite like the British variety.

2

A Mob Of Starlings

OUR LODGINGS WERE adequate for sleeping, but cold and damp for studying during the daytime. The trade-offs were the low rent, living close to the amenities in Hull city centre, and the short journey to the university campus. For Anton and me, it was an ideal relocation. During the previous two years we had lived on the far east-side of Hull, remote from anything that interested us as undergraduates. Using my car during the second year had given us some access to student activities, but our landlord's close supervision and doors being locked as part of a night-time curfew limited how late we could stay out. Now we could enjoy the freedom to do what we wanted when we wanted and as late as we wanted. Not only was it a time to prepare to graduate in my chosen disciplines, but it was also an opportunity to strengthen my interpersonal skills and broaden my general knowledge.

The attic consisted of a small kitchen and living area, plus a bedroom with three single beds, a wardrobe and personal storage space. The bathroom was on the floor below and shared with the tenants on that floor. They were also undergraduates, one of whom was a woman who had given birth to a baby who was kept warm in a shoe box. The building was not a place to invite friends; it was old and neglected and about to be torn down. The whole neighbourhood had a reputation as a sanctuary for petty criminals, although we never experienced any crime ourselves, presumably because the burglars burgled elsewhere. Our daytime activities centred on attending lectures on the university campus, socialising in the university refectory, drinking in local pubs and attending parties organised in friends' houses that offered nicer facilities than ours.

My roommates kept an eye on me. Anton, in particular, gave me guidance when I asked for it, and he did not seem to mind if I chose to disregard his suggestions. He was much more scholarly than me and, since we often travelled in my car during the second and third years of undergraduate studies, he persuaded me to stay in the university library longer than I would have liked. He was treated as the resident expert by his fellow geography students, and gave them advice whenever they asked. Physically, he looked a little like me, except that his hair was blonder, he smiled rather than grinned, his teeth were straight and white, his eyes shone a brighter blue than mine, and he spoke with a west London accent. Our friendship was close even though there were times I think when he had no idea of what I was talking about.

Richard was very sociable and I tried to imitate him. He was usually absent from the attic and missing from the library. His height and weight were similar to mine, but his complexion was much darker, and he looked older than me as his tousled hair was already turning grey. I think my accent confused him, and he could not quite understand how someone like me had made it to university.

On campus, the Geology and Geography Departments were in the same building, just off the Cottingham Road, making my commute quick and convenient, with Geology on the ground floor and Geography up on the floor above. Transferring between the two faculties was like leaving and entering two different worlds since I was the only undergraduate studying for this joint degree. The Geology students were all men, except for one female, and they spent their time examining fossils and rocks; they kept to themselves, were usually seen carrying hammers and clinometers to examine the dips of folds and faults and seemed to socialise only during field trips. These were frequent, usually at least once a term, and often involved overnight camping. They taught me to respect the diverse interests of my colleagues and the collaboration and cooperation involved in communal living.

The Geography Department offered a more balanced blend of the sexes and the students were more relaxed and sophisticated. Field trips were rarely longer than a day, and they concentrated on the purpose of the outing rather than enabling new friendships. Socialising usually took place after lectures when debates flourished over what had just been taught.

Outside the classroom, my time was spent in the Students' Union and at the university library during the weekdays. I spent Saturdays in the public library in the city during the daytime, and then attended the Students' Union campus dance in the evening. My social skills had improved as a result of my efforts to develop good manners and communications skills during my second year at university, and now I was confident that I could connect with others, as long as they could understand my accent.

Most undergraduates at Hull were assigned to one of four Halls of Residence, about 2.5 miles (4 km) north-west of Hull, near a place called Cottingham. Each residence was for single-sex occupation; Needler and Ferens were for men, and women lived in either Thwaite Hall or Cleminson Hall, so I was attracted to the latter two. No-one told me how students were selected for these Halls, although I speculated that the fees might be higher than the amount of my maintenance grant. Despite not living there, it was a measure of a male student's success if he was going out with a resident of one of the women's Halls. It was not just about dating the girl, but also about overcoming the rumoured dangers that these Halls were protected by vicious guard dogs. There was gossip that Alsatian dogs roamed the grounds of Cleminson, and other attack dogs had been sighted at Thwaite.

I thought it was important to continue to establish new relationships with women and strive to feel more comfortable in their company. However, competition for feminine attention was intense. Supposedly, under a third of the 3,000 Hull students were women, and the situation was made more difficult for male students of a discipline that had low female representation. Thankfully, the Geography Department had a high percentage of female students.

Another source of female companionship arose from knowing the public library staff. I was familiar to them, and they generously allowed me to check out as many books as I liked, and to keep them for as long as I wanted. Academically I considered this a huge advantage and they were also the nicest group of young women you could wish to meet. Their only complaint was that there were very few employment opportunities for women in Hull. Apparently, alternative sources of work were primarily teaching, nursing, performing clerical work, working in a restaurant or being hired locally on the docks to gut fish. I greatly sympathised with them.

There was one condition attached to my special library privileges: If a member of staff needed a student to accompany her to a social event, I was to be that person. Since graduation was my top priority, I considered the arrangement a fair exchange.

Another way of meeting girls was at the Students' Union dances on Saturday nights. Young women living in Hull (known as "townies") and nurses from local hospitals were invited to these events, and all present had the opportunity to find partners. Thus, the phrase "Saturday night cattle market" was coined.

I never fully adjusted to the hordes of students I saw on campus. It reminded me of the masses of starlings with which I grew up, chattering, squabbling and feeding near my home. Starlings were one of the most common birds around, occupying any cavity or perch they could find and, before I turned to birdwatching, they were a top provider of eggs. I collected their pale blue eggs, speckled with reddish brown dots, and sought out friends at school who were willing to take one or more for their collection.

Watching undergraduates move between lecture rooms and across campus reminded me of these birds. From a distance, starlings look black, but closer inspection reveals the iridescent sheen of their plumage. Similarly, undergraduates who at the time were still required to wear knee-length gowns, looked dark from a distance; however, a closer look showed colourful clothing beneath their gowns. Also, students were everywhere, moving, standing, sitting and talking, sometimes like a murmuration of starlings (a large group of these birds that forms at dusk and is especially visible during autumn and winter).

* * *

The first Friday evening in November found me driving towards Cottingham, where I hoped to enjoy a romantic evening and quell the anxieties brought about by thinking of my future career. I had decided to develop a serious relationship with my new girlfriend, Annabelle, since it was my final year at university, I had reached my twenties, and I assumed that meeting girls would become more difficult once I left academia. Exactly what was involved in a serious relationship I was unsure, but I decided to be honest and straightforward and share my personal life. It was difficult to determine whether my plan was working, however, as she seemed to be fond of me but showed no particular interest in my birdwatching. My hope was that this would change during the course of our romance.

A few minutes earlier I had collected Annabelle from the Students' Union after her last lecture, and we were on our way to a public park to enjoy the annual celebration in Britain known as Bonfire Night, also known as Guy Fawkes' Night. It was named after a seventeenth century Catholic rebel who had tried unsuccessfully to blow up the British Houses of Parliament 360 years earlier. I was delighted to have found Annabelle; she was only the second student living in the Halls of Residence that I had dated; she was a first-year undergraduate studying English and French, and she was very attractive.

Bonfire Night was an event I enjoyed. As a farm boy, I remembered spending days collecting from hedgerows, nearby trees and from our garden, wood and foliage with which to build a bonfire. As a young child, I participated in Guy Fawkes' celebrations on the farm; as I grew older, I attended a much larger bonfire organised by people of the village, and now I was on the way to this urban event which was even bigger. Somehow the festivities appealed to my outdoor spirit, and the smell of burning wood, the flash and crash of exploding fireworks and the chill of a November evening stimulated my senses.

Annabelle and I stopped off at "The Duke of Cumberland" pub on Cottingham Road for a hasty drink before driving the rest of the way to the bonfire. She looked stunning in the dim light of the saloon bar, with an irresistible smile and large firm breasts hidden beneath a powder-blue blouse. I could not decide if it was her smile or her bust that attracted me the most. I had been dating her for about six weeks since the start of term, and early on I thought I had fallen in love. I was no longer sure about that, however, as we had many differences and I felt that our relationship was still in a trial period.

I also felt acutely aware that, a few days earlier, Anton had helped arrange a meeting for me with another girl, someone from the Geography Department, to whom I had been attracted for some time. Her name was Jean-Louise, she came from somewhere close to Manchester and during our lecture discussions I had thought her much brighter than me. Otherwise, I knew nothing about her except for her good looks. How this arranged meeting would work out, I had no idea.

* * *

I knew that events like Bonfire Night did not always end up with love and affection. About 18 months earlier, Nora, a York girlfriend and I had attended a bonfire party in west Yorkshire that had created the opposite of what I expected. It was a St John's Midsummer Night celebration, near Leeds, and I had been dating Nora since earlier that year. She was a bright and opinionated person, and very argumentative. Her parents had fled Hungary with her and her sister eight years earlier, during the failed uprising against the Soviet-backed communist government. On the way home to York, she had asked me about the annual bonfires. Did I know their purpose and the origin of the name? I had no idea, but I wanted to impress her and took a guess at the answer. I said I thought they celebrated important achievements: Guy Fawkes' Night commemorates a Protestant victory over Catholicism, and St John's Eve celebrates Christianity's victory over Paganism.

I received a look of contempt.

"They're nothing of the kind," she contradicted. "They warn of danger. Bonfire Night reminds you not to threaten authority, and St John's Eve alerts you to the dangers of Paganism."

She continued: "If you read books, you'd know that bonfires are used to frighten away witches and warn communities of enemy invasions."

I thought my answer had merit, but she refused to accept any part of it. Usually I was calm and tolerant, but her criticism made me angry.

"You're not very courteous are you," I replied. "Why do you have to be so impolite? My answer is just as reasonable as yours."

"Not if you know anything about etymology," she replied, ignoring my appeal. "Where does the term 'bonfire' come from?"

I could not answer; I did not know.

"It's from 'bane-fyre', a mediaeval English word," she said as she looked at me in contempt. "Bones of dead animals were burned by villagers to stop their use by witches, and the ashes were used for animal feed and fertiliser. It's believed the word originated here in Yorkshire. Didn't you know that?"

I remained silent. I was not sure she was correct, but I realised that, whatever I said, she would disagree. Not surprisingly, as we arrived at her home, she told me to work on my education and ended our relationship.

* * *

Annabelle, on the other hand, was more amicable and usually agreed with whatever I said. Her home was in the small town of Clitheroe, on the western edge of the Pennines in Lancashire. She could understand my accent and seemed not to worry about my lack of any dress sense. I believed that I was her first boyfriend at university, and we had met at a Student Unions' dance one Saturday evening when a band called Herman's Hermits was playing. After chatting at the bar, we took a liking to one another and started to dance.

She was about my height, slim and attractive, with hazel brown eyes set under long, black eyelashes and perfectly sculpted eyebrows. Her lips were delicate, full-bodied and always slightly open. Her high cheek bones, rounded face and honey-coloured complexion were framed by shiny, chestnut-coloured hair worn in a wavy casual bob. There were feathery tresses that touched her shoulders and a fringe that circled her forehead. Her slim body was dominated by those attractive breasts, hidden that evening underneath a pale cream, ribbed turtleneck jumper. Her smile exposed a perfect set of white teeth, and her contoured lips permanently seemed to invite me to kiss them.

She appeared to be aware of her good looks and communicated pleasure through her smile. She transmitted a sensuous affection as her eyes stayed focused on mine, never wandering to inspect other men. My eyes were not so well disciplined, and Herman's Hermits' lyrics of *I'm into Something Good* seemed to fit in with that night's experience. Ever since our first date, I had been a regular visitor to Thwaite Hall, but so far had not encountered any dogs.

We had planned to reach the bonfire a little after 6pm. It was dark and chilly, with a starry, clear sky predicting a cold November night, so we dressed warmly. Annabelle hid deep within a navy-blue duffle coat secured by four wooden toggles, and she wore a wide-brimmed, colour-coordinated hat, held fast by a scarf tightly tied beneath her chin. She walked along wearing a pair of knee-length dark-tan boots. I wore light brown corduroy, slim-leg trousers and unpolished black farm boots, and I was kept warm by a dirty old light-green anorak, which I usually used for early morning birdwatching, as its colour offered camouflage, so that the birds could not see me—or so I thought. The anorak this evening covered my pride and joy, the dove-grey, long-haired, merino wool cardigan. I wore it primarily for warmth, but I also thought that, if I ended up somewhere inside, I could remove my anorak and reveal the showpiece.

So dressed, we arrived at Cottingham's community bonfire and firework display. On arrival, someone offered us hot minestrone soup and indicated where piping-hot jacket potatoes, sausages and roast chestnuts would soon be available. To drink, there was hot chocolate, mulled wine and apple cider. Trudging across the grass, the chill in the air turned our breath into silver puffs of moisture.

As we waited for the fireworks to begin, Annabelle asked about my recent meeting with a university careers officer. I had begun to think about my future and, as a first step, I had made an appointment with one of the people who helped final year students decide what to do. She knew about the arrangement.

"Did he give you any useful ideas?" she wanted to know.

There was much about the meeting that had disappointed me. I had expected to discuss alternative careers and obtain advice on how to prepare employment applications. Instead, my contact only talked about teaching, giving me a list of universities offering post-graduate courses in education. Hull was not one of them, so I would have to move somewhere else and spend a year continuing my education before I could teach. It is possible that I might have irritated him as I had a knack of sounding gormless (stupid and dull) due to my manner of speech and lack of vision regarding my future. I tried to explain to Annabelle.

"He wasn't helpful. Apparently, he thinks teaching should be my vocation and doesn't believe I'm suitable for anything else. Evidently there's a huge demand for teachers in Britain."

I paused briefly before adding: "And something else happened last week. A lecturer from the Geology Department talked to me about becoming a member of its Micropaleontology unit and studying for a PhD in microfossils, such as foraminifera, ostracods and palynomorphs, as a means of stratigraphy dating. It's a science being used at the moment in the North Sea oil and gas exploration. His suggestion was surprising and flattering, but the pay's so low that I can't accept. I can't afford to stay on at university."

I did not share with her my other cause for concern: An upper second-class honours degree (2.1), or higher, was expected for post-graduate studies, and fewer than 25 percent of graduates receive this degree. It was difficult for me to believe that I would be one of them, and it did not register at the time that the offer was also an indication from my professors of their confidence in me that I would successfully graduate. My limited sense of self-esteem still predicted failure.

"So, will you go back to the careers officer?" Annabelle wanted to know.

"I don't think so," I said. "He was adamant about teaching. I asked about engineering, but he said my degree didn't prepare me for that type of work."

"If you end up teaching, will it be here or somewhere else?"

"I would like to move out of Yorkshire, but the careers person warned that my accent might require me to teach in the north of England. Another problem is that I would first have to obtain a certificate of education, and I can't do that here in Hull. Honestly, I'm not sure I want another year of studying. I'd much prefer to start earning, but that's enough about me, what are your plans?" I asked, wondering why Annabelle was so interested in me.

She replied: "It's too early to decide. My parents want me to return home after graduation, but Clitheroe is such a small town. I'd like to move to Manchester, but my father hopes I'll help him out with his dentistry practice. For now, I need to pass my first-year exams."

"And what time do you need to be back in Thwaite Hall?" I asked.

"No later than 8pm, as I have to study," she smiled. That tied with my plan. My intention was to end the date with Annabelle early, so that I could reach the second bonfire before its festivities were over, and there meet Jean-Louise, whom Anton had assured me would be present. However, for the time being I was with Annabelle in Cottingham, and we returned our attention to the bonfire.

*European Starling***:** *this is a chunky bird, slightly smaller than a blackbird (length 21cm/8 in), with a short tail, pointed head, triangle-shaped wings and a slender bill. Its plumage is a dark-coloured, iridescent purplish-green, and it has a yellow bill that darkens in winter. Approximately 900,000 pairs breed in Britain, and over 30 million arrive from the continent for the British winter, all behaving in a sociable, boisterous, noisy and greedy manner. An interesting phenomenon during autumn and winter is their habit of gathering in large flocks late in the afternoon and participating in acrobatic aerial displays called murmurations. Tens of thousands of these birds fly together in huge flocks, morphing into different shapes by swooping, whirling and looping, before descending to their roost. The purpose of such displays is unclear, but it may be to ensure safety in numbers, and deter predators by confusing them.*

The species is known as the European starling in North America, and it was introduced during 1890, with the release of 60 birds in New York. Today it is estimated that there are around 200 million starlings in the United States.

3

The Bonfire And The Firecrest

THE BONFIRE WAS being lit. Several men scurried around its base, stuffing newspapers and straw into the kindling, then pouring small amounts of paraffin onto the dry materials. Following behind were men with lighted bundles of torn paper; they pushed the burning flares into the tinder to start the blaze. After a brief period of crackling and popping, the bonfire roared into life, sending fingers of silvery smoke rising high into the black night sky. Vertical daggers of orange and yellow flames followed. Spectators were bathed in amber light as they looked towards the fire, and they appeared as black silhouettes from behind. In the light from the fire, trees emerged from the darkness and human shadows moved noiselessly, as if controlled by the flickering flames. Soon the fireworks would begin.

During the past few days the community had erected the bonfire out of trimmed tree branches, hedge clippings, planks of wood, old furniture, broken-down cardboard boxes, garden rubbish and other items that were difficult to identify. The mound of rubbish rose 20 feet (6 metres) in the air, and on its summit was an effigy of Guy Fawkes made out of old clothing stuffed with hay and tattered rags. His "head" was a turnip carved to resemble a human face, and balanced on top of the turnip was a tall, dark-coloured, narrow-brimmed hat, similar to those seen in pictures of American pilgrims.

I was raised near the city of York, where Guy Fawkes had lived as a boy 400 years earlier, and during my childhood he had become something of a role model for me. Both of us had attended schools in York and lost our fathers at a young age. Unlike me, he did not go to university; instead he chose to join the European Catholic army and fight for Spain against the Protestants.

Fawkes' error was joining a band of Catholic co-conspirators in Britain who planned to assassinate James 1, the Protestant king at the time. The conspiracy failed, and Guy Fawkes was arrested while guarding nearly two tonnes of gunpowder in preparation for blowing up the Houses of Parliament. He was imprisoned in the Tower of London, tortured mercilessly, then hung, drawn and quartered on 31st January 1606. The pieces of his body were taken to the "four corners of the kingdom" to warn others not to challenge Protestant authority. I had no desire to follow in his footsteps as far as my career was concerned.

To commemorate the failed Gunpowder Plot, an Act of Parliament was passed requiring the lighting of bonfires every 5th November. The first celebration took place in 1606, and here we were, 359 years later, still celebrating the success of the Protestants who had turned away the threat of Catholic domination. Early on, the image placed on top of the bonfire was that of the Pope, but over the years it has changed to Guy Fawkes.

I looked for alternative role models with links to York, but I could find no-one suitable. I found many well-known personalities, but all of them appeared to have failed at whatever they did, and all had been punished by losing their lives. There was Eric Bloodaxe, the Viking king who was ambushed and killed in 954; Margaret Clitherow harboured Roman Catholic priests and was "pressed" to death underneath her own front door weighed down with huge stones on 25th March 1586; Dick Turpin, the famous highwayman, was hanged in York on 7th April 1739; and Mary Bateman, known as "the Yorkshire Witch", was executed there on 20th March 1809.

My thoughts returned to current events and while we watched the bonfire, I reminded Annabelle that I would be spending the coming weekend at the Spurn Point Bird Observatory, so she would be on her own during the next two days.

Spurn Point had become my favourite site for birdwatching. It consisted of a three-and-a-half-mile spit of sand and shingle, situated between the River Humber estuary and the North Sea, and it was the most south-easterly extension of Yorkshire. At its narrowest point, during the time of my visits, it was only 150 feet (45 metres) wide, but it attracted large numbers of migrating birds that travelled along the east coast and preferred to stay close to land. I had been a regular visitor since 1961, and I had arranged my visits to coincide with the spring and autumn migrations, when rare birds might appear. Some I saw, some I did not. Just before my April 1961 trip, a Pallas's leaf warbler was spotted for the first time at Spurn. Its sighting provoked the inauguration of the Observatory's "Lifer Tin" into which birdwatchers paid a penny or threepence (the amount depended on the bird's rarity), for each new species they spotted. Fortunately for me, an impecunious student, contributions were voluntary.

"I hope you don't mind my going; it may be my last chance this year," I told Annabelle.

She shrugged acceptance of my plan, as she knew I would

not change my mind. When it came to birding, I was very stubborn, but she made no offer to accompany me.

"Won't it be cold and unpleasant at this time of year?" she asked, offering the only discouragement she could think of.

"Probably not," I countered. "It will be frosty, but the weather forecast says it will be dry and clear, so there should be all sorts of birds on the move."

"Will you see another of those little birds?" she questioned.

"It's very unlikely," I replied.

I knew she was referring to the firecrest, or fire-crested wren, which was probably the rarest bird I had ever seen, and most definitely the rarest I had observed on my own. I had become very excited when I explained my sighting to Annabelle, although she could not understand my enthusiasm. I had spotted it during the previous month, in a conifer tree just outside my bedroom window, at home in York. I was only three or four yards away as it hopped from branch to branch at eye-level. The single bird, a male, was foraging for insects and presumably had either been blown off course to my part of Yorkshire or had anticipated bad weather by flying westwards. The fact that it was eating so energetically was an indication that unpleasant conditions might be on the way. Being so small, it was vulnerable to strong winds and risked death if exposed to cold temperatures. While the sighting of the firecrest was an unforgettable moment for me, it was of no interest to Annabelle.

* * *

By this time, more people had arrived at the bonfire, and some individuals were beginning to let off fireworks. Someone was wandering around handing out toffee apples, and potatoes were baking at the edge of the fire. One man carried a portable radio playing the Beatles' hit *Yesterday*, which reminded me that, only a few days earlier, the four Beatles were at Buckingham Palace to receive their MBEs (Most Excellent Order of the British Empire) from the Queen.

The flames of the bonfire soon engulfed the stack of rubbish and reached the effigy of Guy Fawkes. Annabelle noticed that someone had hung a piece of cardboard around the dummy's neck with the hand-painted message, "Thank you Sir Alec!". The fire quickly engulfed the writing.

"What's the slogan all about?" she asked, as Guy Fawkes tipped into the flames.

I seized my chance to demonstrate my knowledge of current affairs and replied:

"I think it refers to the ex-Prime Minister, Sir Alec Douglas-Home. He's the one who lost the general election last year to Harold Wilson and the Labour Party. People living here are mainly Conservatives and blame Sir Alec for the change in government. They dislike the Labour Party because of its social policies and pro-union sentiments."

Seemingly, Annabelle was not impressed by my explanation and decided to argue.

"Why blame him? My father says it was not his fault; it was the economic downturn that the Conservative Party allowed to happen, the damage caused by the John Profumo sex scandal and the lack of support for the trade unions that lost them the election. The public became disillusioned."

Annabelle's reply horrified me. My knowledge of trade unions was limited, but she was disputing my knowledge based on her father's opinions. If I implied that her father was wrong, she might become angry, and I was not prepared to fall out with her. I needed to reply carefully.

"That may be so, but he could have intervened. Instead, he acted aloof and ignored what was going on. He also angered some voters by continuing to support Britain's entry into the

European Common Market, despite the French vetoing our application earlier in the year."

"At least he was honest and decent, unlike many politicians in the Conservative Party," was Annabelle's concluding remark.

It was clear that her opinions differed greatly from mine and, to avoid an unpleasant disagreement, I ended the conversation by turning to watch the fireworks. They fizzed, spat, whizzed, cracked and banged all around us, becoming increasingly noisy and dangerous. Rockets rose high into the night sky, and boys ran around throwing penny bangers and two-penny cannonballs in all directions, to frighten the girls. The spinning coils of Catherine's wheels occasionally flew off their wooden stakes, as if objecting to the martyrdom of St Catherine of Alexandria by the Roman Emperor Maxentius, circa 305. (Originally she was tortured on a spiked wheel to force her to recant Christianity, but when that failed because the wheel broke, she was then beheaded.) There were other colourful fireworks such as Roman Candles, Traffic Lights, Vesuvius Volcanoes and the bright, white lights of Snowstorms.

Annabelle suddenly screamed as a rocket hissed past within inches of her leather boots. While it had been positioned to travel vertically, at the last moment the milk bottle in which it stood fell over. This near miss and the incessant bangs of other fireworks prompted us to retreat to the car.

I owned a sand-coloured, two-door 1956 Ford Popular, purchased at the end of my first year at university. The car had no interior heater, nor a radio, and its single windscreen wiper slowed down the faster the car was driven, which was a serious problem in heavy rain. Its only concession to modern motoring was an upgrade to blinker signal-lights in place of the original amber direction indicators, but it was a delight to drive instead of having to ride a bike.

Annabelle told me that she was ready to return to her Hall of

Residence, so we set off. On the way, I invited her to a twenty-first birthday party which was being held the following week and arranged by friends of mine in the public library.

"It's my father's birthday that weekend," she replied. "I'll be at home with my parents."

"Do you mind if I go anyway?" I asked.

I admit that my request lacked foresight. It did not occur to me to think about the complications that might arise as a result of meeting the other girl later the same evening. I always chose monogamous relationships, and I had not thought about the possible outcomes of my date with Jean-Louise.

"No, I don't mind. Your roommates will tell me what you get up to!" She smiled as she spoke and was not jealous. Apparently, she trusted me.

We reached Thwaite Hall and I offered to accompany her to her room. She declined, so I leaned over and gently kissed her on those soft partly-parted lips. I felt the moisture of her tongue and the taste of lipstick, but she pushed me away as my hands tried to caress her more closely. This I took as a signal that for the time being my time with her was over, so I opened the door, helped her out into the chilly evening air, kissed her one more time and said goodnight.

It had been a terrific start to the evening, but ahead lay the meeting with Jean-Louise and suddenly I felt unsure of myself. If no romantic relationship developed with her I would still have Annabelle, but if we did connect, how would I end my current relationship? I was consoled by thinking that I would have the whole weekend at Spurn Point ahead of me to organise my thoughts.

I jumped back into the car and started the journey to the second bonfire.

Firecrest: A tiny, agile, restless bird, (length 9 cm/3.5 in), that competes with the goldcrest to be Britain's smallest feathered friend. The adult bird weighs under a quarter of an ounce (up to seven grams). It has a bright olive-green back, whitish underparts, a bronze collar, black and white eye markings, and yellow and black stripes on its head. The male's most distinguishing feature is its bright orange-yellow crest with a reddish stripe running through the centre. In Britain, it is a spring and autumn passage migrant, typically breeding in central and southern Europe, although a few pairs do nest in the south of England. The first report of the species breeding in Britain was in 1962.

In North America, its nearest relative is the golden-crowned kinglet, which nests in northern conifer forests and winters throughout the continent.

4

The Ugly Duckling

I DROVE EAST ALONG the Cottingham Road, and then south on Newlands and Princes Avenue, wondering about my future with Annabelle and what to say to her if things worked out well with Jean-Louise. It was a clear, cold night with only light winds, and during the journey patches of black ice tested my driving skills. However, the 15-minutes of travel were completed without incident, and both the anorak and wool cardigan kept me warm inside the freezing car.

I eagerly looked forward to linking up with Jean-Louise whose appearance I had found appealing ever since arriving at university. A group of geography undergraduates had arranged to meet with other students at a community bonfire, and Anton had persuaded me to attend by promising an introduction to Jean-Louise. It was to be a casual affair, more of a getting-to-know-you than a regular date. The site of the bonfire was close to her student house, and if for some reason she did not join us outside, I would be introduced later when we congregated for a party in the common area of her living quarters.

I always thought Jean-Louise physically attractive, although she showed no interest in men during her first year at university. Her hair was worn in a frizzy perm, her eyes were obscured by ill-fitting, red-framed National Health Service spectacles, and she wore shapeless, poorly designed, conservative clothes. She appeared to study a lot, usually in her student home.

By late in her second year, however, everything had changed. Her hair was now wavy, darkened and side-parted to tumble to her shoulders, dark-rimmed designer glasses framed her soft green eyes, her clothes were more colourful and the hems of her skirts and dresses were beginning to rise above her knees. Also, for the first time she could be seen with male companions. She wore a pleasant perfume and appeared more mature and sophisticated than Annabelle.

First impressions that evening would be important, so I was planning to use our shared interest in geography as the focus for our conversation, as I doubted that she would find my hobby of birdwatching inspiring. Also, I lacked the courage to discuss current affairs and I wanted to avoid talking about my childhood.

There was also another challenge to my confidence: Jean-Louise was in a relationship with another student, nicknamed "Little Bill", who was also a geography undergraduate, but the seriousness of that relationship was unclear. I had observed them holding hands outside the Geography lecture rooms during recent weeks. "Little Bill" was smaller than me but otherwise appeared to have no visible physical defects. His blonde hair was well-groomed, his teeth white and perfectly straight, he laughed rather than grinned, and he spoke in a refined manner. I would find him a formidable adversary if he competed with me, but Jean-Louise's roommate had reported that "Little Bill" would be away this evening, visiting his family.

I still had little confidence in my academic and social skills, although the latter had improved substantially while at university. My intellectual talents were slow to appear, and it had not been until I was in the sixth and last form at grammar school that I discovered I could compete with pupils who had awed me with their academic abilities during my early years at the school. Indeed, Hull University had been chosen because it made allowances for people like me. It was one of only a handful of British universities that accepted students who had failed their school mathematics and foreign language exams, and I had neglected both these subjects. My failure in French was predictable; while maybe I could pass a written test, it was absurd to expect my Yorkshire accent to allow me to succeed in an oral examination. The problem with mathematics was my disinterest in learning algebra and geometry. I had passed only six out of nine Ordinary Level (O-Level) exams, whereas I later learned that Jean-Louise had passed all nine.

My ability to participate in social activities was rudimentary before attending university. As a youth, I had few opportunities to mix with others because of my need to catch the school bus. I had cycled to school a couple of days a week during my final two years, and this allowed me to spend additional time with fellow students, including girls, at the school next door. Even so, as early as in primary school, the other sex had appeared formidable, different from me and best to be left alone.

While I was growing up, I often read the fairy-tale *The Ugly Duckling* by Hans Christian Andersen. It offered me inspiration, and it gave me hope that the abuse and disparagement I suffered as a boy would be replaced by respect and admiration once I was an adult.

This expectation was strengthened by an incident every year on our farm's several-acre brick pond. The pond was really more like a lake; it had been dug out many years earlier to extract clay for the manufacture of bricks, and it attracted many freshwater birds. Each April a pair of mute swans arrived and built their nest close to the water's edge, and I watched with wonder as each year several "ugly ducklings" were raised, and transformed into graceful white birds. I was warned not to get too near to the adult birds as they would attack if they felt threatened. They were huge, up to 14 kg (30 pounds) in weight, with a wingspan of 180 cm (six feet). Ordinarily they were quiet, but they would hiss loudly, wave their heads menacingly and noisily flap their wings when they sensed danger.

I watched the hatching of the greyish-brown cygnets covered in down that matured into beautiful white swans and usually left the pond during autumn, never to return. Occasionally, they stayed for the winter and departed the following spring.

Recollections of early romantic relationships slipped into my mind, causing me to remember how slowly my social skills had developed. My initial exposure to girls was during my early teens at barn dances where I was taken by my mother who would wait outside until the dance was over. Boys lined up at one end of the room, while girls sat on chairs at the opposite side. Once the music began, male participants were ushered across the room by an adult-in-charge and told to ask a girl to dance. Unnecessary contact during dancing was discouraged and a rule was enforced that partners should not speak to one another.

The Gay Gordons, the Dashing White Sergeant, Strip the Willow and the Durham Reel were popular dances that kept us moving and, as soon as the music stopped, we returned to our own section of the room. I still wonder about the purpose of these happenings, and I developed the theory that they were more an opportunity for parents to show off their teenagers than a chance for teenagers to develop their social abilities.

As I drove onwards, more memories surfaced of the many short-lived romances with girls during my school years. An exception was a relationship with a girl called Sandra, a friendship that had lasted several months. We had travelled on the school bus together during my fourth and fifth years at school, and we lived in neighbouring villages. The bus collected Sandra first, and one day, for no apparent reason, she kept the seat next to her open and invited me to sit alongside her. I assumed she enjoyed my company and wanted to get to know me a little better, nothing more. After all, I was the only boy on the bus who had been selected to attend the local grammar school. Thereafter, for several months, we always sat with each other.

I liked the situation; it made me feel important. Every day we discussed matters of interest to 14 and 15-year olds, such as pop songs, the latest fashion styles, school friends, TV shows and films. My mother knew of the friendship and sometimes took me to Sandra's home. Her mother hosted whist-drives, and she seemed happy for me to provide companionship for her daughter while the adults played cards.

I had thought the friendship platonic, but apparently Sandra had other ideas. One day during late autumn, she asked me to take her to the cinema and said it would be exciting to go out together. We would need to travel by public transport, since the nearest cinema was eight miles away, and neither family could chaperone us. It was my first pleasure trip with a girl, and only my second time at the pictures.

The public service buses ran once every hour. Sandra was the first to catch our scheduled bus, and I boarded it about a mile afterwards after walking three-quarters of a mile out of the village to the bus stop. It was bitterly cold that evening, and by the time the bus arrived I had lost the feeling in my fingers and toes. I was a farm boy and we took pride in not wearing scarves, gloves or warm socks. As soon as the transport arrived, I stepped aboard via the rear platform, climbed the steps to the warmth of the upper deck and found Sandra smiling and waiting for me. As I sat beside her, she grabbed my hand and snuggled close as the vehicle resumed its journey towards York.

The Odeon theatre in Blossom Street was screening the Alfred Hitchcock film *North by Northwest* and this was the film Sandra wanted to see. After leaving the bus, we walked the few yards to the theatre, paid for our tickets and were ushered to the red velvet-covered seats where we sat and waited for the film to begin. In those days there was no counter in the lobby for popcorn and drinks, although during the intermission ladies dressed in white and selling ice-cream did appear in front of the screen. Neither of us smoked, but the auditorium was full of cigarette smoke. We nestled into our chairs, and once again Sandra took hold of my hand.

It was during the famous scene where the crop-duster biplane chases Cary Grant that my ignorance in courtship was revealed. I knew nothing about wooing and could not understand Sandra's behaviour. She moved close to me, tightened her hold of my hand, placed her lips close to my ear, and whispered that the film was scary and I needed to take care of her. I did not know what she meant. I told her not to worry, that the film would end happily, and it was just a story. It never occurred to me that she expected a more passionate response. Even the sweetness of her perfume failed to arouse my emotions. I kept my arms to myself, continued to watch the film and a minute or so later she moved away and dropped my hand.

During the journey home little was said. Sandra told me that she had liked the film, but she then sat silently looking out of the bus window. When we arrived at my stop, I thanked her for the evening, bid her goodnight and left the bus. She looked at me but said nothing.

A day later, the seat next to her on the school bus was occupied by one of her girlfriends. She told me to find somewhere else to sit, and I obeyed her instruction. Shortly thereafter, she and her parents moved away from York, and I never saw them again. The only advice I was given to overcome this humiliation was from a school friend. When I told him what had happened, he said the result was probably for the best. The fact that she had dumped me so quickly without seeking a reason for my lack of response was not the action of a true friend, and the relationship was destined to end regardless.

* * *

Following this failure, the same school friend invited me to his youth club where I met girls who started to fill in the gaps of my knowledge. I was amazed by his ability to attract girls. He would talk to them, flirt with them, dance to make them happy and then accompany them outside. He introduced me at different times to two young women, both very pretty, one of whom was an expert at the physical side of courtship and the other skilled in the language of love. Jointly, they widened my understanding of the female character and introduced me to intimacy and affection. This education was an important milestone in my social development.

My last romantic encounter before starting university was with a girl called Wendy. We dated for several months and she introduced me to her parents, a step that I assumed meant she was serious about our relationship. She moved north to a teacher training college when I started university, but she appeared to want the relationship to continue so I frequently visited her. Anton accompanied me on occasion, and we camped among the nearby sand dunes. Although my amorous behaviour had improved to the point where I could show affection, I could not figure out what women were thinking. Therefore, when Wendy exhibited a lack of enthusiasm and on one occasion completely forgot about my visit, it required my university friends to suggest that maybe she had found someone else and I should not waste my weekends in Northumberland.

These recollections continued for the rest of the journey,

and now I was approaching the second bonfire. I shook off the nightmares of these past romances and started to think about what was about to happen. Across the public garden I saw a cluster of students and recognised one of them as Anton. He noticed my car's arrival and walked over to meet me, accompanied by Jean-Louise. She was wearing a red, cable-knit bobble-hat, red gloves and a matching tartan scarf, an outfit I had seen her wear to geography lectures, but her form was hidden beneath a heavy, knee-length, black parka jacket. Anton introduced us, she smiled at me and we returned to join the rest of the group.

It quickly turned bitterly cold, so a decision was taken to find shelter in the warmth of the nearby student house. I walked alongside Jean-Louise who shivered and complained about the cold but otherwise said very little. Once indoors, we rid ourselves of our coats, grabbed a glass of hot, spiced punch for her and a beer for me, and then we looked around for somewhere to sit. I took charge and manoeuvred us into a quiet corner where there was a two-person sofa. I took off my anorak to reveal the dove-grey, long-haired, merino wool cardigan, and under her parka she wore a cream-coloured, woollen dress over a laurel-green, cable-knit polo-neck jumper.

Once we were seated, she looked at me, obviously expecting me to say something. What should that be? Where should I start? Would this dalliance end up as a one-evening event, or would there be a shared desire for a longer relationship? And if we did continue the friendship, what would happen with "Little Bill"?

Mute Swan: This is the only swan species resident in Britain, where there are about 6,500 pairs, and its cygnets are probably the most famous of all baby birds. The adult is a large water bird, 150 cm/60 inches in length, with pure-white plumage and an orange beak. The beak has a black base and a black knob on top. The swan makes no call when flying, although the swish of its wings can be heard from a long distance. The Queen owns all the mute swans in England and Wales as a result of a mediaeval law passed when swan meat was considered a delicacy.

The mute swan was introduced into North America early in the mid-1800s, and it has become something of a nuisance, displacing indigenous waterfowl and overgrazing aquatic vegetation.

5

A Strange Green Bird

I LOOKED AT JEAN-LOUISE through a sheepish grin, and realised that the challenge I had given myself was daunting. My first difficulty was deciding which aspect of the Geography syllabus would interest her and give her a positive impression of me. I had already concluded that talking about the political aspects of anything was dangerous, and this feeling had been reinforced earlier in the evening by the exchange with Annabelle. It seemed best to start with something safe like discussing our favourite professors. I hoped that my accent would not get in the way of her understanding of me, as her manner of speech was perfect. Yet, before I could begin, a friend came across to offer us cigarettes. Jean-Louise took one, I declined, and in the end it was Jean-Louise who spoke first.

"I thought most men smoked. Is it that you don't want one now, or you don't smoke at all?" She gazed at me, seeming astonished that I had declined.

I told her it was the latter. "I used to," I admitted, "but stopped in the lower sixth when my biology teacher asked me to set an example for the rest of the school."

I worried that she would think there was something wrong

with me since around 70 percent of males smoked and she might regard me as a little odd. In fact I had other reasons for not smoking: I could not afford to buy cigarettes, my mother and stepfather were non-smokers and there was nowhere near my home to purchase tobacco products.

I was therefore pleasantly surprised when she went on to praise my abstinence, and I decided that being different was probably a good thing. She said that she wished she had not begun, and she was concerned now that doctors were linking tobacco to ill health. Her father smoked constantly whereas she smoked only in social situations.

Mentioning her father gave the opportunity to ask about her parents and postpone the topic of geography professors.

"So, what does your father do?"

Considering her refined manners and accent, I expected to be told that he was a professional of some sort, a banker or a civil servant, so I was not expecting the answer she gave.

"He grinds diesel engine parts for an engineering firm based near Manchester. He's done this all his life."

"But that's not work I would have expected, judging by your accent," I blurted out. I was mystified by the reply, and I thought it an unusual occupation.

Her smile forgave my rudeness.

"My father comes from a relatively poor family in Scotland and trained as a metal lathe turner. He met and married my mother who came from a well-off family connected to the Lancashire cotton industry. She moved to Scotland after the wedding, but when her mother died, her father persuaded her to move to Manchester to live close-by. I'm an only child and was three years old at the time. The kids in school bullied me because of my Scottish accent, and my mother gave me elocution lessons until I spoke perfect English."

I asked if she understood my accent. She said she did, but

not some of the words I had used; for example, I had asked her if she felt jiggered and nithered. "What do those words mean?" she asked me. I told her that I was asking if she felt exhausted and cold because she was shivering and walking slowly on the way back to the student house.

The impression I had was that progress was being made because I had shown concern about her wellbeing. I decided to continue talking about her family, but quickly realised my mistake.

"Tell me about your mother. Does she work? What's her background?"

"No, she's never worked, her father wouldn't let her; all she did before she married was paint landscapes, travel and be company for her mother. My parents are happily married but the situation has altered while I've been at university. My mother's been diagnosed with muscular dystrophy, and her condition is deteriorating. She needs my father to do more around the house, and I have to help when I'm home."

Unintentionally, I had brought up a topic that evidently upset Jean-Louise. I fell silent, not knowing what else to say, and she took the opportunity to turn the conversation back on me.

"I have been told you are likeable, but the last time I saw you, you were very unsympathetic towards a woman. Do you remember the field trip to study the chalk landscape in the Yorkshire Wolds? You were with a girl; I think her name was Annabelle. She tripped and fell down the hillside and all you did was watch and grin. You didn't help her to get up or check to see if she was OK. I hope you don't treat all women that way."

I was upset by her reprimand. At the time, I had not realised that I was being watched. Was the comment serious or was she just teasing? Either way, I felt compelled to defend myself.

"I didn't think the fall was serious. She fell on her own, and I could see she wasn't hurt."

"Maybe her dignity was injured," countered Jean-Louise.

That was something I had not considered, and I worried that arguing about it would end our relationship, so I conceded the point. I was feeling uncomfortable and my emotions were probably showing.

Privately, I did not think my behaviour had been insensitive. That autumn afternoon, Annabelle and I had been with a group of students visiting a picturesque dry valley to study its topography. My attention had been drawn to a Late Cretaceous chalk outcrop that had been exposed by a farmer cutting into the hillside to install a new feed bunker for his winter sheep. Unintentionally, a research opportunity had been created for me, as I was able to examine the freshly exposed chalk for fossil bivalves and belemnites, and I was immersed in my studies when Annabelle fell and rolled down the hill. She had wandered off because she had no interest in my fossil collecting, so I did not consider the accident my fault; there were no broken bones and there was no sign of blood. Although she was my girlfriend at the time, it did not occur to me that I would be considered ungentlemanly (and not much of a boyfriend) for not at least offering her a hand to help her up and restore her dignity.

Jean-Louise recognised that she had made her point, smiled at me and resumed her questioning.

"So, tell me about yourself. Why did you come to Hull? Do you have any hobbies? What will you do after graduation?"

I wanted to avoid discussing details about my upbringing, so I told her that I grew up on a farm and I had chosen Hull University because it did not require mathematics or foreign language qualifications. I went on to explain that birdwatching was my favourite hobby and I did not know what I would do after graduation. I mentioned my favourite birding location, Spurn Point, and that I was planning to go there the following morning. I decided not to give her more details because, in my admittedly limited experience, birdwatching was a topic that most girls found boring. However, Jean-Louise was an exception.

"So, you like birds. It's an unusual hobby, why do you find it interesting?" she asked.

I had never been asked the "why" question before, and I wondered if she were truly interested or simply being polite. I gave her the benefit of the doubt.

"I grew up collecting birds' eggs and then shifted to bird-watching when egg-collecting was made illegal. It's something I can do on my own, it's healthy outdoors, there are always new birds to see and it's a hobby that doesn't cost much."

"But why do you find it so interesting?" she persisted.

"Frankly, it's something I can do wherever I am and whenever I have time. There are hundreds of species to see. I record them on my Life List and I enjoy the challenge of identifying each bird. They're living creatures and I can relate to them."

"Then can you tell me what I saw a few weeks ago when I was at home? In a park nearby were two yellowish-green birds, about the size of blackbirds, pecking away in the grass. They had green on their backs and red blotches on their heads. Every so often they fluttered for a few feet, and then dropped back to the ground to resume poking at the lawn. They looked pretty but acted a little unusual, a bit like you!" she smiled.

I did not understand her last comment, but I decided to stay quiet because of the twinkle in her eye. Her description was helpful, but I was curious as to whether the birds had made any sound.

"Yes, it was strange; something like a squeaky bicycle chain!" she replied.

I immediately guessed what she had seen.

"I think they were green woodpeckers. They eat ants, and the noise they make is called a yaffle, a loud laughing sound."

She seemed fascinated by my knowledge and asked to know if the birds were rare, and whether I had seen any. I told her that it was a common species, although in my part of the country, greater-spotted woodpeckers were far more common. A pair of these birds nested in a rotting tree trunk near my farm, and I often visited the site. My mother always warned me not to climb the dead branches to peer into the nest in case a branch broke and I fell. I added that, from the ground, I would watch the birds carry food to their young.

I also mentioned that the lesser-spotted woodpecker was much rarer in Yorkshire, and that I had never seen one. Additionally, there was the sparrow-sized, greyish-brown-mottled wryneck that had become virtually extinct in Britain. It was a migrant which occasionally passed through Spurn Point, but one had never appeared while I was visiting. As for green woodpeckers, I had observed them on Strensall Common near York and on the lawns of Castle Howard. If she wanted to confirm my identification, I suggested she should go to an off-licence (a shop selling alcohol for consumption off premises) and look at a well-known brand of apple cider that used the green woodpecker as its logo.

I thought this would end the conversation on birds, but it did not. She asked if I had a favourite species, and immediately the cuckoo jumped into my mind, but I thought more carefully.

"There are lots to choose from," I replied, "but I think I would select the relatively large wading bird, the curlew, because of its behaviour towards people. Its call symbolises the warm, sunny days of summer and harvest time, and it has a special way of protecting its nest on the ground. Once it sees you, it will try to run in front of you, dragging its wing, hoping you will follow, believing it to be injured, and so guide you away from its eggs or chicks."

Jean-Louise appeared pleased with my selection, but then she switched topics.

"What do you think you'll do once you graduate?" she returned to an earlier question. "Will you stay in Hull or move elsewhere?"

I repeated that I did not know, but I told her what I had earlier told Anabelle: "The Careers Office wants me to teach, and the Geology department has asked me to stay on and conduct research into micropaleontology. I don't believe I can afford to stay at university—I have no money—and I'm not convinced that I'll like teaching."

I had answered honestly, but the money comment worried me because it disclosed more about my background than I had planned, but Jean-Louise did not react.

"So, what does your family want you to do?" Jean-Louise asked.

"My mother is leaving it up to me, and my father (*I did not admit that he was my stepfather*) passed away 20 months ago. Right now, I don't have a plan, but more importantly what will you do, and what does your family expect?"

Jean-Louise had a clear vision for her future.

"My dad didn't want me to attend university. He thinks women should be secretaries and stop work when they marry. My mother disagreed with him strongly, but she did not have the benefit of a university education, so it's my decision to become a professional of some sort and be able to support myself independent of my family."

"So, what will you do?"

"I've been offered a fashion buyer traineeship with the retail chain Marks & Spencer. It's hiring female graduates to manage the selection and purchasing of women's clothing. I love fashion, so it's a great opportunity to do something that

I enjoy and I'm supposed to finalise the details during a visit to its headquarters in January. The one worry I have is that the firm requires trainees to relocate to any store it chooses during the two-year training period, and this might conflict with taking care of my mother."

Her next question devastated me.

"What about Annabelle? Have you finished with her?"

My first thought was that it none of her business. It surprised me that she even knew that I was dating Annabelle—although maybe, if I had thought more carefully, remembering her reference to the field trip should have made me realise that it was not a secret. To avoid conflict, I timidly admitted.

"Not yet! She knows I'm here, but I've not told her about you."

From the look on Jean-Louise's face, I could see that my answer did not please her, but before she could comment, I confronted her with a similar question.

"What about you? Are you still going out with 'Little Bill'?"

She reacted to my question with some embarrassment.

"I thought someone would have told you: We've broken up. He's found a new girlfriend back home."

I wanted more details, but I did not have the courage to ask. Maybe he had finished with her, and, if so, was there something I needed to know about Jean-Louise? Instead, I mumbled that she had just given me the best news of the evening, and then we both moved on to discuss more mundane matters.

"What sort of music do you like?" she asked.

I thought my preferences were innocent enough, and I replied: "Folk songs; in particular, those by Joan Baez, Pete Seeger and Peter, Paul and Mary."

Her response offended me, but I decided not to react.

"I suppose that's because you were brought up on a farm. Folk tunes seem rather simple to me. I prefer the Everly Brothers, Johnny Mathis and ballet music."

The Everly Brothers and Johnny Mathis I knew, but I had no idea of what ballet music sounded like. Her interests in music were not something I could comment upon, so instead I asked the first question that came into my head.

"What's the perfume you're wearing? I really like the smell."

She smiled at my lack of sophistication, but she had the decency to answer:

"It's made by a company called Lentheric and the fragrance is named *Tweed*. It was a birthday gift from my mother."

"Maybe I can buy you some this year?" I volunteered without thinking, but then I realised that she might consider my proposal too personal, premature, and maybe offensive, but she did not. She thanked me and said I was very kind.

The remainder of the evening was dedicated to small talk, although we did manage to include a review of our geography professors. Jean-Louise's favourite lecturer had just returned from Southern Rhodesia's capital, Salisbury (now Harare), and we chatted about the white-dominated government's refusal to share power with the country's black majority. I told her my favourite professor was a Dutchman who lectured in geomorphology.

Towards the end of the evening, Anton came over carrying a fresh round of drinks. He confirmed to Jean-Louise that he had just accepted a PhD research appointment in the Earth Sciences function of the Geography Department, and said he thought I should take up the Geology research opportunity. He also asked to leave the party very soon, and I agreed to meet him at the front door in a few minutes. I first needed to conclude my conversation with Jean-Louise, although I remained uncertain whether she had any interest in me. However, I ignored my misgivings and asked her anyway:

"I'm invited to a party next Saturday. Would you like to come with me?"

I offered the invitation without considering the ethics of asking her to the same party that Annabelle had declined only hours earlier.

To my delight, she replied, "Yes."

We agreed to meet at 7.30pm in a little over a week's time, and thus concluded our first meeting. She gave me a warm smile, and I shook her hand since I considered anything more amorous to be premature.

On the way home, Anton wanted to know how the evening had gone.

"Fine," I replied, not wanting to say much in case he made fun of my interest in Jean-Louise. "She's agreed to go with me to the party next Saturday."

"Do you think she likes you?"

"I'm not sure, but she's asked me to tell Annabelle about our meeting, which I took as a good sign."

I carefully parked the car and we clambered up the stairs to our flat. It had been an exhausting evening, and since I needed to be up early in the morning, I excused myself and went straight to bed. I lay there, tired but kept awake by the pleasant thoughts of the evening and speculating on how the relationship might develop. There were clearly differences between Jean-Louise and me, yet we seemed comfortable in each other's company.

I left for Spurn Point Bird Observatory at 5am, in time to arrive for the morning "fall" of migrating birds. These included linnets, wheatears, house sparrows, redwings, goldfinches, warblers and whinchats. I joined the regular group of birders whom I knew, so that we could collectively verify what we saw and heard.

In my rucksack, I carried the Observer's *Book of Birds*, binoculars, gloves, an extra jumper, waterproofs and, most important of all, my Nature Notebook in which I recorded descriptions of the birds I saw. After the morning migration, I planned to go to the Narrow Neck and Chalk Bank to watch the coastal migration of what was likely to include terns, kittiwakes, fulmars, scoters, divers and probably several species of migrating ducks and gulls. Later, I would move out to the Humber estuary to observe shore birds, including redshanks, greenshanks, black-tailed godwits, knots, golden plovers, sanderlings, dunlins and maybe even curlews.

Usually I volunteered to help with the mist-netting of birds during my visits. This is a means of catching birds in nets suspended between two poles; once caught, each bird is measured and a leg or a wing is banded before the bird is released. Most species caught this way are common passerines, like snow buntings, redstarts, pied flycatchers, whinchats, greenfinches and house sparrows. The Warren, the cottage where my fellow birders ate and slept while at Spurn, also maintained a permanent Heligoland (or funnel trap) to attract a broader range of species; during a previous spring visit, I had been involved in ringing a black redstart, a rare migrant.

To stay warm in the cold outdoors, I wore corduroy trousers and my green anorak over a woollen jumper, and enjoyed detecting on my jacket the smells of bonfires, cigarette smoke and what I thought was Jean-Louise's perfume. I trembled with excitement at the thought of seeing her at lectures the following Monday morning.

(Jean-Louise, November 1965) "He seems a nice person, despite his lack of worldly knowledge, and I'm happy I agreed to see him. He's good looking and I think he's smarter than he

realises. His accent is very strong but I understood most of what he said. It's surprising that at this stage, he has no idea of a career. We are both at Hull University because of free education and failure to pass our foreign language exams. In my case, the language was German.

"Having finished with my former boyfriend (he's gone back to his old school girlfriend), I would like to find someone new before beginning the long days of study in preparation for next May's finals. It was very cold on bonfire night, and I needed to wear warm clothes. Next time I go out with John I'll wear my canary-yellow, baby-doll dress that I've used in the past to attract boyfriends. It's a long-sleeved shift dress, with a V-shaped open back, Peter Pan collar, matching waistband and a flirty skirt with a hem that rests on my knees. I call it my 'dating frock'."

"John's interest in bird watching is unusual, and I can't imagine myself standing outside for hours in cold weather, staring through binoculars, waiting for some bird to pass by, but he's certainly knowledgeable and enthusiastic. I checked the cider bottle and he's correct, they were green woodpeckers. My hobby used to be underground caving until I nearly drowned, and now I'm content to hike across the countryside.

"I'm impressed that John had the determination to give up smoking. All my former boyfriends smoked, yet John didn't smoke a cigarette all evening. That's a good thing, but I'm not sure about some of our other differences. He's certainly not up-to-date in his style of clothes. Also, his choice of music is odd, he doesn't seem to have much empathy with women and his childhood upbringing sounds very different from mine. We didn't talk about politics, but I suspect we'll have our differences.

"However, it's worth dating him a little while longer. My mother wants me to find the right person and not to wait, as

she did, until I become middle-aged. What's most important to me is that I have the freedom to pursue a career. I'll see John next week at lectures when he's back from birdwatching at Spurn Point, and we'll go to his librarian's party in a few days' time.

Green Woodpecker

Green Woodpecker: The largest of three species of woodpecker resident in Britain (length 36 cm/14 inches), with an estimated 52,000 breeding pairs. It spends much of its time on the ground foraging for food, usually digging into ant colonies. Its body is heavy-looking with a short, stubby tail and a long, strong bill. Adults are green on the upper parts, paler underneath, with a bright yellow rump and a patch of red on the top of the head. These birds are sedentary and rarely move far from where they are hatched. Mostly they are seen in parkland, but they increasingly visit gardens.

Woodpeckers are common in North America, but not the green woodpecker.

Eurasian or Common Curlew: **:** *This is a large (length 56cm/22 in), long-legged wading bird, with a heavy rugby-ball shaped body, long neck and small, round head. It has mottled-brown upper parts, greyer underneath, with greyish-blue legs and a long, slender, down-curved beak, and it has a haunting "cur-lee" call. Female and male are almost identical. They nest on the ground in grassland and wet meadows, and the female lays 3 to 6 eggs during spring. They spend winter near the coast and along estuaries. Up until the early1940s, the bird's rich, dark meat was sold in some British butcher's shops.*

A member of the same family, the long-billed curlew is found in North America and is its largest shorebird. It has the same distinctive long, downward-curved bill and the familiar "cur-lee" call.

6

The Fabled Jackdaw

Memories from Friday evening stayed with me throughout the weekend at Spurn Point Bird Observatory, and several birding colleagues mentioned that I appeared unusually happy and asked why that was so. I think they suspected it had to do with a girl, but I told them it was because I was in my final year of lectures—otherwise our conversations involved only bird observations. One of my friends had seen his first male bluethroat (a small migrant bird with a distinctive blue bib) a few weeks earlier in Norfolk, and the warden reported that several "twitchers" (birders whose main objective is to spot rare birds) were monitoring the sighting of a vagrant Isabelline shrike a few miles up the coast, presumably blown westwards off its normal migration route between China and North Africa ("vagrant" refers to a bird seen outside its normal breeding, wintering and migratory range).

During Saturday, I failed to see anything exceptional other than an unusually large flock of waxwings that descended to feast on berries on the promontory, and it was not until Sunday morning that something more unexpected was spotted. A group of us were gazing out to sea when we saw a large seabird hovering above the waves. After careful examination, it turned out to be a black-browed albatross—the first sighting of this species in Yorkshire, and only the fourth recorded in Britain. These birds are usually confined to the southern hemisphere, where two thirds of the global population breed on the Falkland Islands, but occasionally solitary birds can wander or are blown off course north of the Equator.

I stayed at the Warren Cottage, lodging with several experienced birdwatchers who explained the whereabouts of other birding hot spots and boosted my abilities to distinguish between similar-looking species of birds.

* * *

I told Jean-Louise about my success when I saw her after Monday morning's social geography class, and I boasted about spotting the albatross. She was not as interested in my report as I had hoped, and she preferred to discuss the topic of our preceding lecture, China's "Agriculture First" policy and the Great Famine of the late 1950s when tens of millions of Chinese had died of starvation.

Each day of that first week I tried to sit next to her at lecture time. "Little Bill" had returned, but he sat by himself, well away from Jean-Louise. I confess to being smitten with her after our first meeting, but I still had not communicated with Annabelle. Normally, she and I met in the Students' Union, but for the time being, I stayed away because I was unsure of what to say.

The librarians' party was a hit. Jean-Louise was stunning in her yellow dress, my friends approved of the relationship and offered to supply her with any books that she needed. We danced and talked, but not about politics, and at the end of the evening I kissed her. It was more of a peck on the lips than a kiss because I was still unsure of her feelings towards me, but she reacted by grabbing me by the shoulders, holding my face and giving me a long, lingering smooch.

* * *

I ended the relationship with Annabelle during the following week after receiving conflicting advice from friends on how to accomplish the task. One colleague told me to let her "just find out", someone else suggested sending a letter and my roommates counselled that I should tell her directly. In the end I followed their advice and arranged to meet her in the Students' Union. I think she was expecting the news as, although she appeared to be disappointed, she said that my prompt and direct communication was appreciated. We spoke several times thereafter and I stayed friends with her, but generally I kept my distance in case Jean-Louise saw us together.

I suspended my birdwatching activities for six months to give me more time for my studies and my search for a career, but I made one exception during December. I invited Jean-Louise to come with me, but with a forecast of cold and windy weather, she chose to decline.

I joined my usual small group of birders at the Observatory to spend most of the time gazing out to sea, but we saw no more albatrosses—we saw the customary scoters, divers, auks and gulls, but the only highlight was a passing storm petrel, flying close to the surface of the water, about the size of a sparrow, all black except for a white rump. It is unusual to see these birds so close to land, since they live far out at sea, returning only for the breeding season, and then arriving on land, and departing only at night to avoid predation by gulls and skuas.

Late in the afternoon, I wandered up the beach and stumbled across two shore larks searching for food among the sand and shingle. This species was new to me, so I took careful notes and sketched the birds. That evening, when I reported my observations to the warden, my identification was challenged by several colleagues. They suggested that I had seen skylarks or meadow pipits, rather than shore larks, but when I described the birds' yellow and black "bumble-bee" patterns around their heads, the warden accepted my account.

* * *

Anxiety over whether I was making the correct decision about my career worsened after I committed myself to a future in teaching. While it is an honourable profession, it does not pay particularly well and I would have to wait a year before starting to receive an income. However, I did not have the courage to return to the careers officer to discuss alternatives. My only other option was to stay on at university and accept the micropalaeontology appointment, which was Anton's recommendation. Jean-Louise liked the idea of me teaching and assured me that it was a rewarding and secure profession, with teachers providing an important public service. Eventually, I accepted her arguments and submitted to Reading University an application for its one-year teacher-training programme, starting in September 1966. I was confident that I would be enrolled because the government had announced plans to increase its teacher population by around 20 percent.

I selected Reading because of its academic reputation and proximity to London. It would be exciting to live close to the capital, and the duration of the course was only 10 months. Afterwards I could teach either in Yorkshire or elsewhere if Jean-Louise and I were still dating and Marks & Spencer assigned her to another location.

A few days after sending in my application, I was having lunch with the person who had lodged with Anton and me during our second year. He was reading mathematics and he and I had shared the same bedroom. He was a fan of the Everly

Brothers, and especially their hit song *Cathy's Clown,* because apparently Cathy was the name of the girlfriend he had left behind in Lancashire. He was shocked that I was thinking of teaching; he had chosen to join the business community, where salaries were much higher, and he wondered if I had looked at something he called "the milk round".

"What's that?" I was curious.

"It's how companies recruit graduates. Annually, during autumn, they visit universities to talk to interested undergraduates and invite them back to headquarters if they consider them qualified. I've applied to several firms and expect to receive job offers from most."

I had never heard of the process, and only later I learned that the arrangement had started some years previously to allow major employers direct access to undergraduates on campus. It was named "the milk round" because of its similarity to the British practice of delivering milk to people's homes; in this case, it was jobs to undergraduates. I asked my friend for details.

"How do you choose which company to apply for?"

"It's up to you," I was told. "You select the firms you think you are interested in, and there's no limit to the number that can be selected."

"But why would a business employer want to hire a geologist?"

He was amused by my naivety, grinned and volunteered more details.

"The goal is to hire smart people. They don't care about the subject of your degree; they want graduates who have the right personality and ambition. As long as you graduate, you'll get the job if they offer you one. Some firms hire into specific positions and others provide a traineeship. Go and check it out. Applications are managed by the Careers Office."

I wondered if this was the procedure that Jean-Louise had

used to be hired by Marks & Spencer,—and if so, why she had not mentioned it to me. (She later told me that her application was submitted directly and was not part of "the milk round".) I remained suspicious that there must be a catch in the process.

"But isn't it expensive?" I asked. "At least the travel expenses when you visit their headquarters?"

"You don't pay anything," he smiled. "The companies reimburse travel costs and the interviews are free."

It sounded like a fairy story and I had nothing to lose by applying. Although I knew very little about industry, I reasoned that, if I was not selected, at least I would learn something about business and visit parts of the country that I had never seen before. Also, there was always teaching to fall back on.

* * *

The following morning, I returned to the Careers Office, being careful to avoid the careers officer I had seen before. The lady at the reception desk told me that many employers had already attended campus, but she gave me a schedule of firms that were still to come on site. She referred to some business literature and pointed towards a pile of blank application forms. I sat at a desk to look at the list of firms that were still due to visit, to decide if any of them were of interest to me. I selected only those whose names I had heard of, and the final list included Lucas Industries, Pilkington Glass, Massey Ferguson, Unilever, Imperial Chemical Industries, Ford Motor Company Limited, Coats Paton, Shell BP and Electrical & Music Industries (EMI).

I took the paperwork back to our flat and asked Anton to help me complete the application forms. He thought that I was wasting my time but agreed to check the completed documents for spelling errors and to ensure that I had included the required information. The toughest question concerned career interests: What did I want to do? Most functions I had never heard of, but I understood that writing "Anything" was not an acceptable response; I needed to use phrases like "management trainee", "administration", "production" and "engineering".

When I revealed my plan to Jean-Louise, she doubted my success and thought I would be upset by the rejection letters, but it was my decision to go ahead—as much out of curiosity as believing that I could be of value to British industry.

I considered myself to be behaving like a jackdaw, trying to achieve something that I did not understand. As the smallest member of the corvid (crow) family in Britain, the jackdaw is notoriously intelligent and collects items of no particular value, simply because they appear attractive. It likes shiny objects, such as silver-coloured caps from milk bottles and chocolate-bar wrappers.

A flock of jackdaws lived alongside two disused farm cottages near where I had lived on the farm. They were fascinated by anything new and would follow me whenever I stepped into their territory. They were bold birds, willing to go outside their comfort zone in their search for food and shiny items, and I thought I was doing the same. My one anxiety was whether I was being stupid in pursuing a future in business since I knew that jackdaws could behave idiotically. There was the jackdaw in Aesop's *Fables* that unsuccessfully tried to lift a sheep after seeing an eagle lift a lamb, and the vain bird that collected the feathers of other birds to make himself look good, only to be accused of being a cheat. Was I misleading myself in spending time searching for a job in British industry?

I sent in my applications and began receiving interview invitations, although the receptionist dampened my enthusiasm by saying that most companies interviewed anyone who expressed an interest. Interviews took place at the rate of two or three a week, and each of mine usually came to an end when I had nothing to say. Some interviewers had difficulty understanding my accent. Additionally, I typically arrived ill-prepared, could not articulate my career ambitions and was unconvincing when they asked me why I wanted to work for their organisation.

My ego was flattered during mid-December when Reading University wrote to offer me a place on its teaching course. Anton and Jean-Louise congratulated me and suggested that now was the time to abandon "the milk run", as it was unlikely to be successful. However, there were times when I could be obstinate, and this was one of them. With teacher-training already guaranteed, I wanted to enjoy the possibility of the free travel to the headquarters of those firms that found me interesting.

* * *

My final campus interview was with Ford Motor Company Limited (Ford of Britain). It was an unpleasantly cold, damp late-December day and my car refused to start, so I had to cycle approximately two miles to be there on time. I put on my green anorak to protect the tweed sports jacket I always wore for interviews, and I placed clips around my trouser legs to prevent them from rubbing against the oily bicycle chain. I was pleased that this was my last appointment and I would now be able to dedicate more time to preparing for exams. Additionally, there would be greater opportunity to be in the company of Jean-Louise.

The Ford representative greeted me in the interview room and introduced himself as Mr Welsh. I thought his name odd and wondered why he was named after the inhabitants of a particular country when I had never encountered a Mr Scottish, a Mr Irish or a Mr American, although I did recall a cattle-market auctioneer in York who went by the name of Mr English.

Mr Welsh was slim, about the same height as me, and appeared to be in his thirties. He wore a dark blue-striped suit with a white shirt and university tie, which seemed to be the dress code for people in business. His face was narrow, with high, angular cheek bones and a pointed chin so that, in a way, he reminded me of Charles Dickens' Ebenezer Scrooge. He smiled while keeping his lips tightly closed, he constantly squinted and periodically he looked at me menacingly from behind wire-rimmed spectacles. His hair was thinning and cut in a short-back-and-sides style. He spoke without an accent, indicating that he did not come from Yorkshire.

The interview began by him referring to what was apparently a standard script that he placed in front of himself, and on which he periodically checked boxes and scribbled a few words, none of which I could read upside-down.

After making himself comfortable, he began the interrogation: "So, tell me something about yourself."

Recalling the notes I had prepared earlier, I began by saying: "I'm studying Geology and Geography, and I expect to graduate next June. I've been told I should teach, but I want to consider other opportunities. I live near York, but I'm willing to move anywhere for the right job."

I kept my answers brief, based on the advice of my mathematics colleague, who had told me that recruiters preferred short replies.

"And why do you want to join Ford?" was the next question.

This was another topic that I had prepared for: "I believe a traineeship like the one Ford offers will give me a good background in industry and help me find the right job. Also, I prefer to work for a large company, and I would like to live close to London."

"Can you describe your business experience?" was a question I was not prepared for, and I thought it a little stupid. He should know from my application that I did not have business experience.

I could make something up, but that was risky if he asked for details, so I replied, "None directly, except that my class at school once toured Rowntree's chocolate factory in York."

He was not impressed and looked at me with signs of growing impatience. I think he was struggling with my accent and ready to end the interview when there was a serendipitous knock on the door, and the receptionist entered the room carrying two cups of tea. She placed one in front of Mr Welsh, and the other she gave to me. Sugar and milk were provided, and then she departed.

Clearly the interruption had not been anticipated. Mr Welsh looked at me, then at his wrist watch, then glanced at the cups of tea and apparently resigned himself to continuing the interview. Maybe recalling his first question, he went off-script and said: "Tell me something about your academic programmes that you have enjoyed."

I considered his inquiry for a moment. There was much to recall, as I enjoyed both geology and geography, but I thought that my best stories came from the latter. Placing my tea cup on its saucer, I replied: "Probably appreciating our physical surroundings and understanding why the landscape looks as it does."

For the first time in any interview, I had been asked something that interested me. Consequently, I was enthusiastic and sounded self-assured as I continued: "*The Making of the English Landscape* by W.G. Hoskins has been my favourite textbook. It describes how today's landscape reflects the many historic events that have taken place, like the Roman invasion, the Black Death, mediaeval land enclosures and the Industrial Revolution."

I think Mr Welsh sensed that he had aroused my interest, as

he asked, "Can you give me a couple of examples of what you mean?"

I thought more about my answer and settled on two illustrations: "Let's start with Hull. The town is named after the river that flows through it, and it was originally a Viking seaport. In 1293 it was taken over by King Edward to be his supply centre for the military campaign against Scotland, and its name was changed to Kingston-upon-Hull. The town has since developed along the lines of the same street pattern that was established back then."

Mr Welsh told me that he had graduated in history and asked for a second example.

I replied: "When you take the train home tonight, you'll pass along the southern edge of the Yorkshire Wolds. If you travelled north, you would discover evidence of more than 2,000 years of human habitation imprinted on the landscape. Much of it is obscured because of sheep rearing that began on the Wolds during the 1500s. Before then, arable farming flourished until the Black Death arrived in the 1300s and decimated communities, forcing large tracts of the land out of cultivation. As a new source of income, the landowners introduced sheep farming and evicted the remaining peasants. Wharram Percy is the best example of a deserted village."

I stopped talking, although I could see that my storytelling had interested Mr Welsh. He thanked me for the information and indicated that he had a couple of final questions.

"Have you thought about which department you might want to work in?"

I told him I could not decide. From reading the Ford brochures, I thought the sales function was interesting, but possibly also Finance, and I was open to his suggestions.

"What about PP&C?" he enquired.

"What's that?" I asked.

He raised his eyebrows and replied: "Production Planning and Control. It's an important new function in manufacturing, and it's needed because there are so many different components and colour choices in car assemblies these days. We call the system 'Just in Time' because parts are delivered to factories in accordance with assembly-line schedules. The function may interest you because you seem fairly analytical."

I thanked him, we shook hands and he told me I might hear from the company during January. I left the room feeling relieved that the ordeal was over.

That evening I described my experiences to Anton and Richard, who cautioned me that although the interview had gone well, working in industry might not be my strong suit. Jean-Louise was pleased the interviews were over and encouraged me to submit my acceptance of the teaching traineeship back to Reading University. We also talked about our separation during the year-end holidays; she was going home to work in the local post office, delivering Christmas cards, and my mother had found me a job as a van delivery driver in York.

Once home in York, I was kept busy driving right up until Christmas Day, and had little time to call Jean-Louise. I was working in what was called a "closed-shop" that the Labour government had reinstated after the general election at the request of the trade unions. The union representative told me that I was required to observe all union agreements, even though I did not need to become a member, and that my work was driving only; under no circumstances should I load the van or perform other duties. Additionally, if I finished early, I must not return to the shop until 30 minutes before the lunch break or, if it was in the afternoon, 30 minutes before the end of the shift; if necessary, I should park and wait until it was time to return.

Other than driving the van, the holidays were spent with

family and friends. I eagerly looked forward to returning to Hull to resume the relationship with Jean-Louise, but was increasingly anxious at the thought of beginning five long months of intensive study for final examinations. My mother overheard me talking to Jean-Louise on the telephone, and inevitably remarked: "I would like to meet your friend if you keep seeing her." I wondered if the relationship would last that long as I drove my trusted Ford Popular back to Hull.

(Jean-Louise, January 1966) "The relationship with John continues. My mother was eager to hear details about him, although I told her it was too early for him to be introduced. He was a little unhappy when I turned down the visit to Spurn Point, but the idea of standing outside in gale-force winds during a December snow storm is horrifying to me.

"Little Bill and I have not talked since I met John, and John apparently has ended his relationship with Annabelle. I hear about what takes place from my roommate, who in turn hears it from John's roommates.

"John is still deciding on his career, although I expect him to teach. He was pleased when Reading offered him a place on its course, and his trifling with 'the milk round' seems like a waste of time. I expect it to end without a job offer.

"I continue my plans to join Marks & Spencer, but my mother's health isn't improving. The effects of muscular dystrophy seem relentless, and she is clearly weaker than when I left in summer. She tries to do most things around the house, but my father has to help. Also, there are friends living three doors away who call in regularly while my father is at work. I'm worried that Marks & Spencer will be inflexible towards my need for time off to look after my mother, and they may

assign me to a location a long way from home. I've decided to consider teaching and maybe join John in Reading.

"Delivering the Christmas post was fun, and it was the third year I have done this type of work; the pocket-money is useful. I met someone from the London School of Economics who shared his strong anti-war opinions on Vietnam and agreed with my sentiments on Southern Rhodesia; I like meeting people who hold opinions similar to mine. The Americans seem to be escalating the war in Vietnam by sending additional troops and increasing the monthly draft, and the government of Southern Rhodesia has now totally broken away from Britain and declared unilateral independence."

"I expect John to call round at my student home as soon as I'm back in Hull. We're both in for a tough five months of study as well as needing to finalise our career plans."

Jackdaw: *This is the smallest member of the crow family in Britain, being only 34 cm/13 inches in length. The other breeding species are rook, carrion crow, magpie, raven, jay, hooded crow and chough. Its plumage is totally black except for light grey-silvery feathers on the back of its neck. There are around 1.4 million breeding pairs in Britain. The bird is highly sociable, intelligent, curious and mischievous. Its call is a harsh, repeated "tchak" which gives it its common name of "jack". It nests in chimneys, buildings and tree holes, and it has a reputation for being a collector of bright objects.*

It is not resident in North America, although it is reported to be a rare vagrant.

7

Patient Grey Herons

The day after I returned to Hull, Jean-Louise arrived back by train and we were overjoyed to be together again. There was no exchange of holiday gifts, since we had agreed that neither of us had the funds, but we celebrated the reunion by eating at our favourite Chinese restaurant. Jean-Louise told me how a work colleague had invited her out on a date but that she had mentioned me and declined his invitation, so I thanked her.

The health of Jean-Louise's mother was a growing source of distress, and the prognosis was that her muscles would continue to weaken slowly over time. She was insistent that her illness should not interfere with her daughter's education and asked Jean-Louise not to return home until Easter, when the family would celebrate her 21st birthday. Jean-Louise revealed that during the holidays she had submitted an application to Reading University for its teaching diploma course, just in case Marks & Spencer would not provide flexible working arrangements to enable her to take care of her mother.

As soon as we were back on campus, we began to prepare for exams and complete our Geography dissertations that were due by the end of March 1966. Jean-Louise was writing a paper on the effects of train transport on the welfare of Lancashire mill workers during the nineteenth century, I understood Anton to be writing about actions necessary to prevent a recurrence of the 1953 floods along the East Coast of Britain, and my dissertation was titled *The Evolution of Agriculture on the Western Flank of the Wolds in the East Riding of Yorkshire.* Relatives and friends had contributed to my research which examined the evolution of farm management, from collective medieval strip-farming to modern-day mechanised agriculture.

A priority for me was to visit the Careers Office to collect any letters that had been sent during the holidays by company representatives who had interviewed me. Mostly these were turn-down notices, but four firms had invited me for a second interview and all of them were headquartered in the London region. I shared their content with Jean-Louise and Anton, and I told both of them that I would proceed to the next stage in my job search and travel to the head offices of these companies. They thought I was wasting my time.

Locally, the Member of Parliament for Hull North had died, and an election for a successor was scheduled for 27th January 1966. Nationally, the outcome was important, as the Labour government's small majority in the 1964 general election had fallen from five to three seats, and newspaper articles speculated that the Conservative Party would win. Surprisingly, and maybe because it was announced that the Humber Bridge would be built, Labour won with an increased majority. Jean-Louise was annoyed that she was just three months short of being able to vote, and I failed to participate because I had not registered on the electoral rolls.

The Geology Department staff again asked me to consider the doctoral research project, and the invitation was communicated during our last field trip before final examinations. We were studying the coralline oolite (limestone) formation, an important outcrop of the Lower Cretaceous period, on Filey Brigg, along the Yorkshire coast. It is a well-known site for palaeogeographical study (the study of past geologic times) and illustrates the processes of sedimentation, stratification and the fossilisation of bivalves, belemnites and ammonites. Once more, I declined the invitation. Jean-Louise took my decision to mean that I would definitely be going to Reading to be trained as a teacher.

I wanted to visit all four companies that had expressed an interest in me before finally deciding what I should do. It was unclear what opportunities were available in each firm and, if nothing else, I would enjoy the travel. Friends questioned my wisdom regarding the company that was first on my list, asking why I would consider working for an organisation that wanted to hire me as a production trainee in one of its factories in the north of England, when I wanted to move south; also, I would probably dislike the type of work.

Consequently, I wrote to Coats Paton to decline their invitation, but decided to move forward with the other three firms. Shell-Mex/ BP and EMI wanted to discuss unspecified job opportunities, and Ford of Britain requested that I consider its graduate trainee programme.

* * *

Attending these interviews involved travelling by train for several hours between Hull and London, and I used the time to complete my university dissertation. The other feature of these journeys was the number of solitary grey herons I saw from the train window; the birds stood alongside slow-moving rivers and canals, patiently waiting to catch their next meal. These guardians of the waterways had the patience and persistence to wait for long periods until their prey came along. In a sense I felt they were like me, waiting for the right opportunity to arrive and then grabbing their food before it swam away. They were opportunistic, and content to wait; if nothing came by, they would fly to a new target, in the same way that I would "fly" to teaching if nothing came of my business interviews.

The trip to Shell Mex House was a disaster. I had thought I was invited for interview by a large firm dealing with oil exploration and extraction, but it turned out to be a small company set up as a joint venture between British Petroleum and Shell to jointly manage their British marketing function. Worse still, the firm had announced a spin-off of the sales component, leaving the joint-venture company with nothing more than the storage and distribution of petrol to filling stations in Britain. The organisation had no idea what I could do for it, and I had images of driving a tanker lorry for the rest of my life; this, although an honourable occupation, was not on my list of career preferences.

By now it was mid-February, and Jean-Louise had visited Marks & Spencer in London to finalise her traineeship arrangements. She returned, feeling extremely disappointed, and said she had withdrawn her job acceptance. Apparently, the company was unwilling to promise to place her in a store close to Manchester, and they would not guarantee to give her time off if she needed to look after her mother. The firm was worried about creating an unwanted precedent as well as interfering with her training. Jean-Louise therefore wrote to Reading University and accepted its teacher training offer.

In late February, I travelled to west London to meet the EMI recruiters. I had thoroughly researched the firm, in order to avoid a repetition of the Shell-Mex/BP experience, and I learned that I had been invited to the head office because the campus interviewer thought I might make an excellent accountant. I wondered why, since maths was my worst subject, but unfortunately no explanation was forthcoming. At the end of the day, I was asked to join the firm as an assistant in the accounting department and study for an accountancy qualification at night school. For someone who had never passed a mathematics exam in his life, this seemed like a very risky proposition, so I declined.

My university friend studying mathematics questioned my decision and stressed how difficult it was to become an accountant. He told me that accounting firms generally recruit graduates only from leading universities, and give priority to applicants who had a private school education. He believed that I had rejected a once-in-a-lifetime opportunity.

Thus, the second interview with Ford of Britain in early March was my last chance to find a job in industry that was acceptable to me. I researched the firm and studied functional differences such as sales versus marketing, vehicle design as distinct from vehicle development and why financial analysis was separate from accounting.

I caught the train to London from Hull Paragon station and booked a return ticket for the last train home the following day. I expected to be back home a little after 10pm. Jean-Louise wished me luck and told me to enjoy the journey.

The invitation letter from Ford said that the interviews would take all day, and several applicants would participate simultaneously in the process. The interviews would be held in Ford's Brentwood headquarters, so the firm booked rooms for the applicants in a nearby hotel and arranged for a Ford Transit van and driver to pick us up the following morning. I thought the hotel was very fancy and not the type of place I had previously experienced.

I wore my Harris Tweed sports jacket and thought it was being admired when I received stares from the other candidates. My aunt had bought the coat from Hepworth's, a clothing shop in High Ousegate, York. Its design was what was called "houndstooth", a bold series of broken checks, woven in cream, green, maroon and pale brown made to look like the bite marks of a hound. My aunt's husband owned a similar coat which he wore to the weekly York Cattle Market and the annual Great Yorkshire Agricultural Show.

The day's agenda consisted of a series of interviews individually arranged for each candidate. Clearly it was a competitive process. We were told to meet a representative from Graduate Recruitment at the end of the day to hear if we had been accepted or not. If selected, we would be asked to start work in mid-summer, first for a three-week orientation period, followed by pre-placements in different functions until we were placed in a position.

After the initial greetings and introductions, there was time for tea and biscuits. The main topic of conversation was the British Prime Minister's recent decision to announce a general election to take place on 31st March 1966. Most expected Labour to win convincingly because of its economic policies.

The interviews were exhausting. Each lasted for about an hour and involved being questioned by a Ford employee who had been a graduate trainee a few years earlier. It was not unusual for the same question to be asked several times, and sometimes it was uncomfortable sitting in the same position for long periods, causing my feet to go numb, and making me almost fall over when I stood up.

The questions centred on education, business experience, non-academic interests and why I had applied to Ford; no-one seemed interested in functional preferences. I kept my answers short, asked the interviewer to repeat any question I did not understand and responded honestly and with as much self-confidence as I could muster. After each interview, a "Hire" or "Do Not Hire" message was sent to the Graduate Recruitment office which tallied up the recommendations to decide if an applicant should be offered a traineeship.

During mid-afternoon, I returned to the building's ground floor to notify the receptionist that I was ready to meet my Graduate Recruitment representative. The receptionist buzzed the manager's office and asked me to take a seat. I sat on a large leather armchair surrounded by other opulent sofas and chairs, ceramic pots full of evergreen plants and on show, a new Ford Corsair, a Mark 1 Cortina and a Ford Transit van. There were also several flashy posters advertising the "Mark of Distinction" slogan for the about-to-be-launched Mark IV Zephyr/Zodiac.

About 30 minutes later, a rather pretty-looking, curly-haired blonde girl appeared from a side corridor and called out my name. I shook her hand and she asked me to follow.

"Mr Smith is ready to see you now," she said in a monotone. "Sorry we kept you waiting, but it's our busy time of year."

I accepted the apology and told her the delay was unimportant (my train did not depart until early evening). Mr Smith signalled me to enter his office. He was an older version of Mr Welsh, attired in a faded grey suit and with a lampshade-shaped moustache that matched his grey hair. He smiled, asked me to take a seat, then changed my life forever.

"Many people seem to like you," he began, his eyes peering over his metal-rimmed reading glasses as he sought to gauge my reaction. "We've decided to offer you a traineeship, but we would like you to accept it today. We're about to reach our quota for the year, and as soon as we do, all outstanding offers will be cancelled. If you agree, I'll send you a formal employment offer in the post, along with our Staff Handbook."

I was flabbergasted. What could I say? Receiving a job offer so rapidly was not what I had expected, nor was it something that my mathematics colleague had warned me about. My brain raced to think of something to say to give me more time to decide whether or not to accept the offer; I managed to ask: "Don't you first need references from the university and proof of my graduation?"

Mr Smith smiled again. "Our offer is conditional on you passing your exams, but we don't need anything further from the university. The only remaining piece of the process is that you must pass our medical examination. I'll give you a form and you should complete it and return it to the company as quickly as possible. I hope you can accept our offer."

I was in a predicament. If I did not accept, I was likely to be destined for a career in teaching; if I asked for more time, however, I risked sacrificing the only job offer from a company in which I was interested and which was willing to hire me. The only other option that occurred to me was to accept and later withdraw if I had second thoughts, but that alternative seemed dishonest and unappealing.

I wondered how Jean-Louise might react, if we were not both going to Reading after all, but I thought that she would probably understand the situation and agree with whatever decision I took. Also, who knew how our relationship might develop? I did not think I should pass up a once-in-a-lifetime opportunity just because Jean-Louise and I were presently dating. After all, it was my life and therefore it was my decision.

Mr Smith must have sensed my uncertainty as he added, "You should know that we have just increased our annual starting salary to £1,050 *(estimated to be around £38,000, or US$50,000, in today's value)*. Maybe this will help?"

It did. The amount was much higher than any starting salary provided by the other companies on my list, and well ahead of a teacher's pay. Additionally, I would not need to wait a year before starting to earn.

"I accept!" I announced as enthusiastically as I could.

I hoped it was the right decision. I thought my mother

would be proud of me and my roommates would be surprised that I had been so successful. I would explain to Jean-Louise my reasons for accepting, and I would be able to visit her in Reading from time-to-time.

Mr Smith thanked me and advised that I could join the company in either July or August; my preference should be indicated on the acceptance form that I should sign and return.

As the train carried me back to Hull, the more I thought about the day's events the more excited I was about the outcome. I had achieved something in four months that others had considered impossible. I did not know what duties I would perform for Ford, but that could be decided later.

The medical form was completed during the train journey and I dropped it into the railway station post-box. Arriving home, I found Anton and Richard asleep and did not want to disturb them. It had been an exhausting day, so I quietly undressed and slipped into bed, still overjoyed by the outcome of the day's events, and looking forward to boasting about my achievements the following morning.

(Jean-Louise, early March 1966) "I was surprised that John received invitations from four firms for a second interview. I know he is intelligent but he has absolutely no business experience. Maybe his rural accent helps him because it is a good fit with working men. Even so, it's hardly likely that a west London company needs a Yorkshire accent in its Accounting Department, and at Ford in Dagenham, he would be a better fit if his accent was Cockney.

"I've accepted the teaching course that John was offered. Withdrawing from Marks & Spencer was very difficult, but I feared I might be fired if I could not fulfill the firm's training requirements because of my mother's health. It's awful how

some companies treat women and are unwilling to make allowances for family responsibilities and, in some cases, even terminate female staff when they marry or become pregnant.

"I'm studying hard and my dissertation has been submitted. The assistant professor teaching social geography has a crush on me, and although I'm not interested, I have to be careful that he doesn't retaliate by affecting the level of my degree. It's a difficult situation and I've not told John.

"The other annoyance is this pending general election. It takes place only two weeks before my 21st birthday and therefore I'm ineligible to vote. I hope Prime Minister Wilson wins, and so does my father. John will be here in the morning to tell me about his visit to Ford. It's his last interview and, once he knows the results, we can prepare for our move to Reading."

Grey Heron: A mainly resident, large wading bird, typically seen throughout the year in and around wetlands; it stands about 120 cm (47 in) tall and stays motionless at the water's edge, waiting to stab its passing prey. It possesses a powerful yellowish bill, and while it is mainly a piscivore, it is also known to catch small birds, amphibians and little mammals. Its plumage is mostly bluish-grey, with white on the head and a broad black stripe extending from the eye to the black crest; the underparts are greyish-white, with some black on the flanks. When in flight, its long legs are stretched out behind and its head is tucked in towards its body. There are about 13,000 heron nests in Britain, and about 63,000 birds spend the winter here. Most heronries (groups of nests) are in trees, and herons are among the species that nest earliest in the year.

In the United States, a close relative is the great blue heron, which is larger and has a broader wing span than the European variety.

8

The Nightingale

EXCITEMENT CREATED BY the day before roused me early in the morning. The sensation was the same as winning a tightly fought football game or the elation of spotting a firecrest or a black-browed albatross. I lay listening to the occasional snores of Richard and groans from Anton, and I was impatient to share my good news.

Once they were awake, I announced my achievement before they had time to ask. They were astonished that the company had offered me a traineeship on the same day as the interviews. I told them about my starting salary and how I hoped to begin my employment in late August. I now needed to buy a suit, some white shirts and a briefcase before I started work. They were impressed but cautioned that Ford might not live up to my expectations and I should be careful.

"What exactly will you do?" Richard asked.

I confessed that my duties were unclear. "Once the orientation is over, I'll be given some pre-placements until I find a job that I like."

"And what functions are you looking at?"

"I don't know," I told Richard. "However, Ford must have some idea of what I'm good at because it has hired me."

There then followed a barrage of questions which I answered to the best of my ability.

"Who will choose your pre-placements?" I did not know, but I assumed it would be Graduate Recruitment.

"Where will you live?" That was unknown too, but Mr Smith had mentioned that Graduate Recruitment would find me lodgings close by.

"What about buying Ford vehicles at a discount?" Richard probed further.

I was annoyed with myself for not having asked that question during the interviews. I later read that each Ford employee was entitled to purchase up to two new vehicles and one used passenger car at employee prices each year. If the employee disposed of a vehicle within 12 months of receipt, he (or she) had to pay the company the difference between the original price and the regular retail price at the time of delivery.

"When will they start paying you?" was the next question. I replied that I did not know, but I later read in the *Handbook for Salaried Employees* that salaries were paid monthly in arrears.

Anton then asked the most serious question: "What about Jean-Louise? What does she think of your decision not to go to Reading?"

Calmly I replied, "I haven't told her yet, but I'll see her later today. My plan is to go to Reading at weekends and use some of my salary so that we can enjoy life together. I don't think there will be a problem."

Anton looked sceptical. "I think you should tell her as soon as possible. She's expecting you to accompany her to Reading."

His comment made me feel a little uneasy that I had not thought to call her before starting my journey home. I did not want her to hear my news from someone else, so I decided to call in and see her on my way to campus. I believed she would be delighted, as I knocked on her bedroom door and she called me to enter.

"So, what's the news?" she stared at me, expecting that it would be like the other interviews, not good.

I grinned and clenched my left fist. "Guess what! They've offered me a traineeship and want me start this summer."

She waited for evidence that I had not accepted the offer and still intended to accompany her to Reading.

"Congratulations," she responded, "but I assume we're still going to Reading together?"

"Well, not exactly." I could sense her attitude towards me changing. "They wanted an immediate decision, so I've accepted the appointment, but don't worry—I still plan to visit you in Reading."

Her smile disappeared and I could hear a sharp intake of breath. "You've done what?" she exclaimed. "You've accepted the offer without discussing it with me? You're not serious are you? Don't I matter anymore?"

A feeling of dread came over me as I realised that I might have acted prematurely, and I tried to justify my actions. "But I'll earn much more than a teacher, and Brentwood isn't far from Reading. I'll visit you at weekends."

In an instant I knew I had said the wrong thing.

"That's not the point," she scowled at me. "I'm only going to Reading because of you and now you decide to do something entirely different without even talking to me. I care about you but you don't seem to care for me. If this is what you're going to do, we should end our relationship *now*! It's just not going to work."

With that, she turned her back on me and returned to studying. I stood there feeling rejected and heartbroken. This had not been my plan, and I had no desire to break up with Jean-Louise. However, she did not look as though she was about to change her mind, so I did as I was told and left the room.

* * *

Close to tears, I retraced my journey back to the flat and told Anton what had happened. He listened but was not very sympathetic. Accepting the traineeship without first talking to Jean-Louise was unwise he said. I asked for his help, which he agreed to give, but warned me that the quarrel might last a long time, maybe forever.

What was I supposed to do? This was an entirely new experience for me. Should I wait for Jean-Louise to return to her senses and contact me, or was it up to me to redeem myself and heal the broken relationship? Early reports indicated that Jean-Louise had no intention of forgiving me, nor any desire to see me again. The friendship was over as far as she was concerned. She was apparently annoyed with herself that she had not paid more attention to my treatment of Annabelle.

My first act of conciliation was to send her a box of chocolates. It had no effect. The box was returned unopened. Meanwhile, the more I thought about what was happening, the angrier I became. Jean-Louise had known that I was considering employment in industry, yet at no stage had she asked me to stop because she wanted us to go to Reading together. Also, the urgency of the Ford decision was forced upon me, so it was not really my fault that I had not had time to consult with her. Finally, I did not think it unreasonable to accept the offer and arrange to visit her during weekends while she was in Reading.

Eventually, however, I calmed down and decided that I had to do something or our relationship would end permanently, so I needed a plan. I thought back to the innocent looks that I had cultivated at school in order to avoid classroom detentions, and I decided to try to use these to convey respect and concern for Jean-Louise. Also, as I was good at storytelling, with a good sense of humour, I would try to make her laugh. Finally, I would have to accept that I had made a mistake and be prepared to compromise. I would try to reason with her and explain that my actions had been honest and well-intentioned, but at the same time, I would acknowledge that my acceptance of Ford's offer was premature and I should have talked to her first. The difficulty of the situation reminded me of a time when, as a teenager, I had to persuade someone that I had seen a nightingale.

One evening, I saw this solitary bird skulking deep within a hawthorn thicket and listened to its song. It was not supposed to be there, and I did not have my binoculars for a close-up look. However, it was the right size, its plumage was the brownish-olive colour of a nightingale and its bubbling, harmonic song was unmistakeable. Despite this, when I reported the observation my identification was challenged. I concluded that I should have gathered more information and first discussed the sighting with others before deciding that it was a nightingale.

"Nightingales never make it to that part of Yorkshire," I was told. "It must have been a juvenile robin, a blackbird or a song thrush."

However, I knew what I had seen and was familiar with the song patterns of the alternatives. I did my best to persuade the bird recorder of my sighting, and he eventually agreed to hold my report on record in case other sightings were received. My new "nightingale" project was to persuade Jean-Louise why it was appropriate for me to have accepted the Ford traineeship, without talking to her, and convince her that my actions were honest and reasonable under the circumstances. If I could not persuade her, I was prepared to withdraw my acceptance from Ford and become a teacher like her.

* * *

Therefore, it was with great apprehension that I began my evening drive a few days later to meet Jean-Louise in her student room. Her roommate had been tasked by Anton to be certain that she was present. I knocked on the bedroom door and her roommate let me in and then excused herself, knowing the purpose of my visit.

"Why are you here?" Jean-Louise glowered at me from across the room. "If you're here to say you're sorry, you're wasting your time. I once thought you loved me, but clearly you don't. It's not easy for me to break up with you, but I think it's the right decision."

Her immediate stubbornness alarmed me but I resolved not to give up and walk away. I really wanted her back, so I began my plea.

"I'm here to say I'm sorry and that I don't want us to break up. I regret that I made the decision without talking to you, but they made me decide on the spot or risk losing the opportunity. I still think I did the right thing, but I'll withdraw my acceptance if that's what will get us back together again."

"That's not the point," Jean-Louise said, shaking her head in astonishment. "You've made your decision and it forces us to live apart. Inevitably we'll meet new people and our lives will go off in different directions. It seems sensible to end the relationship now, rather than wait for it to disintegrate over the coming months. I'm sorry it has to end this way, but it just won't work if you move to Essex."

Her assessment distressed me but I was going to fight back. "But Reading's not that far from Brentwood, and I mean what I say when I promise to visit you every weekend."

"But it's 70 miles away, and that's a long distance," argued Jean-Louise.

"I know, but it's me that will do the driving, and I'll buy a new car if I have to."

"That's part of the problem," Jean-Louise complained. "You'll buy a big fancy car and all the girls in Essex will want to go out with you. I can see what will happen. How can I trust you after what you've just done to me?"

I told her that she was better looking than any girl in Essex and I had learned my lesson. It would not happen again.

"But why work for Ford?" she appealed. "My father says it mistreats its workers, bullies the trade unions and complains to the government whenever its employees go on strike. Why not come and teach with me?"

"But I don't want to teach", I cried. "You've said yourself that I don't have the patience to be a teacher, and if your father's correct about Ford, I can always change companies."

I then surprised her by adding: "And who knows, I could end up working in Ford's truck plant that's only a few miles from Reading. Maybe I'll ask to be moved there."

"And what if instead you're posted to some other place outside of Essex?" she snapped back. "We'll be further apart, and it will be like what Marks & Spencer was going to do to me."

I searched for a compromise. "What if I promise not to accept any position outside Essex while you're in Reading, other than if it's in the Langley truck plant?" I thought I could honour the commitment because Ford of Britain's main staff functions were based in Essex.

I sensed I was making progress and pushed forward. I needed to win her back. "And what if I agree to always talk to you before making important decisions in the future and pledge not to date girls in Essex? I really do want us to stay together."

She looked at me, shook her head in disbelief, and then slowly allowed her face to relax.

"You really are hopeless. I can't forgive you for what you

did, but I accept that you didn't intend to cause me pain, so go ahead and accept the Ford traineeship. You're so stubborn and such a dreamer; sometimes I can't figure you out, but I still love you. I don't really want us to break up either, but you must never ever behave like that again."

The thought that we would be together once more made me instantly joyful, and I grinned my acceptance of all the promises I had made. We arranged to go out that evening for cod and chips at the Gainsborough Fish Restaurant to celebrate. Our relationship restored, we kissed, said our goodbyes, and I hurried onwards to campus to celebrate.

(Jean-Louise, late March 1966) "He's proud of his success at Ford, but it never occurred to him that I would be upset if he didn't go to Reading. He seems to be empathetic towards birds but not towards women or me. I had serious doubts about getting back together, but he's so intense that it's hard not to feel sorry for him. Also, Anton said our separation was having a negative effect on his studies, and I've no wish to jeopardise anyone's chance of graduating. Also, I think I still love him. Now we'll see what happens at Ford and in Reading.

"He thought that I was going to Reading because of the health of my mother, which was a little ridiculous. It was my decision to teach, but I chose Reading so that I would be with him. It would have been far simpler for me to have applied to a Manchester institution and moved closer to home to look after my parents.

"The chocolates he sent were rather thoughtless because they were fattening, and the bouquet of flowers I expected never arrived. He's clearly repentant, and now he wants me to meet his mother. The relationship still may fail; it's up to him to show me that he cares."

Nightingale: A delicate-looking bird, 15 cm/6 inches in length, and difficult to spot because it prefers to skulk in dense undergrowth. It migrates to Britain in April, sings until June (the male only) a rich and powerful bubbling song and leaves during August to winter in North and West Africa. Both sexes have identical plumage: brown upperparts, buff to white underparts and a broad rufous tail. It is slightly larger than a British robin and half the size of an American one. There are approximately 7,000 breeding males in Britain, but the numbers are estimated to have declined by about 90 percent during the past 50 years because of loss of habitat and climate change. The male's powerful night-time singing has been celebrated by poets and others since classical antiquity as a melancholy and plaintive tune symbolising the sorrowful aspects of love.

Nightingales are not found in North America.

9

Introduction To Spurn Point Bird Observatory

Ford's written offer of employment rested on the kitchen table in the attic for the duration of my falling-out with Jean-Louise. It constantly reminded me that I had probably lost a girlfriend and my career was on hold. I wished to sign it, but was told to wait until the conflict was resolved, and that I should blame the Post Office if there were any difficulties caused by the delay. Once we had made up, Jean-Louise agreed that I should sign the letter and return it to Ford of Britain.

Amid the crisis, I found an opportunity to register my name on the electoral roll prior to the general election. The Electoral Officer collected the information she needed, and then I ignorantly asked if my vote could be transferred to a constituency that traditionally elected a Conservative Member of Parliament. The clerk looked at me in disbelief and told me that the constituency in which I voted was based on where I lived, and that could not be changed.

The general election took place on 31st March 1966 and was won convincingly by the Labour Party, with a hugely increased

Parliamentary majority of nearly 100 seats. A fresh challenge for the government arose almost immediately when public disorder and rioting broke out for the first time since World War 11 in Northern Ireland. Separately, the government announced that it was beginning investigations to determine if the country should submit another application to join the European Economic Community.

There was a different type of chaos in mid-May when seamen nationwide went on strike; they demanded a reduction in their basic "at sea" working week from 56 to 40 hours and a pay raise. It was a very unpleasant dispute. The Labour government opposed the demands because of their likely effect on the British economy, and by late May had declared a state of emergency that allowed Navy personnel to reposition ships and move essential supplies off the docks. Allegations were made that Communists were trying to undermine the country's security and harm Britain's economic welfare. Some student support was given to the Hull seamen, but most of us were busy sitting exams.

My relationship with Jean-Louise remained strong and we openly shared our feelings towards one another, although we did not spend much time together because of preparing for exams. Anton and I studied in the university library while Jean-Louise swotted in her student house. For the time being, our friendships with each other were limited to attending Geography lectures together and taking part in Saturday night dances at the Students' Union.

* * *

Jean-Louise went home to Manchester during early April for the Easter holidays and to celebrate her 21st birthday. Before she left, I took her to our favourite Chinese restaurant and presented her with a small bottle of Lentheric's *Tweed* perfume.

Later, I heard that the birthday celebration with her parents was spoiled because of her mother's failing health. I remained in Hull to swot for exams, and I managed to survive two weeks on a diet of fried SPAM, boiled potatoes and vegetables. Money was in short supply, as usual, and I could not borrow from my roommates who were both away staying with their families.

Jean-Louise gave me some press cuttings from her father when she returned to Hull. He remained sceptical about my decision to join Ford and wanted me to read the articles. They gave an account of a dispute at Ford's Dagenham assembly plant between management and its paint sprayers. The articles reported that the paint sprayers worked in hot, humid, dirty conditions, and when management unilaterally reduced their rest-time outside the paint booths, they reacted by walking off the job, stopping vehicle production and causing Ford to seek intervention from the government. The articles implied that Ford's action was intended to cause a strike so that it could lower production volumes because of reduced sales and at the same time, avoid paying wages to its workers.

* * *

Shortly thereafter, I fulfilled my promise to introduce Jean-Louise to my mother. However, I told Jean-Louise as little as possible about my family, and I did not mention either my father or stepfather.

I explained that my mother lived in a small village of about 20 farms and houses, with no shops or pubs. It was served by one bus a week that came into the village—on Thursdays, for market day,—and there was a travelling library that visited once a fortnight. The community supported itself with basic needs. My mother obtained milk, pigs' lard and butter from a neighbour, grew her own fruit and vegetables, reared chickens for their eggs and meat, and bought whatever else was needed from a grocer whose van came to the village twice weekly.

"Where in the world are you taking me?" Jean-Louise asked as we neared my old home on an unusually cold late April evening. Outside it was pitch black, and she shivered with the chill of a heater-less car. Ahead, as far as she could see, there was nothing but darkness. For me, it was the landscape I was used to; I knew the road was straight and narrow.

I tried to reassure her: "We're almost there. Don't worry, we're not lost."

I am not sure she believed me. She had grown up as a city girl in a neighbourhood of fashionable, semi-detached houses, with many shops within a short walking distance; also, there were buses galore, public lighting illuminated the streets and there was easy access to trains travelling into Manchester.

Soon the scattered lights of the village could be seen, and a few minutes later my mother welcomed us and introduced Jean-Louise to my two younger siblings. During dinner we discussed the status of our final examinations, the health of Jean-Louise's mother and Jean-Louise's 21st birthday. Afterwards, we settled down to drink cups of tea, and my mother carried out the inevitable interrogation about our future plans. Why was Jean-Louise going to teach? When would I start with Ford? How would we stay in contact when we were living so far apart? How did we first meet, and what was Jean-Louise's family background? When my mother heard that Jean-Louise's mother was a deaconess at her local church, she became very excited and explained how she held the same position in her village church. That was all it took to gain my mother's approval.

Towards the end of the evening, my mother surprised us by announcing that she would pay for an overseas holiday for the two of us as her graduation gift to me. We were to decide where to go, so we talked about alternatives and settled on Mallorca.

The following morning, my mother left for work and I took the opportunity to show Jean-Louise some of the sites of my childhood years. There was the garden with its snowdrops and crocuses that were now being replaced by daffodils and the yellow flowers of forsythia. I showed her the conifer tree where I spotted the firecrest, and the hole in the wall where a robin had nested each year for as long as I could remember. During the return journey, I drove past the farm where I had spent my early years and pointed out the lake and areas that once had been woodland and hedgerows.

* * *

The final exams ended in early June, although the results would not be available until late in the month, so the next few days provided an opportunity for Jean-Louise and me to strengthen our relationship, meet friends, shop, enjoy meals, drink at the local pubs and occasionally watch a film. One day Jean-Louise asked:

"There's a protest march on Saturday. Will you participate with me?"

"What's it all about?" I asked.

"It's to object to the Vietnam War, protest against apartheid in South Africa and oppose white supremacy in Southern Rhodesia." (Southern Rhodesia renamed itself Rhodesia, without international consent, when the country self-declared independence from Britain during November 1965; it became known as Zimbabwe in 1980)

I was not sure I wanted to go. I had never been involved in public demonstrations.

"I'd rather not," I replied. "I don't want to be arrested."

"That won't happen," was Jean-Louise's comeback. "It's a peaceful procession from campus to the City Centre and back, that's all."

I was not convinced. I had seen photographs of the Campaign for Nuclear Disarmament and marches with large crowds that had degenerated into civil disobedience. I did not want to fall foul of the authorities and be fired by Ford even before I had started.

It took a lot of effort for Jean-Louise not to laugh at me. "It won't be like those marches; it'll be much smaller, and everyone will be well-behaved."

I was not sure she was correct but could see she wanted my participation. It was not worth another argument.

"All right," I conceded, "but I'll have to leave the march if things get out of control."

The protest march came and went without incident. There was a brief mention of it in the Hull *Daily Mail* but nothing on television, and I actually enjoyed participating. On our open-sided trailer, there were students I had never seen before waving placards saying "Kill Smith not Africans" and "Who's Afraid of Nazi Smith?" There were other trailers with students chanting "Hands off Vietnam" and yet more holding posters saying "Boycott South Africa" and "Remember Sharpeville". I felt awkward standing there, but Jean-Louise was happy that I had agreed to participate. I got my reward for indulging her when I mentioned that I was making another day trip to Spurn Point a few days later, and she volunteered to go with me.

* * *

We left Hull on a cool, windy morning, and we checked in at the Warren Cottage before going off on our own birdwatching expedition. A rare sooty tern had been sighted earlier that morning. We drove along the sand and shingle spit towards the lighthouse, stopping several times while I excitedly left the car with my binoculars, and chased around the buckthorn and stared out to sea. I would return to the car and report to Jean-

Louise whatever I had seen, while she preferred to sit inside and stay out of the raw easterly wind that was blowing off the sea.

For me, the high point of the outing came at the end of the spit of land when I spotted my first nuthatch. This is a small bird, slightly larger than a sparrow, with a beautiful, soft slate-blue back, whitish underparts, chestnut-brown on its sides and a black stripe across its head. Jean-Louise looked at me as if I were mad as she watched me clamber around the dense, thorny sea buckthorn, and I watched transfixed as the bird flitted, head-first, up and down the willow-like shrub.

Thereafter, I parked along the estuary side of the spit to find shelter from the wind. Jean-Louise left the car and walked with me to the muddy shoreline where I pointed out several types of wading bird, including dunlins, redshanks, green sandpipers and several curlews. She was delighted to see my favourite bird, but by late afternoon, the cold had made her hungry, and she was bored with the birds; she wanted to eat. I had brought my small primus stove and some sausages with me, and I quickly organised a cooking site, but I had not anticipated the strong wind and the cold. The stove kept going out and the sausages showed no signs of cooking. Jean-Louise shivered and eventually returned to the car, asking me to abandon the sausages. I complied and drove to the nearby "Crown and Anchor" pub for an evening meal of shepherd's pie and a glass of beer. Cautiously I asked Jean-Louise if she had enjoyed the day.

"I'm glad I came," she replied politely, "but it's so cold and you spend so much time standing and waiting outside. If I had more warm clothes, I might enjoy it, but I'm not sure I want to come again."

* * *

Back in Hull, all that remained was to see if I had graduated. The Geography Department was the last to announce its results, so on the advertised date late in June when the undergraduate Geography degree outcomes were due to be published, Anton and I made our way to the appropriate location. What degree had I been awarded? Indeed, had I graduated at all? I needed to have passed if I was to be employed by Ford. We climbed the stairs, carefully navigating our way through a steady stream of descending students, to examine the noticeboard.

"Congratulations," some of them shouted at Anton as they recognised him in the dim light of the stairwell. Occasionally they added "And you did very well, John" when they saw me in the shadows, trailing behind.

My confidence grew that I had been awarded some form of degree. We were supposed to stand in an orderly queue to reach the notice board on which the results were posted, but much pushing and shoving made orderly progression impossible. Ahead there was cheering, with the occasional sobbing from a disappointed scholar. Eventually, we found ourselves in front of the noticeboard, which we examined in silence to find our results.

"Hallelujah!" I said as I realised that both Anton and I had passed. The degree awarded to me was a joint-honours, second class, upper-division in Geology and Geography. Anton had attained the highest level possible, one level above me, with first-class honours in Geography. I looked again and discovered that Jean-Louise had been awarded a second-class, lower-division degree, and it surprised me that her degree was below mine. I looked around in case she was among the students, but she was not.

Anton and I retraced our footsteps and decided to visit the Students' Union refectory, just a few hundred yards away, and buy celebratory drinks. The feeling of relief was enormous.

I knew my mother would be pleased, and the degree meant that I would be joining Ford of Britain in late August 1966.

We reached the Buttery Bar and ordered refreshments. Anton chose amber ale, brewed by the Hull Brewery Company; I ordered a can of Black Beauty stout. We were not to know that these locally brewed beers would be available only for a few more years. There was a hum of conversation in the bar; everyone was talking about ordering gowns, colours and caps for graduation day, a little over two weeks hence.

It was then that I noticed Jean-Louise, sitting at a nearby table with some girlfriends and sipping what appeared to be a lager and lime, while a couple of her colleagues had rewarded themselves with a bottle of a champagne-styled cider called Babycham. I walked over and gave her my congratulations, she reciprocated, stood up and we hugged each other. I promised to visit her that evening at her student home, and she reminded me that she was spending the weekend in Manchester with her parents. This prompted me to call my mother and deliver my good news.

I found the public telephone box outside the refectory and waited my turn to call. When I finally got through, my mother was delighted and clearly proud of her son, and she asked me to return home that weekend so that we could go out together and celebrate.

After I returned to the Buttery Bar, Anton and I decided to go back to our flat. Soon it would no longer be our home, as I was moving to lodgings in a place called Upminster, Richard was returning to Nottingham and Anton would stay in Hull but had already arranged new accommodation.

Graduation day was 2nd July 1966. The ceremony took place in City Hall, with academic staff occupying the stage and the students seated facing them in the body of the hall, while guests were positioned at the back of the auditorium. I had obtained two visitor tickets, one for my mother and the other for her elder sister. Students were attired in gowns, hoods and caps, and at the appropriate time, each of us was called onto the stage to receive our graduation certificate. It all seemed rather make-believe, but I thought, "Now I can distinguish myself by adding the initials BSc after my name."

Once outside City Hall, my mother had me pose for photographs. During the picture-taking I suddenly felt that I was being watched. Across the street was a man dressed in a dark overcoat, and he appeared to be looking at me, but when I looked back, he stared in the opposite direction. He was about my height, thin and wearing circle-frame spectacles. Maybe I was mistaken; I was not sure. I had a strange, tingly feeling that he was interested in me, but when I next glanced across the street he had disappeared. I said nothing to my mother, but I wondered if he was my father.

Two days later, I was back with Jean-Louise at her student home, helping her pack and load luggage into my car. I was to take her to the railway station where she would catch the train to Manchester. The following day, I would collect my belongings and drive to York.

"I'll see you at the end of the month," she told me as I carried her suitcases onto the station platform. "I'll travel to York so that we can catch the early afternoon train to London."

"That'll work fine," I replied.

So, my three years at university ended. My academic and social development had been remarkable, and here I was about to step into a new episode of my life. I was confident that I could deal with change and determined to be successful. I spent the final few days in York preparing my car for its long journey to Upminster, saying farewell to friends and relatives and carrying out some last-minute birdwatching at Fairburn Ings, an area of open water, marsh and reed beds created from coalmining waste. Grebes, gulls, moorhens and a water rail were seen that day. I had left Spurn Point far behind near Hull, and I wondered if I would ever return, now that I was moving to the south of England.

Nationally, two new developments to control the economy were announced by the government. First was the July 1966 decision to impose a nationwide six-month "standstill" on price and wage increases, although it was unclear how my salary at Ford might be affected. Jean-Louise's father was angry that the government was interfering with wages. Not only did the freeze apply to future negotiated increases, but also to those that were already agreed but not yet implemented, so it seemed both arbitrary and unfair. The second restriction was the introduction of foreign exchange controls to maintain the value of British sterling. Fifty pounds was now the maximum amount an individual would be allowed to take out of the country annually, but, fortunately, the restriction would not be effective until November 1966, after our trip to Mallorca.

The time had come to stop worrying about my future, and prepare for a restful holiday in Spain with Jean-Louise.

(Jean-Louise, July 1966) "So, now I'm a graduate, about to go on holiday with John, and afterwards I will be taught to teach. Thankfully I altered my career plans. My mother's health has deteriorated, and my primary concern is to help my father look after her. I enjoyed Easter with my parents, celebrating my 21st birthday, and I appreciated John's gift of Tweed perfume. Also, I was delighted that the Labour Party won the general election, although it faces huge challenges. The economy is in a mess, events in Northern Ireland appear serious, Southern Rhodesia defies British authority and there are rumours we might join the Common Market.

"John will start at Ford in late August and is not deterred by the doubts my father has mentioned. I'm resigned to going to Reading on my own. Meeting his mother was a little daunting, and the village in which she lives is so small and isolated. It's nothing like where I grew up. His mother seems to like me, and I liked her. Her accent is just like John's.

"Our courtship is steady, and we don't talk about the Ford incident anymore. We share each other's interests. He participated in the 'global imperialism' march, despite his worries, and I went birdwatching with him. I don't think I could ever enjoy the hobby, but it seems very important to him. To me, all the birds look the same.

"My last few days in Hull were difficult, saying goodbye to friends whom I'm unlikely to ever see again. Graduation was a 'sweet and sour' experience; I was delighted to receive my degree but sad that my parents could not attend because of my mother's illness.

"The next stage in the relationship with John is our holiday in Mallorca. We have never been together for such a long period of time, and I don't think he knows what to expect from a 'package' holiday. I want to sit on the beach and enjoy the sunshine while he wants to do some sightseeing and birdwatching."

Nuthatch: This is one of Britain's smallest birds at 14 cm/5.5 inches long, with a dagger-like beak, stubby wings and a short tail. Its plumage is blue-grey upperparts, orange-buff underparts and a black eye stripe with white underneath. The number of breeding pairs has risen dramatically from about 70,000 in the mid-1960s to around 220,000 today. New forestry plantations, warmer winters and garden food provided in bird feeders are the main causes of this expansion. Its behaviour is distinctive when foraging for food in that it prefers to dive from trees and branches head-first, then jump from tree to tree in short leaps. It gets its name from the habit of stuffing and cracking nuts in tree trunk crevices.

It has three relatives in the United States: the red-breasted, the white-breasted and the pygmy nuthatch.

10

La Abubilla En Mallorca

I DID NOT APPRECIATE it at the time, but the visit to Mallorca presented me with several inaugural experiences. It was the first time I had been on holiday with a girl, I had never flown in an aeroplane before and it was my initial trip to Spain, the adopted country of Guy Fawkes.

I had twice been out of Britain; the first was at the end of my final year in school when I travelled by train and ferry to stay in Paris with friends in order to improve my French (unfortunately too late to help with my foreign language qualifications), and the second was a camping holiday with Anton to Italy and Yugoslavia after our first year at university. This had been a frightening experience. We had used World War II maps to plot our route through Yugoslavia, and we kept losing our way on roads that either were not marked or were identified in a language that we did not understand. We were arrested while camping on a beach in Montenegro on suspicion of being locals who were avoiding conscription in the Yugoslav army.

On the flight to Palma, Mallorca, it seemed as if every traveller was smoking, either a cigarette or a pipe, except for me. We could even buy cigarettes from the air stewardess. Jean-Louise sat relaxed alongside me, smoking and reading *The Valley of the Dolls* while I pondered why Guy Fawkes had changed his name to "Guido Fawkes" during his 10 years of fighting for Spain.

Once in Mallorca, it was clear that Jean-Louise's favourite pastime was doing nothing. She was happy lying on the beach, sunbathing and reading books, whereas I found the experience unpleasant and quickly became restless. I turned a vivid pink under the sun, so preferred to wander around the shops and enjoy sight-seeing, leaving Jean-Louise behind to deal with the local males who wanted to practice their English on her. Our hotel was still under construction, and very dusty and noisy throughout the day, hence the need to stay away for most of the time. The swimming pool was not functioning, despite the artist's rendering in the travel brochure.

Jean-Louise developed a friendship with a newly-wed couple from Manchester who were staying at the same hotel as us. We arranged to take a bus tour together into the interior of the island, and all they did was talk, whereas I preferred to look out of the window and conduct some clandestine birdwatching. Even without binoculars, I spotted black vultures, a cattle egret and an Eleonora's falcon.

The most memorable birding event of the holiday was sighting my first hoopoe, or *abubilla* as it is called in Spanish, and adding it to my "Life List" of birds. This is a cumulative list of bird species that I have personally identified. Jean-Louise and I stumbled upon a small flock as we walked to the hotel late one afternoon. They were on a lawn only a few feet away, catching insects with their long beaks, and Jean-Louise watched in amazement as I tried to get closer to them. Each bird was about the size of a starling, and the species is known for its distinct "crown" of orange-coloured feathers tipped with black, and an upper body coloured cinnamon pink. They are residents of Mallorca but rarely seen in Britain.

Otherwise it was a quiet holiday. We took boat trips on the Mediterranean a couple of times, ate what we were told was Valencian paella (made with chicken and rabbit) and Jean-Louise managed to be sick for 24 hours after drinking too much sangria during one of our boat excursions.

* * *

Soon we were back at the airport waiting for the Dan-Air flight to take us home. The twin-engine turbo-prop was comfortable but noisy, and its departure delayed for two hours due to a mechanical fault. During the delay I was beset by anxiety and misgivings about whether joining Ford of Britain had been a sensible decision. I had no idea what I was going to do, whereas the responsibilities of teaching were clear to me because of my years at school. The move to the south-east of England was an additional concern. I had heard that the people "down south" were different from the stoical northerners I was used to. They were supposed to hate the cold, speak in peculiar accents, drink exotic styles of beer, eat strange food like jellied eels, consider the North grim and its occupants depraved, and they had a reputation for being aloof and unfriendly.

An uncle had told me that there was lots of crime in the area into which I was moving. He mentioned gangs of criminals involved in extortion, racketeering and fraud, and said that a murder had taken place in an East End pub in full view of its patrons a few weeks earlier.

To try to banish these thoughts, I started to make a list of the belongings that I would need to take with me to Essex. Because I was driving my trusted Ford Popular, everything that I required would have to fit into the vehicle.

We eventually arrived at Gatwick airport, caught a train to London and then a connecting train on to York. After distributing gifts to my family and a good night's sleep, I drove us to Manchester to be introduced to Jean-Louise's parents for the first time. She and her mother cooked a roast chicken dinner while her father served me Scotch whisky. We talked about teaching, living in the south of England and our university experiences. It was obvious that Jean-Louise came from a much more privileged background than me.

I seemed to make a good impression on her parents, however, and I received an invitation to return at Christmas. Her mother quickly tired, but she was surprisingly mobile, despite her illness.

I left Jean-Louise in Manchester and used my last five days in York to complete packing for the 200-mile drive to Upminster, where Ford had arranged for me accommodation which was only six miles away from its headquarters in Brentwood. It was a hot and humid day when I began the journey, but by the time I was nearing my destination, I was driving through violent thunderstorms and torrential rain. Amid the downpour, I discovered the home of my landlord, who turned out to be much friendlier than I expected, and I could understand what he said.

Graduate Recruitment had told me that there were two other trainees sharing the same accommodation; one was called David and he came from Liverpool, and the other was Chris from Nottingham. We were about the same age, and all three of us had graduated from university a few weeks earlier. Only David was present when I arrived, and he told me that Chris was expected around lunchtime the following day.

That first evening, David and I discussed our university experiences, families, personal interests and why we had chosen Ford. We did not appear to have much in common; he came from a city environment, his father was a factory worker and he supported the Labour Party. His plan was to find a job in production so that he could move to Ford's Halewood plant to be close to his family; I told him I did not know what I was going to do, but at the time that did not trouble me.

Chris arrived at lunchtime the following day, and once David and I had helped him carry his belongings into the house, he offered to buy us a drink. The landlord suggested we go to the nearby "Masons Arms" pub, where I was surprised to find that the beer was not as bad as I had expected. The young, blonde-haired barmaid who took our orders was pretty to look at and seemed fascinated by me. While I remembered my commitment to Jean-Louise I thought that "looking" was not part of the promise.

Once we began drinking our Toby's Ale, Chris asked, "So, why did each of you join Ford?"

It was a straightforward question, and I spoke first to try to impress my colleagues. "Because of the firm's reputation and its starting salary." I did not care to mention that Ford was the only firm to offer me a job that interested me.

David spoke next. "I want to stay in Liverpool and work in Ford's Halewood factory. It's close to where my family lives."

Chris answered his own question. "My dad says the firm is the best business school in Britain, and he wants me to start here and then leave to take charge of his transport company."

This exchange was followed by a discussion regarding our personal situations. Only I had a girlfriend, and Chris and David were curious, so I explained why Jean-Louise and I had ended up living on opposite sides of London. They said it would be difficult for me to hold the relationship together, and David laughed when I told him about my agreement not to date girls in Essex.

"Pretty stupid," he suggested with a chuckle. "Did she give

you the same promise for men in Reading?" and I realised that she had not.

We next discussed sports, particularly football. David was a loyal Liverpool Football Club fan, whereas I supported Leeds United because it was the only First Division club close to my York home. Also, I was proud that the team was managed by Don Revie, who had masterminded the promotion of Leeds from the Second Division two years earlier. Chris dismissed both our teams as unworthy and was adamant that Nottingham Forest would be the country's champions for the current season. Last of all we discussed hobbies; I mentioned birdwatching, Chris talked about motor racing and David admitted that his only interest was football.

On our return to the lodgings, I thought how different we each were. Our backgrounds were dissimilar and each of us had unique reasons for joining Ford. Prospectively, we would compete with one another for jobs at Ford, but hopefully we would remain friends.

My mind returned to the girl at the bar. Where do you come from and why do you speak so oddly, she had asked, and I worried that fulfilling my promise to Jean-Louise might not be as easy as I had anticipated.

I realised that my life would now proceed under very different circumstances, beginning the following morning at Ford of Britain's headquarters, and I wondered what would happen.

(Jean-Louise, August 1966) "Well, he should be in London by now, and I'll hear from him shortly. I'm busy preparing to move to Reading, and I have promised my parents to come home every other weekend to help look after my mother. My father still doubts that John has made the right decision

in selecting Ford. The trade union to which he belongs has a scathing opinion of the firm's management and the way it treats its workers.

"Our holiday in Mallorca was a happy time. John was worried by the air travel and seemed to be happiest wandering off on his own. Sometimes I wish he could be more sociable, and not hide behind his birdwatching. Nonetheless, we didn't fall out, we met some nice people from Manchester, and we did a lot of talking. His choice of hotels was unfortunate but he apologised. The food we were given was very mediocre; I became tired of sherry soup, yellow rice and a piece of chicken in olive oil that was supposed to be paella. The sangria was like vinegar, despite the added sugar. Luckily, during the last few days we had enough money to eat out most of the time. We slept in the same room in single beds, an arrangement that his mother had insisted upon.

"What I did learn is that it's impossible for him to sit still in any one place for more than a few minutes. He's constantly on the move, wanting to visit shops or explore the town. I appreciate that he doesn't like the sun; however, he doesn't like to read, he refuses to wear a hat and prefers not to use sunscreen. He says he never used these things on the farm. I'm expecting him to fulfil his promises while I'm in Reading, and I've told him that he must visit me because I can't drive, and my parents expect to see him again at Christmas."

Hoopoe: This is a colourful, medium-sized bird of 25-30cm/10-12 inches in length, and is noted for its distinctive fan-like "crown" of orange feathers tipped with black. The upper body is cinnamon pink, and the wings are barred black and white. Both the male and female possess nearly identical plumage, and their flight is undulating like that of a butterfly. They are named after their soft, carrying song of "hoo-poo-poo". They are not common in Britain, where there are around 100 sightings each year; these are usually single birds, most typically along the south and east coasts. Whenever British sightings are reported, the birds attract a lot of excitement and a throng of twitchers.

In North America, it has been spotted in Alaska but is only a rare vagrant.

11

Caught In A Mist Net

THREE FRESHLY-TRAINED GRADUATES travelled in Chris's car from Upminster to Ford of Britain's Brentwood headquarters on Monday morning, 22nd August 1966, arriving a few minutes before 8am. Chris's vehicle was used because it was the most reliable of the three vehicles parked outside the lodgings. The departure was delayed for a few minutes because of Chris's interference with my business attire, when he told me to take off the sleeveless, multi-coloured pullover I was wearing under my suit jacket. My aunt had knitted it and it reminded me of my Yorkshire roots, so his criticism annoyed me.

"You can't dress like that in the office," he declared.

I was ready to ignore his remark until he told me I would look strange in front of the other trainees who would wear suits only, and he persuaded me to go upstairs and remove it. He also said that my brown shoes did not match my dark blue suit and I should wear black ones. I did not have a pair of black shoes but promised to buy some at the weekend. Jean-Louise had helped select the suit and my mother had paid for it. It was a good fit except that the sleeves were longer than my arms and the cuffs grazed the backs of my hands.

I made certain that I had the necessary documents to take with me, and especially a copy of my Birth Certificate which Mr Smith had said was essential. My mother had given me a duplicate copy that permitted me to see the details of my birth for the first time. Her name, occupation and signature were in the appropriate boxes, but the spaces for my father's details were left blank. I asked why the spaces were blank and was told only that my father was unavailable on the day my birth was registered. I also had a copy of a Deed Poll changing my surname from my mother's maiden name to my stepfather's surname.

My other important task was to open a bank account into which my monthly salary would be deposited. At home, my banking arrangements had been with a small, regional organisation that had no presence in Essex. Chris suggested that I open an account with the National Provincial Bank since it had a branch across the street, right opposite Ford's headquarters.

It was a cool, cloudy but dry day as we drove through the Essex countryside. After parking in the staff car park, I took my first walk through the tunnel under the road to emerge in the basement of Ford of Britain's headquarters. It was a remarkable building. The two-year-old structure provided office space for about 1,500 employees, and consisted of six floors, each decorated in shades of light brown and with similarly coloured offices, furnished with matching steel cabinets, desks and boardroom-style chairs. The building's external curved architecture was constructed of glass and Portland stone, and highlighted in pale blue, light green and cream. The conspicuous, oval-shaped Ford logo stood on the front lawn, and a large Union flag flew from a tall flagpole.

The foyer was as I remembered it from my interview, except that a new Zephyr Mark IV was on display, following the model's launch during April, and the Transit van had disappeared.

The three of us approached the receptionist who, after we had introduced ourselves, directed us up the escalator to a first-floor conference room. The closer I came to the meeting room, the more fearful I felt. I still believed my decision was correct, but there remained a niggling feeling that I might fail at Ford. About 20 graduates were gathered in the room, none of whom I recognised, and only one was a woman. All wore shirts under their suit jackets, not pullovers, and I hung my suit coat on the back of a chair to wait for the orientation to begin.

The Graduate Recruitment Manager welcomed us by describing the building's amenities and what we should expect during the three weeks of orientation. He talked about the company's products, stressed the importance of obeying the firm's work rules and told us that Ford was obsessed with productivity. When the building was constructed, beverage machines were installed on every floor so that staff did not have to go down the escalators to the cafeteria for refreshments. The firm had also encouraged shop owners to establish outlets across the street from headquarters, and an Employee Suggestion Scheme was administered by the company to encourage employees to participate in the firm's efficiency. For example, Ford worldwide spelled "employee" with one "e" at the end, which saved thousands of pounds because of less typing and reduced paper use.

We were asked to introduce ourselves, which was contrary to what I had hoped because I did not want to say anything with my strong accent. To my surprise, however, when my turn came, the anxiety disappeared and I introduced myself without embarrassment.

The manager next regularised our status as employees. He gave us each a folder coloured in corporate blue containing a welcome letter, several employment forms, a brochure illustrating the present line-up of Ford cars and trucks, and the meeting agenda for the next three weeks. Attached to each folder was a small salmon-pink card stating our name and home address, and assigning to each of us a personalised Ford identity number. We were instructed to sign the cards and carry them at all times, as they would be inspected to confirm our identity when we required access to Ford of Britain's offices and factories.

This process seemed a little too bureaucratic for me and conjured up thoughts of my mist-netting days at Spurn Point Bird Observatory. We caught birds, measured them, placed bands around their legs and then released them so they could be tracked for the rest of their lives. I kept a log of all the species I banded along with the identity numbers I used, and I thought we trainees were being treated in a similar manner. Each of us was assigned a unique number that would forever identify him or her at Ford. It occurred to me that the main difference between the trainees and the birds was that trainees were carefully selected, whereas birds were indiscriminately caught by chasing them into the mist net.

Once the registration cards were signed, a general discussion took place involving Ford of Britain's organisation and the company's expectations of its staff. During the mid-morning break, we had a chance to chat with each other and talk about our backgrounds and areas of interest. I was surprised at how many trainees knew what they wanted to do and were ambitious enough to have researched Ford's grading system. Someone asked me, "Which grade are you planning to be placed in, six, seven or eight?" I had no idea what he was talking about.

It turned out that graduate trainees were usually placed in jobs at these grades, and the bigger the grade number, the higher the salary range, with some functions offering better grades than others.

I told the person that I wanted first to find the right function.

I soon discovered the jobs with the highest grades. Those appointed as Buyers in Purchasing, for example, would be grade eight, and the same grade was used by Product Planning for its analyst positions. Finance, Sales and Marketing more usually placed trainees in grade seven, and most other functions typically adopted grade six.

The rest of the day consisted of a series of departmental presentations. Before lunch, we heard from an organisation known as Staff Personnel and Organisation, and this was the only time during the whole three weeks when a woman manager spoke to us. Her department was responsible for the development and administration of Ford of Britain staff policies.

During the afternoon, we were given a tour of the mainframe computer facility. We were able to peer through the glass walls to observe what was going on, but we were not allowed entry because of the temperature-controlled, air-vented environment. The guide told us that the new IBM 360 was handling all Ford of Britain's information needs.

Following the end of the final meeting, the three of us drove back to Upminster, and I asked Chris about some things I did not fully understand. For example, why was Systems part of the Finance organisation? What was the difference between position evaluation and performance evaluation? Where did Graduate Recruitment fit in Ford's organisational structure? He answered that information technology helped Finance do its work, position evaluation focused on job responsibilities whereas performance evaluation measured employee contribution, and Graduate Recruitment was part of Staff Personnel and Organisation.

Once back at our lodgings, I walked to the public telephone kiosk near the Upminster underground station to call Jean-Louise. I slotted the required coins into the meter, then dialled her home number; I pressed button A to start the conversation as soon as she answered.

"I survived the first day," I announced gleefully. "It's a huge building, with lots of people, and it's very complicated, and I miss you. Are you okay?"

"I'm fine," she replied, "but tell me about Ford and Essex."

I explained that it had been long and lonely journey to Upminster two days earlier but that the landlord and his wife were kind to their lodgers. I had met my roommates and they were very friendly, and all three of us had gone to a pub on Sunday afternoon. I didn't mention the barmaid.

"And what about your first day at work?" she asked.

I told her that it had been a series of presentations, and a little boring because we had to sit in the same place for most of the day. I was one of about 20 trainees in the group, and I had worn the suit that she helped me select. There was a lot of stuff at the meeting that I did not understand, but my lodging colleagues were helping me.

"How many trainees are women?" she wanted to know.

"One," I replied.

"That's awful," she commented. "I would expect Ford to be more enlightened."

I was not sure what she meant, since what mattered to me was that I had been selected. I considered gender unimportant, so I changed the subject.

"Do you miss me?"

"Yes, but I'll be in Reading in a fortnight's time and you'll have to come and see me. Also, Anton has written to me and says he is dating a female friend in Hull. Additionally, I went to the pictures with a girl companion this past Saturday, and saw a film called *Alfie*."

It seemed odd that she had selected that film. It is about a man in London who finds a job as a chauffeur and uses any opportunity provided by his work to engage in a series of frivolous relationships with various females. I wondered if Jean-Louise thought I might do the same.

She added, "Don't forget your promise to stay away from other women while you're in Essex."

I told her I would not forget, and that I was looking forward to seeing her in Reading.

With that, the Pay-On-Answer telephone ran out of coins and the call ended. As the telephone booth door automatically closed, and I began my walk back to my lodgings, I reflected once more on the choices I had made and what I had done to myself. The accents of the passers-by were very different from mine, and the shops had names that were unfamiliar. Everything that I was used to had been left behind; everything here was new.

* * *

The rest of the week was spent listening to presentations from managers explaining the functions of their departments and trying to persuade trainees that their responsibilities were the most important in Ford. It was wearisome and often beyond my comprehension. Many questions were asked, and I tried to listen, but I often found myself daydreaming about Jean-Louise or drifting off to sleep.

I was surprised by the number of support services flourishing in the company: Finance, Industrial Relations, Public Relations, Legal Affairs, Programme Timing and even something called General Services. This last department was responsible for functions that it seemed no one else wanted, such as transport, facilities management, building security, publishing and courier services. The most memorable presentation of the week was on Friday when I saw Mr Welsh. He accompanied a senior director from Industrial Relations Staff, who talked to us about changes in the company. I did not think Mr Welsh recognised me.

The director's talk was lengthy and sometimes difficult to understand. I thought it foolish to finish the week this way because most of us had become tired of listening and were looking forward to leaving early to start the Late Summer Bank Holiday weekend. However, some parts of the talk's content were interesting. I had not realised that Ford of Britain was a wholly-owned subsidiary of an American company. Apparently, the parent company, Ford Motor Company in Dearborn (a suburb of Detroit), had purchased the remaining 46 percent of Ford of Britain's shares in January 1961; consequently, the company now had access to its parent company's technology and financial resources. Mention was also made of a new company called Ford of Europe that was about to be established and would oversee all of Ford's European subsidiaries. We heard that Mr Ford wanted his European national businesses to work together to design and market vehicles, rather than compete with one another.

There was also talk about how Industrial Relations Staff hoped to transform the firm's traditional adversarial relationship with its trade unions to one that was more collaborative and trusting. I thought the change would please Jean-Louise's father, especially when the director referred to the paint sprayers' dispute and gave a very different story to the one contained in the newspaper reports.

According to the director, late during the previous year, Ford had increased its working conditions pay allowance for paint sprayers in return for an agreement that they would reduce their rest periods outside the paint booths. The changes were implemented in Halewood, but when management made the adjustments in Dagenham, the paint sprayers accepted the higher pay allowance but refused to observe the new relief times. Management threatened to discipline them, causing the paint sprayers to go on strike and close down production. A third-party investigation eventually came up with a compromise that persuaded the men to return to work but which was not welcome by the company. Immediately thereafter the foundry workers threatened similar action, demanding that their working conditions pay allowance also be increased. An interim settlement was reached, with the unions agreeing to cooperate with management to develop a new company-wide job evaluation system and wage structure that would avoid these problems in the future.

The discussion droned on well after lunch, despite many trainees having left already to start the three-day Bank Holiday weekend. Realising what was happening, the director eventually suspended the presentation mid-afternoon and allowed everyone to leave.

Thus, my first week at Ford was completed, and I had just enough time to drive to Romford and buy some black shoes before the shops closed. Ahead of me lay three days during which I would learn more about Essex. My plan was to tour Brentwood and Romford during Saturday, investigate bird-watching locations on Sunday, and possibly attend the Bank Holiday Monday Sports Car Championship racing at Brands Hatch at which Chris was going to be present. First, however, I needed to call Jean-Louise for a second time.

(Jean-Louise, August 1966) "John is about to telephone me after his first week at Ford. I'm surprised I miss him so much. He called me earlier to say that he's finding his orientation complex but helpful. His lodging friends are guiding him on the things that he doesn't understand; apparently, they are nice people. Ford sounds like a male-dominated organisation, just

like the engineering firm my father works for. Only one female graduate trainee in his class suggests discrimination. However, according to John, women trainees are paid the same starting salary as men, and the firm uses the same salary ranges for both sexes.

"He's lucky to have started working, whereas I'm sitting here in my bedroom, deciding what clothes to take to Reading. I'm impatient to start the new segment of my life. I thought about my yellow dress, and I've decided to take it with me, just in case. The film my friend and I watched a few days ago suggests that men in the south can be disrespectful towards their girlfriends, and maybe John might develop that way.

"The Bank Holiday weekend is approaching, and my father will be off work. He has promised to take my mother and me for a picnic in the Peak District. It feels strange to think that, this time next week, I will be in Reading and occupying a student house with three women I have never met before."

The Mist Net: For many birds, the mist net is the first human intervention in their lives. It is the most commonly used method of studying songbirds and other perching passerines. After being caught in the net, the birds are disentangled by hand and then measured, banded and released back into the wild. They may also be weighed. The banding process involves attaching a small, individually numbered metal or plastic tag to a leg or a wing in order to track the bird's movements. Migration routes, geographic range, physical health, breeding patterns and years of life are all measured.

The net itself is typically made of fine nylon or polyester material (like that used for making hair-nets) suspended between two poles, and it is usually a standard size of 2 x 9 metres (7 x 30 feet). Horizontal string lines are used to create loose, baggy pockets in which the birds become entangled when they fly into the net. Guy ropes attached to the poles keep the net upright, and the equipment is usually coloured black because it absorbs rather than reflects light.

12

The Absent Peregrine

THE HIGHLIGHT OF my Friday evening telephone call was announcing to Jean-Louise that I had seen Mr Welsh again and that his colleague's description of the Dagenham paint sprayers' dispute was very different from the newspaper accounts.

"How's it different?" she sounded sceptical.

"It had nothing to do with surplus production. It was about an agreement that the unions negotiated with management and then their members in Dagenham refused to honour it. There wasn't much else the company could do." I believed I was beginning to grasp business matters!

I think she doubted the trustworthiness of my version but was not prepared to disagree. "If you say so, but you shouldn't believe everything you're told. Companies twist the truth. We have an engineering firm near here that an American bought and the new owner says that, to keep the plant open, he has to replace some of the men with women on lower wages. It's disgusting how women are treated. The union's fighting the proposal."

I decided to shift to a neutral subject.

"Where should we meet next weekend?" I knew she would

be living with three other lodgers and thought she might want to arrange an alternative location; also, I did not know the whereabouts of the house.

"Meet me at my lodgings, that will be fine, but I can't give you directions so you'll need to buy a map on the way." She gave me the address and then shifted topics.

"What are you doing this weekend?"

She sounded a little envious when I replied, "I plan to shop tomorrow and look around the neighbourhood. On Sunday, I hope to go birdwatching but I don't know where, and on Monday, Chris has invited me to go with him to Brands Hatch to watch the sports car racing."

"It sounds as if you're having lots of fun," she said, and I think she was envious because I had begun to enjoy my new life while she was still waiting for hers to start. The pips sounded once more on the telephone, causing me to end the conversation as I had run out of money. I told her I loved her and would call again on Monday evening.

"I love you," she said, and the 'phone went dead.

* * *

I bought my work shirts in Romford market. They were cheaper than those in the shops, although they were the same brand—Rael-Brook, and I also purchased several pairs of black socks to match my shoes. The street market reminded me of the one at home, except that the accents of the vendors were very different. It was also newer; York had established its market in the eighth century during the Viking years, whereas Romford's dated back only to 1247 when it began as a livestock market.

Birdwatching on Sunday was something of a disappointment. I had decided to drive north and once I reached Chelmsford, head east close to the picturesque Chelmer Valley to Maldon by the Blackwater estuary. However, August was not the best time for spotting birds, since the autumn migration was not yet underway. I occasionally detoured to inspect the Chelmer River in the hope of spotting kingfishers and reed warblers, but I saw neither. Instead, I observed only common varieties such as wood pigeons, blackbirds, song thrushes, skylarks, magpies and crows. Occasionally, pinkish-brown jays would screech at me when I parked too close to their habitat.

The tranquillity of the countryside eventually changed into open expanses of intertidal mud banks, sand flats and shell banks edged with saltmarsh grass and coastal shingle as I neared the Blackwater. My bird sightings therefore also changed and I saw redshanks, grey plovers, oyster catchers, black-headed gulls and several species of tern. Overhead were swallows, swifts and house martins, and at one stage a solitary kestrel fluttered overhead looking for food.

Another species I wanted to see that was rumoured to be a visitor during autumn in this part of Essex was the peregrine falcon, nicknamed "the wanderer" because of its long-distance migration. It occasionally had been seen at Spurn Point, but not on the days when I was present. In recent years, the British population had dramatically declined, with nearly four out of five peregrines perishing either because of pesticides, being shot by gamekeepers or their nests being robbed and their eggs smuggled to the Middle East where the chicks were raised as hunters and racers. I later discovered that a pair of these birds wintered in the Chelmer Valley, but I was there too early in the year to see them.

* * *

On Bank Holiday morning, Chris and I left Upminster for the Guards Trophy sports car races at Brands Hatch; we drove south through the Ockendons to the Dartford tunnel, which was opened in November 1963 as a way of by-passing London.

We paid the toll of two shillings and sixpence and drove beneath the river Thames on a rather congested, compacted dual carriageway. I told Chris about my Chelmer River visit and how I had looked for peregrine falcons but not seen any. Apparently, this falcon also once occupied the part of Kent through which we were then driving, although we saw none that day.

It was an extraordinary day for car racing. I had never seen anything like it. We paid our entry fee and chose a spectating spot close to the protective rail, just beyond the grandstand. We had a good view of the three-mile circuit, with its series of twists and turns through Druids, and the long uphill sweep of South Bank into Clearways. At first, I was unsettled by the large crowds, but Chris redirected my attention by describing what was taking place.

The crowd became excited once the racing car heats were underway, and the cheering and yelling became deafening. At the backs of the stands were food tents and displays of souvenirs, while around the race track there were large billboards advertising everything from Guards cigarettes to Castrol oil. The pace of the cars was exhilarating, and the smell of burning oil and rubber intoxicating. Engines roared, and their pops and bangs mixed with the screams of the crowd. I was introduced to a range of cars that I had never seen before, including the Lola Chevrolets, McLaren Elvas, Brabham BT8s, and the Ford GT40 fresh from its win at Le Mans on 19th June.

The weather turned grey during the afternoon, and torrential rain was falling by teatime, making the final Formula Three race dangerous and spectating difficult because of fading light, so Chris and I decided to leave early to beat the traffic. On the way, he asked about my job interests, adding that he intended to stay in Brentwood, either somewhere in Sales or with Personnel

Management. I told him I had not discovered enough to decide what I wanted to do.

Soon we were home and preparing for our trip to Dagenham starting the following morning. Chris volunteered to drive all three of us during the week, so early on Tuesday morning, we drove the eight miles (13 km) to Power Train Operations where our induction resumed in the factories' conference room. Power Train, we were told, was the operation responsible for manufacturing engines and transmissions. Rain was still falling, and the rain-soaked industrial complex appeared dreary and dirty. Factories were scattered across nearly five-hundred acres of former marshland, with the river Thames running alongside the southern edge, and a major road between central London and the Tilbury docks along its northern perimeter. The buildings were separated by a crisscross of roads, pathways, creeks and railway tracks, and within the complex raw materials were transformed into moving vehicles.

It was another "first" experience for me. I had never seen a place like it. The nearest thing that I had experienced previously was during my first year in Hull when I cycled through the Stoneferry industrial estate to reach the university campus. That complex was much smaller than this one, but it made up for its size by producing a much greater variety of smells through the manufacture of glue, reducing fish into fish-meal, soap production and the crushing of oil seed.

Each day in Dagenham was dedicated to explaining a different manufacturing process. Whoever set the agenda had cleverly sequenced our experience from the conversion of raw materials to the pouring of metal castings, the assembly of engines, then the pressing of body panels, ending up with the manufacture of the finished vehicle. We began Tuesday morning with a tour of the Blast Furnace that used coal, iron ore and limestone, delivered by barges to the nearby Thames jetty, to produce pig iron. Next door, the Power Station generated enough electricity to serve a town of 180,000 people.

In the afternoon, we were shown the Thames Foundry. We watched as molten metal was cast into engine blocks and other components. Sand, dust and particles of metal were everywhere, and in some places I found it difficult to breathe. We were given protective eyewear, but nothing to protect our lungs. During late afternoon, we returned to the conference room to receive a senior management presentation.

Various managers boasted of their success, causing me to stop listening and divert my attention to a nearby waterway outside the nearest window. This was formed some 250 years earlier when the river Thames had burst its banks, and it was known as the Dagenham Breach. I could see flocks of waders feeding in the shallow water, but I was too far away to identify any species.

That evening I called Jean-Louise to describe my visit to Brands Hatch and the first day at Dagenham. She was a little annoyed that I had not called on Monday evening, but she forgave me when I told her about the weather. She said she was packed and ready to leave for Reading on Thursday afternoon.

* * *

Four days later, I drove across London to visit her in her new home and found the address without difficulty. I probably should have taken a gift, but I did not think to do so, and Jean-Louise did not seem to mind. Her house companions had not yet arrived, so we enjoyed a splendid two days by ourselves. On Saturday, most of the morning was spent clothes shopping, and in the afternoon we toured the university campus. During the evening we had a romantic dinner at an Indian restaurant.

On Sunday afternoon, both of us found it difficult to say

goodbye. It was painful and made me feel sad, but at least we were close together again in the south-east of England and I volunteered to return the following weekend. Our time with each other had gone quickly, but I needed to return to Essex for my third and final week of orientation. I still had no idea of what sort of work I wanted to do.

(Jean-Louise, early September 1966) "At last we are back together. John is less attentive than he was at university, but presumably this is because he's preoccupied with his work. He doesn't like failure. We've parted with the promise that he'll return next weekend. It was a blissful and romantic two days and I expect the relationship to continue. He hasn't been paid yet, but he took me out and bought me a blouse and some fishnet-style tights.

"My new lodgings are clean and spacious, but the other three girls apparently know each other from previous years at Reading, so I don't expect them to have much time for me. That's probably not a problem; with weekly classroom instruction and weekends with either John or with my parents, I won't have much time to build new friendships. According to the doctor, my mother is moving into the final phase of her illness and finding it increasingly difficult to perform most household chores.

"I'm envious of John having the opportunity to find new friends and enjoy the social aspects of living in Essex, and I've asked him to take me to Brands Hatch sometime in the future. His birdwatching might be suffering, but I'm sure he'll find new places to visit.

"Apparently, he dislikes the dirtiness of Dagenham but finds the working environment appealing, probably because everything is so new to him. I don't think my father would

agree. John might end up working there, although he still hasn't decided which functions he likes.

"He continues not to have much dress sense, although at least he's wearing a suit for work. I need to help him. I like his good looks, but he has to dress better. My intention is to take him to London sometime soon and coach him on how to become more fashionable."

Peregrine Falcon: This bird is known as the peregrine in Britain, and the duck hawk in North America. It is a medium-sized bird, 45 cm/18 inches in length and about the size of a crow; it is a very powerful falcon, with a blue-grey back, barred white underparts and a black head. It hunts medium-sized birds (pigeons, grouse, water birds, ducks, gulls and songbirds), and catches them while in flight by executing intricate manoeuvres high above them, then plunging head-first in a spectacular stoop at extreme speeds of up to 325 kph (200mph). While still in mid-air, it strikes its prey with its talons, often hard enough to create a cloud of feathers, and then bites through the neck of the prey to make certain that it is dead. The species almost disappeared in Britain during

the mid-20th century, but has since recovered. Britain has an estimated 1,500 breeding pairs, with a growing number becoming urbanised.

In the United States, the peregrine disappeared from the east and was endangered in the west by 1970. However, through banning the use of crop spraying with DDT, introducing legal protection to prevent persecution, and allowing the birds to colonise urban structures, the species has since been taken off the endangered list.

13

Territorial Robins

THE FINAL WEEK of orientation was based back in Brentwood, with site visits to the nearby Basildon tractor plant and the Aveley parts depot. Returning from Aveley, we diverted for a tour of Ford of Britain's in-plant printing facility near the Dagenham estate. It apparently produced all print and copy needed by the company, including brochures, magazines, forms and packaging, and managed a central companywide mailing system. There was no notable part of the company that I had not heard about, I now felt comfortable talking with other trainees, and I no longer felt self-conscious about the way I spoke. Jean-Louise received an update of what was happening every other day, and she told me how she was progressing.

Early in the week, I met with my Graduate Recruitment representative to discuss pre-placements. I still had difficulty identifying areas of interest in respect of my future with the company, and my number one fear was being sent to an area of activity where I would fail.

The representative adopted an oblique approach in his discussions with me. "Tell me about your outside activities and maybe they'll help me decide what would best suit you."

I described my love of birdwatching and interest in geology.

"Think about the skills you use," he replied. "What makes these hobbies interesting?"

I understood the question, but I found it difficult to answer, so I took my time and eventually replied, "I think I like organising things, I love the outdoors, and I'm analytical and detail-oriented. Also, hard work doesn't bother me, I enjoy accomplishing a particular goal and I like helping others."

He appeared satisfied with my reply and promised to have a list of pre-placements for me by the end of the week.

Before the meeting ended, I found enough courage to ask: "Could one of my assignments be in the truck assembly plant at Langley?"

He looked a little surprised and asked me why. I was too embarrassed to be truthful, so I answered, "Trucks interest me, and I have relatives living on the other side of London." The last comment was, of course, a surrogate for mentioning Jean-Louise.

* * *

In Reading, Jean-Louise had quickly adapted to her daily schedule. Everything was new she said, but she liked her teaching instructor and was assigned to a comprehensive school nearby for her practical work. Her housemates had arrived, they were mixing well, and she appreciated that I had asked for a pre-placement in the Langley truck factory.

I told her that I was still unable to identify any function that particularly interested me, but I hoped the situation would alter during the coming weeks. She worried that, if I did not decide soon, all the jobs would be filled. It turned out that she had been reading about business difficulties in other parts of the British motor industry. The British Motor Corporation had announced the redundancies of several thousand employees, and she wanted to know if the same was likely to happen at Ford of Britain. I said I did not think so.

* * *

On Friday morning, I returned to Graduate Recruitment and received a timetable of pre-placements; the first would be in headquarters Staff Personnel Policies, the next in Production Planning and Control (PP&C) and the third in the Purchasing Department. Each would last for two weeks and I was told that all three functions matched my abilities. I recalled Mr Welsh's comment that I might be a good fit for PP&C, and meanwhile my contact was still waiting to hear from the truck plant.

On returning to the conference room, the Personnel Director was concluding the three weeks' orientation by thanking everyone for their commitment to Ford. He assured those present that job security was not an issue in Ford of Britain. There was no surplus of unsold cars and everyone should expect to be placed within a few weeks.

Someone asked how the government's pay freeze would impact our salaries. He said it was unfortunate that the government was meddling in business matters, but as far as we were concerned, we should not worry. Future merit (performance) awards and promotional increases were exempt from the pay restrictions; only general awards and across-the-board cost-of-living adjustments were frozen.

* * *

That evening, Chris and I discussed the fastest route to drive to Reading early on Saturday morning. I wanted to take the North Circular Road to the newly opened M4 motorway, and then the trunk road from Slough to Reading. He disagreed and believed that on a Saturday morning it would be quicker to use the

Mile End Road and drive directly through central London. He suggested I take some flowers if I really cared for Jean-Louise.

When I arrived in Reading, Jean-Louise cried with delight as I presented her with a posy of white roses and red and pink carnations. She introduced me to her housemates, and then we went shopping. First we bought a casual shirt and a matching pair of trousers for me, and in return, I bought her a dark blue blouse to go with the chocolate-brown button-front suede miniskirt she had bought before leaving Manchester. We ate out, went to the cinema, visited the local park and talked a lot.

She had to return to Manchester the following weekend and sadly explained that there was no improvement in her mother's health. We talked about where she might teach after graduation the following July, and she explained that it was her intention to find a position in the Manchester area in order to be close to her parents. I stayed silent, but I felt unhappy that she was not thinking of moving to Essex.

We talked about current events, and especially the country's celebrations after winning the football World Cup at the end of July. We were surprised at the official apology from the Beatles to the people of the United States for claiming to be more popular than Jesus, and shocked that the founder of apartheid in South Africa had been stabbed to death. West Germany apparently was asking Britain to delay its application to join the European Economic Community because the French would veto the request. I complained about having to pay higher income tax, but acknowledged that the annual cost of living in Britain was rising by under 4 percent and this should be more than offset by a salary increase I would receive on placement.

Driving back to Upminster that Sunday evening, I pondered the next stage of my relationship with Jean-Louise. We were falling into a routine, now that we were both living near London, and it hurt to think of her going back to the north of

England. She had valid reasons to move close to her mother, but where did I fit in with her future plans? Should I act now to make our union stronger or wait until she qualified as a teacher and her mother's health improved?

* * *

The following morning, Chris, David and I left our lodgings for our first pre-placement. All three of us had been assigned to Brentwood headquarters: Chris to Graduate Recruitment, David to Production Planning and Control, and I would start in Staff Personnel Policies. We arranged to meet at the end of the day in "The Thatchers' Arms", a pub nearby, to talk about our first day's experience.

The pre-placement process introduced me to a new set of behaviours among my fellow trainees. Suddenly they were very secretive and withheld information when I asked about experiences and positions that were open in their pre-placement departments. They were unwilling to share details and treated whatever knowledge they had as proprietary. They were carving out their own areas of interest and protecting what they learned as a bird would protect its territory.

Their behaviour reminded me of the territorial robin, a small, brown bird with a vivid red breast that has a reputation for establishing a territory and defending it against all other robins. I observed these birds during my childhood, and once conducted a study to delineate each bird's territorial limits. I found that they kept moving the boundaries. By contrast, they seemed to enjoy the presence of humans and would often follow them in the hope of being fed. This seemed to me to be like some of my colleagues who tried to ingratiate themselves with their bosses in the hope of increasing their chances of a permanent placement.

Each trainee was told to report to the manager named on

their pre-placement schedule. Mine was the woman who gave the presentation on our first day of orientation, and this caused me some anxiety. She had a reputation for behaving aggressively and verbally attacking her subordinates, and I expected her to have little patience with me. I was not mistaken. When I arrived, she was not in her office, so I took the opportunity to obtain a cup of tea from the nearby vending machine. When she arrived a few minutes later, she seemed surprised to see me and immediately delegated me to someone else.

"Follow me; I want you to spend your time in Job Evaluation. The supervisor will explain what we do."

With that, I was taken to the supervisor's office where I was introduced. She then excused herself and I never saw her again. There was no mention of job openings or the qualifications necessary to work in the department. The supervisor explained the purpose of job evaluation and then assigned me to a desk, gave me some reading materials and warned me not to use the telephone for personal calls. Ford of Britain's telecommunications department was monitoring long-distance conversations, and any non-business usage was reported to managers. I was off to a poor start, but as the day wore on things improved, the analysts in the office befriended me and began to describe their work.

* * *

I was the first to arrive at "The Thatchers' Arms" and Chris appeared a few minutes later. Before David appeared, we talked about Chris's visit to Nottingham the previous weekend, and how he had attended a football match between his team and Leeds United. The result was a draw, and I told him that I thought the result was a good outcome for my team.

His next comment surprised me. "I also met someone who says you and he lived together in Hull last year. He's called Richard and is a former school friend of mine. Do you remember him?"

I told him I did and that we had shared a flat. I was about to ask what Richard had said about me when David arrived, and instead we turned our attention to the day's experiences. Chris had been introduced to the "war room" in Graduate Recruitment that tracked each trainee (I worried what it might have disclosed about me), and the department staff had taken him to lunch. David had been handed lots of paperwork and then left on his own, and I told them I sat at a desk most of the day reading a "how to" guide on job evaluation.

Later in the conversation, we discussed our weekend plans. David was going to visit his parents in Liverpool, I did not have anything to do because Jean-Louise would be in Manchester, and Chris announced that he was going to a party on Saturday night.

"Why don't you come with me?" he suggested.

I declined, remembering my promise to Jean-Louise, but asked who had arranged the event.

He told me a secretary in Graduate Recruitment was organising a welcome party for all current-year graduate trainees. He thought I ought to attend because it was an opportunity to get to know my Ford colleagues socially. Although the idea interested me, I still thought I should stay away because of my commitment to Jean-Louise not to meet girls in Essex.

"Jean-Louise wouldn't want me there," I claimed. "I'd be having a good time while she's looking after a sick mother."

"Rubbish!" said David. "Don't be so stuffy!"

I scowled but said nothing. On the way out, Chris asked us if we were interested in moving to rented accommodation in place of our lodgings in Upminster. Apparently, Graduate Recruitment kept a list of local houses and flats that were available for rent, and he would research what was available if we were curious. We agreed that it was an excellent idea, but we should wait until we knew where we were being placed. We each then drove home to Upminster in our individual vehicles.

(Jean-Louise, mid-September 1966) "I've been too busy settling into my academic work to think much about John, and he's been busy preparing for his pre-placements. I hope he'll find a job in Langley. I plan to teach Geography and my course is helping with classroom management and curriculum design. The situation with my mother at home is worrisome and I'll spend this weekend in Manchester.

"John visits me when he can—and has even brought me flowers! Otherwise, it's a quiet time. I'm not sure what he'll do this weekend while I'm away, probably go birdwatching."

Robin: *This is Britain's favourite national bird, known as "Robin Redbreast" and is featured regularly on Christmas cards. With their bright red breast, brown upperparts and whitish belly, both male and female look alike, but juveniles have a brown breast, not red. The birds are approximately 14 cm /6 inches in length, and the number of breeding pairs in the UK is around 4 million; each territory is about 2,000 to10,000 square yards (1670-8360 sq. metres). As well as their song, they use their red breast in a threatening behaviour to defend their territory, and they have been known to fight intruders to the death. During summer, their territory is defended by the mated pair, while each bird holds an individual winter territory. Territory boundaries are fluid and change as circumstances alter. Robins appear friendly towards humans, often watching them while keeping a lookout for food.*

The American robin is not related; it was named as such by early settlers because of its reddish-orange breast, but it is about twice the size of a European robin.

14

The Courtship Display Of The Pied Wagtail

CHRIS REMAINED DETERMINED to have me attend the Saturday night party. He said he wanted someone to accompany him in case his date with the party organiser did not work out, although I kept telling him that Jean-Louise would disapprove of me partying while she was looking after her sick mother. Her parents had originally planned to meet us in Reading but the doctor had refused to give her mother permission to travel, so Jean-Louise decided to leave by train on Friday afternoon and would not return until Monday.

Chris was insistent. "But you'll never make friends with your colleagues if you don't meet them socially. Going to this party is safe."

"But Jean-Louise wouldn't want me there," I responded, although I could feel his frustration at my lack of cooperation.

"Why wouldn't she?" he challenged. "Virtually every other trainee will be there."

"I promised her I would stay away from other women."

"But you don't have to meet other women. You're going

with me, and you can talk to just your Ford friends. I'm sure Jean-Louise would tell you that's OK."

"But I may go birdwatching early on Sunday morning."

"You can do that any time. This is a unique opportunity. If you come with me, I'll drive you there and bring you home."

Chris kept up the pressure, and eventually I succumbed on the condition that I travelled with him and he would bring me home as soon as I was ready. However, I still felt rather guilty, especially as there was no time to inform Jean-Louise who was already in Manchester.

Approximately 60 people were at the party, including about 25 trainees from two intakes, and the conversations focused mainly on experiences at Ford. I did not dress particularly well, although I did wear my favourite dove-grey, long-haired, merino wool cardigan. There was plenty to drink, but not much food, and I drank beer rather than wine. Probably I drank a little too much because of my nervousness about being so close to other women, but I stopped as soon as I became happy, sociable and wanted to talk. The brand of beer provided was advertised by the jingle "Double Diamond works wonders, so drink one today", and by the end of the night the jingle had taken on a very special meaning for me.

Chris introduced me to his date, the secretary who had organised the event, and she turned out to be the blonde, curly-haired, diminutive person who had escorted me to the Graduate Recruitment office on the day of my final interviews. She smiled and took me to meet some of her friends. One of them was called Vanessa, who was a nurse working in Chelmsford and who apparently was at the party on her own. After talking and enjoying a couple of drinks with her, I invited her to dance out of what I thought of as natural politeness. I confess I did not give much thought to what Jean-Louise might think, as I had no intention of cheating; it was just social dancing, or so I thought at the start.

Vanessa wore a knee-length, white, halter-neck dress with a gold-coloured braided belt and matching shoes. She smiled sweetly and seemed very interested in our conversation. We were about the same height, and she was slender with a dainty, slim waist. She was also very attractive, with a small nose, delicate lips, gentle blue eyes and golden blonde hair flowing in waves down her back. Also, unlike Jean-Louise, Vanessa did not smoke.

I quickly realised how physically attractive I found her, and it was not the response that I had expected. As we danced, my feelings intensified, my thoughts turned irresponsible and my desire grew stronger as we danced closer. She smiled as we moved rhythmically from side to side, facing and circling each other. She came close and leaned forward, and the halter-neck of her dress opened low enough for me to be able to see her breasts rising and falling to the rhythm of the music. I found her perfume intoxicating and pulled her closer, and soon we were embracing one another, dancing cheek-to-cheek.

When I look back, I realise how stupid I was, becoming so infatuated with Vanessa and not being able to distinguish between love and lust. As the effects of the beer wore off, I realised that our dance movements had taken on more than just the features of a sociable dance. Here were Vanessa and I, facing one another, crouching and jerking to the Twist, fluttering and shuffling to the Shake, twisting and turning to the Jive and inventing new movements to gyrate to the Locomotion and Mashed Potato. The craving for something more physical became stronger, and our desire for each other intensified.

We were like a pair of pied wagtails. These are small, long-tailed, and lively-looking black and white birds that I first saw during my sixth form school geology trips to Stainforth and Crummack Dale areas in west Yorkshire. We would pass them by as we hiked to collect specimens of Carboniferous Great Scar Limestone, examine Silurian Grits and Flagstones, and search for trilobites among the Ordovician Ashgillian shales. Pairs of these birds would shuffle, run, flutter, crouch, jerk and droop their wings in front of each other as a prelude to mating. Our dance movements were almost as elaborate, and suddenly I realised that I needed to do something to change the situation before it was too late. I was shocked to think that emotionally I could feel such passion towards another woman when my brain felt committed to Jean-Louise, so I suggested we stop dancing and secure more drinks, and I asked Vanessa to introduce me to some of her friends.

During the respite, I spotted Chris in the distance and, after excusing myself, went over to tell him I was ready to leave. He said it was too soon and I should return to my friends, although I think he noticed that my pointed looks were communicating a wish for early intervention. He mumbled something about ten minutes, and I returned to Vanessa and her friends.

I sat with her on a nearby sofa, hoping that the two of us could just sit and talk, which was much safer than dancing close together. However, she slid close to me, locked eyes and kissed me. Her lips were soft and moist, and her tongue gently slipped into my slightly open mouth. Once more, I felt myself losing control and pulled away before temptation got the better of me. I felt obliged by my commitment to Jean-Louise, yet at the same time I was confused by the pleasure I felt in Vanessa's presence.

Fortunately, moments later Chris arrived and announced that we needed to go home.

"I'm sorry," I told Vanessa, "but Chris is my lift."

"Why not stay and call a taxi?"

Chris answered on my behalf: "I promised to take him home so that he can go birdwatching in the morning; he doesn't want to stay out too late."

Birdwatching was obviously the last excuse that Vanessa had expected, and she gave me that bewildered look I normally receive when someone hears about my favourite hobby. Even so, she did not want me to leave.

"Can I see you again?" she asked.

I scribbled her telephone number on a piece of paper and promised to call her, and then I excused myself . . . although there was time for one final kiss.

It was not until the following morning that I realised how stupid I had been. The effects of the alcohol had worn off, and I worried that I had likely put an end to my relationship with Jean-Louise, if she ever found out. It was not the dancing and talking that was the issue, it was the kissing. She would regard that as cheating and I had not lived up to my promise to stay away from Essex girls. I could gamble that she would never find out, but many people had seen my behaviour and there was always a risk that someone might tell her. I could not wait for that to happen; I had to do something before she heard about it from someone else.

It seemed that the best way was to admit to my indiscretion as soon as possible. I would have to conduct a very difficult conversation with her, and while Chris arranged to have the party host tell Vanessa I would not be calling, I prepared for my next meeting with Jean-Louise.

Our arrangement for the following weekend was to meet in central London and go shopping along the Kings Road in Chelsea and then on to Carnaby Street. Jean-Louise had never visited these places, but she had read about their many boutiques containing fabulous clothes and outrageous-looking people. During the outing, I paid for an orange and grey miniskirt for

her to wear at college, and a pale cream leather pinafore dress for her to wear when we went out together during the cold winter evenings.

I planned to make my confession during dinner at a newly opened Indian restaurant just north of Oxford Street. We found a quiet corner table as Jean-Louise excitedly re-examined her purchases from earlier in the day. Once the poppadoms and beer had been served, I looked her in the eyes, and began.

"I need to tell you something about last Saturday." I spoke quietly, so that we would not be overheard. "Chris asked me to go to a party with him last weekend. I didn't want to go, but he said I should because it was arranged for this year's intake of graduate trainees." I could hear myself beginning to blame Chris, and that was not my intention, so I went on: "Anyway, I decided to go with him, and during the party his girlfriend introduced me to one of her female acquaintances. I wasn't thinking at the time, but we talked and danced, and I maybe danced with her longer than I should have. She was pretty but nothing took place because I asked Chris to take me home. I'm sorry that I broke my promise to you and spent time with another woman. What I did was wrong, and it will never happen again."

She looked shocked and, judging by her reaction, she was more hurt than angry. I waited for her response, and in a few seconds it came.

"That really wasn't a nice thing to do. I told you in Hull that something like this might happen. How would you like it if I said that I'd gone out with a friend and met another man in Manchester? You'd be jealous and disappointed, wouldn't you? Well, that's how I feel, but at least you're telling me, and you sound penitent. I've so much else to worry about at the moment that I don't want us to fall out right now, but let this be a warning to you, and never let it happen again."

I felt a wave of relief hearing that our relationship was still intact, and the incident had made me realise how fond I was of Jean-Louise. I started to think that maybe the time had come to do something more with our relationship, and not wait until she finished her teacher training.

As I travelled by underground back to Upminster, I pondered our future. I was still awaiting placement in a permanent job, and she had not even begun to search for a teaching post in Manchester, so maybe now was the time to become engaged. I thought that it might encourage her to think about teaching in Essex and lessen her distress if I was not placed in Langley. Proposing our engagement did not require setting a wedding date, but her answer would indicate whether she cared for me or not. Also, at the back of my mind I admit to having thoughts that, if Jean-Louise turned me down (something that I was not hoping for), at least I would have opportunities to meet other girls like Vanessa.

* * *

My assignment in Staff Personnel Policies finished without a job offer, and I transferred to Production Planning and Control. My work there was mundane, repetitive and not what I liked but, fortunately, no-one mentioned an open position. My third pre-placement involved sitting alongside a senior buyer and listening to him negotiate contracts that seemed almost unachievable by the supplier without losing money. He was very helpful, but by the end of the assignment I had decided that I did not possess the ruthlessness to be successful in Purchasing.

Near the end of my time in the third assignment, I was called to Graduate Recruitment to hear about my next round of pre-placements. The arrangements were for three weeks in the Finance Department in headquarters, followed by two weeks at the Aveley parts depot and then a fortnight in the Basildon tractor plant. Unfortunately, the representative passed on the very bad news that Langley did not have any openings for someone like me. I quickly informed Jean-Louise and I promised to visit her that weekend so we could commiserate together.

The last day of my second week with the senior buyer coincided with some terrible news. On my way to lunch, I chanced to meet a fellow trainee headed in the same direction.

"Have you heard?" he asked me. "There's been an awful accident in South Wales. Lots of children have been killed."

I had heard nothing and asked for details.

"A coal tip in Aberfan has collapsed and destroyed a school and many homes. Over a hundred people are dead, mostly children, and rescuers are still digging out bodies."

The scale of the disaster was difficult to comprehend. After very heavy rainfall, a man-made mountain of slurry from a colliery spoil tip had slid down a hillside and destroyed the community in the valley below. For a while, I felt terrible that I was so anxious about my career when others were dying so horribly. The disaster was the main topic of conversation with Jean-Louise when I arrived in Reading at Saturday lunch-time. There had been an outpouring of grief among her class friends for the unimaginable trauma that the school-children had suffered.

To take our minds off the tragedy, we visited Windsor Castle and detoured past the Langley truck plant to have a look at the factory that was unwilling to place me. Jean-Louise told me that her mother's condition remained serious, and how thankful she was to have decided to teach. She was still worried about my job security because of the latest developments in Britain's motor industry. Nissan, a Japanese company, had been given government approval to start importing Datsun Sunny saloon cars at a time when British-based vehicle manufacturers were still announcing redundancies.

On my way back to Upminster the following day, my thoughts returned to my future relationship with Jean-Louise. In two weeks' time, it would be Saturday, 5th November, exactly one year since we had started dating. Maybe this was the moment to propose to her, provided I could buy an appropriate engagement ring in time. We had already arranged to meet in central London to see the film *Dr Zhivago*, and I thought it would be romantic to propose to her over dinner afterwards.

Back at work, I sacrificed my lunch-hour to visit jewellers in Brentwood. I had no idea what I was looking for, but I knew that Jean-Louise liked opals; they were also her mother's favourite gemstones. Eventually I was shown a gold band set with a medium-sized opal surrounded by a cluster of small diamonds. The opal shone brightly in a multitude of colours, from brilliant reds to greens and blues, on a pale cream background. My budget was stretched, but not broken, and the jeweller told me that he would adjust the band if it did not fit Jean-Louise's finger. He placed it securely in a square, red velvet-covered box.

My plan was to watch the film during the afternoon, and then propose over dinner at the *Quo Vardis* restaurant in Soho. When we arrived at the restaurant, we were ushered to a window table by the headwaiter, and I nervously talked non-stop during the meal. By the time dessert arrived, the fluttery feeling in my stomach was under control so, breathing deeply, I prepared to ask Jean-Louise for her hand in marriage. I believed I sounded awfully nervous when I began.

"It's our first-year anniversary today, and I want you to know it's been the best year of my life, thanks to you. I know I do strange things occasionally, but please don't consider this one of them. I would like to ask you to marry me."

I reached across the table and passed the red velvet box to

her, then waited for her to open it, terrified that she would turn me down. She looked first at the ring, then at me, and then beamed in a way that I had never seen before. She reached over, took my hand, squeezed it affectionately and to my intense relief said, "Of course I will. I love you despite your eccentricities. The ring is perfect."

I leaned over the table, removed the ring from the box and placed it on her finger. It was an almost perfect fit.

We were both speechless with delight. I paid the bill, and as we walked along the streets of Soho, I embraced her. We kissed and clung together under street-lamps that threw huge shadows across our path. We stopped and kissed many times, soft passionate kisses, and it did not matter that people were watching. It was very difficult to part. I took her to the underground station to put her on the tube to Paddington, from where she would catch the train home to Reading. We lingered for as long as we could, but eventually we bid each other goodnight with one final kiss, and she disappeared down the escalator.

I stunned Chris and David the following morning with the announcement that I was engaged. They immediately asked when the wedding would take place, but I told them that the date had not been fixed, as it would depend on the health of Jean-Louise's mother.

* * *

After the weekend's excitement, I completed my last week in the Finance Department, and hoped for a placement. Instead, I was told that the department had already filled its trainee positions for the current year, and I felt cheated. If Graduate Recruitment had sent me to this function earlier, I might have been given one of those jobs. Chris had by now accepted an appointment in Graduate Recruitment and David was under offer from Production Planning and Control, but so far nothing had been offered to me. Many other trainees had been placed and I began to fear that I might be the last 1966 graduate trainee to be placed. Maybe the Aveley parts depot or the Basildon tractor plant would like me. Meanwhile, Jean-Louise was on her way to Manchester to show off her engagement ring.

(Jean-Louise, November 1966) "It's been a life-changing 60 days here in Reading. I'm settled into my teaching program, and John has visited me regularly since I arrived. The incident with the Essex girl was more embarrassing for him than it was annoying to me. I wonder if the encounter accelerated his decision to ask me to marry him. It was cute using our first anniversary, and I had no hesitation in saying 'yes'. He's the right person and I can now start planning the wedding. My mother wept when I told her; she's so very ill.

"The ring is gorgeous, albeit the band is too large, but John says we can return it to the jeweller who'll fix it. The prospect of marriage raises lots of complications: Where will I teach? Will my mother be well enough to attend the wedding? Do we need to move back to Manchester so that I can look after her? How long should we wait before marriage? Will I have time to organise the wedding? Also, my father says he wants John to ask him formally for my hand in marriage; it's an out-of-date custom but I'll respect his request.

"I can't help but think how fortunate I am despite my mother's illness. It's in awful contrast to what happened to the teachers and pupils in Aberfan. The school in which I'm teaching has started a disaster fund and collected food and clothing. I contributed some money.

"John is finding it difficult to find a job and worries that he may become the last trainee to be placed. Most upsetting

has been the absence of a position for him in Langley, but currently the inconvenience of living apart has lessened now that he has proposed to me. I'm sure things will work out. In the meantime, I'm on my way to Manchester to show off the engagement ring."

Pied Wagtail: This is a smallish bird of only 18cm/ 7 inches in length, with a long tail and largely black and white plumage, and it is primarily found in Britain. In winter, the birds move into suburban areas and gather in large roosts where artificial light is present, supposedly for safety reasons. There are around 400,000 breeding pairs in Britain. The birds are highly active and, when not standing still and frantically wagging their tails up and down, can be seen dashing across grassy areas, lawns and pavements in search of insects. They have a strange, jerky walk, a comical running style and an undulating flight during which may be heard its call of "chiss-wick". They are well known for their mating displays, when their elaborate courtship rituals range from the male simply pursuing the female to a series of complex running and flying behaviours that come to an end when the female participates in the dance. The European variant is paler in colour and is known as the white, or alba wagtail.

North America is home to four separate varieties of wagtail (citrus, grey, white and eastern yellow) whose habitat is largely restricted to Alaska and parts of Canada, although some may appear as vagrants along the West Coast.

15

The Lucky Kingfisher

Both families were overjoyed by our engagement and Jean-Louise delighted in showing off her betrothal ring and discussing possible wedding dates with her parents. She also invited several of her former school friends to be bridesmaids. My mother offered to assist with wedding arrangements. Her lifestyle had changed dramatically since I had left home to attend university. After nearly two decades living in a difficult marriage, she had rediscovered her freedom after the death of my stepfather and begun to live the life she had always wanted, including taking frequent overseas holidays.

My first day at the Aveley parts depot turned out to be a disappointment. Early in the morning, I was given a list of relocation benefits and asked to draft letters explaining the arrangements to employees who were willing to move to a place called Daventry, about 95 miles (150km) to the north. Apparently, the parts business, including the department for which I was working, was transferring to this new location. Since Daventry was well outside the boundaries of Essex, my promise to Jean-Louise disqualified me from considering any opportunity that I might be offered.

That evening I called her from the usual telephone kiosk

to find out what had happened in Manchester. She sounded happy.

"My mother loves the opal and my father wants us to marry during August next year, after I've finished my teaching course. He's suggested 12th August. Also, he wants a small wedding ceremony because of my mother's health, and he expects you to ask him formally for my hand in marriage."

I was more than willing to do that but it was unusual for Jean-Louise to abide by old customs that fostered male supremacy. I told her that I would ask and hope he did not say "no".

"Oh, he won't," she replied. "My mother won't let him."

I turned my attention to other matters. "Did your friends agree to be bridesmaids?"

"Two have, but the third is ill and doubtful. What about Anton. Will he be your best man?" I was asked.

I told her I did not yet know because I had not had time to write to him. An invitation would be sent during the next few days and I expected him to accept.

Her best news came last: "My father wants me to teach in Essex. He says he can cope with my mother and I should look at teaching posts close to where you live. I'm supposed to tell the university placement officer later this week. If he asks where in Essex, what should I say?"

"Tell him Brentwood for the time being," I proposed. "It depends on my first job, but it's likely to be either in headquarters or Dagenham."

"You sound a little disheartened," she commented.

I told her I was. "Aveley has turned into a flawed hope and, now we're getting married, I need to find something soon."

"Stop worrying! Everything will turn out fine; be patient," she tried to encourage me.

I realised that I required more than just the patience and persistence that I had used to find my employer; now I needed some good luck to find a job. It was an expertise greater than that offered by the grey herons I had seen from the train at the time of my interviews. Instead, my thoughts turned to the kingfishers I had watched along the river Nidd in Yorkshire during my childhood years. These birds possess the watchful qualities of herons, but they also chase after the fish rather than just waiting for it to swim by. The brilliant flash of orange and blue the bird creates in flight is supposed to bring good luck and symbolise prosperity. I concluded that I needed to be more enterprising, confident, enthusiastic and tenacious to find the right placement.

* * *

December arrived and I was working in the Basildon tractor plant, a recently built facility located on the outskirts of town. A 125-feet (35 metres) tall, white, onion-shaped water tower advertised its presence. Demand for tractors was very high and the plant was hiring, so having been brought up on a farm and being able to drive a tractor, I was sure this was the place for me. I communicated my interest to my mentor and said I was willing to accept any job in the Personnel Department

I was mentored by a person who introduced me to both hourly and salaried employment issues. One of the major topics concerning the hourly-paid workers was the new wage structure that Mr Welsh's boss had mentioned during our orientation, and this was in its final phase of negotiation. Apparently, the new pay structure cost much more than the current wage arrangements and therefore it violated the government's wage freeze. Under these circumstances, it could be implemented only if Ford and its unions could demonstrate to government-appointed officials that productivity improvements of a value at least equal to the additional costs could be put into effect.

What was called a "Plant Productivity Agreement" was being negotiated.

I felt thoroughly at home, and towards the end of my two weeks, my mentor told me there was an opening for an additional personnel officer because of the extra hiring necessary to meet production requirements. Apparently, I was a strong contender, but the decision would not be made until after I finished my pre-placement.

Thus, the following Monday morning after completing the assignment, I visited Graduate Recruitment in the hope of hearing that I had been offered a job. Again, I was disappointed. My representative informed me that the Personnel Manager wanted to recruit me, but at the very last minute he was told by his American superiors to reduce his 1967 budgeted headcount. He had done this by eliminating the position for which I was under consideration.

The fear that Ford of Britain was about to end my employment became very real, although I was assured that there were other opportunities. A new pre-placement had been arranged for me in Ford of Britain's Sales Department. If that was not successful, I would be assigned to the Industrial Relations Department in the Dagenham engine plant for another personnel officer opportunity.

* * *

You can imagine that it was with some relief that I said farewell to Essex on 23rd December 1966, still unplaced, to begin a ten-day holiday, first with my family in York, and then with Jean-Louise at her home. She had travelled to Manchester directly because of her mother's condition, and said she would not visit York.

My mother was keen to hear how I was progressing. I assured her that I would soon have a job, and once I knew where I was working, Jean-Louise and I would begin looking for a home. I was given a letter sent by Anton who had accepted my invitation to be best man and wished me a merry Christmas. The rest of the time in York was spent celebrating the holidays by visiting relatives, exchanging gifts and attending church with the family on Christmas Day. I was not a strong churchgoer, but it was standard practice in our family to always attend services on Christmas Day, Easter Friday and Easter Sunday, and the October Harvest Festival.

My first task, once I was in Manchester, was to ask Jean-Louise's father for his daughter's hand in marriage. He beamed, said 'yes' and thanked me for telling him that he had raised a beautiful daughter.

Sadly, her mother's health continued to deteriorate. She was suffering periods of fatigue and walking with some difficulty. Much of the time she was confined to her bed. Close neighbours helped out in their home and I felt guilty when I left to resume my Sales pre-placement.

Chris was already in our lodgings when I returned and he said he had rented a house in Basildon from the start of February. Neither he nor David wanted to wait any longer, now that they were both placed. I agreed to join the move, despite being worried that I might be placed far away from Basildon. I consoled myself with the thought that at least Jean-Louise would be able to visit me in Essex.

The first half of January passed with no change in my job status. The Sales Department made no offer, despite my telling Graduate Recruitment that I would accept any assignment it presented.

Once more I was transferred, this time to the Dagenham engine plant, and it was on the morning of 19th January 1967, just as I was leaving my lodgings, when the landlord intercepted me.

"Do you have a job yet?" he asked. He knew I was the only one of his lodgers still looking. "I bet you're finding it different in Dagenham than at headquarters," he added.

I agreed. "It's noisy, dirty and congested, especially on rainy days, and the people look so very different from those in the Ivory Tower, and no, I don't have a job."

Reference to the Ivory Tower caused him to smile. It was the name given to Ford of Britain's headquarters, in part because of the colour of the building, but also due to its reputation for coming up with impractical, worthless ideas.

"You'll do fine down there," he said, adding to my self-confidence. "You'll be a good fit."

* * *

Clive, the senior personnel officer and my mentor, was in the office when I arrived. I knew he had worked himself up from the Industrial Engineering Department and transferred to the Personnel Office a couple of years previously. Apparently, about half the company's personnel officers came from the shop floor, and the others had been graduate trainees like me.

The engine plant was huge. It lay on the south side of the Dagenham estate and employed several thousand workers. I could see the engine assembly lines from where I worked on the mezzanine floor. They seemed to stretch forever, as part-assembled units moved slowly past workers who carried out the same simple task many times an hour.

"Go and get yourself a cup of tea and something to eat," Clive told me, "and then we'll talk about what you're going to do today."

When I returned, he passed several safety reports to me and told me to prepare an account of each accident and recommend what should be done to avoid a recurrence. It was real work, and I appreciated the assignment. As I was about to leave, Clive's manager Jack arrived.

"We're going to have trouble today," he announced. "You need to organise an emergency meeting with the senior shop stewards," he told Clive. "The convener tells me his members are going on strike if a Japanese delegation comes into the plant today."

"Why?" Clive asked.

Jack replied: "Some of them were prisoners in Thailand during World War II, and they are still bitter about how the Japanese treated them and their friends. They're not prepared to forgive Japan for what it did, and if the delegation enters the factory, they'll walk off the job."

The day turned out to be extremely busy. The meeting of management and shop stewards was futile; there was no empathy on either side, nor any willingness to seek a compromise. It came down to an ultimatum: If the Japanese came into the plant, the men would walk out. Management argued that they were only obeying orders from the higher-ups.

For the first time in my life I was involved in a work stoppage, and at the end of the day I had the experience of driving through a picket line. I was not sure what a picket did, and I thought I might be stopped and abused for staying in the factory. Instead, the strikers were orderly, did not try to dissuade me from leaving and waved at me as I left. I thought perhaps it helped that I did not look foreign. Some of them waved banners carrying messages that were, to say the least, inflammatory, abusive and very anti-Japanese. By the following morning, the pickets were gone, the Japanese delegation had left and engine assembly was back to normal.

As this pre-placement came to an end, my hopes of an appointment were raised once more. I had enjoyed working with Clive, and told him so. He advised that there was a vacancy for a personnel officer, and while a couple of internal candidates were under consideration, I also qualified and was under review. No decision had been made by the time I finished my last day, but a call from Graduate Recruitment told me to meet its representative at 8am the following Monday.

Over the weekend, I was optimistic that the position would be offered to me, and I was prepared to accept a commute to Dagenham. I told Jean-Louise what was happening and she was excited for me. Unfortunately, my confidence was premature. On Monday morning, I was informed that the job had gone to one of the internal candidates. Local management wanted someone with factory experience, and it had doubted my credibility because I looked so young.

I thought I had reached the end of the road because, as far as I was aware, everyone else had been placed. I was expecting termination, but it did not come. Instead, I received a huge surprise.

"We have a placement for you," the Graduate Recruitment representative beamed. "It's here in headquarters, working for Industrial Relations Staff in an office called Forward Planning. The unit doesn't have the headcount, so we're placing you as a supernumerary. Congratulations!"

"What's a supernumerary?" I asked, worried that the placement was temporary.

"It means we carry you on our headcount and fund your salary until the unit has the budget authorisation. It may take several weeks, but it will happen. You're to report to a Mr Welsh."

I was flabbergasted. Not only was I being placed, but with none other than the person who had interviewed me in Hull. I thought back to how something as insignificant as a cup of tea was able to change a person's life. The reason for the placement was not given and I thought it might be wise not to ask; maybe Mr Welsh was being punished for recruiting me, or maybe I was the last trainee and the unit did not want to lose the only resource available.

Naturally I accepted the appointment and was asked to report to Mr Welsh at 10am that day. My head spun with the suddenness of the development, but by ten 'o' clock I had managed to get my whirling thoughts in order as I arrived at Mr Welsh's office. I could not wait to tell Jean-Louise what was happening and that I would be staying at Ford and working in Brentwood. I was overcome by a huge feeling of relief that both my career as well as my private life were moving forward satisfactorily. I told Chris what was happening and waited in the cafeteria drinking tea until it was time to see Mr Welsh.

(Jean-Louise, February 1967) "John has just called, thrilled that he has been placed in Industrial Relations Staff, working in Brentwood. Apparently, his new boss is Mr Welsh, the person who first interviewed him. He thinks it's a good placement, although he's not sure what he's supposed to do; apparently, it's something connected with 'forward planning'. I know it's been a difficult few weeks for him, and the delay in placement has slowed his interest in preparing for our wedding. It's now up to me to find a teaching post close to Brentwood, and he says we should start looking for a new home fairly soon. I hope he'll relax more now and spend more time with me. It's a long train journey, but I'll start travelling to Essex to familiarise myself with the place, and maybe be able to watch the Formula One Race of Champions at Brands Hatch next month.

"It's difficult concentrating on my studies while I worry about my mother's health, and I must visit home as well as Essex. Already she finds it difficult to stand, climb stairs

and maintain her balance. The doctor says the illness will eventually affect her digestion and breathing. My father is resigned to the fact that her health will not improve, although I hope she will make it to my wedding day. It's always been her dream to see me marry.

"My parents chose 12th August to allow me to finish my teaching instruction and before I start my first job. Everyone's excited about the ceremony, and my two closest friends at school will be bridesmaids. Anton will be John's best man and it will be nice to see him again after a year of absence. It's to be a traditional wedding, with a church service, white wedding dress and a veil to cover my face. I'll also fulfil my mother's request to wear 'something old, something new, something borrowed and something blue'.

Kingfisher: This bird has a stout, sparrow-sized body (about 16cm/6 inches in length), a short tail, rounded wings and a large head. It is usually found near slow-moving or still water, and it is conspicuous because of its bright metallic blue and orange plumage. It may be seen perching motionless on the branch of a tree next to the water, waiting to spot its prey in the water beneath, but close-up views are not easy as it is very shy. In Britain it catches sticklebacks and minnows, and it may also take other small fish, shrimps, tadpoles, frogs and insects. It suddenly dives head-first into the water with its wings outstretched and its beak pointing at its prey, snatches its food and then disappears as a bluish streak. To survive, it must eat its own body weight in food each day. There are

around 6,000 pairs breeding in Britain, and most of them are resident, but a small number migrate during spring and autumn to the coast and estuaries.

There are four types of kingfisher in North America, with the belted kingfisher the most common, and it is also a water bird. Tradition has it that the kingfisher was the first bird to leave Noah's ark and was coloured orange by the setting sun and blue from the sky.

16

The Voracious Gannet

Mr Welsh had changed very little since I first met him. He wore a different suit made of dark and light grey herringbone tweed, and I noticed for the first time that his teeth were nearly as crooked as mine. There was no mention of our earlier meeting in Hull; had he forgotten, or was he too embarrassed because he had caused my hiring at Ford? After some opening pleasantries, he explained the role of Forward Planning. First, he mentioned that his office was staffed only by himself, his secretary and now me, and its function was to develop industrial relations strategies affecting Ford of Britain's 42,000 manual workers.

"My unit was established a couple of years ago at the insistence of the Americans," he told me. "Its purpose is to find ways to avoid conflict and disorder on the shop floor by introducing long-term industrial relations strategies that enable collaboration and cooperation with our trade unions. It isn't easy, but we've made a start with the development of the new wage structure."

He went on to say that my responsibilities would be monitoring and reporting on shop-floor disputes, assisting with industrial relations research and helping prepare for negotiations during major disputes. I was given a stack of documents and told to study them.

"This is the way things used to be," he declared. "Maybe it can be changed."

The first two documents were reports from government-sponsored Industrial Courts of Inquiry involving previous Ford of Britain work stoppages. Each Court consisted of a small group of people brought together to identify the cause of a walkout and recommend appropriate remedial measures. The first Inquiry concerned a 1957 stoppage at Briggs Motor Bodies, now part of Ford in Dagenham. It was known as "the bell ringing dispute" and involved a senior shop steward who had been fired for using a hand bell to call unauthorised meetings of workers; his union members had gone on strike to protest his dismissal. The second Inquiry concerned a 1963 Dagenham assembly plant stoppage, when 70 so-called shop floor militants had been fired for inciting industrial anarchy.

In both cases, the findings of the Court supported the company's actions, and I deduced that shop stewards exercised significant power over workers, to the extent that sometimes they were more interested in pursuing political agendas than representing their members' interests. It also seemed to me that managers were sometimes provoked to a point where they acted vindictively.

During the next few days, I was given more paperwork. Included were brochures describing the government's incomes policy, reports on how to improve job evaluation in manual occupations and details of the Contracts of Employment Act, 1963, which had established for the first time that employers must provide employees with written terms and conditions of employment. I was eager to learn as much as I could, and I asked questions of Mr Welsh whenever I did not understand something.

My thirst for knowledge was like that of the gannet seabirds, gone fishing: voracious. These large birds are summer visitors to the towering chalk cliffs along the Yorkshire coast, just south of Reighton Gap, where I spent the occasional summer holiday. Walking along the cliff-tops, I would see these white birds flying above the sea before suddenly ending their onward flight, hesitating for a moment and then plunging vertically down into the water with closed wings at breakneck speed, only to reappear seconds later with a fish or other food in their bills. They swallowed whatever they caught and later regurgitated it to feed their chicks. Later in the season, young gannets would follow their elders and be taught how to fish by trial and error. Mr Welsh was my elder, and the documents he gave me were my fish.

* * *

When Chris, David and I moved to Basildon, we invited a fourth graduate to join us, Tony, who worked in the nearby tractor plant. We had moved into a recently built, two-storey, semi-detached, four-bedroom house that was fully furnished and included oil central heating. I had never experienced the comfort of having a whole house constantly heated, so, to me, it was luxurious accommodation.

When Jean-Louise began her visits, there was much for us to organise. Where would she work? Where would we live after we married? Could we finance the purchase of a new home? If we did, how should we furnish it? The top priority, however, was finding Jean-Louise a job.

The people at Reading University identified a geography post at a school just north of Brentwood and arranged for Jean-Louise to apply. She was quickly invited to a panel interview but found it disheartening when she received a barrage of questions concerning her marriage plans and what she would do when she was pregnant. Back in the 1960s these inquiries were considered normal, and women's employment was frequently terminated when they became pregnant. Employers were loath to go to the expense of hiring and training women who might need time off—or, indeed, leave work altogether—to give birth and bring up their children; there was no such thing as maternity leave. Although Jean-Louise thought the questions unnecessary and intrusive, a few days later the school offered her the position, which she accepted.

We celebrated each other's appointments with a meal at a local Chinese restaurant, although the differences in our experience were stark as Jean-Louise had succeeded on her first attempt to find a position, whereas it had taken me six months to find someone willing to give me a job.

House hunting was our next priority, but our plans were delayed when Jean-Louise's mother became seriously ill, and nurses were required to look after her. Jean-Louise visited home each weekend and watched helplessly as her mother's health deteriorated. She had difficulty swallowing as well as being unable to walk. During the Easter holidays, I took Jean-Louise to Manchester by car and was astonished at how frail her mother had become, yet she had not given up organising the wedding. While we were there, the local vicar arrived to agree the order of service, and the hotel venue was chosen for the reception. Everyone hoped that Jean-Louise's mother would be well enough to attend the ceremony, even if it was in a wheelchair.

National catastrophes went unnoticed, including that involving an oil tanker, the *Torrey Canyon*, that ran aground off the Cornish coast on 18th March 1967. It seemed unimportant to us, despite the 119,000 metric tonnes (131,000 US tons) of crude oil that it discharged, resulting in dreadful effects on birds, sea creatures and wildlife, and bombing of the ship ten days later to sink it.

* * *

When I returned to work, Mr Welsh sat me down to discuss the contents of a binder holding summaries of every Ford of Britain work stoppage, overtime ban and work-to-rule during the past 12 months. Each statement was titled "Incident Report".

"I want you to prepare these in future and give copies to all Brentwood-based senior managers. Top executives need to know whenever production is disrupted by industrial action," Mr Welsh told me.

He asked to review my reports before they were circulated, and he would correct my grammar, spelling and punctuation, as well as altering the description of the dispute, if necessary. As part of the review process I also received help with my writing abilities. I was shown how to communicate more clearly, frame my sentences in a more logical manner and avoid mechanical writing errors. Quickly, I began to understand why manufacturing workers went on strike: Their work was tedious and repetitive, their tasks were changed at a moment's notice, they had no say in line speeds, their working practices were frequently altered by management without explanation, working conditions were dirty, noisy and sometimes unsafe, discipline was one-sided and workers could be laid off without pay in circumstances beyond their control.

I also received a set of booklets published by "Incomes Data Services", an organisation that had begun a publication reporting all industrial relations developments in Britain. These were important documents for my research; anything serious enough to affect Ford of Britain had to be notified to senior managers in Industrial Relations Staff.

Initially, I did not know if my work was satisfactory, as

nothing was ever said, but my uncertainty disappeared at the beginning of April when Mr Welsh sat me down and gave me my first performance appraisal. He had rated my contributions as "satisfactory" (meaning that I had fulfilled his expectations) and suggested ways I could do better. He recommended that I resume my education and enrol in a part-time or evening course to learn more about industrial relations and personnel management. I soon found a three-year correspondence class managed by the Institute of Personnel Management, in partnership with the Metropolitan College, St. Albans, and I signed up for the course to commence in September 1967. I gave Mr Welsh all the paperwork, and Ford of Britain reimbursed me for the cost of the classes. Mr Welsh also confirmed that the headcount for my position had been approved, and my salary expense was now carried by Forward Planning. I was legitimately placed at long last.

* * *

Jean-Louise and I began to search for a home that we could afford, and we regularly received descriptions of various properties for sale. My savings would cover only a small deposit, and Jean-Louise was not earning at the time, so the mortgage company that we approached told me that, while I would qualify for a loan, Jean-Louise's future income would not be included. The general expectation was she would stop work when she became pregnant, and therefore her salary could not be used to justify a 30-year mortgage—the type of loan for which we were applying.

A month after our Easter trip, and only four months short of our wedding, real tragedy struck. Jean-Louise called me in tears early one Tuesday morning to tell me that her mother had passed away during the night. She was leaving for Manchester immediately and asked me to join her as quickly as possible.

Mr Welsh approved a week's leave, but because I was as yet unmarried, it did not qualify as bereavement time-off; I had to use my holiday entitlement.

The funeral service was a small, sad family affair in the church that her mother regularly attended and was to be the venue for our wedding. It was a difficult time for everyone, including me, and although I desperately wanted to support Jean-Louise, I did not really know how. I persuaded her to recall happy memories of her mother and the trips she had shared with her parents, but this only made her cry more. It seemed wrong to marry so soon after her mother's death, so we suggested a delay to her father.

"Absolutely not," was his emphatic reply to his daughter. "Your mother had looked forward to the wedding, and she'd never forgive me if I delayed it. She told the vicar to proceed, even if she wasn't with us, and she was very proud of you. She looked forward to seeing you happily married and even asked me to give you the money that we had saved for your education but never used; it's her way of helping you to buy your first home."

Neither of us wanted to argue, so we agreed that the wedding should go ahead as planned. The financial gift was a wonderful surprise and made it certain that we could afford to buy a home.

The two months between the time of the funeral and Jean-Louise receiving her teaching diploma was a difficult period. We spent the weekends together, in either Basildon or Reading, and I suspended all birdwatching.

The house search ended when we found a small, two-bedroom, semi-detached bungalow in a place called Pilgrim's Hatch, a mile to the west of Brentwood, and took ownership in late July. To our delight, the money gifted by Jean-Louise's parents covered the deposit.

My work continued at Ford as I read about the government

extending its national incomes policy. The wage freeze was carried over from 1966 to include the first half of 1967, and it was announced that the second half of that year would be a period of "incomes moderation". Only productivity-based awards and increases for low-paid workers would be allowed. The restrictions were accepted by the trade unions as necessary because of the state of the economy, but they warned there was no guarantee that their members would comply.

Concurrently, the British-owned motor industry was struggling with its complex system of piece-work wages and trying to convert them into hourly rates, despite worker opposition. Stoppages and other industrial actions were being taken by groups of workers to press for higher hourly pay and to oppose the thousands of redundancies that were taking place. The advantages of Ford of Britain's wage structure were now clearer, and its newly designed vehicles were selling well. The situation was not so optimistic elsewhere in Britain.

The government's application to join the European Economic Community had begun to make progress. A request was submitted during May 1967, and two of the six member countries announced their support almost immediately. Another more serious world event occurred early the following month. One Monday evening at the start of June, I arrived home in Basildon to find Tony's attention glued to the television. The newscast was reporting the beginnings of the six-day Arab-Israeli war. Tony's reaction was that what was happening would impact the world for a long time to come.

Jean-Louise received her Diploma in Education at the beginning of July and returned to Manchester to stay there until our wedding day. I moved my personal belongings to the Pilgrim's Hatch bungalow and bought locally some second-hand furniture. Chris helped with its transfer by using a Transit van that he had been able to borrow. I visited Moss Brothers in Romford to rent my wedding attire, and Mr Welsh took me to lunch the day before I left for Manchester to thank me for my work and to congratulate me on my marriage. It had been a hectic six months at work, but now I was a respected member of Industrial Relations Staff. The future challenge was to see whether I could also become a respected husband.

(Jean-Louise, July 1967) "It's been a very difficult few months coping with my mother's death; I've cried a lot and John has been as supportive as much as he can while working in Essex. I've my teaching diploma and will start work in the classroom during September. In the interim, I need to finish arranging the wedding.

"My father has helped me relocate back to Manchester. He drove down for the Diploma of Education ceremony, and then we loaded all my belongings into the car and returned to Manchester the following day. During the journey, my father said he'll retire in two years' time, and I invited him to consider living with us. I don't think John will mind.

"I'm slowly getting to know Essex. It's a bit flat and dirty, but not much different from places near my home in Manchester. Basildon New Town is sort of barren, with poor shops and not a lot to do, but Southend-on-Sea, just down the road, has lots of shopping and plenty of places in which to eat. The house the four boys live in is new and I've met John's colleagues, all of whom I like. Chris is a little impulsive and outspoken and David is quiet and thoughtful. I'm not sure about Tony; he has a girlfriend in London and spends most of his weekends with her.

"My new school, just outside of Brentwood, is only five years old and a coeducational secondary institution. It's close to our home in Pilgrim's Hatch, and I can easily catch the

bus, but eventually I want to learn to drive. The bungalow is small, with two bedrooms, although it's all we can afford, and without the deposit from my parents, we couldn't have bought it. It's at the end of a cul-de-sac and very quiet. I've also been introduced to motor-car racing. John took me to Brands Hatch during my first visit to Essex to watch the Formula One Race of Champions.

"I hear from Chris that John works hard during the week and he's usually the last one home. Apparently, he's much more confident now, and he admires Mr Welsh. He's learning to defend Ford and its industrial relations record, and I think my father has given up arguing with him because there's chaos throughout the motor industry.

"Once we're married, John says he's starting a three-year personnel management course; it seems ironic that just as I finish my education, he goes back to school.

"For now, I'm counting down the days to our wedding. John says that 12th August is 'the Glorious Twelfth', the start of the red grouse shooting season. That seems to fit with the Scottish roots of my father, he adds. I've told him it doesn't matter; what matters is that my mother won't be present at the ceremony."

Gannet: *Adult gannets are large, white-coloured birds, about 95 cm/37 inches in length, with pale yellowish heads, distinctive black-tipped wings and long, dagger-like bills. Most of their life is spent out at sea, but from March to September they create dense nesting colonies called "gannetries" on cliffs and rocky islands. There are about 220,000 breeding pairs in Britain, which accounts for around 56 percent of the world population of this species. In flight they are thin and angular, with a long neck and a pointed tail and wings. At sea, when not fishing, they glide low over the water, flapping their wings intermittently. To cope with the impact of hitting the water head-first at high speed, the bird's strong bill breaks the surface of the water.*

In North America, there are nesting colonies in Quebec, and birds can be seen along the eastern and southern coastlines of the USA during winter.

17

Two Turtle Doves

I LEFT BASILDON FOR west London early on Friday morning, the day before my wedding, first to collect Jean-Louise's veil from her aunt, and then to pick up Anton at his parents' home. It was a cool day with plenty of sunshine, and my car was functioning perfectly as Chris had helped me the weekend before to change the spark plugs and replace the ignition leads. The number of wedding guests had been restricted to 30 family and friends, and neither Chris nor David was included.

The prospect of marriage excited me, and I no longer moped over losing the opportunity to meet new girlfriends. Jean-Louise had managed the organisation of the wedding and was a little stressed that everything might not happen as planned whereas I simply needed to turn up. My own anxiety was caused by having to meet strangers, especially Jean-Louise's relatives from Scotland, whose language I might not understand. I thought they should be able to figure out what I was saying, since my accent had softened somewhat during the year in Essex and my Yorkshire expressions were now replaced with genuine English words, but mostly I hoped that Jean-Louise would take charge of the conversations. Earlier she had asked me not to call her "turtle dove" in front of her relatives; it was a nickname I used sometimes when we were on our own.

"Have you ever been given a pet name?" she asked me.

I told her that an earlier girlfriend had called me "petal" (I think she came from Durham and used the word as a term of endearment), and I defended my use of "turtle dove" as an expression of love towards her; and from where I came, turtle doves were symbols of affection and commitment.

This adorable small dove had a special meaning for me as a young boy. During my one-mile walk home to the farm from Sunday School, I passed by a copse of mixed oak and ash trees that was home to a pair of these birds every summer. During April and May, the woodland floor became an ocean of bluebells, and I would stand amid this blue haze and listen spellbound to the couple of doves making their gentle "purr-purr" sound. One dove would perch in a nearby tree, watching me, while the other was barely visible, crouched on a nest made of thin twigs and incubating two eggs. These weekly detours ended in August, when the birds left on their arduous journey to winter in Africa and the bluebells had long disappeared.

On the way to Anton's, I collected the wedding veil from Jean-Louise's aunt. She was a retired seamstress, formerly employed by Elstree film studios, and had offered to embroider the bridal headdress. It was a soft, delicate, two-layer, fingertip-length creation, made of champagne silk tulle and adorned with gold lace in the form of floral and leaf patterns, and Jean-Louise planned to use it as her "something new" during the wedding ceremony.

Because her aunt could not attend the wedding, I promised to send her a piece of the wedding cake. She gave me the veil neatly attached to its bridal hair comb and resting in a white cardboard box, and after exchanging a few pleasantries, I left to collect Anton.

I had not seen him for over a year, yet we reconnected immediately. I was surprised by how little he had changed; only his dark-rimmed spectacles were new, whereas his long, curly blonde hair and happy smiling face remained unchanged, although he was developing that glassy-eyed look that is often associated with academics. As we loaded his suitcase and wedding suit into the car, his mother asked to look at the veil. I obliged by handing her the box, which she opened, looked inside, and lovingly stroked the headdress. Then, after a cup of tea, we departed for Manchester.

There was much to talk about during the journey. Anton gave me the latest news about the people I knew in Hull and spoke enthusiastically about the woman he was dating. He reminded me that I had frequently seen her in the university library during our final year, and that I should expect a wedding invitation very soon.

"I still think you should have accepted the PhD in micropaleontology," he told me. "It's an important new science for hydrocarbon discovery and—who knows?—you might have ended up working for an oil company and be exploring the North Sea."

I told him I appreciated his confidence but did not regret my decision.

"I'm happy where I am," I said, and he just smiled.

"Tell me about your research project." I wanted to learn more about his studies.

He spoke enthusiastically: "It's hydrology and all to do with measuring land degradation and soil erosion caused by human interference with water systems that alter the balance of nature. We carry out all sorts of analyses and find solutions to improve land stewardship. Currently, I'm studying several locations in Yorkshire to find ways to improve the balance of water and avoid soil deterioration.

I hope to complete the studies within 4 years to obtain my doctorate."

He went on to discuss statistical measures he was using to evaluate changes in water-borne sediments in his study catchment areas which frankly I did not understand, and was relieved when he eventually changed subjects.

"But tell me about you and Jean-Louise." He returned to questioning me.

I explained how she would teach near our home, that we had bought a small bungalow near Brentwood, that I was now working in industrial relations and would soon return to education to study for a qualification in personnel management.

"And the honeymoon plans?" he continued.

"We're going to Glyfada, just outside Athens, and we have to be in Luton tomorrow evening to catch the flight out on Sunday morning."

His questions caused me to check that I had brought the wedding ring. I had, and I asked him to take care of it until the wedding ceremony.

Our discussions then shifted to more general stuff, such as the Six-Day War which had allowed Israel to take possession of the Sinai Peninsula and Gaza Strip from Egypt, annex the West Bank and East Jerusalem from Jordan, and seize the Golan Heights from Syria. An inquiry into the Aberfan mining disaster had concluded that the National Coal Board was at fault, the Wimbledon tennis tournament was televised for the first time in colour, and there was still no political settlement in Southern Rhodesia. Meanwhile, the British motor industry continued to transform itself; after experiencing financial difficulties, Rootes had been taken over by Chrysler, Leyland-Triumph had acquired the Rover car company, and Jaguar joined the British Motor Corporation.

By now we were north of Stoke-on-Trent, and I needed him

to guide me by mapping the rest of the way. It was still daytime, but I was unfamiliar with the roads that lay beyond the Jodrell Bank Observatory. We ended our conversation and arrived late during the afternoon at Jean-Louise's home, where a surprise was waiting for me.

Even before the car came to a stop, Jean-Louise ran from the house looking very unhappy. "How could you?" she complained. "You've left the wedding veil at Anton's. You have to go back and collect it."

My stomach sank. I looked over on the back seat and could see the box was missing. I knew its importance to Jean-Louise, and immediately assumed there was no option but to return immediately.

"I'm sorry," I said very contritely. "I took it out of the car to show Anton's mum. I'll return right now and collect it," and I turned to climb back in the car.

"That won't be necessary," she said, taking my arm, and her expression changed into a smile.

"Anton's mother called after you left, and she's taken it to Euston terminal to put it on the train. My father will collect it in the morning from Manchester Piccadilly station. Thanks to Anton's mother, everything should be OK."

I was so relieved at this news that I could not be cross about her little trick.

By the following morning the weather had turned overcast and it was raining. About 45 minutes before the ceremony, Anton and I arrived at the church carrying umbrellas. There were no ushers or groomsmen, so we stood in the church doorway, welcoming guests and guiding them either to the right side of the aisle, if they were my relatives, and Jean-Louise's to the left. I walked my mother to her seat and when it seemed that everyone was in attendance, we stepped forward and stood waiting at the altar. A few minutes later the two bridesmaids joined us and a cousin of mine arrived to act as the flower girl.

A few moments afterwards, Jean-Louise appeared at the church door, holding onto her father's arm, and the two of them began to walk down the aisle. She looked radiant, dressed in an elegant, floor-length white wedding dress with a cream-coloured lace overlay. I tingled with excitement as she moved towards me and stood to my left as her father sat down in the front pew. The service was flawless. Jean-Louise winked at me when I lifted her veil, there were more loving smiles as I slipped the wedding ring onto her finger, and I kissed her after the formal marriage vows. (Back then, it was unusual for the bridegroom to be given a wedding band.) The paperwork was signed, and then the processional walk took place down the aisle.

Outside the church, we were greeted by a cold, blustery and very wet Manchester. The photographer gave up taking pictures as we scrambled into the waiting car, with Jean-Louise frantically holding onto her veil as the wind tried everything to rip it away. Once in the reception hotel, the festivities took place without mishap, except that the rain outside turned heavier and heavier. After speeches and photographs, we left our guests and went to change into our going-away clothes. That was when we encountered an unexpected obstacle. As Jean-Louise reappeared, her father became upset.

"A daughter of mine should not go on honeymoon dressed in green," he said agitatedly looking at her emerald green jacket. "You need to wear something else."

"What's wrong?" Jean-Louise asked, very surprised by his criticism.

"It's an unlucky colour. The Scots don't wear green. They're Protestants and unionists, and they boycott the colour because of its connection with Irish republicanism. It'll bring you bad luck."

Fortunately, Jean-Louise's aunt interceded and told him not to be so old-fashioned.

A few guests ventured outside to wave us goodbye, but most stood inside watching our departure through the rain-streaked glass as the downpour continued. The storm stayed with us as we drove south, and I battled with my car's single wiper blade and the inside of the car's windows steaming up. Visibility externally was limited to a few yards but, even so, I did not want to abandon my plan to reach Luton later that evening. However, just south of Stafford, Jean-Louise spoke up.

"Please stop," she implored. "It's dangerous and the weather scares me."

At first, I preferred not to change my mind. "It'll stop soon," I said, "It's just that I don't want us to miss our flight."

"We won't be alive to catch it if you keep driving in this weather," was her comeback.

She was right. I was already having difficulty seeing through the blurred windscreen, made more hazardous by the bright headlights shining through the rain as vehicles came towards me. Eventually I pulled off the motorway a few miles north of Birmingham, and as my stress level rose because I did not know where I was, Jean-Louise calmly removed the Automobile Association route book from the glove compartment and mapped us to the cathedral town of Lichfield. She spotted a coaching inn with a "Rooms Available" sign, and on entering, the receptionist greeted us and assigned us to the honeymoon suite.

Thus, our first night of married life was spent in a large four-poster bed recovering from physical exhaustion and surrounded by a confetti-covered floor; someone at the wedding had stuffed Jean-Louise's suitcase with the contents of several boxes of the small bits of coloured paper.

By morning, the rain had eased, and it had stopped completely by the time we reached Rugby. Thereafter we made good time to Luton and managed to catch the flight to Greece, and soon we were flying across continental Europe. Jean-Louise read her book and smoked, while I looked out of the window, with both of us silently wondering what lay ahead of us now that we were married. Four months earlier, a military coup had taken place in Greece, but our tour company had assured us that Athens was safe for tourists. I was anxious that, if something went wrong, it would be my fault as I had chosen Greece as the honeymoon destination.

(Jean-Louise, mid-August 1967) "I'm married and on my way to Greece. All the wedding arrangements worked well, except for the weather, and it'll be a long time before John forgets leaving the veil in London. I was happy we stopped overnight in Lichfield; the rain was awful, and it was especially difficult to see the road ahead of us, although John would have kept on driving if I'd have let him. John blames the confetti in my suitcase on his uncle.

"Now I'm wondering about my changes in life: living with John, starting a career in teaching, having enough money to live on, and no longer having my mother to guide me.

"My father was depressed during the reception and nervous when he gave his speech. He misses my mother. He and I were pleased that our relatives came down from Scotland, and we were glad that John's aunt, uncle and family drove across from York. My father's reaction to the green jacket was unexpected; I knew he didn't like me visiting Ireland when I was a young girl, but I hadn't realised how superstitious he was. I suppose it

was the way he was brought up and my mother always stopped that behaviour.

"It was a delight seeing Anton, although I didn't have time to talk to him, and my bridesmaids' support was appreciated. One of them gets married in a week, but I can't attend her wedding because I'll be in Greece. Anyway, I'm pleased to be with John, and he shows the same feelings towards me. He says he won't call me 'turtle dove' anymore."

Turtle Dove: This is Britain's only migratory species of dove, which has a range covering most of Europe, the Middle East and North Africa. It is a dainty bird, smaller and slighter in build than most other doves, and a little larger than a blackbird (length about 28 cm/ 11 in). Its wings are mottled with an intricate tortoise-shell pattern, and it has wedge-shaped black tail feathers with white edges; there is a distinct black-and-white-striped patch on its neck, its breast and head are pale grey-lilac and it has orange eyes and reddish legs. It is well known for its "purring" call on warm summer days, and around 14,000 pairs breed in Britain, mainly in southern and eastern England. The species is becoming increasingly rare in Britain, however, with an estimated 96 percent decline in the past 50 years. Turtle doves have long been a symbol of love, and in poetry they are usually associated with fidelity and trust.

The mourning dove is its closest relative in North America.

18

A Family Of Owls

NEARLY EVERYTHING WAS perfect during our honeymoon. Life was joyful, and even unanticipated annoyances were thwarted by our love for each other. Lunn Poly arranged the chartered aircraft out of Luton and the flight was nearly full, despite the coup in Greece and the £50 spending limit that was still imposed on holiday makers. My passport showed the number of Greek drachmas I had bought a few days earlier. The young and attractive air hostesses first served us hot food and drinks and then pushed carts around offering us duty-free cigarettes, alcohol and perfume. In those days, the recruitment criteria for their position were "female, single, aged 21 to 27, excellent health, good eyesight, neatly proportioned figure and pleasing appearance".

It was a short journey from the airport to the hotel, and after checking in, we were directed to our bedroom and told our suitcases would follow. It was on reaching the room that we realised why the journey had been so short: Just outside the window, across the road, was the landing strip for the airfield! As aircraft arrived, the walls of our building shook and the noise was so loud it would be impossible to sleep. Jean-Louise looked at me for an explanation. I remembered the advert in the holiday brochure stating that the hotel was "fair-priced and a newly constructed resort facing the beautiful and clean sandy beach of Glyfada". It made no mention of "adjacent to the airport runway".

Jean-Louise laughed anxiously. "I don't know what you have in mind, but I'm not going to stay awake all night."

I was in an awkward situation as Jean-Louise obviously expected me to do something, so I decided to complain to the front desk.

The receptionist could not understand what I was saying, and the nervous waving of my hands did not help. She summoned a person who spoke English and appeared to be more senior than her who, after apologising for the noise, gave us a room on the opposite side of the hotel. She promised it would be quieter and had a view of the beach. Jean-Louise was delighted.

There was no shaking of the walls in the new room, and the noise was significantly less, although not entirely absent. With extra pillows provided by the hotel, we cuddled together at night, holding the pillows over our heads until we fell asleep. Eventually we saw the funny side of our predicament, and Jean-Louise forgave me for my hotel choice. Fortunately, from midnight to early morning very few 'planes arrived, and we kept the windows closed because of the air conditioning, as well as to keep out the din.

We still could not prevent the noise of early-morning aircraft becoming our alarm clock, and on the first day, Jean-Louise was eager to don her bathing suit and start sunbathing before other tourists arrived. For breakfast, we grabbed some sesame bread rings and yoghurt from the hotel restaurant and took them to the beach.

The seashore extended over 100 yards from the hotel to the water's edge. Essential items were packed in our beach bag, and I carried the straw mats and blue mini-parasol that we had purchased the year before in Mallorca. As Jean-Louise lay at the water's edge in direct sunlight, happy to read her novel and coat herself with sunscreen, I huddled under the umbrella desperately trying to keep out of the sun. Jean-Louise took the occasional dip in the sea to cool off, but I did not like to bathe. By late morning, my fair skin was reacting to the sun's rays and parts of my body were beginning to burn. I told Jean-Louise I needed to go back to the hotel and that is when we discovered the second blunder of our holiday.

The sun had climbed high into the sky and turned the way back to our hotel into an expanse of scorching sand. In the early morning it had been much cooler, and we had walked barefoot to the water's edge; now we needed to sprint 100 yards across burning sand with no footwear. After a brief paddle to cool our feet, we began the journey and howled and grimaced as we chased towards the hotel like a pair of mad dogs. When our feet became unbearably hot, we dug them momentarily into the cooler sand just beneath the surface, before resuming our trek back to the hotel. By the time we arrived, the skin on the soles of our feet was red and sore. We spent the afternoon soaking our extremities in cold water and coating each foot with aloe-vera gel. Rehydration was provided through a visit to the hotel bar.

For our second day, we were better equipped with sandals, shirts and towels, and we did not go out until mid-morning because the sun from the day before had tired us out. Back on the beach, Jean-Louise once more stretched out, deepening her tan, while I used the umbrella to cover as much of my sensitive skin as I could. By early afternoon I had lost the battle. Despite the sticky suntan lotion and the partial shade, most of my body was burning, feeling hot and tender, and parts of my back and legs had turned bright pink. That was enough for me. From my childhood days, I knew the next stage would be painful blisters. I gave Jean-Louise the choice of continuing to sunbathe without me or leaving the beach and going sightseeing in Athens with me. She chose the latter.

Each day, we travelled by public transport and investigated the various historic sites in Athens: The Acropolis, the Parthenon, the Acropolis Museum, Constitution Square and the ancient Agora of Athens. We booked a day tour to the Oracle of Delphi because we read that the Beatles had been there four weeks earlier and we were keen to see what had attracted them.

Something that caught my attention during our sightseeing was the many representations of a small owl that was apparently called Bubo and was the sacred bird of Athena, the Greek goddess of wisdom and strategy. They were on statues, on vase paintings and reliefs, on coinage and on weights and measures displayed in the museums. I wondered why, and I visited a bookstore to find out. I read that in Greek mythology the owl sat on the blind side of Athena, so enabling her to see the whole truth.

Many Greek legends exist about owls, especially on the battlefield. For example, an owl was supposed to have settled on a ship's mast before the Battle of Salamis in September, 480 BC; its presence was believed by Greek soldiers to be a message from Athena to support their fight, and they went on to achieve a famous victory over Xerxes the Great of Persia.

Jean-Louise asked which species of owl we were looking at. Judging by its size, and from what I read, I told her it was the little owl.

"Do we have those in Britain?" she asked.

"Yes," was my reply, "they're even occasionally seen on the Yorkshire Wolds."

In fact, I had observed a little owl late one afternoon just outside a Wold village, a few miles from Hull, perched on a telegraph pole and bobbing its head up and down. Although it is normally nocturnal, the species sometimes is seen in daylight, usually perching on a tree branch, telegraph pole or rock.

"What other types of owl do we have?" was the next question.

I told her that four other species were resident in Britain, and I had seen them all. There was the tawny owl that I watched flitting around the farm at dusk, a barn owl that once came down the chimney in our home (we captured and released it) and there were the long-eared and short-eared owls that I had seen roosting in trees. I had a strong fondness for owls as beautiful, serene and wise birds—all qualities that I saw in my wife!

* * *

It was during our visit to Constitution Square that we found ourselves talking to a group of students who were supporters of the Greek socialist Andreas Papandreou. One was a teenage girl and the other three were young male adults in their early twenties. Armed soldiers and tanks were all around us and made the students feel nervous. They asked to move away from the square to a place where they would feel much safer. Each understood some English, and the girl acted as the group's communicator. She explained that the person with whom they sympathised had been incarcerated after the right-wing military coup that had taken place four months earlier. It was apparent that they were aspiring young revolutionaries committed to resisting the military takeover and overthrowing its leaders.

Our friends spent time talking about what they saw as brutal oppression, censorship of the news, government by dictatorship and the suppression of individual freedoms and free speech. They also believed that the United States had backed the coup in order to prevent the spread of Communism.

We chose an outside street table at a taverna, so that we would not be overheard, and enjoyed a feast of moussaka, souvlaki, pita bread, ouzo and beer as we talked. The dissidents spoke sadly about their lost colleagues and said that many thousands of left-wing supporters had been arrested and imprisoned in local detention centres and on remote Greek islands, or "Greek Gulags" as our friends called them. Some had been detained close to our hotel, and each detainee was being "re-educated" to try to erase their communist ideals. At the end of the evening I paid for the meal, we said our goodbyes and the four students slipped away into the darkness of the night. We never saw them again, and it was not until July 1974 that democracy was restored in Greece.

Once in the seclusion of our bedroom, Jean-Louise remarked, "I hope they're successful. They're very brave. Can you imagine Britain abolishing human rights, censoring the press, banning gatherings of people except to attend church and imprisoning people without trial? What an awful place."

I asked if she thought I had chosen the wrong country for our honeymoon. She replied she did not think so, and added that it was important to learn how other people live and, if possible, help them.

"Now you know why you can't wear a mini-skirt in Greece and why I can't have long hair," I added. "Both are banned by the military junta."

Thankfully, the rest of our stay was peaceful and uneventful.

* * *

Too quickly it was time to return home. We collected the car from Luton airport and drove the 170 miles (270 km) to Manchester to briefly visit Jean-Louise's father. The following Monday was a Bank Holiday, and the day after that I was expected back in the office by Mr Welsh. Also, Jean-Louise had school papers to prepare. She admitted feeling anxious about her new job, but she was pleased when the school secretary wrote notifying her that the school had appointed a mentor, a woman in the geography department, to help her during her first year.

Our other reason for visiting Manchester was to open our wedding gifts and send out thank-you notes before taking the presents back to Essex.

"Who's this one from?" asked Jean-Louise.

We were halfway through the unwrapping, and this particularly large and heavy parcel showed no name. It had come directly from the Derbyshire manufacturer and consisted of a lovely stoneware dinner set of six lidded soup bowls and the same number of salad and dinner plates, all glazed in pale grey with soft brown stripes.

"I have no idea," I replied, as I unsuccessfully searched for a card. Jean-Louise's father suggested we prepare a list of everyone we thought might send us a gift, and then compare the names with the presents received. We did, but there was no name missing.

That night, as Jean-Louise slept beside me, I wondered about the dinnerware. It was an expensive gift and must have been sent by someone who thought a great deal of us. Was it a work associate or a former friend at university? I could not think of anyone who could afford to be so generous. Then I recalled the strange man across the street at my graduation in Hull, and the unexpected letter I had found in my mother's desk. Were these clues? Was the gift from the same person? I could not be sure, but I concluded that this was the most likely solution to the puzzle. My next thought was: Should I tell Jean-Louise or shield her from my personal situation and not say anything? Did she have the right to know? My conclusion was that she did.

After lunch, we bid farewell to Jean-Louise's father and left for the long drive to our new home in Essex. It was a warm, dry, sunny day, and a few minutes into the journey, I plucked up the courage to share my thoughts with Jean-Louise.

"There's something I need to talk to you about," I began with slight hesitation.

"You sound serious." She looked at me in surprise.

"I am," I replied. "There's something you should know. It's about me, not us, and maybe I ought to have told you sooner. It's a secret I've never shared with anyone until now."

"It all sounds very mysterious. What is it?" she asked, giving me her full attention.

"Well, you need to keep it a secret too. No-one else knows, not even my mother."

"Go on then," she encouraged me.

I took a deep breath. "I think the dinner set is from my father, my real father. I've never met him, but I know he exists because of a letter I found among my mother's papers. My mother doesn't know I found it."

"But your father died nearly four years ago!" objected Jean-Louise.

"No," I replied, "that was my stepfather. My mother always told me that he was my real father, but it's not true. I know nothing about my true father, I've never met him, and he's never communicated with me. I'm sorry; I should have told you sooner."

Jean-Louise responded sympathetically. "No, it doesn't matter. It has no effect on our relationship, and I appreciate your openness. It's better to know now than if a stranger knocks on the door in the future."

I told her that it was still a guess on my part, I could not be certain and there was nothing more I could tell her about my father.

Eventually, we arrived in Pilgrims Hatch. It was the first time Jean-Louise and I had been in our new home as a married couple. She giggled as I carried her across the threshold, and she gave me a huge kiss as I set her down in the hallway. Married life was off to a good start and I would resume my career the following morning.

(Jean-Louise, late August 1967) "It would've been fun to spend more time on the beach at Glyfada, but clearly John's body wasn't up to it. The sun was hotter than in Mallorca, and there was nowhere close to the beach for John to wander around. We both have an interest in history, so the visits to Athens and Delphi were very fascinating. I couldn't wear my bikini, as I would have risked being arrested but, luckily, I took with me some long skirts to wear in town. John was considerate throughout and stopped for rests when I asked him to.

"The political turmoil and the presence of military people in the streets was not what I expected. The students we met were incredibly courageous. I enjoy supporting the underdog, whereas John is much more down-to-earth and considers both sides of an argument. It seems the world is full of political unrest, with the Red Guards and Cultural Revolution in China, Americans fighting in Vietnam, Biafra at war with Nigeria, the Middle East battles, the Guatemalan Civil War, military dictatorship in Argentina and the uprising in the Congo. I'm happy to be safe and back in Britain.

"I'm going to love my new home. It's small and intimate, but already I have plans for interior design and replacing the chocolate-brown exterior paint. Presently there is very little furniture, so I'm looking forward to buying more.

"I worry about leaving my father in Manchester, now he's on his own, but expect to visit him often and he'll come and

stay with us. He insists on working until his retirement at age 65. John's mother said she might call in on us during one of her trips to catch a passenger ship for a cruise, and I hope to make my own friends in Essex as soon as I start teaching; presently I know only John's colleagues.

"John's confession about his father was a shock. Who'd have thought that someone who'd never cared for him would send us a wedding gift? I felt respected that he told me rather than keeping it to himself, and it's become our secret; it will bind us closer together.

"Now that I'm home in Pilgrims Hatch, my first priority is to prepare lesson plans for teaching and then I'll start my career in a few days' time."

*Owls Generally***:** *they are silent, stealthy, solitary, mostly nocturnal (crepuscular) birds of prey, considered by some as sinister and omens of death and by others as symbols of wisdom, protection and prophesy. All the species are characterised by an upright stance, a large, round head with a conspicuous circle of feathers surrounding a flat face, a facial disc around each eye and large, sharp talons. Their head is capable of rotating 270 degrees, they have acute hearing, and the layout of their wing feathers makes them adapted for silent flight. Most owls swallow their prey whole.*

Owls in Britain: The attractive looking tawny owl is the one responsible for the familiar "to-wit-to-woo" call and the most common, with around 50,000 breeding pairs. The elegant barn owl is possibly the most easily recognised, with its white underparts, heart-shaped face and screeching call; it is widely distributed with about 4,000 breeding pairs. The wise-looking long-eared owl possesses an authoritative stare, and there are about 3,500 breeding pairs. The camouflaged short-eared owl usually nests on the ground, is medium-sized with ears that are difficult see, and hunts during daylight. There are around 2,000 breeding pairs in Britain but thousands more arrive from the continent for winter. Around 5,000 pairs of the comical little owl are resident, mainly in England and Wales. The giant eagle owl, which looks like overgrown long-eared owl, is a recent arrival in Britain; it has been known to attack a deer fawn and other raptors, as well as kill a fox. There are only a couple of dozen breeding pairs, mainly in Yorkshire.

Owls in North America: There are at least19 species, some regional and others habitat-sensitive; the great-horned owl is one of the more common and the barn owl is the most widespread.

19

The Domesticated Mallard

Mr Welsh surprised me with some unexpected news as soon as I returned to work.

"Well done; you've been promoted to grade seven and will receive a promotional salary increase at the start of September," he told me.

I stared at him and allowed a large grin to spread across my face; what a way to return to work. Eventually I found the manners to say, "Thank you!"

Here it was, the end of August 1967, and I was successful at home with my marriage and now increasingly prosperous at work. I could not wait to pass on the glad tidings to Jean-Louise, but more immediately, I needed to know what had happened in the office while I had been gone.

"Two things," he replied. "The first is that the government has approved our new wage structure, thanks to the Plant Productivity Agreements, and we'll backdate the pay adjustments to March 1967. The unions are delighted because their members are receiving pay increases averaging a little over 10 percent when the rest of the country is subject to a wage freeze. You'll need to monitor reactions to the new grades and publish Incident Reports whenever a dispute arises. We hope there won't be many, but you need to be familiar with the job evaluation process."

With that, he passed to me a copy of the Hourly-Paid Job Evaluation Manual and told me to study it and refer any questions to the manager responsible for its implementation.

"And the second happening?" I inquired.

"Ford of Europe has been created. Dearborn is filling most senior positions with Americans, and a new Vice President of Industrial Relations has been appointed. *(Dearborn is the site of the 12-storey Ford World Headquarters/Central Staff Office Building located on the outskirts of Detroit)*. Our director is to report to this new Vice President as well as to the Chairman of Ford of Britain. In future, we will have to review all major disputes with the Vice President and obtain Ford of Europe's concurrence on any policy change. We have been asked to prepare an analysis of shop-floor industrial action that occurred during the past twelve months so that the director can share the study with his new Vice President. Since it's time for you to take on additional responsibilities, I want you to complete this work."

* * *

At home, Jean-Louise was preparing lesson plans for her fourth and fifth-year classes. She developed her teaching notes by topic, and each subject was supported by exam readiness assessments. She worked late into the night, and as the days passed, we established a routine of taking our evening meal together, and afterwards separately finishing our day's work. When we had time, we discussed financial arrangements and responsibilities for domestic duties.

A couple of days after she began teaching Jean-Louise asked me: "What shall I do with my salary? The school wants my bank account changed so it's in my married name and not in my maiden one."

The advice from my bank was not simple. My wife could not open a bank account in her new name by herself. I had to co-sign. Married women back then were unable to independently manage their finances unless authorised by their husbands. It seemed easier to convert my existing arrangement into a joint account which Jean-Louise could then access once she received her own cheque book. We agreed that any large withdrawals, other than home maintenance expenses such as the mortgage, home insurance, community rates, electricity and coal would be discussed before they were made. Even so there were credit difficulties. On one occasion, Jean-Louise found a dining table and a set of matching chairs at the Times Furnishing Company in Romford, but we had insufficient funds to pay for them. Instead she requested a hire purchase (credit) agreement but was told that I had to go to the store first and co-sign before the loan could be approved. It was not until 1975 when these archaic rules were changed because the British Sex Discrimination Act made it illegal to discriminate against women financially.

Another priority was to decide who would be responsible for which tasks around the house. I accepted garden maintenance, home repairs and washing the car, while Jean-Louise offered to carry out the weekly clothes wash and house cleaning. Cooking and shopping would be shared, and home decorating would be apportioned as necessary. However, not everything in our relationship went smoothly. We were constantly learning more details about each other's character, and there were times when our differences caused major disagreements.

For example, Jean-Louise wanted the garden maintained to the same high standard as the inside of the home. Outside was mostly a large area of grass, criss-crossed by concrete paths. During August, the grass had become overgrown and Jean-Louise wanted it mowed to look tidy. We did not have a lawn mower, so I invited several work colleagues to come over one Sunday afternoon to use hedge shears and scissors to trim the lawn. In return, I supplied them with beer. Jean-Louise did not like the results and quickly approved my purchase of a second-hand grass cutter.

There was also a minor tiff over the "yellow dress", the frock that she occasionally wore at university, and which somehow had made its way to Pilgrims Hatch. One morning she appeared dressed in the garment ready for school. I suggested that it was too provocative and too revealing to wear in front of teenage children. She disagreed and said that its knee length was within the boundaries of the school's dress code, and she was going to wear something smart that day because she was going out after school with her school mentor.

A more serious exchange arose over replacing the Ford Popular. It had become unreliable and its annual repair costs exceeded its value. Chris had bought a Lotus Cortina and I wanted to do the same. It would be second-hand of course, but Jean-Louise instantly objected.

"You don't need such a powerful car," she said crossly. "It'll cost too much, and I don't want to be taught to drive in a vehicle like that. It will probably kill both of us. I think we can afford to buy a new car but let me choose which one."

This was the first time she had mentioned me teaching her to drive. It was not a responsibility I looked forward to, and I could imagine us screaming and arguing with one another as I had seen other couples do. On the other hand, it was unreasonable to expect her to use public transport for the rest of her life, and I felt that it was my obligation to provide support now that we were married. After further discussion, we agreed that she would choose the car and I would begin giving her driving lessons once the fine weather returned in spring.

A few nights later, she called my attention to a light blue, low mileage Ford Anglia 105E advertised in the local newspaper. It was the smallest vehicle in the Ford range, and the least powerful, but it was inexpensive because its owner was anticipating the release of its successor, the Ford Escort, in a few weeks' time. The vehicle came with a heater, two windscreen wipers and a radio, and we negotiated a reduced price. The Ford Popular was sold by advertising it in Ford of Britain's employee newspaper.

Family planning had been resolved before we married. We agreed there should be no children until our careers were established and we could provide a comfortable home. Jean-Louise took the initiative and discussed contraception with the general practitioner who treated her mother. His recommendation was to use the recently introduced oral contraceptives because they were the simplest and most reliable.

* * *

I completed the Incident Report project for Mr Welsh, and it showed that most Ford of Britain disputes occurred in large plants and involved only a small numbers of workers who, because of the nature of their work, could close down a plant whenever they walked off the job. Ford had more than 20 unions, and no single organisation seemed to dominate. Major causes of disputes were changes in work practices, factory working conditions and worker discipline. Pay disputes were less frequent, although their incidence was rising because of the new grading system. Most pay grievances involved changes in wage relationships between different groups of workers, rather than the wage amount, because there were now five grades instead of three.

After the project was completed, Mr Welsh gave me a new assignment. The Industrial Relations Vice President had asked to see a review of collective bargaining practices in all Western European countries, or at least those in which Ford had a presence. Its purpose was to identify processes that Ford of Britain could adopt in order to improve its relationship with its trade unions. I was asked to prepare the study by the end of the year.

* * *

Jean-Louise wanted to know more about the new wage structure once she knew I had read the Job Evaluation Manual. It was a complex document that included many terms that were unfamiliar to me (for example, datum jobs, profiling, job characteristics and weightings). Mr Welsh explained these terms, and the project appeared to have created closer management-union collaboration.

I was proud to tell her: "Ford of Britain is in the forefront of modern personnel management, being one of the few British companies using objective job analysis to compute appropriate wage rates for its manual workers."

"So how does the new structure differ from the old?"

I explained as best I could. "Manual work used to be divided into four categories: unskilled labourers, semi-skilled production workers, craftsmen and women. I think these were a carryover from Victorian times when blue collar workers were segregated into craftsmen, machine minders, labourers and women. Treating women separately hasn't been a big issue for Ford because it employs less than 1,000 of them."

I continued. "We evaluate each job in the same manner and assign one of five grades. All workers are placed in grades A through E, including the women."

"So, women are paid the same rates now? That's good, but

why are there so few of them?" Jean-Louise continued her quizzing.

"Women are not paid at exactly the same rate as men, but close," I admitted. "We now use 87 percent of the equivalent male amount instead of the old system where women received 90 percent of the lowest men's wage rate. On average, the women have received pay raises about the twice the average 11 percent as a result of the new wage structure. As for numbers of female workers, since most factories work shifts and British law prohibits women from working nights, we can't hire them."

I do not think Jean-Louise was impressed by my explanation. She shrugged her shoulders, "OK then, how many of these women are in the higher grades?"

Looking sheepish, I answered, "None. There are no women in the top two craft grades, and only a handful in the semi-skilled classification Grade C. Most are at the production worker level Grade B."

I think she was appalled. She ended the discussion with: "If women teachers can receive equal pay, why can't Ford do the same for its female workers, and hire more women for the dayshift only?"

I suggested that if she wanted further details, we should invite Mr Welsh and his wife to dinner. It would also be a way of thanking him for his support during my first few months in Forward Planning. She agreed.

* * *

Meanwhile, our contact with Chris and David continued. Tony had married a few weeks after me and moved to west London. Consequently, Chris and David chose to relocate to a smaller house in Hornchurch, and they invited us to visit their new home. Early on Saturday evening, 18th November 1967, we arrived.

Even before we were out of the car, Chris ran down the driveway, excited to tell us that the Prime Minister had just announced a devaluation of the pound. He has made this decision despite many earlier assurances to the country that the government would never devalue the currency.

"Do you mind if we don't go out?" asked Chris. "I'd much rather watch the television."

I had hoped we could visit the pub, but I deferred to Jean-Louise who agreed with Chris.

What we heard was something unprecedented in our lifetime. As well as freezing incomes, the government was now devaluing what we were already paid. The Prime Minister said that the pound in our pocket would not lose its value, but everyone realised that a devaluation of 14 percent would lead to higher prices. The excuse given was that serious adverse economic conditions were affecting the country, and we were assured that the nation would become great again as a result of the devaluation. Little did we realise that inflation would increase several-fold during the next few years and, although the devaluation provided a short-term boost to the economy, the country's growth rate remained below that of its international competitors.

More bad news arrived a few days later when Charles de Gaulle, the President of France, announced his veto of Britain's second application to join the European Economic Community. He claimed that Britain's economy and its alliance with the United States were incompatible with the interests of Europe, and Britain would collapse economically if it was admitted into the Community. The British government protested, stating that it would continue to pursue membership.

Quickly the trade unions demanded higher wages to compensate for the currency devaluation, despite the government's wage restrictions, and union leadership from the political far left became more militant. In response, it was rumoured that the government was investigating ways of restricting union power and would likely use the recommendations of the Royal Commission on Trade Unions and Employers' Associations (named "the Donovan Report" as the Commission was headed by Lord Donovan) to achieve this goal. The Commission had been appointed by the government some 30 months earlier "to consider the role of trade unions and employers' associations in promoting the interests of their members and in accelerating the social and economic advance of the nation".

The shop-floor situation in Ford of Britain was similar. Despite Ford's national unions supporting the new wage structure, groups of workers began to protest their grades, usually when they found they were in classifications lower than colleagues who had previously been on the same wage rate. Most often impacted were craftsmen who formerly had occupied one grade, and who were now distributed across three levels. Improving the grade classification assigned to a job was the simplest way of increasing wages during the period of the government's pay restrictions.

* * *

As Christmas arrived, Jean-Louise and I encountered another of our small disagreements. It began when Mr Welsh and his wife accepted the dinner invitation, and Jean-Louise decided to serve duck with orange sauce.

I confess I was a little mystified by her question: "Should I cook one or two ducks on Saturday?" she inquired. "I want there to be enough meat to go around."

I had no idea, but I thought one was best because it was the cheapest. Also, remembering a superstition from my family, I added that she should purchase a female duck.

"What in the world for?" she asked, looking astonished.

"My mother says that hen ducks are plumper and tastier. That way, we'll have more meat on one bird."

I think she thought I was mad, but on Saturday morning I realised that she had accepted my advice—or at least she thought she had; I had no idea how the butcher had sexed the bird if it arrived without its feathers; maybe it was shot in the wild on the marshes of the Thames Estuary and came to the butcher with its plumage intact.

Mr and Mrs Welsh duly arrived, and after introductions we sat down to eat. The tomato-ginger bisque turned out to be perfect, but then, as we prepared for the main course, Jean-Louise called me into the kitchen.

"Look," she whispered, as she pointed to several small pieces of dark duck breast and two skinny duck legs. "There's not enough meat to go around, so I'm going to give most of it to our guests and serve us with more potato, cabbage and orange sauce. You mustn't say anything."

It turned out that our guests enjoyed their dinner and did not seem to notice the virtual absence of duck alongside our mashed potato and vegetables. We talked about Essex, families, marriage, the devaluation and Ford of Britain, and then Jean-Louise asked the inevitable question about women's wages.

"Why doesn't Ford implement equal pay?" she asked Mr Welsh. "If jobs are evaluated using the same criteria, it would seem the right thing to do. And because there are so few women, it wouldn't cost the company very much."

Mr Welsh was surprised by her advocacy, glanced at me and then replied: "It's really what the unions agreed to. The women have received increases double the percentage awarded to men, and no-one thought equal pay was necessary. Market conditions differentiate between men and women and support a gender wage difference."

"But if the evaluation system is equal, shouldn't the pay be the same?" Jean-Louise insisted. "Ford is supposed to be in the vanguard of leading management practices."

Mr Welsh became defensive as he tried to explain: "But men and women don't work in the same manner. British law prohibits women from working night shifts, and there are legal limits on the amounts of overtime they can work. Also, their absentee rates are much higher than for men."

I could see that Jean-Louise was about to erupt. I needed to think of a different topic to deflect the conversation, and I came up with the recent outbreak of foot-and-mouth disease. Probably it was not the best subject to mention over dinner, but it was something of importance to me because of its potential consequences for my farming relatives. I timidly added that we had chosen to serve duck because beef, pork and lamb might be contaminated by the disease. At the end of the worst outbreak in Britain during the twentieth century, nearly 450,000 farm animals had been slaughtered.

After the Welshes left, I worried that Mr Welsh might have found the cross-examination offensive, but I need not have worried. The following Monday, he told me that he had enjoyed the conversation and found my wife refreshing and high-spirited.

A few days later Jean-Louise and I left home in our Ford Anglia to spend Christmas with her father. This was his first year-end holiday without his wife, and he had also lost his daughter to me. Jean-Louise did the cooking, and our conversations stayed away from contentious topics like wearing green jackets, Ford's attitude towards its trade unions and when her father might expect a grandchild. We would return to Brentwood before the New Year for me to return to work in Forward Planning, and Jean-Louise would prepare for her second term of teaching.

(Jean-Louise, December 1967) "I feel as though the honeymoon continued after we returned home. Increasingly we understand each other and find compromises when we're on the verge of disagreement. Sometimes I wonder what I might be doing if I were a fashion buyer for Marks & Spencer, but then I realise that looking after my father is my top priority. John's commitment to Ford grows every day, and he works very hard. There are times when I wish he would stand back and be a little more objective. However, he probably needs to obey orders and express opinions that suit the company if he hopes to be promoted. If his mother can persuade him that a female duck is plumper than a drake, I'm sure Ford can convince him that management is right all the time.

"I enjoyed meeting Mr and Mrs Welsh, despite the problem with the amount of meat on the duck. Mr Welsh came across as very intelligent, almost too intelligent; he seems to be able to invent an excuse for anything.

"My work is satisfying. I have completed the first term, and my salary is helping with our expenses. The car was a large commitment, and the mortgage uses up a substantial portion of our monthly income, but the only other big expense is new furniture.

"When the spring weather arrives, John has agreed to teach me to drive. I worry that he can be impatient, and we'll see if that affects his instruction skills.

"Current national events seem sort of lousy. The prices in the shops are going up because of the devaluation, Ford of Europe is talking about moving the production of British vehicles overseas, the French President has vetoed Britain's application to belong to Europe (my father says that, whatever you do for the French, they are never thankful), factory unrest is worsening as workers oppose wage controls, and we still can't take more than £50 sterling when we travel overseas.

The only piece of good news is the government's decision to introduce tax relief on mortgage interest payments.

"John and I have talked about staying in Britain for next year's holidays and visiting Scotland so that I can see members of my father's family who couldn't attend the wedding. Also, it will save money. Meanwhile, it's back to teaching in a few days' time."

Mallard: *This fairly large duck (length 50-60 cm/20-24 in) is one of the most abundant breeds of wildfowl in the world. It can be seen on and near salt- and fresh-water ponds, streams, lakes, estuaries, marshes and other wetlands. The wild mallard is the ancestor of most domestic ducks. The male, or drake, is identified by its vivid glossy-green head, chestnut-brown chest and a white ring around its neck. The female, or hen, has a dull, mottled yellowish-brown plumage. Mallards usually pair up late in the year, and the female lays its eggs in early spring. At that time, the male leaves to join up with other males, so it is the female that incubates the eggs and takes care of the ducklings, and only the female makes the familiar quacking call. There are about 150,000 breeding pairs in Britain but an estimated 700,000 individual birds winter here.*

This is also the duck most often seen throughout North America, with about 10 million birds of breeding age. They are mostly migratory, breeding in northern United States and Canada, and wintering in the south and in Mexico.

20

Flocks Of Chaffinches

WE TRAVELLED HOME after Christmas, bringing Jean-Louise's father with us to visit our bungalow for the first time. He had stopped long-distance driving due to eyesight problems, dislike of the dark and the lack of a companion since his wife's death. We gave him the spare bedroom and I went out of my way to make his stay as comfortable as possible by providing lots of cups of tea, having a daily newspaper delivered, cleaning up the tobacco ash he left behind and respecting his preference to watch television and snooze rather than talk. He admired our home, although he thought it small and poorly furnished.

A few days after we had returned, the weather turned frosty, and the bungalow was chilly because of its reliance on a single small coal fire in the living room to provide heat. We occasionally returned from work to find Jean-Louise's father crouched in front of the fire, dressed in his overcoat, trying to stay cosy. He complained that the room was also damp because there was no carpet, and he took matters into his own hands one Saturday morning by accompanying us to Romford and buying a low-pile, wall-to-wall carpet in a rich burgundy colour that was installed in our front room the following Monday.

Travelling to school became particularly unpleasant for Jean-Louise as the icy weather arrived. She stood in freezing temperatures, waiting for buses that sometimes never arrived, and occasionally I had to drive her to school to avoid her missing classes. She continued to talk about learning to drive.

My birdwatching was confined to the local neighbourhood, and it was not helped by the wintry weather that caused birds to seek shelter, but because we fed our back-garden species with food scraps, I was able to spot blackbirds, blue tits, chaffinches, wrens, robins and house sparrows. We took Sunday walks in the neighbouring Weald Park, once the sun had melted the ground frost, and I was rewarded with sightings of a variety of ducks, geese and gulls.

One of the most abundant and colourful birds that I identified by its loud and varied song was the chaffinch. It is a bird whose eggs I took and traded as a child, and it is supposed to be the second most common breeding bird in Britain, after the wren. The more colourful males generally stay near their breeding grounds during winter, whereas the females separate and migrate further south. Indeed, in winter, British birds are joined by large flocks of chaffinches from Scandinavia, and a feature of these flocks is that they are often single sex. Consequently, the name "bachelor bird" is sometimes given to the chaffinch. This gender segregation also was affecting humans during the first half of 1968, as several groups of women got together to pursue collective community crusades, irrespective of the attitude of their menfolk.

The first of these was an initiative known as "I'm Backing Britain". The campaign was started in London by five female secretaries, intent on improving British productivity, and the initiative was announced on television during the year-end holidays. It was calculated that, if the British workforce worked an extra half-day a week, for no extra pay, the country's economic problems would be solved. It quickly gained momentum and thousands of hours were volunteered, the sponsors received strong government support, newspaper reports were very positive, badges and T-shirts were handed out, and the Post Office created a new franking mark to advertise the campaign.

It was during January 1968 when I gave Jean-Louise one of the lapel badges that I had received in Industrial Relations Staff.

"So, is it having any effect?" she wanted to know.

I told her I did not think so. "We're not circulating the badges, and it's up to individuals to support or ignore the campaign. Ford needs everyone to participate to make the initiative effective, but the unions have told their members not to work unpaid overtime. They think it's a gimmick."

"Well, at least the secretaries were listened to," Jean-Louise commented. "Maybe they would have been more successful if their supporters hadn't had the T-shirts manufactured in Portugal with 'Made in Portugal' labels; that was a huge embarrassment."

A few weeks later, the campaign was subsumed into a "Buy British" movement, and the five secretaries ceased to be interviewed and returned to their regular work.

* * *

Anton announced he was getting married and sent us a wedding invitation. At the same time, he mentioned the recent sinking at sea of three Hull trawlers during bad weather, with the loss of 58 lives. There had been an outcry among the men's wives, mothers and daughters, complaining about unsafe working conditions and demanding improvements from the boats' owners. Nothing had been done, so after collecting signatures and arranging public rallies, the women switched their attention to soliciting support from the government.

I asked Jean-Louise if she knew what was happening in

Hull. She told me that her fifth-form pupils had asked for an explanation during their studies of British agriculture and the fishing industry. They especially wanted to know why the girlfriends of fishermen in Hull were called "tarts", when in the south of Britain this was a nickname used only for prostitutes. The use of the word had been a feature in one of the newspapers.

"What did you tell them?" I asked.

"I explained that many of the women were employed on the docks, gutting fish, while their menfolk worked at sea, and some of the men never returned because their ships foundered and they drowned. I answered the 'tart' question by telling them it was local slang for 'pretty woman' and a reference to jam tarts and curd tarts (open pastry cases with a sweet filling) that are specialities of the Hull region of Yorkshire.

"I also described how the women typically wear headscarves at work, and consequently the protestors had become known as 'the headscarf army'. We discussed the importance of the fishing industry to Hull, and why not all trawler men approved of the women's actions. Even so, I told my class that the women never wavered in their struggle, and persuaded the government to create a 'Fishermen's Charter' that concedes all the improvements the women were demanding, including more safety equipment on ships, full crews and the availability of a medical vessel near to where they're fishing. Unfortunately, some of the men have become angry because a few trawlers can no longer put to sea or their sailing date is delayed because of the new requirements. Men have jeered the women on the streets, and even punched one in the face. Some of the women have received anonymous death threats, and their leader has been fired and blacklisted from future employment.

"We still live in a man's world," lamented Jean-Louise, "but I hope Barbara Castle will change that situation." (Ms Castle was in the process of being appointed by the Prime Minister as the Secretary of State for Employment.)

* * *

It turned out that everyone liked my report on Western Europe, and my director wanted it presented at the next meeting of the plant Industrial Relations managers. Its delivery was delegated to me. The study covered 11 European countries, excluding Ireland because it followed British practices, and I also excluded Greece, Portugal and Spain where trade unions were either banned or repressed. Unlike the voluntary approach in Britain, the countries studied typically controlled collective bargaining using statutory regulations.

Jean-Louise coached me on how to make the presentation, suggesting that it would be like delivering instructions in the classroom. I brought home the transparencies, and she asked me to talk her through the content. She told me the messages were clear, but I should be more relaxed, speak with greater confidence and appear more exuberant.

On the day of the talk, I entered the conference room and could feel many pairs of eyes looking at me, possibly trying to understand why someone as young-looking as me would present such an important subject. The director explained the purpose of the study and asked me to begin.

It was a very long 60 minutes. Regrettably, nothing new was decided, although I did receive compliments on my work. It was a weird feeling, standing in front of 30 managers who had far more experience than me, telling them what I thought they should do.

They accepted the idea of reducing the number of trade unions. Britain possessed around 600, whereas other countries had far fewer and many were organised by industry, whereas in Ford of Britain, four or more unions could represent the same small group of workers. However, those present concluded that such changes were a matter for the unions to address.

The idea of introducing incentives and legal restrictions to limit the number of shop-floor disputes was welcomed, but Ford could not introduce these changes on its own. Cooling-off periods before a strike, secret ballots and imposing financial consequences on union members who disregarded agreements were all very well and good, but they would be fiercely opposed by the unions. The decision of the managers was to do nothing until the results of the Donovan Report were published. The Ford of Europe Vice President warned those present that if Ford of Britain continued to do nothing, more manufacturing activities would move overseas because the current level of shop-floor disruption was unacceptable to senior corporate management.

* * *

Shortly after the presentation, I started teaching Jean-Louise to drive, and the inevitable happened. We would start calmly and respectful of each other, albeit a little nervous, and emotionally go downhill from there. By the end of the lesson, we were shrieking at one another, I would be told to shut up and accused of giving stupid instructions. Eventually, we would drive home in silence. However, the anger would have worn off and we would have settled our disagreement and apologised to each other by nightfall.

The worst experience was teaching Jean-Louise hand signals, especially for the right-hand turn. She insisted on signalling quarter-of-a-mile ahead of the change in direction. She approached each junction at full speed, suddenly braked and stamped on the clutch as if it were an insect, and then tried to force the gear lever through a gate that did not exist. She claimed that it was impossible to steer a car while she had one arm waving outside the window and the other fighting the gear lever; she said she did not have a third hand with which to steer. Fortunately, we eventually worked out the sequence and timing for these turns, and then reversing became her most dangerous manoeuvre. We would jump the curb, almost collide with someone's garden hedge and then sit there arguing over whose fault it was.

We gradually advanced from country-lane driving to motoring on busy main roads, and I stayed silent as Jean-Louise stalled in front of traffic lights turning green, suddenly stopped at pedestrian crossings without any pedestrians and practiced her parallel parking on streets that prohibited parking.

Eventually we decided that, if our marriage were to continue, it was necessary for Jean-Louise to receive lessons from a professional instructor. Thereafter she booked her driving test and passed at the first attempt. The L-plates were donated to one of her school pupils, and she began talking about buying a car.

* * *

Ford was prospering because the Mark 11 Cortina had become the best-selling car in Britain since its launch in October 1966, and sales of the Ford Escort were double the volume of its predecessor. These successes were despite the Zephyr/Zodiac Mark IV production remaining low and the demand for Corsairs starting to decline.

Ford's achievements were not shared by its competition. Because of financial difficulties, British Motor Holdings announced its merger with Leyland Motors, to create the British Leyland Motor Corporation, and the former Rootes organisation, now American-owned Chrysler UK, was trying to redesign its vehicle range to sell in the United States.

Nationally and globally, other news included the increase

in Indian and Pakistani refugees arriving in Britain from east Africa, protests in London against the Vietnam War and the assassination of Martin Luther King Jr on 4th April 1968.

For recreation, Jean-Louise and I watched films such as *The Graduate* and *Far From the Madding Crowd* at the local cinema, and we occasionally visited central London for sightseeing, but more often we shopped for fashionable clothes.

* * *

We attended Anton's wedding and enjoyed the drive to Wales. It was a beautiful event, with the couple looking very happy, and relatives and friends everywhere. We had little opportunity to talk to Anton but did hear that his research was progressing well and that he hoped to be appointed as a lecturer the following year. Thereafter he and I fell out of touch with each other since neither of us enjoyed writing letters and our priorities shifted to our respective careers and family lives. It was a shame that we lost contact.

David was the next social casualty. This event occurred when Chris and I happened to arrive at headquarters at the same time. During our walk through the tunnel, Chris made a surprise announcement: "David told me this morning that he's decided to leave Ford and join Chrysler UK in Coventry."

"Why would he do that?" I asked. "That company's in serious financial trouble."

Chris did not have an answer, but he volunteered to call David and arrange for the three of us to have drinks together that evening in the local pub called "The Horse and Groom".

When I arrived a little after 6pm, Chris and David were already drinking. It was a quiet pub, ordinary-looking on the outside, and sparsely furnished inside, but adequate for our needs. Chris and David were at a corner table, and I joined them after buying a beer at the bar.

"So, what's going on? Why are you leaving Ford of Britain for Rootes?" I asked David, and my tone must have indicated my disapproval of the move.

"Why don't you congratulate me?" said David, scoffing at my indignation. "I'm receiving a huge pay raise, the firm will reimburse my relocation costs and I'll have Europe-wide responsibilities, including Simca in France."

"But aren't you worried?" Chris interrupted. "Rootes almost went bankrupt. Aren't you concerned that might still happen?"

"No, I'm not," countered David. "Chrysler plans to become a major manufacturer in Europe and, like Ford, it has the financial muscle and technical knowledge to succeed. I think I'll be fine."

It sounded as if David knew what he was doing, although both Chris and I had our doubts. Anyway, David went ahead with his change of employer, and I never heard from him again. Chrysler Europe continued to struggle into the 1970s, and in 1979 the parent company sold the entire operation to Peugeot Citroen.

* * *

Summer was just around the corner, and Jean-Louise and I were preparing for our holiday in Scotland. Home life was perfect, and I had tamed my job. The Ford two-year wage agreement was in place until March 1969, and management and the unions were jointly resolving grading grievances using a formally agreed procedure. Where practical, jobs were redesigned so that higher graded positions could be spun off to provide career progression for the more skilled workers in that occupation. The system also received external support when the carpenters and joiners took their grievance to an outside Industrial Tribunal that confirmed the correctness of grade C.

It was hoped that this new era of calm and cooperation would continue. Days lost to work stoppages across the company had fallen by 50 percent. What we did not know, as May 1968 came to an end, was that this period of relative peace would end with extreme militancy from an unexpected source, and the integrity of the job evaluation system itself would be severely challenged. The Dagenham sewing machinists were tired of waiting for an upgrade to grade C and being treated by the company as unequal women alongside their male colleagues.

(Jean-Louise, May 1968) "Not much to say at the moment, except that I'm pleased I passed my driving test. John was probably more nervous than I, sitting in the car, and it was a wise decision to take my last few lessons with the British School of Motoring. Now all I need is a vehicle to drive.

"John increasingly enjoys his job as he learns more. Because of his responsibilities, he's in contact with the personnel officers in all Ford of Britain plants, and his Western Europe study exposed him to overseas industrial relations contacts. He hopes this will help his advancement. My fifth-form pupils met him, and several said they loved his accent. He came to school to talk to them about careers in return for my help with his presentation, and to support the Industrial Society that is assisting school leavers to decide what to do with their future.

"I continue to enjoy my work, and I'm making more friends. Recently I've become friendly with the physics teacher, and she's invited me to her home.

"My father's first visit was a success, although he found our bungalow very cold. We've just bought an electric fire for him to use in his bedroom the next time he stays. He and John seem

to be getting on well together. He likes the house we've bought, and his gift of the carpet was totally unexpected. Home life has fallen into a pleasurable routine, we are careful with our money and both of us are committed to being successful in our careers."

Chaffinch: This is one of the most common and widespread species in Britain, with approximatcly six million breeding pairs. The British birds are mostly sedentary, but during autumn are joined by large numbers of chaffinches from Scandinavia that can double the population. It is 15 cm/ 6 inches in length, and the male is brightly coloured with a pinkish-orange chest and face, black and white wings, brown back, a green rump and bluish-grey on its neck and head; these colours modify during winter. The female is a dull sandy-brown, with a grey-brown neck and underparts of pale grey. The bird is well known for its short and simple "pink, pink" song and it is commonly seen in woodlands, hedgerows, fields, parks and gardens. The two sexes separating outside the breeding season may have something to do with competition for food.

In the past the chaffinch was introduced to New Zealand where it is now the most numerous species. It is only seen as a vagrant in North America.

21

The Rookery

MY DEPARTMENT'S MOOD of calm and confidence began to change dramatically on 22nd May 1968, when the Dagenham River Plant personnel officer telephoned to tell me that nearly 200 female sewing machinists had begun an overtime ban, and were threatening to go on strike for one shift in a week's time. They said they were sick and tired of waiting for management to reclassify them as skilled workers in grade C, instead of keeping them at the same level as line production employees in grade B. The personnel officer knew that I needed to publish an Incident Report, and that it was without precedent for a group of women workers to take on this level of industrial action.

There was an immediate flurry of management activity. The job analysis people committed to processing the grievance quickly, as long as the sewing machinists withdrew their overtime ban. This was done, but there was no immediate resolution of the women's claim, so the work stoppage went ahead, prompting angry reactions from my superiors. The trim workers, as they were called, refused to observe the jointly approved grading resolution procedure and took independent measures, knowing that these would quickly affect vehicle production.

I was asked to coordinate the preparation of a disciplinary letter to warn each machinist that she could be fired if she walked off the job again. The letter caused fury, and every sewing machinist handed her copy back to the supervisor.

On Friday 7th June, the conflict escalated. The Incident Report that I prepared on that day informed management that the sewing machinists had met in the works' car park and voted to begin an indefinite, all-out strike starting the following Monday. They would not return to work until their job classification was changed from grade B to grade C. The women were convinced that the original job profile had been "manipulated" as a means of devaluing their work, they were being mistreated because they were women, and now was time to fight for what they believed was justified.

The women worked dayshifts, with three men working nights to handle urgent sewing requirements for the car assembly nightshift. Their responsibilities involved sewing the backs and cushions of car seats, preparing door and fascia pads and stitching headliners (the fabric covering the inside ceiling of vehicles) for installation into Dagenham-assembled Cortina and Zephyr/Zodiac models. During development of the job evaluation system, two job profiles had been prepared: An intermediate post for rough-stitching the cut-out pattern, and a finisher post for completing the product for installation. Management had combined the two descriptions into a single job before the evaluation was conducted because the machinists were required to move between the two posts. Local union representatives did not support this decision, and the women believed that the action had been taken solely to rob them of their rightful grade classification because they were women.

The Dagenham trim shop was located in a remote and dilapidated asbestos shack known as the River Plant. It boasted a leaky roof, ill-fitting windows and an unpleasant work area that was hot and humid during summer and cold and draughty in winter. Job applicants had to pass a skill assessment during their recruitment, and each operator was given an output quota that was frequently inspected for quantity and quality. A similar number of sewing machinists worked in Halewood, supporting the Escort and Corsair production, but they did not participate in the dispute during its early days.

Resolving the grievance was made difficult because four different unions represented some of the women, and they held no common point of view. My River Plant colleague explained: "Most machinists belong to the National Union of Vehicle Builders, which has told them to stay at work until the grading grievance negotiations are concluded, but the women are tired of waiting. A few trim workers belong to the engineers' union, and that union hasn't decided what to do. Also, there are two other unions, the transport workers and the general and municipal workers, who have told their members to stay at work and process the grievance through the jointly-approved grading resolution procedure."

Jean-Louise asked me about the threatened strike during the weekend. She was alarmed that the women had been forced to resort to industrial action and sacrifice their wages in order to obtain something that she believed was justified.

"It's good for them," she said on hearing of the planned fight, "But they shouldn't have to sacrifice their pay; sewing is skilled work—I know, I do it—and they should be paid the same as men with equivalent skills."

I tried to explain that it was not that simple. "There's a grievance procedure that the women should follow, and the company won't negotiate while they're on strike. Also, if they want equal pay it's up to their unions to request it. So far, they haven't done so, and no new wage demands can be submitted until the current wage agreement expires next March. At that time, both sides will have to comply with the government's wage policies, whatever they might be."

Jean-Louise chose not to argue, but it was clear from her attitude that her sympathies lay with the women; by Sunday evening the strike had become national news.

* * *

Monday morning began with confusion. Women congregated outside the River Plant, waving banners reading "We Want Recognition for our Skills", "Equal Rights in Pay and Grading" and "Skilled Money for Skilled Work". Everyone obeyed the picket line, since over the weekend the National Union of Vehicle Builders had announced its formal support for the strike, and hostilities had worsened after allegations were published that the company was applying sex discrimination to persecute its female workers.

The women's strength lay in their solidarity and their willingness to act in spite of union recommendations to the contrary. They came together like rooks in a rookery to look after each other and to resist any outside threat that they believed could be harmful. Folklore says that, when a rookery is abandoned, bad things happen to the people who own the land. Bad things began to happen in Ford of Britain as a result of the stoppage, but the women had no intention of giving up on their convictions. They may not have been dressed in all-black like rooks, but their behaviour reminded me of the rookery I had visited as a young child. The birds had made known their displeasure at my intrusion by flying above the tree-tops and using their raucous voices to warn each other of my presence.

Shortly after the National Union of Vehicle Builders declared the strike official, the engineers' union did the same but, oddly, supported only the equal pay claim and not the higher grade demand. The other two unions continued their opposition and wanted the sewing machinists to follow official procedures. Management made the decision to continue vehicle production for as long as possible, and they started to store cars without seats on the Dagenham estate in the hope that the unions would persuade the women to quickly return to work.

My role was to inform management of developments by preparing Incident Reports, and to collect data in preparation for possible negotiations with the trade unions. The latter included comparing the wages of Ford's sewing machinists with those of similar workers in other companies, as well as collecting competitive information on gender pay differentials. I also worked with my River Plant colleague to prepare a personnel profile on each sewing machinist in case this information was needed. My knowledge and perceptions of what subsequently happened is as follows.

Jean-Louise was upset by what she saw on television. Public support for the women, at least initially, was lukewarm; Ford of Britain condemned the strike as irresponsible, and the reaction among the machinists' male colleagues was that they should go back to work; the men's attitude was that the women were only working for "pin money" (money for non-essentials).

A surprise development for me was that I was asked to attend an off-site meeting with the unions that was arranged to try and end the strike. My director wanted someone available to handle the back-up data in case it was needed during discussions. The unions requested the joint meeting to take place as soon as possible, which was arranged for Monday one week after the strike began. I was also told to attend a management meeting arranged for the prior Sunday evening, when the company would finalise its negotiations strategy. This took place in a rather posh Lancaster Gate hotel, where I stayed overnight.

The action plan approved on Sunday evening was to condemn the two unions that had supported the stoppage, refuse to discuss the grading issue any further until the women returned to work, and to be ready to close down the Dagenham assembly and body plants if the unions did not secure an immediate return to work. From my perspective, Ford of Britain's new collaborative industrial relations strategy was in disarray.

Around 11am on Monday morning, I travelled with my colleagues to a hotel in the London Bloomsbury district where the discussions with the unions were to take place. We were greeted outside by a group of boisterous women, all waving placards and shouting rude slogans that accused management of sexism and claiming that the company was cheating them out of their rightful wages. For some reason, I received special attention. One of the female pickets wanted to take me home and adopt me, and another asked if my mother knew what I was up to. I still looked much younger than my age, and while the women might have been angry over their grade, they still had not lost their sense of humour. Eventually we went into the hotel and were escorted by Ford of Britain's security guards to the main conference room.

This was my first opportunity to observe senior-level negotiations. I sat behind the management team as both sides spoke critically of each other. My director condemned the stoppage and pointed out that it was in breach of the joint agreement for handling grading grievances. He was particularly irate during mid-afternoon when a note was passed to him notifying him that the Halewood sewing machinists had just voted to join the strike. He announced petulantly that, if the unions did not act quickly, thousands of workers would be laid off.

In response, the unions accused management of creating the conflict by the way in which it administered its job evaluation system. The weightings used to evaluate the characteristics of the sewing machinists' job were not disclosed, and this undermined any trust in the process. The union representatives were reminded that they had earlier agreed to this condition as a means of protecting the objectivity of the new evaluation process. Eventually, the unions volunteered to instruct the women to return to work provided the company created a joint internal committee to investigate the sewing machinists' claim for their post to be upgraded to grade C. After further discussions involving the composition, purpose and authority of the committee, the proposal was accepted.

Intense emotions surfaced during the meeting. At one point, the manager responsible for job evaluation accused a sewing machinist of acting callously towards the menfolk who were about to be laid off. She in turn accused the manager of introducing a job evaluation system that intentionally discriminated against women. He countered that she did not understand job evaluation and was unqualified to comment on the subject. She exploded with anger, leapt from her seat and, screaming profanities, headed straight towards her opponent. Fortunately, as she attempted to climb across the table, several colleagues restrained her, and she was removed from the room and never returned.

By late afternoon, a Works Notice had been jointly agreed announcing the end of the strike and the creation of the joint committee. Everyone appeared to be happy except for the sewing machinists present, who surrounded their Vehicle Builders national official to complain about the outcome of the meeting. Also, in the euphoria of the moment, the absence of the national official representing the engineers union was not noticed.

I arrived home to find Jean-Louise marking examination papers in bed. This was the first time she had needed to do this, and she was finding it very tedious. She had seen me on television, walking behind the director when he had announced the settlement to the media. She was surprised by the outcome; why would the women even consider returning to work without any concessions?

Mr Welsh asked me to be in the office early the following morning, in order to prepare an Incident Report confirming that the strike was over. When I arrived, however, he intercepted me, looked serious and communicated some unexpected news.

"The women haven't returned to work. They've disobeyed the unions' instructions, and the Halewood sewing machinists are also on strike. We're going ahead with the Dagenham layoffs, and Halewood hopes to use its supervisors to sew seat covers. Call the River Plant for details and publish an Incident Report as quickly as possible."

I telephoned my colleague who told me that only a handful of women had turned up that morning, and all of them had been persuaded to stay on strike.

"They're as mad as hell that the national unions have tried to force them back to work without any concessions," he said. "They've no intention of ending the strike and say they won't meet for another two weeks."

No further meaningful efforts to resolve the stoppage took place until the end of the third week. By then, thousands of workers in both Dagenham and Halewood had been laid off, and the use of supervisors as sewing machinists in Halewood had failed because of opposition from the workforce. Barbara

Castle, the government's newly appointed Secretary of State for Employment, became involved, but even her request for the women to return to work was ignored. She appointed a Court of Inquiry, which immediately ran in to difficulties when the chairman insisted that the hearings should be in private, whereas Ford management wanted the hearings made public. Simultaneously, the Court failed to persuade the women to go back to work while it fulfilled its duties.

Eventually, the Secretary of State arranged to hold separate meetings with the sewing machinists, their unions and, last of all, with Ford of Britain management to try to find a compromise and persuade the machinists to return to work. The Ford delegation was told that the women felt cheated out of their grade and needed some concessions before they would end the stoppage. Reference was made to another car manufacturer that used a differential of 93 percent for women's wages, and it was suggested that maybe Ford of Britain could do something similar. A potential settlement emerged that, as long as the women returned to work, the company and unions would renegotiate—and the government would approve—the women's pay differential. In addition, the Secretary of State said she would have the Court of Inquiry investigate the claim for grade C in public, and she would introduce an Equal Pay Bill into Parliament as soon as she could.

It was Saturday evening when our home telephone rang. Jean-Louise answered it and then passed the receiver to me. It was Mr Welsh.

"We need you in the office tomorrow morning around 10.30. Is that possible? The Dagenham sewing machinists' shop stewards are holding a mass meeting in the morning, and they'll recommend a return to work. If they're successful, we'll need to notify senior managers immediately."

"I'll be there," I replied.

The call came in at about 11.15 on Sunday morning that the women had voted unanimously to return to work the following morning, but with a condition: The unions and management had to negotiate an improvement in the wage differential. I was directed to prepare costings for each percentage point, assuming the differential was increased from 87 percent to up to 95 percent. Negotiations took place on Monday, and an agreement was reached that altered the differential from 85 to 92 percent. The layoffs ended and car assembly resumed.

The Court of Inquiry recommended that Ford of Britain should appoint a new internal review committee to evaluate the position, but the outcome of this committee's review was to keep the job at grade B. The committee's three management members supported the lower grade, the three union officials endorsed grade C and the external chair voted with management. Although upset, the machinists stayed at work.

The Equal Pay Act was eventually passed by the British parliament during May 1970, but it did not take effect for five years, until 29th December 1975, to give employers time to prepare for the change. About the same time as this Act became effective, discrimination against women in employment was made illegal under the Sex Discrimination Act, 1975.

* * *

Back in the office, it was now time to turn my attention to other tasks; in particular, the report issued by the Royal Commission on Trade Unions and Employers' Associations (the Donovan Report). This had been published during the machinists' strike, but I had no time back then to review its findings in detail. I also began to think about my next job that I hoped would give me front-line negotiations experience. Mr Welsh had taught me a great deal, but now I needed practical experience in industrial relations, which would help my second year of studies with the Institute of Personnel Management. There was much to be decided ahead of me.

(Jean-Louise, July 1968) "It was extraordinary that John was so personally involved in the sewing machinists' conflict. I was proud of him, although I don't like how Ford treats its female employees. Even though he was in a support role, it shows how far his career has advanced in under 18 months. He's learned a lot.

"We talked about many issues that were never reported in the newspapers. For example, the women were appalled that no female sat on the union-management grading grievance committee. How could a group of men understand the skills needed for a sewing machinist? The company was concerned that the sewing machinists' job was one of 50 benchmark positions used to evaluate other jobs, and if its grade changed, there could be repercussions elsewhere. Early on, during the preparation for negotiations, there had been disagreement among the management team; some members wanted to make an example of the women and others proposed that the company quickly concede grade C so that everyone could get back to work. Management in Dearborn appeared concerned that any voluntary concession for equal pay would create a precedent in other countries still using gender discrimination, so it would be better to wait until legislation mandated equal wages.

"My own career is progressing well, and John puts up with me working most weekday evenings. I've stopped preparing lesson plans, but marking exam papers has taken over. Once that's finished, I hope John and I can spend more time together. Maybe I'll accompany him on one of his bird-spotting adventures.

"I'm looking forward to our holiday in Scotland, and especially helping with the driving. There were times during the driving instructions when I thought we would fall out forever, but we always found a way of making up and apologising. I was pleased, and I think John was relieved when I passed my driving test the first time."

Rooks and Rookeries: The rook is a relatively large-sized (45 cm/18 in) member of the corvid (crow) family, which is resident in Britain and in north and central Europe. It has black plumage with some blue and purple gloss on its wings. It is distinguished by a patch of bare, greyish-white skin on its face and around its large, whitish-grey pointed bill. The species is highly sociable and intelligent. There are over one million breeding pairs in Britain, and they live in large communities that do just about everything together: forage, roost and nest. Rookeries provide safety from predators and protection from unwelcome guests, allowing the birds to work together in support of each other.

Rooks are seen as only very rare vagrants in North America.

22

The Avocet And The Osprey

Jean-Louise's teaching performance was rated excellent in every category for her first year in school and she was told that her salary would be raised at the beginning of September 1968. I congratulated her, despite feeling anxious that she was making stronger headway in her career than I was in mine, but I reassured myself with the knowledge that my salary had risen faster than hers. Jean-Louise's mentor contributed enormously to her success and had given guidance to Jean-Louise throughout the year, and helped her with pupil discipline and lesson plans. We decided to invite her to dinner to say thank you. The menu was roast beef and Yorkshire pudding in place of duck with orange sauce. Her friend appreciated the invitation and told us how she spent most of her time on her own at home because her husband travelled extensively overseas on business. Jean-Louise was happy that my work had so far taken me no further than London.

There was uncertainty over which classes Jean-Louise would teach in her second year. The government had decided that 15-year-olds would stay on at school for a further year, but implementation of this decision was being delayed because of the country's economic situation. Retaining the school-leaving at age 15 avoided extra expense on education, and it was not until September 1972 when the school leaving age was raised to 16.

At home, I was managing our finances successfully, thanks to our salary increases exceeding the annual rise in the cost of living, which was now close to 5 percent and which had been pushed up by the November 1967 sterling devaluation. What little money we could afford to save was set aside to buy Jean-Louise a car, to avoid us having to burden ourselves with a loan.

* * *

In the meantime, the Ford's Industrial Relations Staff became calm once more. While my colleagues were busy preparing the company's testimony for the sewing machinists' Court of Inquiry, Forward Planning escaped being given any new assignments. I circulated a summary of the government's Prices and Incomes Act, 1968 which allowed for a resumption of pay awards of up to 3.5 percent annually, with additional amounts for productivity improvements, and I continued to report on new disputes involving the job evaluation system. However, the primary issue in Ford's factories were the recurrent layoffs caused by supplier strikes that disrupted the delivery of critical parts. Jean-Louise could not understand why Ford did not carry a larger inventory to avoid having to send workers home without pay.

The Donovan Report turned out to be a huge disappointment. It concluded that major reforms in British industrial relations were unnecessary, and that everything would return to normal if there were stronger links between shop-floor bargaining and the more formal national-level negotiations. It further claimed that legal controls were unnecessary and contrary to British custom and practice.

Criticisms came from all sides. The national unions opposed the idea of the government monitoring companywide agreements, shop stewards rejected relinquishing authority to their national officials, and the Confederation of British Industry was critical that no importance was attached to industry-wide bargaining. My Ford colleagues concluded that nothing existed in the proposals that would reduce the likelihood of future confrontations with the unions.

Certain government ministers remained fearful that industrial conflict would keep going, and there was speculation that the Prime Minister and his Secretary of State for Employment were considering alternative solutions to curb what they called "excessive union power". Jean-Louise's opinion was that, if industry adopted the same attitude towards the unions that existed in teaching, there would be no need for change.

No-one appeared particularly concerned about Ford of Europe's "Europeanisation" programme. Neither Ford of Britain management nor the unions appeared to be particularly troubled by what was taking place. It had been decided that the new Capri model would be assembled in Germany and Belgium, as well as in Halewood, making it the third British vehicle to be built overseas (the other two being the Transit and Escort).

* * *

A few days before my summer holiday, Mr Welsh called me into his office.

"I don't want to lose you," he said with some disappointment, "but the Dagenham assembly plant wants to consider you for an open position as a personnel officer. Are you interested?"

I was very interested. I told Mr Welsh that a factory opportunity would provide me with valuable practical experience. He agreed.

"Then meet with the manger as soon as possible," he said.

Several days later I travelled to Dagenham, and after a brief meeting with the Industrial Relations manager, the job was offered to me. Jean-Louise knew what I was doing and had not objected, even though the job involved a much longer commute than the one to Brentwood headquarters. It was pleasing that my first job in Ford had taken six months to find, whereas this one was settled in a week. The start date was set for 3rd September 1968, the day after the Summer Bank Holiday, and immediately following our return from the holiday in Scotland. There was no change in my grade, but I would receive a small merit adjustment. Jean-Louise congratulated me and hoped my working hours would not lengthen.

* * *

Once her summer term at school was over, she asked if we could spend a weekend in Suffolk. She knew I was not busy and her friend the physics teacher had recommended that we stay at a hotel in Suffolk that she had visited and which was well-known for its dining excellence. Jean-Louise proposed we drive there on Saturday morning, spend the afternoon birdwatching at the Minsmere Nature Reserve, have dinner and stay overnight at the hotel, and then tour the home of the painter, John Constable (in an area known as "Constable Country") during the return journey. Constable had been her mother's favourite painter.

Arriving at the Minsmere Reserve, I was excited by the prospect of seeing a rare coastal wader, the avocet, that had returned to Britain in 1947 after 100 years of absence. Its disappearance was thought to have been caused by loss of habitat, but during

World War 11, the area was flooded to keep out the Germans, and shortly afterwards the birds started to reappear to breed. By now, half-a-dozen pairs nested around the “scrape”, an area of shallow water and exposed mud flats.

Unfortunately, the bird hides were unavailable on this particular day, and I left the reserve without seeing the object of our visit. However, I did observe the black-headed gulls that are infamous for stealing avocet eggs and attacking avocet chicks, and I heard the fog-horn-like toots of a bittern in the reed beds and spotted a bearded tit and black-tailed godwits.

Jean-Louise was much more engaged the following day when we toured the riverside and rolling hills of the Stour Valley. Included in the tour was Flatford Mill, once owned by John Constable’s father, and East Bergholt, the village in which John Constable was born. She explained to me how Romanticism (the personal expression of the natural world) was a popular art form when Constable was alive, and that he was one of its most famous exponents. I had not appreciated art in the past, and Jean-Louise promised to take me to The National Gallery in London to introduce me to some of Constable’s original works.

* * *

We left Pilgrims Hatch for Manchester on the date of our first wedding anniversary, and we talked and listened to the radio as we travelled northwards. High on the pop music charts were Simon and Garfunkel with *Mrs Robinson*, and the surprisingly successful *I Pretend* by Des O’Connor. Lots of Beatles music was also playing because of the groups recently released animated fantasy film, *Yellow Submarine.*

The news coverage included the technicians’ strike at London Weekend Television, caused by a franchise change, and the last steam-engine in service that was on its final journey between Liverpool and Carlisle. Internationally, there was discussion of Bobby Kennedy's assassination a few weeks earlier, the prosecution of Martin Luther King's alleged murderer who had been arrested at Heathrow airport, and the fact that the Republican National Convention in Miami Beach had nominated Richard Nixon for President. There were also riots and protests occurring in Chicago as the Democratic Party prepared for its National Convention.

Jean-Louise's father was pleased to see us, and, at Jean-Louise's suggestion, took us shopping to a boutique-style home-furnishing shop in Stockport, but unfortunately we could not afford to buy anything. Afterwards, he treated us to dinner at his favourite restaurant, the *Berni Inn*.

Two days later, we resumed our journey north to Scotland. For me, it was a chance to visit parts of the country I had not seen before; for Jean-Louise it was an opportunity to reconnect with her Scottish relatives. She was proud of her heritage and excited to show me off to her uncles, aunts and cousins. During the journey, she explained her Scottish lineage and how she grew up with her mother's relatives in Manchester, rarely meeting her father's side of the family.

We drove along the newly opened M6 motorway and then the narrow A74 trunk road from Carlisle to Glasgow, and next we travelled north along the western edge of Loch Lomond towards Oban. Large parts of Glasgow were in the process of being rebuilt after a deadly storm had wrought havoc during January 1968, when the city was struck by torrential rain and wind gusts of up to 135 miles per hour (217km/h), causing 300 houses to be destroyed, 70,000 homes damaged and 21 people killed.

After a night in Oban, we travelled 160 miles (255 km) to the small village of Kinlochewe in the north-west Highlands, with a population of around 50. Jean-Louise's relatives did not live in this part of Scotland, so we were on our own. It was a wonderful opportunity to share interests and forget about work, combine our hobbies and have fun together. Jean-Louise enjoyed hiking and viewing the scenery while I followed behind, either birdwatching, such as stalking a ptarmigan (a very shy member of the grouse family), or gazing into the sky in the hope of spotting a golden eagle. At other times, I would take out my geology hammer and examine the rocky outcrops along the way, hammering away on the oldest sedimentary strata in Britain, about one thousand million years old, consisting of pebbly sandstone, shale and thin bands of limestone.

We stayed three nights in a charming croft run by a husband and wife. The croft was a stone-built, white-washed, slate-roofed cottage with one bedroom downstairs and four more upstairs. It was spotlessly clean, simply furnished and faced the magnificent Torridon Mountains. Our bedroom was upstairs and accessible only through another guest room, so we became good friends with the occupants of that space. Our hostess spoke some English, but her husband limited himself to Scottish Gaelic. Breakfast consisted of salty porridge followed by eggs, bacon and black pudding (blood sausage). Nothing was familiar to Jean-Louise and she felt foreign because of the way she spoke, whereas for me it was just another holiday.

We ended our stay on a Sunday morning and, before departing, I offered payment for our room to the lady of the house. She declined to accept it, but she gave me a tin can and told me to place the money in the container and leave it behind a large rock just outside the farm gate.

"You mustn't leave it on our property," she stressed. "As a member of the Free Church of Scotland, I'm not allowed to accept money on the Lord's Day."

I did as asked, and I later learned from Jean-Louise that on Sundays the Free Church of Scotland forbids its members to drive, to work or to involve themselves in business transactions. I was relieved when Jean-Louise told me her Scottish relatives were members of the more moderate Church of Scotland.

We set off to drive to Perth on the Scottish east coast, 160 miles (255 km) away, where I was expected to meet for the first time with Jean-Louise's Scottish relatives who had not attended the wedding, but she had another surprise for me before we arrived.

"Why don't we break our journey at Loch Garten," she suggested. "You might be able to see the ospreys."

The location was a freshwater lake surrounded by tall pine trees and was the only site in Britain where nesting ospreys could be seen. This fish-eating bird of prey had been extinct as a breeding species in Britain since the early 1900s because of egg collecting and the practice of taxidermy (preserving the skin and feathers). Only the occasional bird was seen migrating along the east coast between Scandinavia and West Africa before 1954, when the osprey first returned to Britain, and that year, a pair had nested near Loch Garten. On this particular afternoon I enjoyed watching the male circling and calling to its mate, and then hovering over its prey before swooping and skimming low across the water and disappearing into the loch to secure its catch. I was adding a new species of bird to my Life List, and at the same time, I was about to add Jean-Louise's Scottish family to my friendship list.

During the final part of the journey, Jean-Louise counselled me on several Scottish customs that I might encounter when I met her relatives. She explained that "grey pies" (thin-crusted pastry containing minced lamb) may be served for lunch and

I should not ask questions, that the Scottish brogue of her relatives might sometimes be difficult to understand and I should not ask them to repeat themselves (that would be rude), and if I heard negative comments about England, that was simply Scottish humour and I should ignore it.

We stayed two nights with her uncle and family, who showed us the city, introduced us to single-malt whisky and took us out one evening to a ceilidh, a Scottish gathering with folk music and dancing. Then it was onwards 40 miles (65 km) south-west, to visit a cousin living near Stirling, close to where Jean-Louise's parents had originally lived.

We several times visited Stirling, a clean and picturesque town clustered around a large castle seated high on a hill, overlooking the Scottish lowlands to the south and the highlands to the north. It was a city immersed in history; nearby was the site of Stirling Bridge where in 1297 William ("Braveheart") Wallace won a battle against the English, only to lose to them the following year at the Battle of Falkirk. Not far away was Bannockburn, where Robert the Bruce had finally conquered the English in 1314.

Near the end of our stay, Jean-Louise was surprised when her cousin sat us down to share some memories of Jean-Louise's parents.

"Do you know why your father is so happy that you decided to teach?" she began.

Jean-Louise did not and asked why.

"Well, he left school at 14 and could only find temporary work in the local boat yards and, after a period of unemployment, he took up a four-year apprenticeship, beginning 1924, with the British Electric Plant company (later Harland Engineering) in Alloa, as a lathe metal turner. However, he didn't like the work and after a short period of time as a policeman in Kilmarnock, he moved down to London. First, he attempted to join the

Royal Air Force but was rejected for medical reasons, and then, by early 1931, was enlisted in the Scots Guards for 3 years and thereafter transferred into its Reserves. He became unemployed and homeless on the streets of London, causing him to return to Scotland during 1934 where his father found him a job as a chauffeur."

"But he's always been an engineer," said a perplexed Jean-Louise. "When did he stop chauffeuring and become an engineer?"

"He learned the hard way," her cousin replied. "He had to give up chauffeuring at the start of the war when he was recalled by the Scots Guards, and in 1940, he was sent to fight the Germans in Norway. When he returned, he resumed his career in engineering which exempted him from further fighting, and a short time later he married your mother. I think that's why he's pleased you've chosen a safe and secure career as a teacher."

"But how did my parents meet? My mother's family were from Manchester and I think were well off. His family apparently were not. How did two people from very different backgrounds meet each other?"

The story became even more fascinating as Jean-Louise's cousin continued: "During the late 1930s, your father worked as the chauffeur for a very rich couple who lived near here and who owned a coal depot, railway and factories. The wife was a close, lifelong friend of your maternal grandmother whom she'd met in cookery school. Because your father's employer had no children, the wife became very fond of your mother and frequently asked her to visit Scotland. She and your mother were often seen driving around town, with your father as the chauffeur. At some point, the woman suggested that your father marry your mother. No-one knows why and when; maybe the idea came from your mother's parents because your mother was in her mid30s and your father had returned to a safe occupation. Anyway, he agreed and married your mother in Manchester during spring 1942, and continued his engineering career in Scotland."

"But why was he willing to move to Manchester when I was three?"

"In late 1947, your mother was asked by your grandfather to look after him because his wife had died and, in return, he promised to buy your father a house and find him a job. Your father's parents had passed away recently and therefore they moved to Manchester in early 1948."

Jean-Louise was surprised to hear why she had ended up in Manchester at the age of three with a Scottish accent. More importantly, she understood why her father had been so concerned about her welfare. Both she and I had experienced unusual starts in life but had experienced very different upbringings. She was a composite of her mother and father's backgrounds, whereas I had grown up independent and remote from anyone.

The following morning was our final day on holiday. We visited a local craft show where Jean-Louise renewed her interest in art and purchased a water-colour of a nearby loch painted by Birgitte Brondun-Nielsen, a Danish painter who had moved to Scotland after World War II. We really could not afford it, but we bought it anyway. It was a way of taking home a memory of our first trip to Scotland.

It had been a glorious holiday. We had delighted in each other's company, Jean-Louise had learned a lot about her Scottish lineage, and I had added another bird species to my Life List. We arrived home in Essex on Bank Holiday Monday, 2nd September, and the following day I would begin my new job in Dagenham. Jean-Louise would start her second year of teaching later that same week. I had little sense of what to expect in Dagenham, whereas Jean-Louise anticipated that her second year of teaching would be similar to the first.

(Jean-Louise, September 1968) "The school summer holidays were a welcome change. I spent time socialising with my physics teacher friend, made sure that my father was in good health and taking care of himself, and I did some decorating of the bungalow.

"The trips to Suffolk and Scotland were fun, and I enjoyed giving John a chance to catch up on his birdwatching. I had not realised that he had no appreciation of art until we visited Constable Country. The story from my cousin in Scotland explains why I owe so much to my mother; she supported my cultural development (in art and literature, as well as an awareness of women's rights), whereas my politics and bluntness come from my father.

"Both of us seemed to bond with my relatives in Scotland. I knew they existed, but I'd never spent time with them while growing up. They appeared to like John and viewed him as a Yorkshire farm boy rather than a Sassenach from the south of England.

"The history of my parents was a surprise. I was aware that my father served in Norway during the war, but I'd no idea of what he did, nor any knowledge of how my parents met. Both John and I have unusual stories buried deep in our past. Fancy the rich girl marrying the chauffeur!

"Now I'm back at school, I've met the newly-arrived teachers and I'm adjusting to my new classes. There's a different head of the geography department and he seems intolerant towards women. My mentor was passed over for the position because the head of the school expects her to stop work soon because of the success of her husband.

"John's begun his new job and is starting to be absent for very long hours. Hopefully this is just while he gets to know the basics of his new position. The job fits well into his career plan, but I don't think he realised that he might have to work long hours, and the length of his commute doesn't help. Because he's not home until late, I've decided to enrol in an evening Cordon Bleu cooking course and hope he enjoys the new meals I prepare for him. He used to take me to work in bad weather, but now I'm on my own so much, I need a car as soon as we can afford one.

Avocet: This is a strikingly elegant shoreline wader, about 45 cm /18 in. in length, that has a stilt-like walk. It can be seen along the east coast of England in summer and the south-west in winter. The name comes from the black colouration on the birds' heads, which resembles a cap worn by advocates (a term used for lawyers in certain countries). The rest of the plumage is white, with a black band on the wing, black wing tips, and a black-striped pattern on the back. Their other distinctive features are their long, slender, upturned beaks, used to feed on crustaceans, worms and aquatic insects, and their long blue legs. In modern-day Britain, there are about 2,000 pairs nesting, but there can be as many as 75,000 visitors during winter.

The American avocet has a similar beak, but it is distinguished from the European species by an orange-cinnamon coloured head and neck.

Osprey (Fish- hawk): These birds are found on every continent except Antarctica. Their length is around 55cm/22 in, and today there are about 250 breeding pairs in Britain, mainly in Scotland and the north and east of England, and there are two pairs in Wales. It is a spectacular, fish-eating bird of prey with a hooked, powerful beak, and it can be seen hurtling towards its prey and plunge-diving into water at speeds of up to 50 km/h (30 mph). It has a brown back and wings, a white head, a broad brown line through the eye and a black beak. When in flight and seen from below, it displays white or slightly mottled underparts. It is a migrant in Britain, arriving from Africa during late March and April.

In North America, it is mainly found in the north and west, alongside rivers, lakes and coastlines where there are abundant sources of fish.

23

The Cockney Sparrer

IT WAS A bright and clear day for my first morning's commute to the Dagenham assembly plant, but there was plenty of traffic on the roads and the journey took longer than I had expected. Nonetheless, I arrived only a few minutes after the day-shift started, after driving a distance five times greater than that to headquarters. I was already beginning to realise that my small pay raise would not cover the additional cost of travel and wondered if accepting the job had been a financial mistake. Also, my self-confidence that I could accomplish my new duties successfully was starting to fade. As I arrived at the security gate, the guard stepped forward, inspected my salmon-pink identity card and directed me to the staff car park.

Earlier Jean-Louise had wished me luck, but she had remained firmly under the bed covers until after I left. Breakfast was on my own. For the next few months, although we went to bed together, it would be only during the weekends that I would be able to linger with her in the morning and talk. Sensing my stress, she had reassured me I would be successful in my new position, and I had told her to expect me home around 7pm.

The Personnel Department was housed in the main office building, to the right of the reception area. It was quiet outside the plant, as most men were already at work, although a few red, double-decker buses were still arriving to drop off passengers destined for other factories. Simultaneously, lorries and trains loaded with new cars were on the move, and transporters delivering car components were everywhere.

Inside the factory lobby, the receptionist, seated behind her desk and dressed in a Ford outfit with its blue-and-white oval logo, smiled as I entered. I waved back and took a sharp right into the Personnel Office. I met my new boss who asked me to follow him onto the shop floor where he planned to introduce me to some of the supervisors with whom I would work.

"I would like you to meet the day shift trim and final assembly superintendents," he announced. "You'll look after their operations as well as the janitors and quality control departments. There are two shifts, and each works a fortnight on days followed by a similar period on nights. It's important that you stay after the end of the dayshift to deal with problems, and you need to be prepared to come in for the nightshift when requested. Your colleague Wayne takes care of the paint shop upstairs, material handling and the maintenance activities, and each of you has around two thousand workers to support."

Immediately I stepped onto the factory floor, all my senses were engaged. The first thing I noticed was the noise; the consistent hum of the assembly lines, the thuds and bangs of components being fitted onto semi-finished cars, the screech of pneumatic tools and people shouting at each other in dialects that I had difficulty in understanding. Visually, I was fascinated by the clattering feeder lines delivering engines, transmissions and other components, the sparks from the welding guns, the constant tide of men moving between work stations, pallets arriving and leaving on fork lift trucks and partly-assembled Cortina and Zephyr/Zodiac models passing by on the main conveyors. I was surprised by the absence of natural light; the interior of the building was lit only by overhead fluorescent lighting.

The smells of fresh plastic, solvents, car-body solder and burning oil drifted in the air. At the end of the assembly line, I could taste wax in the atmosphere as fully assembled vehicles were sprayed with a fine mist to prepare them for dealer delivery, and everywhere there were different textures of metal, rubber, fabric and moulded parts.

The superintendents welcomed me and asked about my prior experience. Both of them were surprised when I admitted that I had never before worked in a factory. I also heard them comment on my youthful looks, but no-one mentioned my accent which by now was understandable but still noticeable. Maybe they were just as conscious of their own speech patterns as I was of mine. It was my first close connection with people who had been born and brought up in the east end of London. They were very different from the more formal "suits" in headquarters, and I found them refreshing and honest to work with. It might not be easy to share their opinions, but they seemed uncomplicated and sincere.

The remainder of the first day was spent familiarising myself with my workplace. I met the plant's senior shop steward Bill, known as the convener, and his deputy Bernie, who were full-time union representatives. Conflict seemed to be a way of life whenever you talked to them. Wayne and I ate lunch together, and he explained that although normal working had resumed after the sewing machinists' strike had been called off, production was still restricted because of the large number of workers who had resigned during the dispute and the factory was in the midst of a major recruitment campaign. After lunch, my boss instructed me on the office procedures and forms I would need to use, and I encountered "tea ladies" for the first time. These women were employed to serve tea, sandwiches and snacks to workers during the morning and afternoon production breaks. All the food was freshly prepared and pushed around on trolleys holding large tea urns. I was glad that office workers were included in their rounds, and cheese baps (large, soft bread rolls filled with Cheddar cheese) became my favourite mid-morning snack.

I described the new environment to Jean-Louise and I said I was excited about the opportunity to learn more but still apprehensive about my ability to meet the requirements of the job. She said that my doubts were normal but temporary, and I should stop worrying.

My duties were very different from those in headquarters. First, there was the "damage to clothing" programme. Most workers wore their own clothes to their jobs, and a shirt, a coat or a pair of trousers could easily tear on the rough edge of a pallet or become soiled by oil and other fluids. The company reimbursed the cost of cleaning, repair or replacement, as long as the damage occurred on company premises, and it was my responsibility to approve individual reimbursements when requested to do so by the foreman. This was mostly straightforward, but arguments could develop when a worker wanted the torn clothing replaced rather than repaired, or if I questioned hand-written invoices that bore no official shop name or logo.

Another of my duties involved the Ford Suggestion Plan. This scheme encouraged workers to submit ideas to improve efficiency and save the company money. If a suggestion was adopted, the employee received a tax-free lump sum of one-sixth of the first year's labour and materials cost savings. Occasionally I was asked to intervene to speed up an evaluation, determine the status of a proposal, or clarify why a suggestion had been rejected. Disputes would develop when I reported that a suggestion had been turned down either because it was a duplicate (someone else had already submitted the idea) or because it was ineligible for investigation. There was a long list of ineligible subjects, one of which happened to be "industrial relations policies", which I always thought was odd.

Additionally, I had responsibility for handling grievances, which was the most important of my duties. Typically, the personnel officer advised the line supervisor of what to do, but if the foreman did not resolve the problem, the dispute was referred to the Personnel Office, when I would become personally involved. Disagreements were often caused by new work practices, job mobility, adverse working conditions, discipline and concerns over health and safety practices.

Last, but not least, I managed the distribution of disciplinary warning letters to workers who were frequent or long-term absentees, or habitually late. Most absentees never returned to the plant, and those who did often claimed illness as the cause; they were required to report to the Medical Office and be cleared health-wise before being allowed to return to work. The tardiness problem was a little more complex: Workers often blamed unreliable public transport, not feeling well, illness in the family or malfunctioning time-card machines. Some even went so far as to organise a colleague to clock-in for them; if caught, the services of both the employee and his agent were terminated.

* * *

During September, I was approached by the Ford Dagenham Employment Office to assist until the end of the year with its recruitment campaign. Several Dagenham factories were still trying to operate without the labour levels necessary to meet required production schedules. Volunteers were needed to support Saturday selection interviews at Labour Exchanges (nowadays called Job Centres) across the east end of London; interviews began at 10am and finished around 2.30pm, depending on the number of applications received. Two Ford personnel officers had to be present at each location and without thinking, I accepted, believing the experience would advance my career.

"I wish you hadn't done that," Jean-Louise told me the evening I announced my plan. "I hardly see you during the week, and now you'll be missing most of Saturdays."

I tried to reassure her: "It's only for three months, and it'll help my career."

"But you're beginning to work too much," she grumbled. "I'd like to see more of you. Can we at least do something together on Saturday evenings?"

"What do you have in mind?"

"Well, for example, I'd like to see the new musical *Hair*. It's opened at the Shaftesbury Theatre in central London and I hear it's a witty and fabulous show."

What else could I do? I agreed.

We saw *Hair* the day before yet another Vietnam march in London. On 29th October 1968, 25,000 opponents turned out to march against the war, and earlier in the year a similar gathering had ended with violence and 250 arrests. Jean-Louise supported the demonstrations but never participated.

* * *

I was assigned to conduct interviews at Labour Exchanges close to the Central and District lines of the London Underground, the assumption being that applicants living in these locations would have easy access to Dagenham via public transport. I partnered with Dick, a personnel officer from the engine plant, but not the person who had successfully competed with me during my pre-placement in that factory. We travelled as far west as Hackney, but the majority of our interviews took place in West Ham, East Ham, Plaistow, Becontree and Barking. In order to be hired, an applicant was interviewed after completing an application form which needed to show evidence of previous factory experience (or equivalent), and confirm that he could both read and write in English since this would be the language of his supervisor, and all safety notices were printed only in English. The applicant also initialled an agreement to work shifts and overtime whenever requested.

I had never encountered so many people of colour before. There had been no racial diversity at my school, and very little at university. Immigrants had begun to arrive in large numbers during the 1960s, and many of the white "Cockney sparrers" had decided to leave the east end and move to suburbs and new towns (towns established for the relocation of populations in poor and bombed-out housing after World War 11), to the east and the north of London. This nickname for east-enders originated from their reputation for acting like house sparrows: Ever on the move, always friendly, usually in groups and chirping like the birds. (Although it was not apparent at the time, the birds were also moving out of town; once the most common species in London, the population has fallen by around two-thirds, and in some parts of central London today, they are no longer visible.)

Recruiting qualified applicants was a challenge, not helped by my natural instinct to trust people. It was not unusual for application forms to be incomplete, or for applicants not to be able to remember what they had written. There were times when two people would enter the interview room—one to translate the conversation for the applicant and the other to communicate in his home language. There were also instances of people substituting for candidates who were not present at the interview. Even so, we recruited some very fine workers.

During this three month period, the Race Relations Act,

1968 was implemented and it became illegal to discriminate in employment, housing or public services on the basis of a person's race, colour or national origin.

* * *

Jean-Louise remained displeased with my long working hours and absences on Saturdays. She compensated by spending more time visiting friends and redecorating the bungalow, but not having her own car was a regular complaint, as this restricted her activities. I told her I would look for one as soon as I had time. I added to her annoyance when I turned down her invitation to attend the school's Guy Fawkes celebration on 5th November 1968 that she was helping to organise. I needed to stay behind to meet the nightshift that particular evening, so she attended Bonfire Night without me.

I was at home when she returned late that evening, smiling and smelling of cigarette smoke and alcohol. She admitted that, after the fireworks, several teachers had gone across the road to "The Rose" pub to get to know each other socially, and one of them had given her a lift home. "The Rose" was an old-fashioned public house, originally a terrace of four cottages that had been converted into a comfortable and well-decorated pub many decades earlier, and it was just across the road from the school. I told her the television was predicting that Richard Nixon would become the next President of the United States, but she did not seem to be interested. Instead, she was far more eager to tell me about her evening.

"I've met our new Economics teacher," she said enthusiastically, "and he's promised to find me a car."

I felt indignant that my wife was expecting someone else to do what I thought was my responsibility. "Who is he and why would he want to do that?" I asked.

"He's just arrived at school and he fixes cars as a hobby. He says he can find me something reliable and cheap. He lives in East Ham and he's called James."

It seemed a kind offer, but I was not sure I liked the idea. I think she read my mind because she added: "You don't really have time to help, and he says he has friends in the second-hand car market."

I accepted the arrangement, provided she chose a car at a price we could afford, as I knew she needed her own vehicle, and there was no sign that my work would slow down long enough for me to help her find one. A brake supplier had gone on strike and Ford was having to lay-off most of the assembly plant's workforce. Soon, the weather would turn cold and icy, making public transport uncomfortable and unreliable.

A week later, I returned home to find a tweed-grey Morris mini-van parked in our driveway and Jean-Louise waiting to show off her new purchase. It was five years old, with two side doors and double-doors (with small windows) at the back, giving access to a dingy-looking storage area. The front side-windows were made of two sliding glass panels, and the side-doors opened from the inside by pulling on a wire chord. It had a manual transmission and an 850cc engine. Jean-Louise was particularly proud of it because of its cost; technically it was considered a commercial vehicle and therefore attracted a much lower rate of purchase tax (changed to VAT or Value Added Tax in 1973) than a regular car.

Apparently, James was going to install a radio and side-windows in its rear side panels. Understanding that this was going to be done the following Saturday, I wanted to meet him but realised I would be interviewing, so I asked if he might still be around when I returned home.

"No," replied Jean-Louise. "He's fixing the car in East Ham and will bring it to school on Monday morning, but if you want to meet him, come to one of our socials at "The Rose" pub."

Apparently it was becoming a regular practice for a group of teachers to stay after school on Friday evenings and go across to “The Rose” when it opened, in order to meet socially. I accepted the invitation, and three weeks later, a little after 6.30pm, I arrived at the venue. Jean-Louise’s mini-van was parked outside, and I parked the Anglia alongside it. Jean-Louise welcomed me, introduced me to some of her girlfriends and then took me across the room to meet James.

My first impression of the young man was that he was the classic “Cockney sparrer”. The people around him seemed mesmerised by his energetic conversation and chirpiness; he constantly moved his hands and arms around while talking and his face was a kaleidoscope of expressions. He stood about my height and was as slim as me, dressed in khaki trousers and a blue pullover. His accent clearly came from London’s east end and he had less hair than me.

I thanked him for finding Jean-Louise’s mini-van and for fitting the windows. He told me the vehicle had originally been owned by his cousin who had used it only for local deliveries. He talked about where he had grown up, that he was married and that he and his wife were planning to relocate to Essex. This was something of an adventure for them because they had always lived in East Ham. He also told me that he belonged to the National Union of Teachers.

In turn, I described my background and my work at Dagenham, and told him why I had chosen Ford. We discussed the sewing machinists’ strike, and James confessed he did not understand the grading issue but thought that equal pay was long overdue. I told him that the unions had not originally demanded equal pay, so they should be blamed for the dispute as much as Ford, and he just smiled.

I asked him why he had chosen to teach and was surprised by his reply.

"I didn't plan to. I originally intended to join the Metropolitan Police, but friends dissuaded me."

"What happened?" I queried.

"Someone I knew had joined the police force a couple of years earlier and become involved with crooks and gangs in the neighbourhood. They threatened that, if he didn't keep taking their bribes, something nasty would happen to his family. Since I was planning to marry, I didn't want to take the same risk."

"And," he added, "therefore family safety is another reason for leaving East Ham, as well as teaching."

At the end of our conversation, I wished him a merry Christmas, said I hoped we would meet again and thanked him once more for helping Jean-Louise. He promised to maintain the vehicle for her and said she had asked for it to be resprayed a bright colour, primrose-yellow, as she considered the current grey was dull and boring, and she wanted it to look bright and happy to stand out in car parks so that she could find it. James said that a friend of his would do the work, but they needed to wait until the warmer weather arrived in order to avoid having problems with the paint.

The Christmas holidays gave me five days of rest. Jean-Louise's father spent the time with us and talked about retiring in 15 months' time. He said he would not move to live with us; he wanted to stay where he was, but he did want the three of us to go to Norway as soon as he retired. We watched television as the Apollo 8 spacecraft successfully reached the moon on 21st December.

I was back at work on 30th December 1968, preparing for another busy year. Ford's wage negotiations were beginning and the government was enforcing its maximum 3.5 percent incomes policy. Simultaneously, Barbara Castle was presenting to industry and the trade unions, draft legislation proposing the legal reform of British industrial relations. In the plant, layoffs continued because of supplier shortages, and Wayne and I speculated whether the company might try to address the problem of layoffs in its March 1969 wage negotiations.

(Jean-Louise, December 1968) "The big news is that I now have the freedom to drive my own vehicle. Even when it's cold and windy, I can go to school, visit friends and do the shopping. A few days ago I had my first experience of driving through snow and I survived by travelling slowly.

"James, the new Economics teacher, made the purchase possible. He's very kind and lots of fun to talk to. We have a similar political outlook and both of us support trade unions. I think he respects my background because of my father's affiliation with the engineers' union. He's also an excellent mechanic, and his friend's installation of the rear side-windows has made the mini-van brighter and safer to drive.

"John has virtually withdrawn from my life. He's so consumed with his job, and he stays behind at work whenever there's a problem in the plant. It's very different from when he was working in headquarters. The decision to interview on Saturdays was a little thoughtless, although I've met him outside a couple of Labour Exchanges, and we've gone up to London for Saturday evenings. I've also introduced him to Constable's paintings in the National Gallery and bought him an art book for Christmas. My only consolation for his long working hours is that he has also neglected his birdwatching as much as he has me. His Life List is on hold and his binoculars have stayed in their case for the past few weeks.

"Teaching is straightforward, even though the behaviour of my sixth-form pupils can sometimes be difficult; also, I haven't warmed up to working with my new head of department.

"My father's spending Christmas with us and, so far, he

remains in good health. He's asked me to plan his dream holiday to Norway in the summer of 1970; he wants to visit the places where he fought during the war.

"There's no plan so far for having children, and I think we should wait until at least after the Norway trip."

House Sparrow: These small birds (about 5 cm/6 ins. in length) are noisy, gregarious and probably the ultimate avian opportunists. They exploit human rubbish and habitation, and they have colonised most towns and cities, so that they are now the most widely distributed species of birds in the world. They eat any scraps of food and seem happy to live and breed near people. If a small bird is seen with a black bib and grey crown, and the feathers on its back are streaky brown, it's almost certainly a house sparrow. There has been a serious decline in numbers since the 1970s, when the population in Britain was around 12 million, but that number is now halved. Scarcity of food, unsuitable nesting sites and an increase in predators are all probable causes.

In North America, it is known as the English sparrow and was originally introduced to attack the larvae of the linden moth. Today's estimates are that there are around 150 million English sparrows in the United States.

24

Bird Idioms

My weekdays at work during early 1969 remained long, but there were no Saturday interviews, allowing me to spend the weekend with Jean-Louise to help with the shopping and to share the chores, as well as continuing my Institute of Personnel Management studies. We found time to attend the local cinema on Saturday evenings to watch films such as *The Lion in Winter*, starring Katharine Hepburn and Peter O'Toole, and *Bullet* with Steve McQueen.

The commute between home and Dagenham became much more difficult and took far longer as the weather deteriorated. It soon turned cold and frosty, with sleet or snow on some days, and fog on others. There were times when I had to lower the car's front window in order to see the edge of the road and avoid oncoming traffic, and I was forced to drive at only a few miles per hour especially when it was icy.

I had lost contact with Mr Welsh and unexpectedly I found myself also losing connection with Chris. A few weeks after I transferred to Dagenham, he had called me to announce his departure to Northern Ireland where he was to become a Ford field sales manager. Like me, he wanted practical experience, and he did not seem to be concerned about the conflict between Catholics and Protestants that appeared to be escalating.

At school, Jean-Louise was tiring of lewd comments from some of her sixth-form boys. Her short skirts and colourful blouses elicited unwelcome remarks, so she switched to more seasonal woollen dresses and long-sleeved jumpers, and threatened disciplinary action if the behaviour continued. There were also difficulties with her head of department's prejudice against women. He ignored ideas from female staff, while at the same time requiring their loyalty in support of his own decisions. Jean-Louise conspired with her former mentor to ignore changes the head of department made without consultation, and she accepted James' advice to join the teachers' union to safeguard her employment status.

* * *

In the plant there were plenty of grievances to handle, and a one-day strike was organised by shop stewards to object to recurring lay-offs. Exactly why workers complain about losing wages by sacrificing even more income has always perplexed me. In January 1969, Barbara Castle, still the Secretary of State for Employment, published a White Paper titled *In Place of Strife*. It proposed making collective agreements legally binding, introducing cooling-off periods before industrial action could be taken, imposing financial penalties on unions for any breach of an agreement and requiring secret ballots before work stoppages could be carried out. There was strong opposition from the unions and also from some members of the government, and ultimately the proposals were replaced by a "solemn and binding" undertaking from the unions' leadership that it would "voluntarily" limit unauthorised strikes. At the time, 45 percent of British workers were members of trade unions, and that percentage was rising.

My former colleagues in Industrial Relations Staff had begun contract negotiations with the unions to establish a new wage settlement that would be effective in March. Management offered a 5 percent increase along with what it called an "income security plan". The latter would be used to justify an award above the government's 3.5 percent ceiling by incentivising workers not to participate in unofficial strikes. As long as they had not been involved in any unofficial action during the previous twelve months, they would receive a portion of their wages if laid off because of a dispute elsewhere. At first the national unions rejected the proposal, but they changed their minds when the wage offer was increased to 7.5 percent and eligibility under the "income security plan" was decreased from 12 to 6 months.

Unfortunately, the Ford plant conveners opposed the "income security" provisions and regarded them as a set of "penalty clauses" that interfered with shop-steward authority. Even so, the national unions approved the contract and asked for implementation; seven unions had approved and five objected to the settlement; the remainder abstained.

The situation on the shop floor turned ugly. The engineers' union broke away from the national vote and demanded a renegotiation of the agreement. The company refused. At about the same time, I bumped into the plant convener, who was waiting to see my boss.

"I thought we had an agreement, Bill. What's going on?" I asked him.

"We're angry with our national officials," he responded adamantly. "There's been no consultation with the shop floor, and several important unions rejected the deal."

"But how can you oppose a majority decision?" I queried.

"We don't accept the so called 'penalty clauses'," he replied. "The conveners met last Sunday and decided to call a companywide strike starting next Monday, 24th February, unless the company withdraws its proposals."

I could not tell if he supported the conveners' decision, and he made no comment on my suggestion that, if the company withdrew the provisions, the wage increase would violate the government's incomes policy. The situation in the plant became confused; it was unclear what would take place companywide, and my management worked late into the evening to develop contingency plans in case the stoppage took place.

I was in the office at about 6.30am on the day the threatened strike was due to begin. It was not particularly early for me, given what was happening, but it was one of the few occasions when I did not arrive ahead of my boss. My regular work practice was to be in the office before my superiors, and leave only after they had left.

As I reached the plant security gates, pickets stood outside waving placards and making lots of noise. Vehicles were being turned away, and the pavement entrance was blocked to stop pedestrians walking into the plant, but my staff parking permit gave me access. Many workers obeyed the pickets, but some gathered in clusters and resolutely walked through the picket lines. They were accused of being "scabs" and "black legs", and told there would be retaliation once the conflict was over.

The term "black leg" was a phrase new to me and I checked into its origins. There are many stories, none of which has anything to do with racism, but the one I favour is that the term was created long ago based on the black legs of a crow. This bird is known for stealing food from other birds, and the men walking through the picket lines are considered by their striking colleagues to be stealing from them. Whether the avian culprit was the British rook or the carrion crow is unclear, as both have black legs, although the rook wears black feathery "trousers" on its legs and congregates in flocks, whereas carrion crows are mainly solitary birds.

This was one of many bird idioms that I read about. For example, I learned about a "swan song", describing someone's final accomplishment at work or in life based on folklore that a swan's most beautiful song is the one sung just before it dies. Then there is "bald as a coot", describing a completely bald person and referring to the white-feathered markings on a coot's head which looks like baldness. Some birds' names are used to describe human behaviours; there is "a snipe hunt" (searching for something that cannot be found), "a gannet" (name for a gluttonous or greedy person) and, my personal favourite, "a jenny wren", said in folklore to be the stereotype for a chattery, scolding woman who is usually small, pretty, noisy and energetic, like the tiny wren.

Once in the office, I checked with my boss to find out what was happening.

"We're opening up the production lines," he said. "Half the men have ignored the pickets and are being moved around to fill critical jobs. We'll assemble only the Cortina today."

The telephone kept ringing, as workers called to see if they should come to work. I encouraged their attendance, but I left it to each person to decide, given that it was necessary to pass through the picket lines. For some men, that didn't matter, but for others it was a point of principle never to cross one. That evening, as I watched television at home, reports suggested that the strike was collapsing, and earlier in the day, the unions had collectively reaffirmed their acceptance of the settlement.

Jean-Louise continued to criticise me for my long working hours and started to complain that I was of no use at weekends because I was mentally and physically exhausted. She knew she could not change my behaviour so, rather than continue to complain, she found activities that did not require my involvement, and her mini-van helped. I would find notes that she was out either with her physics teacher friend or with her former mentor, or that she was at another Cordon Bleu cookery class. She even went up to Manchester to see her father. She read more at home, and James seemed to come around more frequently to fix her mini-van and help with other things around the house that she could not do on her own. I was concerned by what was taking place, but there seemed to be little I could do about it.

Unfortunately the dispute at work went from bad to worse. The morning after the strike began the engineers' union declared it official and instructed its Ford members to stop work. Shortly thereafter, the transport union took similar action; its national official had supported the settlement, but when asked to withdraw his approval by the union's General Secretary, he declined and was quickly replaced by an alternative representative who reversed his decision.

Thereafter the picket lines became much more numerous, extra rowdy and more threatening, with eggs thrown at cars, fists thumped on vehicle bonnets and paintwork intentionally scratched. All production ceased, with training and building cleaning taking priority as work for those left behind. Wayne and I were expected to coordinate both shifts to keep people busy.

The conflict became more inflamed when Ford of Britain took the unusual step of suing the unions in Court for breach of contract. A few days after the submission, the Court rejected the suit and declared that labour contracts in Britain are always "gentlemen's agreements", and not legally enforceable.

It was early in the third week of the strike that I came face-to-face with the human suffering that is sometimes caused by collective action. A janitor foreman visited me, accompanied by a tall, slimly built, middle-aged, rather damp and dirty looking labourer.

"He's just shown up for work," the foreman told me. "It's his first time here and he came through the sewer system into the plant, so no-one saw him. What shall I do, give him work or send him home?"

I looked at the employee who spoke in his own defence.

"I can't afford to stay out," he said pleadingly. "My union's not one of those making the strike official, so there's no strike pay. I've debts and a family to feed. I need to work."

"Have you any tasks for him?" I asked the foreman.

"Yes, there's clean-up work in the Paint Shop, but I'm worried about his safety."

"Let him work," I replied, "and give him the option of staying here overnight or going home. Also, provide him with overalls to make it difficult for him to be identified otherwise there'll be retribution when the strike's over."

The employee was delighted. He smiled and thanked me for the decision, and I never heard from either him or the foreman again.

Once more, it was Barbara Castle who initiated the solution. Separate meetings were held with the three parties involved: the unions supporting the strike, those opposed to it and Ford management. The company agreed to alter the formula for lay-off pay from individual participation in industrial action to collective plant-wide involvement. In reality this was an empty promise because it could be guaranteed that a dispute would occur somewhere each week in a factory the size the Dagenham assembly plant. Nonetheless, the workforce accepted the revised offer and returned to work on 20th March 1969.

My long working days continued as new grievances were submitted and shop stewards became more hostile. Jean-Louise continued to organise her life separate from me although we did try to connect during the weekends. On a positive note,

I received my first ever general salary increase. The company extended its union-negotiated percentage wage award to salaried employees, partly because clerical and technical staff were unionised, but also to maintain pay differentials between workers, their supervisors and other salaried staff.

* * *

On one of those rare days when Jean-Louise and I had time to talk, she asked about our summer holidays. Where should we go? We thought we should save money by not travelling overseas, but she insisted that I take a break from work and spend time with her. She suggested we visit the south-west of England, a region she had not seen.

Clumsily I raised a topic that I knew would be provocative. “I don’t think we can drive that far using the Anglia,” I said, “it’s too slow and becoming unreliable; I think it needs to be replaced.”

I had my reasons. Ford had begun offering one year-old Cortinas at a special employee discount because the model was being returned by managers who were switching to the newly launched Capri. A plant colleague said he could find me one in good condition and with low mileage.

“But we can’t afford a new car,” she replied, although she did not sound determined.

I had done my homework. “Actually, we have the money because of my recent salary raise. If we buy the car now, it will cost less, and we’ll have a vehicle that’s sturdy enough for an English holiday this year and one which we can use for the Norway trip next year.”

Jean-Louise did not argue, so by late May we were the proud owners of a four-door, saluki bronze, Mark 11 Cortina 1600E, with only six thousand miles on the clock. It was comfortable, fast and good looking, with a black vinyl roof, chrome trim and additional driving lamps mounted on the grille for bad weather. I washed and waxed it most Sundays as a diversion from my Institute of Personnel Management studies.

* * *

At home our living standards were being maintained as British inflation stayed at around 5 percent. A new opportunity to enter the European Economic Community arose when the French President, Charles de Gaulle, lost a constitutional referendum in April 1969 and resigned. His successor, elected a few weeks later, was much more supportive of Britain's prospective membership. There was also the passage of the Representation of the People Act that lowered the British voting age from 21 to 18 (to be implemented in February 1972). Additionally, the maiden flight of the Concorde took place on 2nd March 1969.

The annual Ford factory shutdown in August was only a few days away, and I was exhausted and looking forward to spending time with Jean-Louise and finding out a little more about what she was up to during my long days at work. I knew we needed to reconnect, and I resolved to leave all business in the office and do whatever Jean-Louise wanted me to do. I also needed to have a serious conversation with her about James. Although he was likeable, I thought he was spending too much time with Jean-Louise and I could not believe that her mini-van needed that much attention.

It was close to my first-year anniversary in the Dagenham assembly plant and I was beginning to think about my next job. After 12 months, I was free to consider new opportunities and hoped I would find something that improved my work-life balance. The recruitment process at Ford was for managers wishing to hire new staff to approach candidates directly, in order to determine interest, once the one-year eligibility period had been fulfilled. I wondered what I should do next.

(Jean-Louise, August 1969) "John's commitment to his personnel career has become excessive; I rarely see him except for weekends, and then he's usually tired and doesn't want to do anything. It takes all his energy to go outside and cut the grass.

"Apparently, he's very successful, and the more praise he receives, the harder he works. I wish he would be more sensitive to my needs. Now that I'm in my second year of teaching, there's less preparation work and little else to do at home except read and watch television. The Cordon Bleu cookery lessons are taking me out of the house two evenings a week and I frequently visit my friends. The Friday evenings in "The Rose" continue, but John hasn't made it to one this year. I think he's a little jealous of James, but that's his fault for neglecting me. James helps me to do things around the home, as well as maintaining the mini-van, tasks that John either isn't here to help with or can't do.

"Regarding world events, Southern Rhodesia's decision to break all ties with Britain and become a republic and rename itself Rhodesia, is very disappointing. I wonder what the lecturer at Hull who came from that country thinks. In contrast, I'm pleased with Charles de Gaulle's resignation. I also supported Barbara Castle's efforts to establish order in the collective bargaining process, but it seems that once again the men took over and decided to do something entirely different.

"I'm looking forward to our holiday. We plan to visit parts of Hampshire, such as Stonehenge, then drive to Cornwall, and I've booked bed and breakfast accommodations for the duration of the journey. I've also included some birdwatching

on the agenda, as John's been unable to go bird spotting this year because of his job.

"The new car is comfortable and fast, and it will be reliable for long journeys. During our tour, I will take photographs of the physical landscapes we drive through to use at school, and I'll begin my third year of teaching with the hope of seeing more of John."

English Wren

Wren: This is a small (about 10 cm/4 inches long), active, round-bodied, brown-coloured bird, with a short, upright tail and pale eyebrows. Its underparts are pale grey with brown barring. It is the most common breeding bird in Britain and generally does not migrate, except to move to more sheltered habitats during winter. Its numbers in Britain are estimated at about 17 million. In spring, the male builds several delicately constructed nests, each with a small opening, and allows the female to choose in which nest to lay her eggs; the spare nests are known as "cocks' nests".

There is only one species in Europe, whereas there are nine in North America. The family is common across the United States, and the species closest in appearance to the European wren is known as the house wren.

25

The Cornish Chough

Our suitcases were stowed in the boot of the car, and the Ordinance Survey maps covering the route of our journey had been placed in the glove compartment. It was the day before our second wedding anniversary, and the weather was sunny and warm as we drove south-west out of London towards Hampshire. I had left my work papers in the assembly plant and was clearing my mind of all thoughts associated with tasks that still required my attention. I knew there would be no calls from my bosses because it was Ford of Britain's annual factories shutdown. Jean-Louise had already liberated herself from teaching matters, and the plan was to dedicate our time to sharing each other's hobbies. Our itinerary included geology and history excursions, studying the social geography of the places we were visiting, surveying the physical landscape through which we drove and possibly conducting some birdwatching.

During the drive, I apologised for not spending more time with Jean-Louise. The past year had been an important period in my career, and I had learned a lot, but I acknowledged that I needed to manage my working hours better. I promised to look for a new position once the holidays were over, and Jean-Louise said she hoped that I would find something closer to home. She said she had appreciated the support of James; he was a wonderful friend and she was thankful for his assistance but it would be inconvenient for him to help out after summer because he and his wife were relocating to the other side of Essex. Fortunately, her remarks gave me the opportunity to question his character.

I began tactfully, knowing that I did not want to fall out with my wife and then have to sit alongside her for the next several hours, saying nothing because we had disagreed.

"You seem to have become very close to James and I'm feeling a little jealous. It's one thing to have a friendship, but I'm wondering if it might be developing into something more serious."

Jean-Louise did not to know whether to be angry with me or sympathetic. At the very least she seemed shocked by my accusation.

"You've no reason to feel jealous," she replied, sounding ruffled. "He only comes over when I invite him, and that's only when there are things to do that I can't do on my own. We see each other every day at school, so it's a professional relationship. If you were home more often, you'd know that we are just the best of friends. We see eye-to-eye on most things, but he's happily married, and so am I."

I immediately dropped the subject, as I found it was an unpleasant topic to discuss and I did not want to provoke a controversy. I concluded that, if a closer relationship was developing, it was just as likely to take place at school as at home, and it was up to me to trust Jean-Louise, to pay her more attention and to allow more time for her needs.

* * *

Our first stop was at Winchester, about 70 miles (110 km) south-west of London, and one of the most beautiful cities in Britain, with layers of history that are visible across the urban landscape. It had served as a provincial capital during Roman times and flourished as a fortified town during the Saxon period. The Norman conquerors had built castles and a cathedral, and the city had later established itself as a centre for wool and cloth-making. Its population was decimated by the plague (Black Death), but the city returned to prominence during the 18th century when much of it was rebuilt, and prosperity returned after the railway reached Winchester in 1840.

It was also the home of Jane Austen at the end of her life, and we visited her tomb in the cathedral where she was buried in 1817. I was not sure who she was, but Jean-Louise explained.

Then we travelled to Stonehenge for a close-up look at the monument, a circle of bluestone rocks dating back to around 2,000BC, and the 80 or so larger sarsen slabs of silicified sandstone erected a few hundred years earlier. The latter came from nearby quarries, whereas the bluestones supposedly originated 125 miles (200 km) away in north Pembrokeshire in Wales. Like the many millions of visitors before us, we could only speculate on the purpose of the circles as religious, ceremonial or funereal, or maybe as a solar calendar. The whole site is a fascinating and very closely guarded national monument, so although my geology hammer was in the car, Jean-Louise told me to leave it there.

Our first night was spent in accommodation just outside Salisbury. It was a time for romance and celebrating the start of our holiday. The following morning, we drove to the New Forest, about 10 miles (16 km) to the south. This is an area set aside by King William I in 1079, to be used for the Royal Hunt. Many small hamlets, parish churches and farmsteads were destroyed so that the area could be converted into unenclosed pasture, heathland and forest. For us, it was like walking back in time; we could almost hear the noise of the hunt, the swish of the arrows and the scuffles of wild pigs and deer trying to make their escape. I could hear birdsong, but its source was difficult to spot high up in the canopy of trees. I tried to find breeding siskins and wood warblers, but Jean-Louise was impatient to get us back on the road.

It was a long drive to Cornwall. On the way, I explained what I had read about Cornwall's Coat of Arms and its emblem, a bird known as "the Crow of Cornwall", but which is actually called a chough (pronounced "chuff"). The bird is all black, other than for a very distinctive, curved, long red beak and red legs. Some call it the red-billed chough. The species had not yet made it onto my Life List because it is not a migrant bird and is confined to the west coast of Britain. I wondered if I might be fortunate enough to see one during our holiday, but unfortunately I did not. At the time of our visit, the bird was virtually extinct in Cornwall, as it had been hunted as a trophy, its eggs taken by collectors and its feeding habitat destroyed. At the time I knew of only one resident pair, and one of those birds had apparently been found dead a year earlier. Jean-Louise indulged me by allowing me to reveal my knowledge of birds in order to take my mind of work issues.

After arriving in the quaint fishing village of Mevagissey, we lodged nearby in a converted farm building. There was time to stroll among the attractive shops in the town's labyrinth of narrow streets and alleyways that twisted and turned down to the twin harbours, where the crying of herring gulls and the smell of fish and salt water took control of our senses. The town was first recorded as a fishing port in 1313, and traditional fishing was mainly for mackerel, herring and pilchards. Today it harbours a multitude of small fishing vessels catching everything from lobster and crab close to shore, to bass, sole and plaice out at sea. Mackerel are still caught and the smaller pilchards are now fished as Cornish sardines. During our ramblings I bought Jean-Louise some fudge and a poetry book.

The following day, we walked together along the rugged coastline, occasionally stopping to study the Lower Palaeozoic stratigraphy. This time I was permitted to use my hammer and chisel, while Jean-Louise took photographs of the sheer cliffs, picturesque coves, tidal creeks and shingle beaches, and I collected rock specimens to take home with me.

After that we went sightseeing again. Cornwall was once the largest tin-mining region in the world, boasting two thousand mines, and we spent a day in the St Just mining district, where we stopped off at the still-functioning Geevor Mine. By the time of our visit, tin-mining had virtually ceased, and the local villages and hamlets had restructured their economies to favour agriculture, fishing and tourism, although evidence of past mining for tin, copper, lead, tungsten and mispickel (arsenic) was visible everywhere.

The most noticeable geological feature was near the old market town of St Austell where the tall, white peaks of china clay, otherwise known as kaolin, dominated the landscape. These deposits, created by the decomposition of feldspar and mica in granite, had once been the largest in the world, and were used in the ceramics industry and, more recently, in paper manufacturing as filler and for coating.

As a final surprise at the end of our holiday, Jean-Louise revealed her secret arrangement for a ferry trip to St Mary's in the Scilly Isles, about 28 miles (45 km) off the Cornish coast. She said it was an opportunity for me to do some birdwatching, and her ambition was to see the Prime Minister who was supposed to be on holiday there.

As the ferry departed Cornwall, I spotted fulmars and

more herring gulls along the granite cliffs of Land's End, and out at sea there were kittiwakes, shags and razorbills. At St Mary's, I spotted wheatears, little buntings, ringed plovers and oystercatchers. We hiked around the town and along the beach, finally glimpsing the Prime Minister with his wife and their dog. A few days earlier, the PM had directed British soldiers to Northern Ireland for the first time, to quell the spiralling sectarian violence between Catholics and Protestants, and I wondered if Chris was safe.

On the trip back to Penzance, I looked for puffins, the smallest member of the auk family that nests on nearby islands, but I was unsuccessful. Puffins are shy, elusive birds that fly out to sea in late summer and spend eight months swimming, diving and floating, all well away from land.

We spent our last night in Tintagel, on the north coast of Cornwall, to see the castle where the legendary King Arthur (who was said to have ruled part of Britain in the late 5th and early 6th centuries AD) was supposed to have been conceived. It was difficult to imagine Uther Pendragon seducing Igraine in such an inhospitable place by having Merlin make him look like her husband.

Thereafter, we took a detour across the granite moorland and peat bogs of the Bodmin area to visit the castellated tors (free-standing rock outcrops) produced around 100,000 years ago by the periglacial actions of repeated freezing and thawing. There Jean-Louise took her final photographs of the holiday, and our return to Essex was then all too quick.

* * *

Back in the Dagenham assembly plant, I found relationships on the shop floor peaceful, in part because of worries that short-time working was imminent due to declining car sales. Overtime had already been cancelled. Nationally, industrial unrest was rising and disputes over wage claims were more frequent. Despite this militancy, the Labour government remained committed to its prices and incomes policy and was rumoured to be looking once again at legal measures to control collective bargaining and discourage unauthorised industrial action.

The dustmen of London took unofficial action late in September 1969 to press a wage claim. As a result, we stayed well away from the city for the duration, as piles of rubbish accumulated on the streets of London, rats were sighted, children were sent home from school because of the stench and there was a risk of fires breaking out.

This dispute was followed by one involving coal miners who were demanding higher wages and shorter working hours for surface workers. So-called "flying" pickets were organised for the first time to travel to work sites and intimidate workers into joining the dispute. Cars, vans and buses full of striking miners and sympathisers arrived at pre-determined sites to stop miners entering the pits. The strike ended after two weeks when the National Coal Board conceded to the strikers' demands, and fortunately before our supply of coal for the living room fire was exhausted.

Jean-Louise decided to invite James and his wife to dinner to demonstrate to me that they were a happily married couple. James confirmed that they had moved to Essex, although his wife was having doubts about living in the countryside and was sad at leaving her job as an office clerk on the Royal Albert Docks. Her home had always been in East Ham. There was not much we could do to help, but I thanked James once more for his work on Jean-Louise's mini-van. Otherwise, we talked about teaching, trade unions and my work, and I was relieved to detect no suggestion that there was anything more than a professional friendship between Jean-Louise and James.

* * *

Following my first anniversary at Dagenham, I began to receive job offers. My biggest concern was whether to continue to specialise in industrial relations or broaden my experience into other areas of personnel management. One evening, at her insistence, I discussed the alternatives with Jean-Louise.

"Tell me about the choices," she began.

"There are three," I responded. "The first is staying in Dagenham and moving to the River Plant where I've been asked to replace the senior personnel officer who's retiring. It'd be a promotion for me, but the work is similar to what I do now, and the commute will not change. Also, I'm not sure I want the visibility of taking care of the sewing machinists because of their militancy, and I'm told they're notorious for harassing people in the plant with indecent comments. The only advantage I can see is that I would have more control over my hours.

"The second job is at the Dunton Technical Centre; that's much closer to home and gives me salaried personnel experience, but it's not a promotion.

"Finally, there's a corporate position in Salaried Personnel Policies, based in headquarters, that would broaden my knowledge of salaried staff policy development, and it's a promotion."

It didn't take long for Jean-Louise to communicate her preference.

"It's obvious. Accept the Brentwood job. You promised during the holidays to spend more time with me, you'll be back close to home, it's a promotion and it will broaden your experience.

"Also," she added, "if you work closer, maybe we can begin to look for a bigger house? The bungalow is fine, but I want my father to spend more time with us after his retirement, and the bungalow is too cramped."

I supported the idea but suggested we wait until after her father had stopped working and the visit to Norway was over, and Jean-Louise agreed. The following day, I accepted the Staff Policies Analyst position in headquarters and arranged a start date of 3rd November 1969. During the following few days, I said my farewells to colleagues in the Dagenham assembly plant and probably received the best compliment in my life from Bill, the convener. He praised the support I had given his members during my 14 months in the plant and said he thought I had a very promising career ahead of me.

(Jean-Louise, October 1969) "Well, I'm expecting to see more of John now he's moving back to Ford of Britain's headquarters in Brentwood. It sounds as if his work will be very different, but he'll be much closer to home and will have more control over his working hours, and he's promised to join me at 'The Rose' pub for some of our Friday evening gatherings. For myself, I've just received another seniority salary increase, and John will receive a promotional adjustment, so I hope these will help us to afford a new house when we're ready. I'm beginning to think about children, and I'm ready to change schools.

"John doesn't need to worry about James although his fears probably helped persuade him to accept the Brentwood position. James is my best friend but it's a professional relationship, and his willingness to look after my mini-van saves lots of money.

"The holiday was something of a reunion and a chance for us to do things together that we like. The highlight was the ferry trip to St Mary's. I managed to spot the Prime Minister, and John saw razorbills. The Cortina was comfortable, so we've decided to use it next year when we visit Norway."

Chough Bird

Chough (pronounced "chuff" and sometimes known as the Red-billed Chough): This resident bird is Britain's rarest crow, approximately 40 cm/15 inches in length, currently with an estimated 500 breeding pairs, mainly in the south-west of Scotland, Wales and Northern Ireland. After the species had been absent from Cornwall for 30 years, three birds arrived in 2001, and a pair nested the following year. Numbers have slowly increased to around 50 birds presently. It is a shy bird that rarely moves far from its breeding site. As well as glossy black plumage, bright red legs and a long, curved, red beak, it is distinguished by its high-pitched call of "chee-ow" and its habit of diving and swooping from the clifftops. It feeds on invertebrates found just below the surface of grazed grassland. Its general distribution is in Morocco, north to Spain and east across to the Himalayas. It is resident in mountainous regions and along coastal sea cliffs, and there is an Alpine Chough with a yellow beak, but there are no choughs in North America.

26

The Skylark

It was after my second day with Salaried Personnel Policies in Ford of Britain's Brentwood headquarters on Tuesday 4th November 1969. I had worked late the previous evening, but tonight I was eating dinner with Jean-Louise after arriving home at 5.30pm. She was delighted. It was our first weekday evening meal together since our holiday in Cornwall and I told her to expect me home even earlier the following day. I wanted to go with her to the school's Guy Fawkes bonfire night party, and to join her friends afterwards in "The Rose" pub to celebrate James' move to his new home in Essex.

"And how's your new job?" she was impatient to know.

There was not much to say. It was what I had expected—a desk job involved in policy development—and a little like some of the work I had done for Mr Welsh. It was much quieter than Dagenham, so I replied: "It's very different from what I'm used to but I think I'll like it. The people around me are smart, and I worked with Anita for most of today." The last comment was a bit of a tease for Jean-Louise.

Her response was predictable. "Who's she? I didn't think Ford employed many women graduates."

"She's not a woman!" I smiled. "Anita's an electronic desktop calculator that we use for analysing salary surveys. She does the maths after we input the numbers." I was not sure that Jean-Louise appreciated my humour, as she sighed, narrowed her eyes and resumed her questioning: "And why's that work important?"

I told her that my new department managed all of Ford of Britain's employment programmes for salaried staff. We conduct a salary survey each year among a group of competitors, we research trends in remuneration and benefits, and we annually recommend salary and employment condition changes to senior management. Currently, the March 1970 general salary increases are under preparation.

Immediately switching topics, Jean-Louise told me that the dates for our trip to Norway had been booked for June the following year, and she had arranged ferry tickets for the three of us, plus the car, travelling between Newcastle and Bergen. She also said that her father would stay with us for Christmas and return over Easter, after he retired.

Shortly after this, I received an unexpected telephone call from my mother. Since our marriage, I'd had little contact with her, as she was either working at the hospital in York or taking cruises overseas. However, once or twice she had called at the bungalow to see us en route to board a cruise ship to somewhere. Just after we were married, she had introduced us to a man whom she had started dating; they had since become engaged and were planning to marry at the end of July 1970. Her telephone call was to confirm that I would be back from Norway in time to give her away.

* * *

At the bonfire the following evening, I was introduced to many of Jean-Louise's school friends, and I was impressed by the number of parents who came up to her to express thanks for teaching their children. Her patience, enthusiasm and knowledge were repeatedly complimented and, clearly, she was very successful.

Later in the evening, a group of us walked across the road to "The Rose" pub. We gathered informally, bought our own drinks and most of the teachers were accompanied by their spouse. It was a brief affair. Someone stood up and made a short speech, congratulating James and his wife on making the move to Essex. James responded by introducing his wife and admitting that the relocation had been something of an ordeal. Both he and his wife had left many friends behind and were adjusting to the lack of public transport and the quietness of the countryside in their new location. At the end, everyone toasted the couple with whatever remained in their glasses.

As we were leaving, James' usual chirpiness reasserted itself and, grinning at Jean-Louise, he asked if she had shared something with me that I knew she had not.

"No," she replied sheepishly, "but I will when we're home."

"There's no reason to wait. Tell him now while your friends are here."

Jean-Louise looked a little embarrassed and I wondered what was so important that James wanted her to announce it before the party was over.

She began hesitatingly: "I hope you don't mind, but I've adopted an eight-week-old kitten. One of the girls brought it to school, and I've agreed to take care of it. It's named Treacle because of its colour and it's adorable. Please can we keep it?"

Her public appeal made it difficult for me to say no, although my reaction was to feel annoyed because everyone else seemed to know what was going on except me. I faced a dilemma; I could either accept Jean-Louise's proposal or be critical of her in front of her friends. James had constructed a very difficult situation for me, but first I wanted to be sure that Jean-Louise understood that she was making a long-term commitment.

"Who's going to take care of it while we're on holiday?" I said, thinking this might be a consideration she had not anticipated. I was mistaken.

"I'll take care of it, if none of your neighbours will," volunteered the physics teacher.

Clearly, there had been prior consultation and I was not going to win the debate. I conceded the inevitable and yielded to peer pressure.

"OK, that's fine by me," I admitted, and tried to grin my agreement at Jean-Louise's friends.

Jean-Louise hugged me, and I do believe I heard a ripple of applause.

On Friday evening, Jean-Louise brought Treacle to live with us. The kitten was given the run of the house, breakable objects were moved out of reach and the necessary items for her to eat, sleep and play were purchased. Treacle spent most of the daytime outside, but at night, slept on our bed. Jean-Louise was thrilled, stroking and talking to her, and I felt pleased that I had made the right decision. Jean-Louise's father had his doubts about the wisdom of adopting a cat but suffered its presence during his visits.

* * *

For the next few weeks, I focused on learning every aspect of my new position. I was assigned responsibility for one of the specialist staff groups that was administered outside of Ford of Britain's standard pay ranges. These were employees in the Ford Airline Group that included pilots, mechanics and cabin crew. They ferried Ford's senior executives around Europe, and I soon became a frequent visitor to Stansted Airport.

The chief pilot took care of Mr Ford during his European trips, and he would frequently justify his salary proposals by claiming: "I mentioned the proposal to Mr Ford, who said it was a good idea."

I needed strong reasons and personal courage to turn down the chief pilot's recommendations.

The March 1970 union negotiations at Ford took place without disruption. The government had eased its incomes policy to allow settlements of up to 4.5 percent, but the limit was widely ignored, especially in the engineering industry where awards were averaging around 18 percent. The Ford of Britain's shop stewards urged their members to reject the company's 15 percent offer and demand pay parity with the British Midlands motor industry. There, hourly wage rates were replacing piece work (wages paid for the amount produced) and were higher than Ford's. However, the workforce rejected a work stoppage, and an agreement was signed with the unions. My department distributed a Staff Memorandum implementing the same award percentage for salaried staff, and once more I saw my remuneration move upwards as a result of trade union intervention.

During the sunny, warm work-days of late spring, I found time after lunch to wander through the woods and open farmland adjacent to the Brentwood headquarters. It was an opportunity for me to reflect on the tasks I had left behind in the office. Sometimes I heard a male skylark singing its extravagant song, high in the sky, reminding me of those childhood days when I helped with the harvest by stacking sheaves of wheat into stooks that eventually were loaded onto carts and taken away for threshing. I reflected on how everything was so different now. From roaming the fields of Yorkshire, I was now roaming the factories of Essex.

Nationally, the Labour government tried to dampen down

domestic demand and increase taxes to assist with the country's exports. Simultaneously, there was a fight with union leaders to comply with national wage guidelines, and there were suspicions that the government might renew its efforts to introduce legal controls over collective bargaining.

The situation reached a crisis in late May 1970 when the Prime Minister dissolved Parliament and called for a general election on 18th June. A comfortable Labour victory was predicted because of improvements in the economy, and local council elections had shown a strong preference for Labour. There was also speculation that the election was being held earlier than necessary because otherwise it might conflict with the introduction of decimal coinage scheduled for early 1971. The expectation was that the currency conversion would be unpopular and might jeopardise Labour's likelihood of winning.

However, to many people's surprise, a late swing among voters brought the Conservatives to power (the Conservatives won 330 seats versus Labour's 288) under the leadership of Edward Heath. Jean-Louise was shocked, but I was pleased, so we said little to each other! The Conservative manifesto contained a promise to reform industrial relations through what it called an Industrial Relations Bill, as well as commitments to abandon formal prices and incomes policies and resume negotiations for Britain's entry into the European Economic Community. In contrast, Labour wanted more democracy in the work place, including appointing workers to company boards, and questioned the need to negotiate with Europe because of the likelihood that any agreement would have adverse effects on our trade relationships with British Commonwealth countries.

Explanations for Labour's surprise loss included negative trade figures released during May, union indiscipline, rising prices (annual inflation was now slightly over 6 percent) and England's unexpected loss to West Germany in the football

World Cup quarter-finals four days before the election. There were suggestions that the loss had caused some disgruntled Labour supporters to vote against their party, blaming the Prime Minister for the result.

* * *

Meanwhile, I finished my Institute of Personnel Management studies and travelled to London to sit the final examinations. I passed and was told that I would receive a graduate member certificate early in September.

By now, we had reached mid-June, the weather had turned warm and sunny, and Jean-Louise's father was looking forward to his holiday in Norway. We drove to Manchester two days after the general election to meet him. Jean-Louise was not sure what to expect during the holiday since, for as long as she could remember, she had never been away with her father for longer than a weekend. She asked me to bear his welfare in mind and make allowances for his heavy smoking, his need for early and frequent rests and his fussiness over the food he ate. I told her I would do my best.

On the way north, we listened to the radio and the many voices speculating over the ramifications of the new Conservative government. They predicted a battle between the government and the trade unions, and they praised the former Prime Minister, Harold Wilson, for his past efforts to reduce the country's debt, take control of inflation and return Britain to positive economic growth. On a lighter note, there was discussion about the future of the Beatles, as Paul McCartney had announced his departure from the group.

On arrival in Manchester, we were greeted by Jean-Louise's father with a pot of tea on the table, and we sat down to finalise our plans.

"Are you ready?" his daughter asked him.

He smiled enthusiastically and then walked across to his hand luggage and extracted an envelope out of which he took a black and white photograph and a three-inch-square of tissue paper. He was eager to start the holiday and proud that he still had records saved from his encounters with the German soldiers 30 years earlier.

"These are the places I would like to see," he announced, showing us the two documents.

The black and white photograph depicted four soldiers marching in front of a raised balcony outside a building surrounded by deep snow. The soldiers wore white camouflage battledress, carried skis and rifles and were walking along a pathway with snow piled up on either side. Another dozen or so men were standing nearby, observing the soldiers. Everyone was warmly dressed, and most of the men wore tin helmets.

"This was taken during the war," he told us.

"Where is it? What's happening?" I asked him.

"It's a photo of a place called Fossbakken in north Norway, well above the Arctic Circle. I was stationed there for a few days during the war. In April 1940, I was a member of a small group of Scots Guards that sailed from Scotland to a port in north Norway. We trekked many miles to this place and found Norwegian soldiers defending it from the Nazis who were advancing north from Narvik. Our purpose for being there was to capture Narvik from the Germans."

"What happened?" Jean-Louise asked him.

"We were moved elsewhere and never made it to Narvik. The town was retaken by other Allied soldiers but eventually re-occupied by the Germans when Norway surrendered to Germany on 10th June 1940. We transferred to a place called Mo i Rana, about 200 miles (320 km) to the south. It was freezing cold with deep snow, and some of us suffered frostbite while others encountered snow-blindness. None of us had skis, and most didn't know how to use them anyway. We ended up fighting the Germans just south of Mo i Rana, and I had to retreat north to Bodo. On the way, we slowed the German advance by shooting at them whenever we crossed a river. Here's the map of where we started the fighting."

He passed the piece of tissue paper, and I saw that it was dated "17 and 18 May 1940". It illustrated a hand-written list of locations such as "The Dalsklubben Position", "To Hemnes", "To Mo", "the Dals River" and "Stein".

"What was it for?" I asked

"It showed us the location of the Germans and where to go when we were told to retreat."

"You actually fought the Germans?" a mildly astonished Jean-Louise asked him. "You never talked about this before."

"It's something that's hard to talk about because of the friends I lost, but it's why I want to go back to Norway," he replied, and then he completed his story.

"During May 1940, we moved to Mo i Rana from Fossbakken to stop Nazi reinforcements advancing north. Several hundred German troops had been moved by coastal steamer from Trondheim to a port near Mo i Rana, and they were receiving artillery and air support. We were no match for them. There were casualties, and eventually orders were given to retreat to Bodo. Whenever we came to a bridge, we would blow it up and control the high ground to shoot at the Germans until they brought up reinforcements. Sometimes they sent soldiers on bicycles so that, when we shot at them, they knew where we were and called in artillery and air support to attack us. Fortunately, I survived and was shipped out of Bodo by troopship at the beginning of June, the same time as the Dunkirk evacuation. Luckily, the port of Bodo was accessible to naval ships and bad weather kept the Luftwaffe on the ground."

It was a fascinating story and Jean-Louise was proud of her father's contribution. Tracing his war route was the main reason for the visit, but we also planned to do some sightseeing, and I had packed my binoculars in the hope of a little birdwatching although Jean-Louise had asked me not to wander off and abandon her father.

The following day we started our adventures by driving to Newcastle to catch the ferry to Bergen. We were not sure what to expect.

(Jean-Louise, June 1970) "Well, I'm looking forward to a fortnight in Norway. I hope my father and husband will get along since they've never been together for such a long period of time. John's supposed to look after him, and I've reminded him about my father's chain-smoking, and that he'll need to smoke in the car during the long journeys. I've told John he can do some birdwatching, but his top priority is looking after my father.

"I haven't seen much of John's mother since we married, although when she does call by, it's like a whirlwind of activity. She wants everything explained and usually has a list of things she wants to do and needs my help in accomplishing. I'm usually exhausted by the time she leaves. I plan to attend her wedding.

"It's worthy of note that most of our friends are my friends. John never seems to become close to people; he's happy on his own and this maybe because of how he grew up. He talks about his associates at work, but I rarely meet them.

"I never realised that my father was involved in so much fighting, although I knew he lost some friends during the war, which was why he was motivated to return to a career

in engineering. Because his job was grinding engine parts for battleships, he was exempt from serving in the army.

"Harold Wilson's surprise defeat in the general election was deeply disappointing. He tried hard to save Britain economically and I don't think it was right that he was voted out of office. For the first time in a general election, I could vote.

"I have kept James away from our house and he now maintains my mini-van at school during lunch times. I always appreciate his help and consider him a friend and work colleague.

"Owning a pet kitten has long been a dream of mine, but my parents would never allow one in the house, so I'm glad that's now changed. Treacle is a fluffy bundle of joy, and John plays with her almost as much as I do. Our neighbours look after her while we're away."

"My next ambition is to move house. We'll see how willing my husband is to relocate when he returns from our holidays. Also, I need to spend more time looking after my father, now he's retired."

Skylark: This is a brown, rather dull-looking bird, slightly smaller than a starling (16 to18cm/6 inches long). These birds are migratory, but they do not move long distances between seasons. Their plumage is mainly brown, streaked with black above and buff-white below, and they have a short, blunt crest on the head that is raised when the bird is excited or alarmed. In flight, it displays a short tail and small, broad wings, both edged in white. Its preferred habitat is open farmland and heath. It is well known for its rich, sustained song, which can last for 2 or 3 minutes and which is delivered by the male while hovering at heights of 165 to 300 feet (50 to 90 metres) above the ground. Skylark numbers have declined dramatically during recent years, due mainly to changes in farming practices.

In North America, efforts to introduce the skylark have generally been unsuccessful, but it has become resident on the southern tip of Vancouver Island in British Columbia. It is also found at the higher elevations on some of the Hawaiian Islands where it was introduced during the late 1860s.

27

A Bird That Walks Under Water

We checked in well ahead of the sailing time, ate a late lunch and boarded the ferry for an evening departure. Most of our personal belongings were left in the car. The ferry maintained a leisurely speed and was expected to arrive in Bergen the following afternoon. The crossing at first was gentle and the bunk beds comfortable. After eating a snack, we retired for a good night's rest and were greeted in the morning by a glimmering green sea watched over by a dark, threatening sky.

By the time we were in sight of Norway, the weather had deteriorated, as if to welcome us to the country's rugged and menacing landscape. There was driving rain, a bitter wind, rough seas and swirling mist ahead that obscured most of Bergen, sparing only the outlines of wooden houses along the waterfront, adorned in a palette of reds, oranges, blues and white, against a background of grey. The towering emerald green forests beyond the city were shrouded in a silvery grey cloud, and large, belligerent herring gulls scavenged and patrolled alongside our ferry boat as they were pounded by the wind. I invited Jean-Louise onto the deck, but she chose to stay in the warmth of the passenger cabin, and smoke with her father.

Our first overnight stay was inland at a hotel located in Voss, a town bombed by the Luftwaffe during April 1940, two weeks after Germany invaded Norway. It was difficult to believe that 30 years before our visit the town centre had been destroyed in retaliation for its occupants resisting the German army, and that Bergen had fallen on the first day of the Nazi invasion.

Now it was a picturesque, quiet community, nestled among green fields near two calm blue lakes, and surrounded by mountains and fjords. The following morning, the weather had improved and we ate our first Norwegian meal consisting of rye flat bread (called "lefse") served with pickled herring, smoked salmon, fermented trout and "brunost" (brown cheese). Jean-Louise's father was appalled, as he preferred porridge, eggs and bacon for breakfast. I spoke with the waiter who nodded his understanding and disappeared into the kitchen. A few minutes later, he returned with a bowl of porridge, two poached eggs on toast and a broad, beaming smile. Jean-Louise's father was delighted and Jean-Louise thanked me for my intervention.

This was the beginning of a daily routine. At each hotel, I ordered a special breakfast for my father-in-law, one that consisted of food he could recognise. It soon expanded into a second request, made practical by my foresight to bring a Thermos flask with me. Each morning I asked for it to be filled with hot tea for our day's drive. For lunch, we typically stopped and purchased bread, cold cuts, fruit and tomatoes, and for dinner, most hotels served fish that Jean-Louise's father could identify, the only condition being that it was served without its head.

Another challenge arose on the way to Dombas, some 225 miles (360 km) away. Jean-Louise's father continued to chain-smoke and was joined by his daughter who enjoyed the occasional cigarette. The smell in the car was so bad and the smoke so thick that I looked forward to the bathroom stops and breaks that permitted me to leave the car. However, there was much to observe on the way, and when the scenery became less interesting, Jean-Louise would read, while her father fell asleep.

Four days after our ferry docked in Bergen, we had driven 500 miles (800 km) to the north-east and arrived in a town called Steinkjer. This is where Jean-Louise's father suddenly became very attentive. He told us this was as far south as his comrades had reached in their attempt to delay the German advance from Trondheim, about 75 miles (120 km) from where we were. He believed that 80 percent of the town was destroyed by the Luftwaffe during its attack on the British forward base. By the time of our arrival, it had become a picturesque municipality along the edge of the Trondheim fjord, surrounded by gently sloping fields, undulating hills and a dense spruce forest covering the higher elevations.

The battle involving Jean-Louise's father had taken place many miles to the north as part of the Allied strategy to stop the German advance at the narrowest part of the country, and force the Nazis to either withdraw or cross the border into Sweden, thereby bringing that country into the war. The plan did not work because the Germans were far better equipped and had easily pushed aside the Norwegian and Allied opposition.

Driving north, we stopped for a night in the enchanting village of Mosjoen on the banks of a fjord. Here the British and Norwegian troops had fought alongside each other but had ultimately been forced to withdraw. The British forces were evacuated by ship along the coast to Bodo, while the Norwegians travelled on foot across the inhospitable mountain terrain.

Eventually we arrived in the small village of Korgen, about 30 miles (50 km) north of Mosjoen, and close to Mo i Rana, a few miles ahead of us. We were enjoying lunch on the grassy banks of the River Rossaga when a Norwegian family overheard us, and a man spoke to Jean-Louise in heavily accented English.

"Where are you from? Is this your first time in Norway?"

Jean-Louise answered that we were British, and that it was her first trip to Norway. She added: "We're here celebrating my father's retirement by returning to where he fought in the war as a Scots Guard. He wants us to take him as far north as Bodo."

The Norwegian looked at Jean-Louise's father with admiration and as if he had seen an apparition.

"You mean your father was here at the time of the German invasion? I was a teenager then, but I remember the fighting and bombing. We owe a great deal to the Scots Guards for helping us."

He hesitated for a moment, and then continued: "My family would be privileged if you would join us for dinner this evening. We live close by in a village called Bjerka."

Jean-Louise looked at me, silently asking if we could accept the invitation. It seemed genuine, and I could not think of a good reason to decline; it is not often that people invite you to their home while you are on holiday.

"It's not that far to Mo i Rana and people in Norway don't eat until late in the evening," I told her. "We can check in at the hotel and then return for dinner."

Jean-Louise accepted the invitation with grateful thanks.

That evening, a few minutes after six, we found ourselves at the home of our Norwegian hosts, where we were served a dinner of poached cod, carrots with swede and boiled potatoes, followed by apple cake. Jean-Louise's father only nibbled at his food despite knowing what he was being served.

Our companions spoke very little English, so it was left to the man we met by the river to lead the conversation. We told him about our itinerary, where we lived in Britain and how we planned to drive to Bodo to catch the ferry back to Bergen. He lavished praise on Jean-Louise's father and recalled his own experiences.

"Back then I lived in Mo i Rana. The Luftwaffe destroyed our town and my family moved here. Once Norway surrendered, we were required to support Hitler and show loyalty to the German flag. It was difficult. Some of my friends joined the German SS, but most refused to cooperate. While you are in Mo i Rana, you should visit the small churchyard; it has the graves of several Scots Guards."

Jean-Louise's father was deeply moved by the attention he received and graciously acknowledged the recognition, and said he would visit the church. He also said he regretted that the Scots Guards had not been able to do more, and he praised the Norwegian soldiers for their bravery in travelling through inhospitable terrain. Reference was made to the terrible weather that spring, and how the Scots Guards had stayed close to the road because of the deep snow and their lack of skis.

It was a very special evening for us. Here was a family thanking Jean-Louise's father for risking his life in the service of their country. They did not need to thank him, but they chose to.

As we were leaving, our host asked if we knew that we would be travelling on the "Blood Road" once we passed Rognan on the way to Bodo. We expressed our ignorance and asked him: "What's that?"

We were told, "During the German occupation, about 30,000 prisoners of war were moved to this part of Norway. They were mainly Russians, Poles and Serbs, and thousands of them died. They were forced to build new roads and railways under awful conditions. They were underfed, given inadequate clothing and treated brutally by their guards. You'll be travelling along one of the roads they built."

* * *

Earlier in the day, Jean-Louise's father had become very excited as we neared Mo i Rana. He asked me to stop when he realised where he was. It was the place his fighting had begun during the war.

"This is the road we guarded," he declared. "The Norwegians retreated over the mountains from Mosjoen to Mo i Rana, and we were supposed to keep the road open for them. Then suddenly the Germans arrived; they came from over there," (he pointed towards the mountain and continued): "There's a fjord on the other side of those mountains where steam ships and sea planes had brought them. That's when the combat began."

Despite the day being very cold, he wandered up a short trail to look back and gaze at his surroundings. We followed him and recognised how emotional it was for him to remember his wartime exploits.

"They came at us from that direction," he said, pointing to a small river. "Our backs were to the mountain and we used the forest for cover. They attacked during the afternoon. One group crossed the river on our eastern side, to charge our left flank, and where the river is widest on the west, German paratroopers were dropped to attack us. The fight continued into the night because of the Arctic daylight. We were given orders early in the morning to evacuate to Mo i Rana, and a day later we abandoned the town and retreated to Bodo."

He sat on a rock staring around him, looking upset and probably experiencing survivor guilt. We walked away to give him space and allow him time to recall his friends and the fighting.

* * *

The morning after our dinner with the Norwegian family, we visited the church in Mo i Rana to inspect the graves of the fallen Scots Guards. Jean-Louise's father thought he recognised the names on two of the gravestones.

Our last day of driving was the excursion to Bodo. We crossed into the Arctic Circle and stopped to allow Jean-Louise's father time to gaze at an area where he had been chased by the German soldiers. He was astonished at how much the area had changed, and on this occasion he was able to enjoy the scenery. The people in the tourist centre were as pleased to greet an ex-Scots Guard as the Norwegian family who had invited us to dinner, and they presented him with a "Polar Certificate" which they said gave him the freedom of the Arctic Circle.

Finally, we reached Bodo, the port from where he had been evacuated, and which was the final purpose of his visit. Afterwards we took him to watch the midnight sun settle on the horizon, and then immediately rise again. A long way to the north was situated the village of Fossbakken, but we did not have time to drive that far.

Soon it was time to catch the Hurtigroten coastal steamer back to Bergen, and I drove the car to the quayside for loading onto the ship. The steamer was no cruise liner; it was a working boat, ferrying people and cargo to and from a dozen or so ports along the Norwegian coast. We watched as my car was winched upwards, swung across the forward area, and then slowly lowered onto the deck, where it was secured by ropes and chains for the journey. The Cortina was the only vehicle on board, and I watched with some alarm during the journey as dripping boxes of salted cod were swung over its vinyl roof and lowered onto the deck.

The ferry took us south among some breath-taking scenery. We entered long, spectacular fjords, passed soaring mountains of granite rising vertically out of the water, and chugged slowly past silver waterfalls and red farmhouses clinging to bluffs overlooking the water. I was able to do some birdwatching, spotting auks, kittiwakes, eider ducks, puffins and a white-tailed sea eagle.

During the road trip, I had spotted a dipper (sometimes called the white-throated dipper and known as a "fossekal" in Norway), a delightfully small, rotund bird that inhabits the rocky banks of fast-running, freshwater streams. I saw it for only a few seconds, and it was unclear whether the bird flew out of sight or simply submerged itself in the turbulent waters, but it disappeared before I had time to tell Jean-Louise. It is the national bird of Norway and has a unique ability to survive in the barren landscape of that country, and it can fly and swim simultaneously to hunt its prey under water. The little brown and black bird, with a white throat and white upper breast, reminded me of the one I had seen on the River Devon, between Dollar and Tillicoultry, during our holiday in Scotland. It exemplified the determination to survive that Jean-Louise's father and colleagues had shown during their fight to protect Norway.

The weather remained mainly cold, so that viewing on deck was sensible only when there was something exceptional to be seen. We were challenged by the sport of chair-hugging engaged in by the other tourists on board, who were all Germans. Before dawn, they crept onto the deck, carrying towels, books and spare clothing to place on the chairs commanding the best views, and thereby laying claim to prime deck-side seating. Once so marked with their personal belongings, they believed the deckchairs to have been rendered out of bounds for use by anyone else. However, not to be outdone, sometimes I would rise even earlier to beat the Germans at their own game; at other times, I would remove their belongings and move the deckchair to another location. I thought it bizarre that, 25 years after fighting a war, we were now fighting over deckchairs.

Finally, we reached Bergen. The Cortina was lifted onto the wharf, and I was dismayed to see it was covered with fish spatter, which turned out to very sticky as well as very smelly. We quickly found somewhere to have it thoroughly washed, even though the rain had returned. It was our last day and a final opportunity to do some shopping, so when we discovered a market selling Norwegian knitwear, we spent our last remaining kroner.

We disembarked at Newcastle and drove back to Manchester, all the while talking about our adventures and what each of us would remember most from the trip. For Jean-Louise's father, it was overcoming his fears and returning to the place where he was almost killed during the war. Memories of the war were still vivid for many people and they had not forgotten the atrocities that they had witnessed. He thanked us for our company and said he would not have liked to have gone on his own. He had found it emotionally stressful to think of friends who had died in front of him 30 years earlier.

Jean-Louise's memories were of the glacial landscape and the opportunities to take pictures of drumlins, cirques, eskers and moraines that she could use in her geography classes. I had obviously enjoyed the birdwatching and sightseeing, but the most important element was getting to know her father more closely. I had discovered that he was quiet and thoughtful and preferred time to himself. He could not be hurried, but he was always punctual.

Jean-Louise appreciated my willingness to take care of him, and knowing my temperament, said she admired my patience, my willingness to help whenever difficulties arose and putting up with his heavy smoking, and I think my efforts deepened her respect for me. It was the future care of her father that now concerned her. As an only child, she knew it was her responsibility to look after him, but she was not sure how to do that. For me now, the holiday was over, I needed to reengage with my responsibilities in Ford of Britain's headquarters. I also expected to hear more from Jean-Louise about moving to a larger home.

(Jean-Louise, July 1970) "I've discovered so much about my father that I didn't know. Norway was the first time he and I went on holiday together, and I never realised how close he'd come to being killed. It was amazingly kind of the Norwegian family to invite us into their home like that. Thanks to them, he feels proud of what he did.

"John took good care of him and was very patient. There were no arguments, no falling out and no selfish birdwatching. Now I need to decide how best to look after him in retirement. He's healthy enough, despite his smoking, although he's a bit of a hypochondriac. He can be obstinate as well, and so far he says he won't leave Manchester. Maybe it's up to John and me to move closer to him.

"I enjoyed the time away, although the sea on the return journey to Newcastle was rough. John claims he was sea-sick, but I think it was the bottle of Bols schnapps he drank with a Dutchman in the ship's bar. Beating on the roof of the cabin from the upper bunk scared me in the middle of the night.

"Our hobbies continue to fit with each other's interests, and while I'm busy researching geography, John's either watching birds or hacking away at pieces of rock.

"Now that we're home and John's back at work, I've several weeks before resuming teaching for my fourth year. Maybe I should move schools. On the other hand, John and I possibly should first find a new home. I'm about to spend time with my father in Manchester, and will go with John to his mother's wedding later this month."

(European) Dipper: It is a short-tailed, plump, small bird about 18cm/ 7 inches long, and is unique for its ability to hunt and feed under fresh water. It jumps or dives into shallow streams, where it can walk and fly to hunt its prey. In order to do this, it uses its wings to push downward against the currents while it holds onto stones with its feet. The birds eat aquatic insects, fish eggs and small fish. Although they do not possess webbed feet, they are physically adapted for life under water by having well-developed wing muscles, eyes that function under water, blood that stores large amounts of oxygen and specialised flaps over their nostrils to prevent water entering. Usually they dive from a rock or simply walk into the water. The species has a distinctive white throat and white breast that contrasts with its dark brown/black plumage over the remainder of its body. The bird flies rapidly and

straight, making a whirring sound, or it glides while emitting a shrill "zil, zil, zil" call. Approximately 10,000 to 20,000 pairs breed in Britain, mainly in Scotland.

There is an American dipper, mainly living in the mountainous areas of the western North America, and it is a dark-black colour all over. It does not migrate, but if its food source freezes over it will move to a larger expanse of available water.

28

Swifts Flying High

ON OUR RETURN from Norway, events directed Jean-Louise's attention towards the health and comfort of her father. A labour dispute broke out on the docks, causing her to travel to Manchester to be sure that her father had enough to eat. Nearly 50,000 dock workers stopped work on 15th July 1970 to pursue a substantial pay raise; major ports were idle, meat prices soared and supplies of many foodstuffs were interrupted. Fortunately, her father had a good store of groceries, and Jean-Louise's presence was not needed. The government eventually declared a state of emergency on the docks, and troops were deployed to replace striking workers.

At home, Jean-Louise used her newly acquired Cordon Bleu cooking skills to change our menu from difficult-to-find New Zealand lamb to locally produced pork, and replace our lemon soufflé (dessert) with blackcurrant syllabub. Normal food supplies were re-established in early August after the dock workers accepted of a 7 percent pay raise.

Later in the month, we attended my mother's wedding. It was a happy occasion, and the newly-weds left for a four-month world cruise, having arranged for my siblings to be looked after by my maternal grandmother. On the way home, Jean-Louise confronted me with a life-altering proposal.

"I'm very worried about my father. He's adamant that he won't leave Manchester and says he'll move into a retirement home if he has to."

I thought that was the end of the conversation, but I was mistaken.

"I think we should live closer to him," she continued, "and I wonder if you'd be willing to leave Essex."

It was a startling proposition and not a good time for me to quit my job. The British economy was stressed, unemployment was starting to rise, albeit from a low level, and competition for jobs had increased because more people were entering the labour market.

"That seems rather extreme," I said. "I'd need to find a new employer, sell our home and look for somewhere else to live. Isn't there someone living near your father who can look after him?"

I sensed that her mind was made up. "Possibly," she replied, "but I don't like being so far away. Couldn't you find work in Ford at Halewood?"

"I don't think Halewood is an option. It's a manufacturing location and the jobs there don't fit with my career. I'd need to find a job outside Ford."

"Would you be willing to try? I know it's an enormous favour, but it would make me very happy." She understood what she was asking of me.

We agreed that my looking for another job did not mean I would find one, and therefore we might not be able to move, so it was with great apprehension that I began my search. Also, I disliked the thought of leaving my current employer. The company was successful, I enjoyed my work, there was a good career ahead of me and new international opportunities were opening up in Ford of Europe that had headquartered itself in Brentwood. On the other hand, I knew that some of Ford's vehicle manufacturing was shifting out of Britain across the North Sea to other parts of Europe, and capital investment from the parent company had been diverted to locations other than Britain. It was well known that the platform for the Mark 111 Cortina would be used in West Germany for the Taunus car, and the Granada, planned as the replacement for the Zodiac/Zephyr, was to be assembled on the continent as well as in Dagenham. Dearborn had announced that its new European automatic transmission plant was to be built in Bordeaux, France and not in Britain.

I thought that transferring elsewhere in the motor industry was unwise. Conditions were chaotic at British Leyland as it battled with inter-union rivalries, restrictive work practices and never-ending wage demands, and Chrysler UK (formerly Rootes), was in similar disarray. Also, workers in a major car components firm had gone on strike during the previous month, and a supplier of vehicle plate-glass was experiencing a stoppage by 8,000 of its workers.

Finally, I did not want to approach firms that were members of the Ford Salary Survey group and risk my employer finding out that I was looking for a job elsewhere. Therefore, it was under these rather restrictive conditions that I began my search.

The following Sunday, I studied the job opportunities advertised in the *Sunday Times* newspaper.

"Is there anything of interest?" asked a curious Jean-Louise.

"Nothing," I told her, "but I'll keep looking, and I'll search in other publications too."

I did as I had promised, but there seemed to be very few opportunities available. I heard about a Merseyside company in the Wirral that did not advertise its vacancies, but it had a good reputation as an employer, so I wrote to it. An officer of the firm replied that it was not recruiting at the present time but my paperwork would be held on file. I never heard from the organisation again.

I received a more serious response from an American-owned cereal manufacturer with a plant located in Trafford Park, only 30 minutes' drive from the home of Jean-Louise's father. I was not sure that the opportunity made sense for me, but I applied nonetheless and was called for an interview during which my suspicions were confirmed. The interviewers revealed that the job was primarily administrative and involved only employee welfare. It would pay less than I earned at Ford and there were limited career opportunities. I decided that the company was acceptable, but not the job, and a few days later I was relieved to receive a letter telling me that the firm had appointed someone who worked locally in the Manchester area.

By the end of the year, Jean-Louise had reconsidered and decided to manage her father's welfare from a distance while having him spend more time with us. The idea of our moving to a larger home was resurrected.

Meanwhile, the government was acting on its electoral promises. The European Economic Community approved Britain's latest application to become a member, but with the proviso that it must first negotiate terms satisfactory to all current participants, especially those concerning financial contributions and involvement in the Common Agricultural Policy. At the same time, the Community began parallel negotiations with Denmark, Ireland and Norway.

* * *

I continued as a Staff Policies Analyst during the period of my job search. One of my more unusual duties was to help Ford of Britain prepare for the decimalisation of Britain's currency that would occur on 15th February 1971. The former currency of pounds, shillings and pence would be replaced by pounds and new pence, and there was a host of Ford of Britain personnel policies that had to be altered because of the switch in currency. In fact, the changes involved more than just a currency conversion, as each policy had to be examined to make sure it remained competitive with other firms.

Jean-Louise's worries about the welfare of her father were highlighted once more when power-plant workers implemented a work-to-rule, causing periodic electricity black-outs lasting two to three hours. Hospitals and other critical organisations used back-up power generators, while industries, shops and homes used batteries, candles and whatever else they could find. Enterprising butchers made candles out of string covered in lard, and a black-market in European candles emerged. Jean-Louise's father stayed at home and a neighbour supplied him with torches (flashlights). We sat and talked in our bungalow during the dark, and we drank hot chocolate and Bovril courtesy of the paraffin primus stove that had survived my many visits to Spurn Point Bird Observatory. Fortunately, the industrial action was called off after only a week because of general public criticism, but it was clear once again that the comforts of home life were vulnerable to interference from labour militancy.

We spent Christmas in Pilgrim's Hatch and Jean-Louise's father stayed with us. The house was seasonally decorated, we prepared turkey and trifle, listened to the Queen's Speech, watched television and showed each other the slides we took during our tour of Norway.

Adjusting to the new coinage system was straightforward, as the halfpenny, half-crown (two and a half shillings) and ten-shilling note had already been taken out of circulation. The threepenny coin was to cease being legal tender at the end of August 1971, but the sixpenny piece (valued at 2.5 new pence) would be kept in circulation until June 1980. There were few problems, but suspicions existed that some shops were using decimalisation to round up their prices and the government had used the change-over to cover up the effects of sterling devaluation.

The next industrial dispute to affect our life at home came from the postal workers, who demanded a 15 to 20 percent wage increase and went on strike on 20th January 1971. They stayed out for seven weeks. Important correspondence, such as insurance premiums and utility bills, somehow found their way to our letterbox, thanks largely to private postal services, but most personal correspondence never arrived. The government took a hard line, and the union ultimately ran out of funds. Without financial support, the postmen went back to work, without major concessions, on 8th March 1971.

* * *

Meanwhile, Ford's Industrial Relations Staff had begun its annual round of wage negotiations. The unions resumed their demands for pay parity with Midland car workers, now that they had the freedom to negotiate without any statutory wage increase limit. In response to their claim for a basic £10 a week raise, Ford offered £2, arguing that the company was unwilling to behave like the rest of the British motor industry and risk financial ruin. This time the workforce supported its unions, and a nine-week official stoppage began on 1st February 1971.

A stubborn Henry Ford declined to become involved, but he warned that he would no longer approve new investments in Britain unless the country remedied its industrial relations practices. The Prime Minister assured him that the government's plan to bring order to collective bargaining through its Industrial Relations Bill would resolve the situation. Eventually, as the cost of strike pay escalated, the General Secretaries of the two main unions (engineers and transport workers) negotiated a settlement with the company of £8 a week, spread over two years. The first instalment was an average raise of 24 percent, the second raise gave a further 10 percent six months later, and the final payment was 6 percent in a year's time. Annual inflation at the time was still around 6 percent.

Jean-Louise expressed shock that Ford had agreed to settle at four times the award it had originally proposed.

"What's going on?" she asked me. "I don't understand what your firm's up to."

"It's what we have to do to get the men back to work," I admitted.

"No, that's not it," she countered. "Ford pays its workers so much less than British Leyland, but puts up with a lengthy strike over pay, only to have the men go back to work after a huge settlement. They'd have avoided the loss in production if they had made a more sensible offer in the first place. It doesn't make sense."

I did not have a good answer so decided not to argue. Instead, I told her that my office had announced the same percentage increases for salaried staff, so my salary would rise too.

* * *

The top priority for the Conservative government was the introduction of its Industrial Relations Bill to restrict the powers of trade unions, and the House of Commons approved the Bill as the Industrial Relations Act. Its proposed regulations were condemned by the trade unions who promised to fight them using a strategy of civil disobedience if they were implemented. The law required unions to register for legal protection, made collective agreements legally enforceable, outlawed closed shops, required secret ballots before industrial action could be taken, created a Court to oversee industrial activity and avoid harmful strikes, and it also imposed penalties on unions and their members for non-compliance. Before the law was passed, the unions engaged nationally in a "Kill the Bill" campaign. James asked Jean-Louise to participate, but she declined because it interfered with her teaching, and ultimately the protests had little effect on the passage of the law.

James was no longer a regular visitor to our house, now that his home was in the opposite direction to the school, but occasionally I saw him at "The Rose" pub. He was busy with union business as his organisation adapted to dealing with the new Secretary of State for Education, Margaret Thatcher. She was accused of not consulting with the union and came under fierce criticism when the government announced the abolishment of free milk for children aged 7 to 11 years.

Our savings were sustained by my general salary awards although annual inflation was beginning to take off and quickly rose to near 9 percent. We had funds available for entertainment, and watched newly released films like *Love Story, Cromwell* and *Ryan's Daughter,* and we attended theatres in London to see musicals like *Oh! Calcutta* and *Godspell*, as well as the new farce, *No Sex Please, We're British.* We also decided that we could afford an overseas holiday to Italy during August 1971. More and more people were choosing holidays overseas, and the £50 annual spending limit had been abolished, making foreign travel more attractive.

There was one final piece of positive news before we left for our summer holiday. My manager called me into his office late one afternoon.

"You may not know," he began, "but your supervisor has accepted a new position in Ford of Europe. I want you to replace him at the start of September 1971. There's a promotional increase, and you'll receive a management roll lease car." (This was a company vehicle that was also available for private use, with a monthly payment to cover the cost of insurance and Road Tax.)

"Will you accept?" he added.

I was delighted; I had not expected a promotion so quickly.

"Yes," I replied enthusiastically, "but first may I talk with my wife?"

The condition was accepted.

"What's not to like?" was Jean-Louise's reaction. "You stay close to home, you know the work, you like your staff, there's another pay raise <u>and</u> you qualify for a company lease car! If we're going to stay in Essex, it's about time we started to look for a new house because of all your salary increases."

The following day, my boss announced the promotion, and I received the congratulations of my colleagues.

It was then time to prepare for our two-week holiday in San Remo on the Citta dei Fiori in Italy. Our flight took us to Genoa, from where we were taken by bus to our hotel. We spent the time relaxing, eating and enjoying the abundance of flowers typical of the region, but birdwatching was not on my agenda since I had heard that only house sparrows frequented this part of Italy. Ahead of me lay the challenges of becoming a supervisor and beginning the search for a new home, but for the time being I was going to rest and enjoy the Italian sunshine, take a glass of Italian Vermentino and "salute".

(Jean-Louise, July 1971) "I'm proud that John's being promoted to a manager position after only five years with Ford. With his latest pay increase and the money from selling the Cortina (I want to keep the yellow mini-van), we should be able to afford a larger home and I'm ready to start a family. I remain uneasy that we didn't relocate to Manchester but I have an aunt and neighbours who are keeping an eye on my father.

The plan seems to be working, but he remains my number one responsibility.

"Education is an important profession, but teaching is very demanding and exhausting. Sometimes, there's an overwhelming amount of work, and I'm thinking of going part-time.

"John's birdwatching has suffered during the past year. There's really nowhere nearby for him to see new species, and we've been so busy with work and our families that his hobby has taken a back seat. With a promotion, I've told him that he's 'flying high', like the 'big swallows' I used to see above tall buildings in Manchester. He tells me these are swifts that spend most of their life airborne. He says they even mate and sleep while flying. I find that hard to believe.

"James remains a good friend and is looking forward to becoming a father since his wife became pregnant shortly after they moved to Essex. He's the local representative for the National Union of Teachers, and I think he'd like me to become more involved.

"Italy is a place I've never visited, and without the currency controls we should enjoy a peaceful holiday. John tells me he wants time to read up on how to be a successful supervisor, and while we're gone our neighbours will take care of Treacle.

"I think it's going to be an interesting time for the Conservative government, as they seem already deep in conflict with the unions. We're experiencing the consequences at home, such as sitting in the dark without electric power, missing our postman for several weeks and worrying about fresh food supplies."

Swift: This was historically known as "The Devil's Bird", probably because of its high-pitched, screaming call. It is a medium-sized (16 cm/6 inches long), sooty-brown bird, known especially for its aerial acrobatics. It is typically seen on the wing (its wing-span is approximately 48 cm/18 in), swooping and diving high above buildings. It has long, arrow-like wings and a short, forked tail. A summer visitor to Britain from central Africa, it arrives when the weather is warm and there are abundant flying insects on which it feeds. There are about 85,000 breeding pairs in Britain, although the population is in decline because of loss of nesting sites. It feeds, drinks and preens itself in flight, and it is the only species of bird that mates on the wing. It also sleeps in flight, often at a height of around 10,000 feet (3,000 meters), where it shuts down half its brain, continually corrects its flight path for wind drift and wakes up in the place where it fell asleep.

Four types of swift are resident in North America. The chimney swift is the most common in the east, and the white-throated, Vaux's and black swifts in the west.

29

The Long-Distance Tern

I SOON ACCUSTOMED MYSELF to delegating work to others. Content-wise I knew what was needed, and once I overcame my fear of ceding control, it was easy to dictate outcomes, timelines and expectations to my subordinates. However, there was controversy. Politely, my staff accused me of micro-management, establishing unrealistic goals and altering requirements half-way through assignments. At first, I denied the allegations but after listening more carefully, I decided to provide additional information to clarify my requests. Jean-Louise sympathised with me while suggesting that maybe my expectations were too high.

It was usual for newly promoted supervisors to keep pet projects that they had been assigned in their prior position, and I was no exception. I retained responsibility for the Ford Airline Group, which allowed me to take time out of the office to visit Stansted. It was a busy period, as the Civil Aviation Act of 1971 had prompted a major reorganisation of the British Overseas Airways Corporation (BOAC) and British European Airways (BEA), which were to be integrated and become British Airways. Pilots' pay rates were to be renegotiated, and it was expected that these would be related to the types of aircraft flown. However, the Chief Pilot at Ford wanted his pilots to be paid on the basis of what aircraft they were capable of flying, and not on the model of aeroplane they were actually flying.

My boss processed the promotional increase which, with recent adjustments, resulted in my income having risen by 35 percent during a five-month period. The additional spending power was appreciated since it was well ahead of annual price inflation that was nudging up towards 10 percent and showed no signs of slowing down. We also benefitted from government tax cuts and the government's efforts to hold down mortgage interest rates. Thus, I was unable to argue against taking on a higher mortgage to purchase a new home, and Jean-Louise became increasingly impatient to begin the search. Immediately on appointment, I had ordered a Cortina Mark III lease car and was allocated a vehicle already built because of quality defects that early production of this model had encountered.

My superiors decided that, to strengthen my decision-making skills, I should attend a course that taught methods of gathering and organising data, looking at the causes of problems, conducting decision analyses, and identifying potential problems that might arise during implementation of the decision. The course was delivered in the Brentwood headquarters building during late September 1971, and while I found it useful, I realised that intuitively I had adopted most of the taught skills during my earlier years at Ford.

One day Chris surprised me by showing up in my office to congratulate me on my promotion. He had been visiting his friends in Graduate Recruitment, and they had mentioned my appointment. The purpose of his visit was to attend a sales conference that was preparing all sales zone managers for the relaunch of the Cortina Mark III, because initial problems that had plagued early production had been corrected.

It was wonderful to see him again. I knew he was still living in Northern Ireland, and he surprised me by announcing that he was married to a woman called Angela. They had met at a dance shortly after his arrival in Belfast, and married 18 months later. The wedding had been restricted to family because of the Irish "troubles", but he said we were welcome to visit them at any time. I talked to Jean-Louise about the invitation that evening.

We decided to accept and not to worry about potential violence in Belfast, knowing that Chris and Angela lived outside the city. We chose to travel during the last week in October because Jean-Louise would not be teaching, as it is the period when schools in Britain are closed to permit pupils to harvest potatoes before the frosts arrive. With modern farm mechanisation, the need for the holiday has become outdated, but the tradition continues.

We caught the ferry from Liverpool to Belfast, where we were met by Chris who drove us to his home without incident. He introduced us to Angela, an attractive, petite, outgoing person who entertained us with a wonderful sense of humour and spoke with a thick Ulster accent. We caught up with each other's news and enjoyed several sightseeing trips, although we stayed well away from the city. We also avoided the border with the Republic of Ireland since earlier in the month the British Army had begun demolishing roads for security purposes.

One of the big political decisions that took place during our visit was a House of Commons vote approving Britain's entry to the European Economic Community on 1st January 1973. After 15 months of negotiations, the Conservative government considered the terms to be acceptable.

"Well, it seems we're in," Chris announced over breakfast, as we prepared for a day's outing to Portaferry and Strangford Lough.

"Not quite," I replied. "Membership is still 14 months away, and the Labour Party has threatened to renegotiate the terms if re-elected. There's also talk of a referendum for the people to decide whether to stay in or pull out."

We spent the rest of the day sailing on Strangford Lough. Our efforts to catch herring and mackerel were unsuccessful, probably because it was a little too late in the season, at least for the latter. Jean-Louise and I were amazed by the geography of the lake. It was a large, shallow sea inlet, about 16 miles (25 km) long, 4 miles (6 km) wide and about 30 feet (10 m) deep, and it was surrounded by the remnants of the last ice-age in the form of drumlins (egg-shaped hills), some of which were partly submerged and formed small islands in the lough.

The lough was an important autumn destination for migrating wading and sea birds, so I was delighted to have an opportunity for some birdwatching, even though I had not brought my binoculars. There were flocks of migrating light-bellied Brent geese and wigeons, and shore birds such as oystercatchers, knots and redshanks. Unfortunately, it was too late in the year to see many of the breeding species, such as the Arctic, Sandwich and common terns, although Strangford Lough is one of the more important nesting sites for these birds in Britain. The Arctic terns had already left for their autumn migration to Australia, and the common and Sandwich terns had departed for their winter homes in the southern hemisphere. Previously, I had seen all three species at Spurn Point Bird Observatory, but this was the first time I had witnessed their nesting sites. The chance to do some birdwatching gave me feelings of freedom and accomplishment.

* * *

Once back home in Pilgrims Hatch, Jean-Louise and I began a search of nearby towns and villages to identify the preferred location for our new home. First, we contacted the mortgage company to find out how big a mortgage they might approve. Next, we compared our must-have and nice-to-have lists and found them surprisingly similar. There was no conflict as we agreed that our ideal home had to have been built recently, be detached, have four bedrooms and be located in a nice neighbourhood close to shopping facilities. The one important aspect I overlooked was school amenities, which caused Jean-Louise to remind me that one day we might have children, while she failed to consider the requirement for a reasonably sized garden. As for price, she was conservative and wanted us to purchase something that we could readily afford, whereas I was willing to stretch our finances to purchase the ideal home.

During late November 1971, we thought we had discovered the perfect house. It was in a village called Highwood, about 10 miles (16 km) north of where we lived. We made an offer to the agents, and it was accepted by the seller, but a few days later we were "gazumped". We were both unfamiliar with this term for something that happens when a seller accepts an offer from one buyer, then chooses a higher offer from an alternative buyer, and subsequently invites the original bidder to either increase his or her price or back out of the transaction. We were furious and completely disillusioned when we discovered that gazumping was apparently both widespread and legal. After accusing the estate agent of negligence, we heard that the other buyer had offered to pay in cash, whereas we would have had to seek a mortgage. We therefore withdrew from the transaction and continued our search.

Another house that we liked was a few miles to the east, and we took a second look at it during early January 1972, when Jean-Louise's father was staying with us. The house was almost new and had four bedrooms, a landscaped garden, an immaculately designed open-staircase and a marble fireplace in the front room.

The house had been given a name, and we asked during our second visit why the name had been chosen.

"We called it after the farm we once owned near here which burned down," was the response. "The farmhouse was an 18th century timber-framed building, but we found it cold, draughty and damp. No-one knew what caused the fire, and since we wanted to give up farming, we sold the land to Ford as part of its Dunton Technical Centre development. This house was then built with all the modern comforts that were not present in our old home, and we named it after the farm."

We liked the house very much, especially the central heating, so we made an offer, and at the end of January were told that it had been accepted. At first, the owners were worried that we were too young to afford the property, but the mortgage company assured them that the funds were available. The Pilgrims Hatch home was sold during March, and Jean-Louise and I moved into the new property at the start of May 1972. The sellers were building a new home nearby which caused the three month delay in completing our purchase.

The move was an opportunity to rid ourselves of belongings that we no longer needed. Out went several boxes of unwanted clothes, including my green anorak, the moth-eaten dove-grey, long-haired, merino wool cardigan and Jean-Louise's little yellow dress. Initially, she did not want to part with it, arguing it reminded her of so many wonderful times in the past. I said she was being too sentimental, as the dress had outlived its purpose, and she reluctantly agreed. Treacle moved with us and was given the run of our new, securely fenced back garden.

After the relocation, James became a regular visitor since our new house was on his commute route between his home and the school. He continued to help Jean-Louise with her mini-van, and he also assisted with some re-plastering of our downstairs ceilings. A group of friends was asked to help, and he checked in regularly to ensure that the work was being done to Jean-Louise's satisfaction.

* * **

Meanwhile, nationally the requirements of the Industrial Relations Act were under constant attack from the unions, as were the government's efforts to voluntarily limit the size of wage increases. Earlier in the year, on 9th January 1972, 280,000 coal miners went on strike and stayed out until the end of February. We were still living in Pilgrims Hatch and relied on coal to heat our home. Our supply of coal was quickly used up, and since the miners targeted supplies to power stations, there was a series of power cuts. Evening meals became either beans on toast if the power was on, or a cheese and pickle sandwich if not. We wore our warmest clothes and used candles for lighting, and Jean-Louise's father stayed with us until the strike was over.

Shortly after the miners went back to work, the train drivers began a work-to-rule to support their wage demands. Both passenger and freight services were disrupted. The government insisted on applying its legal 60-day cooling-off period and the secret ballot provisions to the train drivers, with miserable consequences. The compulsory ballot resulted in six out of seven drivers supporting the work-to-rule, and the cooling-off period was simply ignored as part of the trade unions' strategy of civil disobedience. Thankfully, there was no direct impact on Jean-Louise and me, other than having to drive on more congested roads.

Next it was the turn of Britain's dock workers, whose demands for increased job security in response to the use of shipping containers were being ignored. The national workforce had fallen by about a third, to around 42,000, and instead of addressing their grievances, the government was allowing port employers to implement new redundancies and move additional work off the docks. The dispute turned unpleasant when the dock workers tried to shut down several container yards, and the owners reacted during June 1972 by seeking Court injunctions.

We watched the worsening dispute on our television. At first, the Court decided to impose fines on the union, but the union argued that it had no power to stop secondary picketing. Consequently, the fines were quashed and instead the Court turned its attention to the pickets and they were told that, if they did not cease their actions, they would be arrested. They refused, and eventually five shop stewards were jailed in Pentonville on 21st July 1972.

The public outcry was instant. Mass demonstrations were organised to support the release of the so-called "Pentonville Five", and there was talk of a General Strike. Then suddenly the pickets were let out, which prompted the dock workers to walk off the job again, continuing to demand improved security of employment. Thousands of boxes of fruit and vegetables rotted on the docks, and ships heading for British ports were diverted to continental ones. The government declared a state of emergency and by mid-August the violence had become so severe and the arrests so numerous that the union called off the work stoppage and watched as the men trickled back to work.

At home, we ate tinned fruit and vegetables until we left for a holiday in Portugal's Algarve at the end of the first week in August. We thereby avoided the worst of the dispute and were relieved to learn that Jean-Louise's father had sufficient resources on hand for the duration. By the time we returned from holiday, the dock workers were back at work.

* * *

We stayed in Albufeira, an ancient Portuguese fishing village on the Atlantic coast, nestled between vertically rising sandstone cliffs. We spent most of our days strolling along the nearby sandy beach or walking the streets of the town, but there was little opportunity for birdwatching because we did not rent a car.

We mostly ate sardines or other fresh-caught fish that we bought in the local fish market and cooked ourselves, with Vino Verdi to drink. We enjoyed the evenings dancing and sampling the different wines at local nightclubs, and it was a time of high fashion. I wore rust-red, hip-hugging bell-bottom trousers with a fitted blue and lemon-yellow striped satin shirt, while Jean-Louise looked elegant in her halter-neck, patterned maxi-dress with a white shawl. My hair was long and groomed, whereas hers was styled, mid-length and shaggy.

* * *

As we returned home, another lingering labour dispute was intensifying. Nearly 300,000 building workers had by now joined a national pay strike that began during May 1972 with selective stoppages. The conflict had turned violent, as flying pickets shut down building sites, and employers accused pickets of preventing workers from working. In mid-September, an agreement was reached awarding wage increases averaging around 25 percent, but retaliation followed as certain employers built up dossiers of evidence to demonstrate in court that unlawful assembly and intimidation had taken place. For Jean-Louise and I, the dispute had no direct effect on our lives, except that we often drove past groups of pickets demonstrating outside building sites.

The disruption caused by this militancy and the resulting wage settlements pushed inflation up to an unacceptably high level, and the government decided to reverse its decision and introduce statutory wage controls. As a result of so many disputes, in late October, the government announced a 90-day pay and prices freeze, taking us back to the situation that had existed during the Labour government days, and which I always regarded as ineffective.

* * *

About the same time, a tragic event took place in my department at work. It was one of those incidents that all supervisors dread. On this particular day, the weather had turned very wet and my boss asked to borrow David, a former graduate trainee who had recently started work on my team, to collect some important documents from Dagenham. David was a valuable addition to my department and was always willing to do whatever was requested. He left for Dagenham under a drizzly grey sky.

It was around four o'clock in the afternoon when my manager returned looking very troubled, and asked me to be prepared for some bad news.

"I'm afraid David's been killed in a road accident," he reported, obviously upset. "An on-coming lorry hit his car when the driver lost control, braked and skidded across the road. David was killed instantly. I've talked to his parents and you need to tell your staff as soon as you can."

The news was devastating, and it made work suddenly seem unimportant. It was difficult to know how to react. I wanted to pretend that everything I had just been told was false but finally struggled to ask, "What do you want me to do?"

"Tell your staff what's happened and let them go home early. Be sensitive. There's not much anyone can do, but his parents have been told and the funeral is on Saturday in north Wales. I'm going to attend and you should be there if you can."

"I will," I immediately answered.

"Then let's travel together, and I'll arrange the rail tickets," he said as he disappeared.

Passing the distressing news on to David's colleagues was an unreal experience. Everyone was shocked and upset. No-one felt able to return to work. They talked about what had happened, and then passed on the news of the tragedy to people who had worked with David in other departments. There was a general feeling of disbelief and shock that a friend and close work associate had been lost. Meanwhile, as I gathered up his personal belongings to take with me to the funeral, I wandered around in a daze.

That evening, my mind was totally distracted. Nothing could stop me from thinking about the "what ifs"; for instance, if I had refused permission to my boss, David would still be alive. Jean-Louise was enormously sympathetic. She listened to what I told her, supported my grief and reassured me that it was not my fault. Even so, I experienced waves of guilt and irritation with myself. Everything had seemed to happen so suddenly that I was convinced there were other things I should be doing, but I did not know what they were. Jean-Louise tried to take my mind off my distress by telling me much more welcome news.

"Angela called today to say that she and Chris are moving to Essex. Chris has a new job in Sales, and they've bought a house in Braintree. They want us to visit as soon as we can."

She also told me that her best friend, the physics teacher, was pregnant—and she sounded a little envious of her friend's condition.

* * *

On the day of the funeral, the weather seemed to be out of sync with the reasons for our travel. It was a lovely sunny morning when my manager and I started the five-hour train journey to north Wales. Thoughts of David returned, and I remembered my last conversation with him. He had been looking forward to going home to see his girlfriend.

I felt awkward about being alone on the train with my boss for such a long period, and I worried over what we should talk about. It scared me to think that he would want to discuss David, but I need not have been concerned, as no mention was made of him.

My manager began the conversation as soon as we left Shenfield, talking about his family and their plans for while he was away. He asked about my wife and home life, and I told him how I had ended up at Ford; he laughed at the role Mr Welsh had played.

Eventually, we exhausted that topic, and I decided to change the conversation and take the opportunity to talk about my career. Anything was better than having to mention David or sitting there in silence thinking about the reason for the journey.

"What are your opinions on my next career move?" I asked him. "What should I do?"

His reply was helpful. "It depends on your interests. There are several options. Firstly, you can stay in Central Staffs, and possibly move into Ford of Europe to gain international experience. Secondly, you could utilise everything you've learned and become a plant industrial relations manager, which probably is the most obvious next step. Or you could specialise and move into a function such as training or recruitment. It's up to you to choose."

I thanked him for the alternatives but had doubts about overseas duties since I could not see how these would help my long-term career. Most British companies appeared to delegate control of personnel management to executives in their offshore subsidiaries. Moving into Ford of Europe might result in an immediate promotion, but in the long term I could end up trapped in international work.

Changing the subject, although I did not want to dwell on what had happened, I asked rather worriedly, "How shall we replace David?"

"I'll take care of that," he replied quickly, "but you need to do something for me. Ford of Europe wants us to prepare a Foreign Service Manual for Americans assigned to work in Britain. Expatriate numbers are increasing, and they want consistent communications. You need to see the manager responsible for expatriate management and develop a plan with him."

We had been travelling north and now west since leaving London, and I began to notice the fine views of the Welsh coastline as the journey came to an end. On arrival at the station, my boss said he was travelling to Halewood that evening, so I would be on my own for the return trip, and we hailed a taxi to take us to the funeral. We expressed our sorrow to David's parents, and told them how David had been liked by his colleagues, and then I gave them the few belongings I had found in David's desk and brought with me. A woman came over to thank us for returning David's things, but I was not sure if she was his girlfriend or his sister. We then chose to be inconspicuous while the family grieved. It was one of the saddest days of my life.

Back in the office, my feelings of guilt and anxiety continued, and resuming normal work was difficult. Perhaps I should have shared my thoughts with my colleagues, but there were no employee assistance programmes to help me, so I told only Jean-Louise and otherwise suffered in silence. Slowly, as I immersed myself in specific tasks, I shook off the feelings of culpability and managed to return to my usual routine of working.

* * **

November brought the realisation that 1972 had been a year of great change. Jean-Louise and I had moved house, I was now an experienced member of the management team at Ford of Britain, I had dealt with the worst possible situation a supervisor could encounter, financially we were comfortably well off, I was benefiting from very large Ford wage settlements and Chris and Angela were about to become part of our lives.

Industrial chaos continued at the national level, thanks to the relentless opposition from the trade unions to the Industrial Relations Act, and now due to their disapproval of wage controls. It was difficult to predict what would happen next, either at home or at work.

(Jean-Louise, November 1972) "At long last, John seems to have found a friend in Chris. I thoroughly enjoyed meeting Chris's wife and being shown the sights of Northern Ireland. What a wonderful place; it's just a shame there's so much violence. Now that Chris and Angela are moving to Essex, I hope we'll see much more of them.

"Recently, I've been busy decorating and furnishing our new home, teaching and enjoying the holiday in Portugal. It's a wonderful house and I hope to become pregnant sometime soon. John's salary keeps going up, so I think we can afford to have children and I'm a little jealous of my teacher friend who's already pregnant. Her baby's due next year and she's giving up teaching.

"John's work is going well, but the death of his colleague in the office was awful. I don't think he's fully recovered from the shock.

"My father likes our new home and is a frequent visitor. In particular, he enjoys the central heating. With so many trade

union disputes, I'm pleased he can stay with us and I can take care of him. He's happy not to be working.

"John's preparing for our entry into the Common Market; he's installed a freezer in the garage to store New Zealand lamb and Australian butter because he thinks these items will become much more expensive and difficult to find once we're in Europe at the start of January next year. There's a lot of speculation about prices going up. Denmark and Ireland are also joining the EEC but, surprisingly, Norway chose to stay outside. There was some talk about a referendum to allow people to decide if the terms of entry are satisfactory, but the current government has rejected the idea. Many Labour Party members still oppose entry, and Labour leaders say that, if they're elected, they will renegotiate the terms and ask the British people to vote to either stay in or leave.

"I hope to find a new teaching position closer to home now we've moved. James has been helping me with the redecorating, along with some of his friends from East Ham, and he and John seem to be getting on well together."

Tern Family: These small to medium-sized birds are more compact than most gulls and are mainly known for the great distances they travel during migration. Most of them are pale grey and white in colour, except for growing a black cap in summer. The Aleutian, Arctic, Caspian, common, little, roseate and Sandwich terns all have long tail streamers and webbed feet, and they skim low over the sea before diving to catch fish. The black and the white-winged inland or "marsh" terns are blunt-tailed, with almost black underparts in summer, and they dip into the water to pick up their food.

Arctic Tern: This member of the family (length 34 cm/13 in) moves between its summer northern hemisphere breeding grounds and Antarctica where it spends winter. It feeds on small fish in shallow coastal waters and it nests on beaches and offshore islands. The birds' journey south takes place between late July and early October, and the record distance travelled is apparently held by a bird that wintered in the Weddell Sea in Antarctica, before returning to the Farne Islands, off the Northumberland coast, clocking nearly 60,000 miles (96,000 km)over the course of its yearly migration.

The species also breeds along the coasts of New England and Washington, and migrates along both North American coasts, but it is seldom seen from land.

30

Dabbling And Diving Ducks

OUR FRIENDS HAD relocated to Braintree, and early on a Sunday morning during late November 1972, we set off to visit Chris and Angela, but first made a brief detour to a reservoir near our home that attracted a large number of waterfowl during autumn and winter. I was driving my newest lease car, a Cortina Mark 111 GXL 2.0, sprayed bright Daytona yellow, with a black vinyl roof. Somehow the primrose colour had come to symbolise our union, with Jean-Louise's yellow dress, the primrose-coloured mini-van and now my latest company vehicle.

The water was difficult to inspect from the road, and therefore duck spotting required me to clamber up the causeway. Jean-Louise watched, choosing to remain warm in the car.

In addition to the native coots, grebes and noisy black-headed gulls, there were other species, but so far away that it was difficult to recognise them, even through binoculars. However, I had been taught how to identify ducks from their profiles, the speed of their wing beats, their flight patterns and by watching how they feed. Some species search for food by tipping forward into the water, bottoms-up, and they are known as dabbling ducks; others feed beneath the surface by diving.

From what I could make out, there were gadwalls and mallards plus wintering pintails and small teal representing the dabblers, while pochards and goldeneyes were the diving ducks. Jean-Louise was amazed that I could identify what she described as tiny dots in the distance as we drove along the short length of the roadway that was close to the reservoir.

* * *

Our hosts greeted us with smiles and handshakes, and they immediately showed us around their new home. The property was a little smaller than ours, recently decorated, very private and with a view of the countryside at the rear. We then sat in the kitchen to drink tea and talk while Angela prepared lunch. I asked Chris how long they planned to be in Braintree.

"I'm not sure," he replied. "My father wants me to leave Ford very soon and take over his road-transport business in Nottingham. Moving on will be difficult, especially since Ford's done so well this year, and the Cortina is outselling British Leyland's top model."

This led to a discussion on the continuing chaos in the British motor industry and especially the ten week strike that had just ended at Jaguar. We agreed that labour disputes in the engineering industry were helping Ford improve its sales ranking. I told Chris my plan was to remain in my current position for about a year, but after that I was not sure what I would do.

"Will there be a salary increase next year, now that the government has frozen pay?" Chris asked.

"I think so," I tried to reassure him. "The freeze is supposed to end in March, and we expect the government's Stage 2 to allow for modest adjustments".

"And are you still teaching?" Chris turned his attention on Jean-Louise.

"Yes, until next summer," she answered. "Then I hope to go part-time. There should be lots of opportunities because the school-leaving age is finally being raised to 16."

Chris asked about our holiday. I told him we had loved Albufeira with its white sandy beaches, incredible rock formations, lots of sunshine, fresh fish and the late-night bars and cafés, and I added that most things were cheap. I confessed that we both felt guilty for supporting an authoritarian dictatorship, although this may have explained why the people had been so kind and careful to take good care of us. About 18 months after our visit, the "Carnation Revolution" took place in Portugal, so called because civilians gave soldiers carnations to celebrate the arrival of democracy. We talked about travelling together the following year to the same place.

Angela apologised for the absence of furniture that was still in transit from Northern Ireland. She and Chris were happy to have left behind the violence of Belfast and she hoped that she could bring the rest of her family to England very soon.

Over lunch, after discussing the implications of joining the Common Market in 5 weeks' time, the conversation shifted to our new home and what had we done since moving in. The discussion generated a tiff between Jean-Louise and me over money, a topic that was the most likely to cause disagreements between the two of us.

She began: "We've re-plastered most of the downstairs ceilings and re-wallpapered the bedrooms with the help of a friend from school."

"I'm not sure all that work was necessary," I interjected. "It cost a lot."

Jean-Louise gave me a look of disapproval, and continued: "My friend James found some people he knew to do the work, and I'm happy with the results."

"Who's James?" asked Angela.

"He's a teacher at my school and lives nearby, although originally he came from East Ham."

Angela sought clarification. "Why would a teacher help you decorate?"

"He didn't," responded Jean-Louise. "He asked some out-of-work dock labourers that he knows to help. They're former stevedores (longshoremen), who have been made redundant and now can find only casual work. They're nice people and fun to listen to."

Accepting the answer, Angela shifted her interest. "What have you done about furnishing the house?"

Once more, Jean-Louise replied. "I discovered an interior decorator listed in the *Sunday Times*. She did wonderful work, although the materials she selected were high-end. The curtains came from Harrods, the floor and bedroom furnishings from a Pimlico boutique called Casa Pupo and the light fixtures I bought at Habitat."

Again, I could not help adding a comment that the amount of money we were spending was excessive. "Everything was very costly even though the results look good," I contributed.

"Ignore what he says," Jean-Louise appealed to Chris and Angela. "He moans about everything I spend on the house, but ask him about the hi-fi system."

Angela looked at me for an explanation, so I confessed: "She's referring to the Bang & Olufsen hi-fi system I purchased to replace our old record-player. It was expensive, but it'll last a long time."

Jean-Louise and I were never going to agree on money. I was willing to stretch our finances for a mortgage on the best house we could find, but I did not want to spend money on furnishings. She, on the other hand, worried about the loan but, once we had bought the house, was preoccupied with making it look the best she could, at whatever cost. Chris ended the conversation by taking us on a drive to show off his new golf club, and by the time the tour was over, we were ready to head home. On the way, I was gently reprimanded.

"I wish you wouldn't complain about money all the time," grumbled Jean-Louise. "It makes me feel like a spendthrift and you sound like a meanie."

"I'm sorry," I replied, "but we can't keep spending at your current level."

I was gently taken to task for being critical and told that I should not worry about things before they happened. It was clear that we were unable to agree, so I apologised and shifted the conversation to other things. Jean-Louise said that she was applying for a part-time job at a school near our new home, and she hoped to hear back very soon.

* * *

Our 1972 Christmas holiday was spent in Manchester. We visited Jean-Louise's father because of the unreliability of train services for him to come to us. He treated us to dinner at a local restaurant on Christmas Day and to the pantomime at the Davenport Theatre on Boxing Day.

He came back with us in the car, and we arrived home in time to celebrate the country joining the Common Market. The public were told about the advantages of membership, including greater protection of the environment, improvements in working conditions, introduction of consumer safeguards and the availability of funds for vocational training. Early on, there was little change in food prices, although certain cheeses and meats became scarcer to find. The Labour

Party remained divided over the wisdom of the country's membership.

The government's wage freeze ended with the introduction of Stage 2 that allowed pay increases of up to 4 percent, plus one pound per week (a total of about 6 percent). Union opposition continued to be intense because of the argument that workers' standard of living was being eroded by inflation that was higher than the percentage for wage awards. As a result, there was more militant behaviour. In February 1973, some 29,000 railway workers began a series of one-day strikes to support their pay negotiations, and for several weeks no-one knew which trains would run. Passengers faced long, frustrating and unpredictable delays.

At around the same time, 250,000 civil servants decided to participate in a one-day strike. This action closed government offices, and shut down air travel because the air traffic controllers participated. On May Day, 1st May 1973, some 1.6 million workers stayed away from work to reinforce the protests against wage controls. Rail travel, car manufacturing, newspaper publishing, coal mining and the docklands were all affected. It seemed that as one dispute ended, another one began.

* * *

Meanwhile, I followed-up on my boss's request to develop an Expatriate Orientation Manual, and a manager called Walt from Ford of Europe worked with me. He was a stout, affable, middle-aged American who spoke with a strong New Jersey accent. We completed a 50-page manual that covered everything from shopping to religion, entertainment to education and health care to road signs. We incorporated clothing conversion charts, addresses of local churches, instructions for driving on the left-hand side of the road and the addresses of shops where American-style food could be purchased. Walt also asked for a glossary of frequently used American words alongside their English counterparts; for example, surgery instead of doctor's office, pavement in place of sidewalk, tap rather than faucet, lift instead of elevator and roundabout replacing traffic circle. I also added words with different pronunciations, like process, schedule, aluminium and lever.

The Ford March 1973 wage negotiations took longer than expected because the plant conveners called for an all-out strike as part of the strategy to wreck the government's incomes policy. However, they encountered stubborn resistance, and an Essex newspaper reported that four out of five workers it interviewed opposed the work stoppage. Eventually management's offer was accepted, and a strike was avoided.

A few days later, my manager approached me with an unexpected proposal. "I don't want to lose you, but two managers want to talk to you about new opportunities."

I thought I was ready for a change but uncertain what to choose.

"If you think I'll benefit, I'd like to know what's available," I replied.

"There are two openings," my boss told me. "The first is with Walt in Ford of Europe; he likes you and wants you to take over his manager position for Compensation Planning and Foreign Service Policies. It's a promotion and you'll gain international experience. The other is as the Industrial Relations Manager for the KD (Knocked Down) Operations in Dagenham. It's a great job, but it would be a lateral transfer for you. They need someone to support the new general manager, who's a high-potential executive but has no personnel management experience."

It was going to be a difficult decision. I was still unsure how my career would benefit from an international assignment, and I already knew that Walt was a demanding manager. On the other hand, I had never been inside the KD plant and did not know much about its business. Nonetheless, each of Ford of Britain's 20-plus manufacturing plants employed an Industrial Relations manager, and therefore there would be far more job opportunities in the future if I moved into KD. It was also an experience that would make me an attractive recruit to other companies if I chose to leave Ford.

I spoke with both managers. Walt expected me to accept his promotion, but I investigated KD Operations and learned that they picked, packed and shipped vehicle parts to overseas manufacturing plants for assembly. Car assembly pieces were packed and shipped and, when combined with locally sourced parts, could be assembled into completed vehicles. Most customers were Ford factories in countries like Ireland, the Netherlands, Portugal, Israel, South Africa and New Zealand. However, what I failed to understand was how KD's products would be impacted by Britain joining the European Community and how the introduction of new shipping technologies would affect the business.

By the time I talked to Jean-Louise, I had decided to resume a long commute to Dagenham and accept the unpredictable hours of KD Operations because it was the post most likely to benefit my career. There was no point in waiting for a similar position to open up closer to home because, in practical terms, there was none. Both the nearby Basildon tractor plant and the radiator plant were likely to promote from within. I think Jean-Louise realised that I had made up my mind before we talked, so she chose not to argue.

"If that's what you want to do, you should go ahead," she said, resignedly. "I'm working closer to home now, so I'll have more time to look after the house. You should do what you think is best for your career."

In retrospect, I believe I made a very bad decision. My new manager did not want to be instructed in personnel management; he delegated everything to me while he travelled overseas marketing KD's services. Simultaneously, the demand for knocked down vehicles declined in countries like Ireland and the Netherlands because of Britain's membership of the Common Market that made importing fully assembled vehicles cheaper. Additionally, so far KD had not used shipping containers to export freight, but had continued to rely on the traditional method of packing wooden crates into ships' cargo holds. Its customers wanted to use containers, since they were cheaper and more reliable, and they were increasingly frustrated that KD would not comply. Lastly, whenever a dispute occurred, Ford's Dearborn headquarters would quickly get in touch with Brentwood to find out what was happening, because the overseas Ford assembly locations would complain about disruption in supplies. I had not done my homework and had been too narrow-minded to see that there was a huge future in international personnel management.

When I told Walt of my decision, he was dumbfounded, and could not understand why anyone would turn down a promotion, especially when the lateral opportunity involved a long and unpleasant commute. Nonetheless, I accepted the appointment in KD Operations with a start date of 1st June 1973.

While waiting for my transfer back to Dagenham, a household problem arose that underscored my foolishness in selecting Dagenham. Late one afternoon, the office telephone rang; it was Jean-Louise sounding very upset.

"What's wrong?" I was worried by the stress in her voice.

"We've been burgled," was the tearful reply. "The house has been ransacked and I don't know what's missing."

"Call the police, and I'll be home in a few minutes," I told her.

I explained to my staff what was happening, and by the time I arrived home the police were present. The thief apparently had forced the lock on the front door, but appeared to have burgled the downstairs only, so the police speculated that Jean-Louise had interrupted him when she returned to the house. It seemed fortunate that the burglar had fled rather than confront my wife. We eventually determined that only my camera and a small amount of cash had been stolen, and large items such as the television set and my Bang & Olufsen hi-fi equipment remained in place. Even so, Jean-Louise was very upset, and I comforted her as best I could. A locksmith came the same evening to repair the damaged door, and the following day I submitted an insurance claim.

The more serious consequence of the theft was the emotional trauma suffered by Jean-Louise. She felt as if she herself had been violated, and her greatest fear was that it might happen again while I was many miles away in Dagenham. I tried to reassure her, but she remained tearful and upset for several days.

* * *

On 1st June 1973, I began my long and tedious daily commute to KD Operations, and soon found myself tired and stressed because of the nature of the work and the long hours. Angela called to cancel the Portugal holiday because Chris's father had been taken ill, and she and Chris were needed in Nottingham. Jean-Louise rearranged our July trip and chose Tenerife, one of the Canary Islands belonging to Spain, instead of Portugal. By the time of the holiday I would be ready for a rest and afterwards I would return to a position that was turning out to be far more difficult than expected and required long hours at work.

(Jean-Louise, late June 1973) "I've completed six years of teaching, and I'm looking forward to changing schools and working only three days a week, but I'll still teach geography. John and I have encountered many changes during the past few months, some good and some less so. I'm still suffering from the trauma of the burglary and don't feel safe at home. John's decision to return to long hours doesn't help; I feel left on my own. James still calls by on occasion to check my mini-van, and I know he'll help me if there's any other need and John's unavailable.

"I'm proud of the house now that it's fully decorated and furnished, and Angela says the person I found to help me has very good taste. I worry that I'm about to lose Angela's friendship, as it seems she will soon move to Nottingham so that Chris can take over his father's business. It's a shame they couldn't accompany us on holiday to Portugal because of his father's illness, but Tenerife is a place I've never visited. I'll enjoy hiking, lying on the beach in the sun and tanning myself beside the hotel swimming pool. Hopefully John will find something to do if the sun gets too hot for him.

"I probably ought to have disagreed with John more strongly when he decided to accept the KD job. I should have pointed out the damage it could cause to our relationship like the Dagenham assembly plant experience. It may help his career, but it doesn't help our family time together. He leaves the house around 6.30 am, and I don't see him back home before 7.30 to 8.00pm. The job apparently is tough and not what he expected; he has discovered that no one on his staff

has the knowledge to deputise for him, line managers expect instant solutions, and the convener is an anti-management person with a fairly hot temper.

"For the time being, I'm going to get on with my life as best I can, and will help John when it's necessary. At least I can enjoy living in my lovely home."

Gadwall: *This is a medium-sized dabbling duck, about 46-56cm/18-22ins. in length. It is similar to a mallard, with a large, square head and steep forehead. Its flight is swift with rapid wingbeats, and it usually flies in small, compact flocks. The male has grey plumage with a mottled white breast, black rump and white bars on its wings. The female is a brown colour and easily confused with the female mallard. Its preferred habitat is reservoirs, farm ponds, gravel pits and lakes with vegetation, as well as coastal fresh and brackish marshes, and about 25,000 gadwalls winter in Britain.*

In North America, it breeds in the north-central United States and on the Canadian prairies, and it winters in the southern United States.

Eurasian Pochard: This is a medium-sized diving duck, about 46 cm/18 ins. in length. It is similar to a gadwall), with a rounded, gently sloping head and an elongated, chunky beak. Its flight is fast and direct with deep wingbeats, and it usually flies in a V formation after forming small- to medium-sized flocks with other diving ducks. The male's colouring is distinctive in winter/spring when it has a bright reddish-brown head, black breast and tail, red eyes and a pale grey body. The female is a pale brown, with a greyish body and brown cheeks, and is easily confused with other duck species. Its preferred habitat is the same as that for the gadwall. About 75,000 pochards winter in Britain.

In North America, there is a separate group of pochards, including the canvasback, the scaup, the tufted duck, the red-head and the ring-necked. The canvasback and the redhead look most like the Eurasian pochard, which is seen as an occasional vagrant in North America.

31

The Kleptoparasitic Skua

A RELAXING JULY 1973 fortnight in a hot, sunny Tenerife was what I needed before returning to the onerous challenges in KD Operations. It took time for me to supress my worries about meeting the requirements of the new position, but eventually the fun of being on holiday eliminated thoughts of work. Jean-Louise had celebrated the end of full-time teaching and was looking forward to starting her part-time employment during September 1973 in a school close to our house, where she would teach three days a week.

We stayed in Puerto de la Cruz, on the north side of the island, and enjoyed early morning rambles through the mist and occasional shower. As the day became hotter, we returned to the coolness of the hotel and made use of its refreshing swimming pool. The first week was active as we rented a car to give us the freedom to go anywhere. We explored the island's stunning mountains, its impressive beaches and spectacular coastline and went hiking in Mount Teide National Park. Birdwatching was restricted to observing buzzards flying high overhead.

During the second week, Jean-Louise complained of tiredness and spent much of her time resting in the hotel. I often stayed inside with her, as I was glad to keep out of the sun. She grumbled about tenderness in both breasts, especially at night, but we decided not to contact a local doctor. Once back home in Essex, she arranged to see her general practitioner, and on the evening following the consultation, I arrived home from Dagenham to find a very radiant wife waiting at the door. Before I could say anything, she announced: "I'm having a baby and it's due at the end of the year. I'm so excited!"

I reacted with delight and gave Jean-Louise a huge hug. Admittedly, we had been trying for something like this since we moved into the new home, but the announcement was unexpected. The predicted birth date at the end of December seemed unusually early and I wondered why Jean-Louise had not realised she was pregnant sooner. Her story was that she had not noticed any increase in her weight, there had been no morning sickness and she thought her body rhythm was reacting to the stress of the burglary. It was unimportant however; what mattered was that we were happily married, proud of our new home, had the funds to start a family and were about to become parents.

We did not know the sex of the baby, and it would not be known until the child was born. It was not until several years later that prenatal scans became routinely available, thus all we could do was celebrate the pregnancy by drinking beer and wine at the local pub. At the time that this was happening, there was no recognition that alcohol was a risk factor for pregnant women, nor was there any standard advice from doctors to stop smoking. Indeed, Jean-Louise maintained both habits throughout the pregnancy. It was not until a few months after Jean-Louise realised she was pregnant that the medical profession recognised the link between physical defects and foetal alcohol syndrome.

Meantime, our families were delighted by the news. My greatest obstacle to supporting Jean-Louise was my obligation to work in Dagenham. It was not so much the type of work, but the long hours; the commute took about an hour each way and working beyond the end of the dayshift was standard. As had happened before, I felt committed to my job and placed my work duties ahead of my personal responsibilities towards my wife. I could have asked for a transfer, or even resigned, but those were unacceptable alternatives that could wreck my career and remove my ability to support the family.

To ease the situation, Jean-Louise's father spent much more time in our home, and the former physics teacher, who now had a child of her own, gave helpful advice as we prepared for the baby's arrival.

* * *

The convener in the KD plant was unrelenting in his pursuit of grievances, and frequently threatened overtime bans and work stoppages to secure concessions. All worker discipline was challenged, changes in work processes had to be discussed before implementation, a complaint was made every time a foreman was seen performing manual work, and the convener insisted that job openings should be filled by employees from elsewhere on the Dagenham estate, not externally recruited. Work in the packing plant was less stressful than in other factories because of the absence of conveyor lines, so according to the convener, men with disabilities or work restrictions should be given priority to move to the KD plant when vacancies arose. However, I often received complaints from foremen that medical restrictions interfered with a person's mobility between jobs once they arrived. Technically, the provisions of the Industrial Relations Act were in force to help me threaten the unions, but Ford senior management ordered that none of the Act's rules should be used to advocate the company's business needs.

I privately nicknamed my convener "the skua", because of his scavenging habits to get what he wanted. He reminded me of the great skuas I had seen at Spurn Point Bird Observatory that live by stealing food from other birds. This rather unremarkable-looking raptor pursues individual birds at sea to attack and steal their fish, sometimes by forcing them to regurgitate, and occasionally by killing and eating the bird itself. The functioning of the KD plant was always at risk when the convener was on the prowl.

It was during this period of constant pressure that I made a decision that nearly cost me my job. I succumbed to a weakness by dishonouring an agreement and not having the resolve to stop a misguided decision taken by my peers. One Friday afternoon, the production manager told the management team that workers in the parts-receiving area had repeated their complaint about draughty working conditions and the need for safety barriers. After the necessary improvements had been scheduled to be implemented during the weekend, the shipping manager suddenly objected, claiming that the changes were unnecessary and expensive.

"It's a long-standing grievance," I argued back. "If we don't fix the problem, the men have said they will strike."

"I don't believe it," he countered. "They're bluffing; the work should be cancelled, and we should save the money."

I knew he was wrong, but I received no support from my management colleagues. Maybe it was because he was from North America that no-one wanted to disagree with him. Therefore, a decision was taken to ignore the commitment and cancel the work—the thinking being that this was no different from the unions' behaviour when they made promises and then occasionally broke them.

Predictably, the following Monday, the parts-receiving workers realised the work had not been done and immediately turned around and went home. Parts picking ceased because of shortages, and several overseas shipments were delayed. When the nightshift workers did not show up either, the decision not to fix the problem was reversed and the improvements installed that same night.

My telephone rang the following morning. It was a call from my manager's American director in Brentwood headquarters since, as usual, my boss was travelling overseas.

"I want you up here immediately," he commanded, and hung up.

An hour later, I sat in front of him anticipating that my career was likely to be at an end. Executives at the US headquarters in Dearborn had complained about the delay in shipments, the KD Operations shipping manager had given his version of what had happened, and I was about to be the sacrificial lamb. I was overcome with trepidation that, after seven years with Ford, I was about to be fired at a time when I was responsible for a huge mortgage and a pregnant wife.

"What in the world were you thinking?" the director was furious. "That was the most foolish decision I've ever heard of anyone taking. We lost a day's production and annoyed several customers. If you allow that to happen again, I'll fire you. If you're overruled in the plant in the future, call me and I'll become involved. Do you understand?"

I nodded and offered to explain what had happened, but he was not interested in my story.

"It's over," he said decisively. "We don't need to discuss it. What's necessary now is for you to negotiate an agreement to establish the use of shipping containers in the Case Marshalling

Area. Customers are demanding we use them; they're cheaper, faster and safer than what we do now."

With that, he waved me out of his office, but I did not feel like going back to work. His reprimand had left me feeling annoyed with myself and upset. Instead, I drove home to tell Jean-Louise what had happened. She was surprised to see me home so early, sympathised and then reassured me that I would never make the same mistake again. I was not the cause of the blunder and I should consider it a learning experience, she said.

"Get over it. You've been taught a valuable lesson," was her concluding remark.

* * *

At home, we had become more cautious with our spending habits because we had lost a major portion of Jean-Louise's income. Additionally, I was funding a more expensive commute and money was needed to purchase baby equipment in preparation for the arrival of our child. The challenge was made more difficult because prices in the shops were rising, not least because of the consequences of joining the Common Market. Food prices had risen in less than a year on average by about 15 to 20 percent, but even higher on items like meat, eggs, cheese and butter. The availability of fish and its price was also affected because Iceland had introduced a 50mile (93km) fishing limit to protect its fishing rights. At first British trawlers ignored the restriction, but by the end of 1973 Britain had conceded.

Jean-Louise more often bought cheaper meats, such as sausages and minced meat, we occasionally used margarine rather than butter and we sacrificed eating cheese except for New Zealand Cheddar. My freezer store of New Zealand lamb was slowly being depleted. Eating out was limited to special occasions, and trips to London were cancelled in part because visits to the city had become dangerous due to the efforts of the Irish

Republican Army to transfer their terrorism from Northern Ireland to England. There were car bombings in Whitehall and near the Old Bailey, and in September 1973 there was a campaign to extend the attacks to London railway stations.

* * *

During October 1973, the government announced its Stage 3 wage controls, with pay increases limited to 7 percent, and an annual individual cash maximum of £350 (US$822, at the exchange rate then). This would last until July 1974 but included the provision that, if annual inflation rose over 7 percent, something called a "threshold payment" would be triggered. It was a complex calculation but it allowed a special award of 40 new pence (about one US dollar) a week for each percentage point that the cost of living rose above 7 percent.

Union opposition to the government's policies stayed hostile and rebellious, and almost immediately, around 260,000 coal miners rejected a 7 percent pay offer and voted for an overtime ban, beginning the following month. Also, power station engineers banned out-of-hours working at the start of November 1973 in protest at the government's decision not to allow the implementation of a pay agreement that had been negotiated a year earlier.

Another hugely important global event took place during October that undermined our standard of living by driving up the cost of petrol. From 6th to 25th of that month, the Middle East "Yom Kippur War" took place, causing major disruptions in the worldwide supply of oil. Following Israel's military successes against the Arab coalition that began the fighting, Arab oil producers took action that caused the price of oil to quadruple and supplies to drop by 25 percent in a matter of days.

Queues formed outside British petrol stations, and I was

occasionally among the motorists in those queues, trying to fill my Cortina's fuel tank to get me to work. By mid-December, the situation was so serious that a 50 mph (80 km) motorway speed limit had been introduced in Britain, some filling stations had run out of petrol because of a 10 percent reduction in deliveries, and the public were told to avoid discretionary travel. Shops were instructed to turn off their heating, specific temperature maximums were imposed on office conditions, floodlighting for sports events was banned and electric power for advertising was prohibited. There were also rumours that petrol rationing would be introduced and that coupons had been printed. In the end, Saudi Arabia helped Britain by providing additional oil supplies.

The Middle East crisis was accompanied by an escalation in bitterness over the miners' pay dispute with the government. On 12th November 1973, the overtime ban was implemented, with coal supplies expected to decline by up to 50 percent. The miners were unwilling to compromise on their 35 percent wage demand, believing that due to the rise in oil prices, future electricity generation would rely more heavily on coal.

The government responded by declaring a state of emergency and countering the union's demands with an improved wage offer of 13 percent. However, the proposal was rejected. At the same time, electricity generation was further jeopardised when the train drivers began to delay the delivery of coal to power stations by implementing a work-to-rule. Britain was headed towards an electricity supply crisis and a bleak and chaotic winter.

On 13th December 1973, the government announced the start of a national three-day working week, to begin 1st January 1974. From that date, commercial users of electricity would be restricted to working only three specified consecutive days each week, and the working hours on those days could not be extended. Domestic power outages were inevitable and these would be scheduled as far as practical on a daily rota basis, and the timetable of power cuts would be published ahead of time. A proposal to force residents to heat only one room in their home was abandoned and the Queen apparently accepted a request not to mention the industrial crisis in her Christmas speech to the nation. Hospitals, supermarkets and newspapers were exempt from the reduced working week although they could be impacted by rolling blackouts. Education in schools continued at five-days-a-week. The Prime Minister announced that it would be the hardest Christmas ever since World War 11, and at home we did not know how these conditions would interfere with the birth of our child.

Power cuts became standard, with daily, at least three-hour rolling blackouts announced ahead of time. The home's central heating system was no longer effective, the availability of indoor lighting was haphazard (we used candles as back-up), and it became dangerous to operate our gas burners for cooking when it was dark. Outside, the street-lamps were either dimmed or turned off, and television screens across the nation went blank at 10.30pm (except over Christmas and New Year when the government relaxed its rules). Shops stayed open when they could, but the supply of essential foods and household items became unpredictable.

Work in the KD plant was expected to be less affected by the miners' dispute than in many other factories. Dagenham estate could avoid the worst of the national power-cuts because it had its own electricity supply, and in anticipation of coal shortages, someone in the company had arranged for fuel to be shipped directly from the continent. KD management planned to maintain production as long as there were parts in stock to pack, and in some situations it would ship cases with absent components and the missing items were to be forwarded by air-freight as soon as they became available.

Jean-Louise's school colleagues worked normal hours and Jean-Louise continued her three-days-a-week employment until the end of the autumn term. We established a plan to take her to hospital if the baby began to arrive while I was away in Dagenham. First, she would call for an ambulance, and if that was not available, she would use a taxi service. The back-up plan was for the husband of her physics teacher friend to take her, since he worked nearby. If that failed, James would be called. Meanwhile, a bag with everything needed for a stay in hospital was placed near the front door. It was a difficult and uncertain time.

* * *

On Christmas Eve, our child had not yet arrived, so we visited the home of the former physics teacher. We ate dinner, drank and talked a lot and, after exchanging gifts, returned home at 1am. Jean-Louise's father was already in bed.

An hour later, I was poked in the ribs.

"It's happening," Jean-Louise said nervously. "I'm having contractions."

I was not certain what to do, so I telephoned the hospital and was told to take her to the maternity ward immediately. A few minutes later, with Jean-Louise and her hospital bag on the back seat of the Cortina, I was driving cautiously north through the Essex countryside with no working street lights, blacked-out traffic lights, and a ground mist swirling across the road to obscure what little was visible in the headlights of the car. Fortunately, there were few other vehicles on the road, so I proceeded without mishap. Half-way to St John's Hospital in Chelmsford, Jean-Louise started groaning much louder, and from her deep breathing, I realised that her contractions had resumed.

We arrived in the warm but dimly lit the hospital, with me feeling thoroughly flustered, and uncertain what to do, but after examining my wife, the nurse simply told me to go home.

"We'll call you when it's time," she said. "We'll keep her here until the baby arrives. Meanwhile, merry Christmas!"

Thirty minutes later I was back home and in bed, but I could not sleep in case the telephone rang. It was just before lunch on Christmas Day when the hospital finally called.

When I arrived back at St John's Hospital during early afternoon, I was shown to the waiting room. There was another husband present whose wife had already given birth, and he was waiting for her to recover. He produced a bottle of champagne and a couple of plastic beakers and offered me a drink. I gratefully accepted and we toasted until a nurse interrupted our celebration and escorted me to the delivery room. The birth was over, and Jean-Louise lay quietly in bed, a little dazed by what she had gone through.

"It's a daughter," she said, smiling at me. "We agreed to call her Louisa."

Moments later, I heard the cries of my daughter as she was brought into the room and placed in the arms of her mother. She was small and fragile, with tiny curled fingers, and her legs kicked underneath the white blanket. The warmth and comfort inside the hospital contrasted with the cold and uncertainty outside.

Jean-Louise smiled, and I could only smile back. We didn't say much, just looked at each other and squeezed hands, but I was very proud of my wife and child. After a while, the nurse told me what I needed to bring the following day to take my family home and suggested there was no point in staying any longer. When I arrived back at the house, my father-in-law was eating baked beans on bread in the middle of another three-hour blackout, although he had been able to use the gas burners to heat up the beans.

On Boxing Day, I returned to the hospital to collect my new family and take them home. I remained on holiday during the Christmas week as daily power outages continued, supplies to supermarkets were increasingly disrupted and the television, when it was available, reported no signs of a settlement. For the first time in England, New Year's Day was a public holiday in 1974, and it was not until Wednesday 2nd January that I would need to return to KD Operations. By then, the country was operating on a three-day working week; no-one knew how long it would last, and at home we faced the additional challenge of taking care of a one-week-old daughter in a cold and often darkened house.

(Jean-Louise, January 1974) "I'm the mother of a precious child and I can't imagine more difficult conditions in which to welcome a baby into the world; the shops are often closed early because of power outages and our home is chilly and uninviting, with no electricity for heating; food is difficult to prepare (when it is available in the shops), and I have to hand-wash the baby's nappies in lukewarm water. Everything has become more expensive just at a time when I stopped receiving a salary. My father complains of the new high prices a year after we joined the Common Market, but his pension has been increased by the percentage rise in the cost of living. Each evening the television stops broadcasting at 10.30pm, and the weather has been dull and cold. The best thing is to go to bed early and hope the situation improves overnight, but it doesn't.

"Even with the early nights, I'm not getting much sleep. The baby wakes me up every three to four hours, and I feed

her. I've adjusted to breast feeding but still have soreness from childbirth. Friends have called to congratulate me, but entertaining is tiring.

"There're still difficult conditions at the petrol stations because of the oil crisis, and that's not being helped by the miners' battle with the government. No-one is willing to compromise. John's exhausted by his work but does what he can to help when he's home. Not only is his job very demanding, but now he has to put up with a crying daughter during the night. Almost being fired a few weeks ago shows how stressed he is.

"I love my father being here. He's in good health, sleeps a lot and is nervous whenever I give him Louisa to hold. John's mother visited us, having spent Christmas with her husband's relatives in Brighton, and enjoyed looking after our daughter. My next task is to arrange the christening but I will do that after the miners' dispute is settled."

Great Skua: This is an aggressive, ferocious pirate of the seas, usually seen either hugging the waves or rising in the air to chase after less fortunate birds. It is known to kill and eat smaller ones, like puffins and auks, and it is a common visitor to cliff-side seabird colonies where it takes eggs and chicks. It is a large, dark-brown bird, approximately 55 cm/22 inches long, with white wing patches, and its underparts are lighter in colour than its back. It has broad, rounded wings, a short, stout tail and a sturdy hooked beak. It nests from May to July on flat ground close to the coast, either in solitary pairs or in loose colonies. It vigorously defends its nest and has a loud "tek-tek" or "ji-ah, ji-ha" call. There are about 10,000 nesting pairs in Britain, mainly in the north of Scotland.

In North America, some skuas are known as jaegers, a Germanic name for hunters (for example, the pomarine, the parasitic and the long-tailed jaegers). The great skua is seldom seen from the shore but may occasionally appear during winter along the coastline as far south as the mid-Eastern states.

32

Grebe Dances With Weeds

THE FIRST TWO months of 1974 were difficult for all of us, but especially for Jean-Louise, as she coped with looking after a young child during the daily power outages. For most of the time I was absent, working in KD Operations, so she persuaded her father to continue his stay with us and become the emergency shopper, allowing her to remain in the house to take care of our baby. My mother had given up work the year before and was still travelling, first to Eastern Europe and then to Denmark.

We purchased a paraffin heater to provide warmth in the living room, and used candles and torches (flashlights) for light early in the mornings and during the evening. Dawn did not arrive until 8.00am, and darkness returned as early as 4.00pm. Warm clothes were worn and supplies of household essentials such as toilet paper, detergents, salt, flour and sugar were purchased whenever we could, and our household became one of many engaged in panic buying.

Bathing the baby and washing all our clothes had to wait until the power was turned on, and powdered infant formula milk was stored in case it was needed. The milkman delivered our daily requirements for dairy products, and soft drinks and alcohol were available for purchase from the nearby off-licence that stayed open, even when the power went out. Maybe we drank more in the evening than usual, but it helped us survive.

There was no point leaving the house for night-time entertainment. Cinemas and restaurants were impacted by the same rolling blackouts and many pubs decided to close. So staying at home to look after our daughter was the preferred arrangement. Spending patterns were adjusted because of our reduced income. While Jean-Louise had been given 12 months of unpaid leave, there was no maternity pay, and her salary ceased immediately she stopped teaching, even though she promised to return to school as a supply (substitute) teacher before the 12 months expired.

Jean-Louise used her hairdresser when needed, while I was at home looking after our daughter. Her hair stylist stayed open during blackouts by selling high-priced cans of vegetables in return for free shampoos, and argued that she was managing a food shop and not a hair salon. If we were lucky, the local chippy was open on Saturday and I would bring home fish and chips for lunch. Petrol supplies improved, although the price at the pump was much higher than before the Yom Kippur War. Fortunately, the weather was kind for the time of year, with mild daytime temperatures and very few overnight frosts. The worst of the experience was being ignorant of when the disorder might end, and rumours grew that worse was to follow.

Reports in the national news remained grim. As well as estimates that several million workers had either lost their employment or were claiming benefits for a shortened working week, companies were reporting financial difficulties and sales in the motor industry fell by over 25 percent. Fortunately, Ford of

Britain was less badly affected than elsewhere, with car production declining 15 percent during 1974 compared to 1973.

Annual inflation moved into double digits and there was speculation that the world, including Britain, had entered into a deep recession as a result of the oil crisis. Only the Irish Republican Army seemed unconcerned by what was happening; it continued its bombing campaign in England by blowing up a bus on the M62 motorway on 4th February 1974, killing 12 people, and later in the year there were explosions at the Houses of Parliament, the Tower of London and two public houses in Guilford and Woolwich. The worst atrocities were committed in Birmingham where 21 people were killed and 182 injured in two pub bombings.

The government failed to persuade the miners to accept its wage offer and the caveat that it would permit further negotiations once the men were back at work. Instead, the union conducted a strike ballot, and 81 percent of its members voted to stop work at midnight on 9th February 1974. The government instructed the army to organise troops to move coal to the power stations, and there was speculation that a two-day working week would be introduced. It was difficult to predict what would happen next . . . and then, suddenly, the situation changed.

The day before the strike was due to start the Prime Minister announced a general election for Thursday, 28th February 1974. As he put it, the poll is to decide: "Who governs Britain—the unions or the government?" The miners postponed the work stoppage and reverted to peaceful picketing during the period of political campaigning.

If elected, the Conservative government promised to modify the Industrial Relations Act but would maintain orderly policies to control pay and prices. The Labour Party pledged a full repeal of the Industrial Relations Act and an end to mandatory wage restrictions. It proposed, with union-support, to introduce what it called a "Social Contract" that would establish national guidelines for dealing with social issues such as food subsidies, employment, rents, public transport and welfare provisions, as well as legal rights to protect unions and their representatives. In return, the trade unions agreed to cooperate with voluntary wage restraint, such as supporting 12-month intervals between wage settlements and keeping pay awards in line with inflation. The government also announced it would renegotiate the terms of Common Market membership and conduct a referendum to determine whether Britain should remain in the European Economic Community under the new terms.

No one political party achieved a majority as a result of the election. The Conservatives polled most votes, but Labour won four more seats. The outcome was a hung parliament. Prime Minister Heath tried to negotiate a coalition with the Liberal Party but failed, and on 4th March 1974 he resigned. Concurrently, the Labour Party returned to governing Britain under the leadership of Prime Minister Harold Wilson. Two days later, the new government authorised a resumption of negotiations with the coal miners and a 35 percent wage increase was agreed. The miners returned to work. On Thursday 7th March 1974, industry was directed to resume normal working and the three-day work week came to an end.

* * *

Ford's wage negotiations had taken place during the period of the three-day working week, and the one-year settlement complied with the Conservatives' Stage 3 incomes policy. Workers were promised that threshold awards would be paid, if triggered, and a commitment was made that the firm would abolish its service increments as soon as it was allowed to do so, and all workers would be paid at the top wage rate. I had no direct involvement in the negotiations, although my convenor told me that the agreement was derisory, given the level of inflation and wages paid elsewhere in the motor industry.

* * *

Once home life was more or less back to normal, Jean-Louise organised our daughter's christening for the same day as her 29th birthday. Family and close friends were invited to the baptism that was held in a nearby church. James and his wife were present and announced that their second child was on the way, and the physics teacher and her husband became our daughter's godparents. Chris and Angela came down from Braintree and told us that Angela was pregnant, and that once the baby was born, they would relocate to Nottingham so that Chris could take over his father's business. In the circumstances, we agreed to delay our holiday together for a further year.

* * *

At work, it was time to negotiate the introduction of shipping containers into the Case Marshalling Area (CMA) of KD Operations. This would affect approximately 30 fork-lift drivers, who worked 7-day, 12-hour shifts. It would also impact the lorry drivers who transported the wooden crates from the CMA to the docks, but these were not Ford employees. Finally, the duties of the dock workers would change because it was far more efficient to operate cranes to lift already loaded containers onto ships, than move individual wooden crates into ships' holds. Because all three of these groups were represented by the same union, and this was the union that had fought on behalf of the "Pentonville Five", I expected very difficult and hostile negotiations. However, it was left to me to create a negotiations plan that would satisfy both management and workers.

My first challenge was with KD Operations management.

"Why do we have to negotiate?" the shipping manager challenged. "Management isn't obliged to negotiate productivity improvements. Why can't we just go ahead?"

"What do you think will happen then?" I asked.

"The men will strike, and the convener will lead them," was the opinion of other members of the management team.

"Exactly," I retorted. "They'll stay out as long as we insist on them using shipping containers, and who do you think will get the blame?"

The protest ended and I was told to go ahead. Unfortunately, my first meeting with the convener and his CMA shop steward was far from successful. I provided an optimistic outlook for shipping volumes and I promised that new equipment and safety training would be provided and that any fork-lift driver with insufficient work would be given alternative duties in the plant. The response was immediate.

"Under no circumstances will you take away work from our members. If you want to use containers, have them stuffed on the docks. That way our members are unaffected."

I had to disagree with the idea. "That's not rational. It makes no sense to load cases onto lorries, transport them to the docks and then unload them and pack them into containers. It's highly inefficient."

"But you get what you want, and we get what we want," was the reply. "If you're not prepared to guarantee us employment, we're unwilling to support the change."

We kept talking, but it was clear their minds were made up. The meeting was adjourned, and later that day the convener called me on the telephone: "The lads have decided to impose an immediate overtime ban to protest your proposals," he told me.

I had been instructed to discontinue negotiations the moment any industrial action took place. I duly did so, but a week later, when the ban was lifted, I arranged a second meeting. This was no more successful than the first. The drivers demanded guarantees of indefinite employment and promises that management would replace any driver who was moved off the CMA. There were threats that, if management took unilateral action, the drivers would go on indefinite strike, and close the plant down.

There was no way to concede to the union demands. I registered a "failure to agree" notice with the union, and undertook to involve the convener's full-time District Official. No progress was made at this level, thus our inability to reach an agreement was referred to national level. I was told by Industrial Relations Staff that there would be a delay of several weeks because the union's national representative was busy working with the government to finalise the details of the Social Contract.

* * *

For the Whitsun holiday weekend in late May 1974, we drove to Yorkshire to show off our daughter to my relatives. It was the first time she had travelled any distance by car, and she spent most of the journey asleep in her maroon carrycot on the back seat of the vehicle. By now she had become aware of whom we were. The weather was sunny and warm, and with surprisingly good visibility because of a strong westerly wind. After visiting my aunt and uncle on the east side of York, I took a short detour to show my family one of the places where I used to go birdwatching as a young teenager.

It was Castle Howard, approximately 20 miles (32 km) from

my home; I had usually cycled there and back and it was a place to which I escaped when conditions at home had turned into disagreements between my mother and stepfather. It is also a stately home, and I showed Jean-Louise the parklands, the walled garden, the Great Lake and the large hall on top of the hill. All my prior visits had been on my own, so it felt very special to be sharing it with my family. My daughter sat in her pushchair and looked around but gave little attention to the birds, preferring to smile and babble at her parents. Only the mute swans and cygnets captured her attention, before she fell asleep.

Of particular interest to me was the single great crested grebe, swimming among the ducks, coots and moorhens. It was a bird that had fascinated me as a schoolboy, when I would watch its courtship displays in February and March. A pair of grebes would swim in front of each other, flicking their heads from side to side, shifting towards each other low in the water, calling, preening and holding in their beaks tufts of water-weed that they plucked from below the water's surface, then paddle furiously around each other, upright and chest to chest.

* * *

I was back at work on 3rd June 1974, celebrating my first anniversary in KD Operations, and happened to be in the office when an unexpected telephone call came in from Walt. I had not spoken to him since rejecting his job offer and was unprepared for what he said: "My compensation manager has to return to his home country, and as a result, his job is opening up again; are you interested? It's like before, and I'm willing to offer it to you if you say you'd like to be considered."

I do not think the offer could have been more serendipitous. After a very stressful year in KD Operations, I was being offered a way of returning to Brentwood and spending more time with my family. I still worried about the relevance of international responsibilities, but this concerned me far less than the chance to move closer to home. Additionally, there would be a salary increase and I would receive a second company car.

I asked to talk to Jean-Louise, and promised to call him back the following morning, but he should expect my answer to be "yes". He accepted my condition and said he hoped I could start no later than 1st July 1974.

Jean-Louise was delighted and could not understand why I had delayed my acceptance. "That's wonderful news. Now I'll see more of you, and you'll see more of your daughter." She reassured me that she thought international work was increasingly relevant in large multinational companies and that I should let go of hoping to move to a larger industrial relations manager position on the Dagenham estate. If that was the career I wanted, then we should move to Halewood where she could live closer to her father.

I told her about the salary increase and how I would also become a member of Ford's worldwide profit-sharing plan. Eligibility for a free company car in addition to the leased Cortina was mentioned, and I offered to trade in the Cortina for a smaller vehicle that Jean-Louise could use to replace the mini-van. It had given good service but was becoming unreliable, and maybe James could help prepare it for sale.

"Well, you'd better hurry and tell Walt before he changes his mind," was her last piece of advice.

The following morning, I accepted Walt's offer and told my boss. He was disappointed, but glad he had a month to find a replacement. For me, everything had taken a turn for the better; my commute would reduce to only 15 minutes each way, both Jean-Louise and I would have new cars, I would be able to spend more time at home, there would be a further increase in my salary and no longer would I have to contend with a difficult convener.

* * *

Nationally, the industrial relations situation appeared to be improving. Action had been taken by the new government to repeal the Industrial Relations Act and the unions were supporting modest wage demands. Separately, the Common Market countries had accepted Britain's request to renegotiate the terms of its membership.

During my last few days in KD Operations, I concentrated on preparing for the shipping container national negotiations. Walt agreed that this responsibility should transfer with me because Industrial Relations Staff had insisted on this as a condition of my move. I was anxious to reach a settlement and excited that my life style was about to improve, both at work and at home.

(Jean-Louise, June 1974) "It's fantastic that John's moving back to headquarters. I think it was a mistake to return to Dagenham and he shouldn't be so cautious about broadening his knowledge beyond Britain. I think he will enjoy the international experience, although he's not sure what to expect when working for an American. He says he'll be surrounded by people from all over Europe, including Belgians, Dutch, Swiss, Germans and French.

"I'm going to miss my yellow mini-van, but the Escort John has promised me should be fine. I'm also sorry to have stopped teaching although possibly I can do some supply work in a few months' time.

"My daughter's now six months old and I'm enjoying every

minute with her. She's sleeping through most nights, smiles and laughs a lot, and she is already crawling. It was tough at first, when we kept losing power and I sometimes had to feed her and change her nappy in the dark, but the christening was a success, with my friends and some of John's relatives attending. I think our daughter enjoyed her first visit to Yorkshire, but I don't think I'll ever get used to the strong Yorkshire accents of John's relatives. His has almost disappeared, although he tends to speak like them when he's back among them.

"His birdwatching has virtually ceased, so it was a pleasant change see him enjoying the visit to Castle Howard and showing it off to his daughter as the place where he spent many of his childhood days. It would have been more rewarding if she had been enthusiastic about the birds rather than reaching for anything that was close by.

"Politically, I'm happy that the Labour Party is back in power, but I suspect there are difficult times ahead. The oil embargo is over, but the price of petrol stays high, and other prices in the shops continue to go up. We struggled through the three-day working week and now we have to contend with bombs and violence from the Irish Republican Army. John's mother was recently close to where one of their bombs exploded in London.

"It's a pity we couldn't go on holiday this year with Chris and Angela, but we hope that can remedied next year, after they have settled in Nottingham. For 1974, we'll spend the holiday at home because of the age of our daughter, and my father will return to stay with us."

Great crested grebe: This is an elegant, diving water bird, the largest member of the grebe family in Europe, and noted for its mating display. It is approximately 50 cm/20 inches long, and an excellent swimmer and diver that can pursue fish underwater. Adults are unmistakable in summer, with a mottled-brown back and sides, a dark brown neck and white undersides. It has a long neck and an erect black crest or crown throughout the year. During the breeding season, on its head it has ornate reddish-orange plumes with black tips. The birds were hunted almost to extinction in Britain during the 19thcentury, because their head plumes were used to decorate hats and ladies' undergarments. Around 5,000 pairs breed in Britain today.

The great crested grebe is not found in North America, although other species are present, such as the pied-billed, least, eared and horned grebes.

33

An American Eagle

DURING MY FINAL afternoon in KD Operations, a surprise awaited me. I received a telephone call from my manager's secretary instructing me to come to his office immediately, but she would not give the reason. I was suspicious because he rarely talked to me and was usually out of town. The purpose was clear the moment I entered his room: He and the staff who reported directly to him had gathered to thank me for my work during the past 13 months. I had always believed that they did not appreciate my contributions, and I was elated to find out how mistaken I was. Even the shipping manager smiled and shook my hand.

After relaying his appreciation and wishing me success in my new job, my boss opened a cabinet, took out a miniature replica of a "knocked-down" case, handed it to me, and said that he hoped the farewell gift would be a permanent reminder to me of my days in KD. It was something that the plant carpenters had constructed out of varnished oak, with a flexiglass window on one side. On top was a brass plate with the salutation "From your Friends in KD June 1974", and inside was a digital clock. Everyone applauded the speech while I stood there feeling somewhat embarrassed about being the focus of attention. I wondered if maybe I was abandoning KD Operations too early, and I left the room feeling rather sad and apologetic.

During my early days with Walt, it became clear that working for a manager like him would be very different from anything I had previously experienced. Unlike my past bosses, he reviewed his subordinates' work in great detail and set very specific goals, not all of which were sensible. For example, he did not want me sending borderline job evaluation recommendations for European-based management positions to the United States in case they might be turned down, as that would reflect badly on his credibility. He also criticised his staff in public (an inappropriate management practice) and did not care how they worked as long as assignments were completed on time. Also, like some other Americans, he had a presupposed impression of Europe and Europeans that could not be changed. He was a private person, not wanting to socialise with his subordinates, yet he had a deep understanding of his area of expertise, enjoyed sharing his knowledge and appreciated that I was unfamiliar with most international matters.

* * *

At home, the effects of joining the Common Market continued, but this time the problem was availability rather than price. We were virtually out of sugar, thanks to the Caribbean countries that had sold their sugar at higher prices to other countries because of our European membership. British farmers could not make up the difference using sugar beet, and therefore there were many days when local supermarket ran out of sugar. Once more, panic buying took place to empty the shelves as soon as new supplies arrived. Even when sugar was obtainable, it was normal to limit each customer's visit to one 2lb (0.91kg) bag. We conserved what we had, and Jean-Louise and I stopped sweetening our tea, a measure not adopted by her father. A group of friends organised a sugar syndicate so that, whenever new supplies arrived in the shops, everyone was told of its availability before it was too late.

Another consideration was that it no longer made sense to save money because annual inflation was about double bank interest rates and had reached 16 percent (despite the Social Contract), stock market values had plummeted and payments on variable rate mortgages had increased to 11 percent. The financial outlook appeared fairly sombre.

* * *

The container negotiations resumed in mid-July with a meeting of the company's senior negotiator, my boss's director who had almost fired me, the district and national officials of the union involved and my former convener and CMA shop steward. The convener was asked to summarise the union's position.

"There's no objection to the use of containers," he insisted, "but they have to be packed on the docks, not in the CMA. That way, redundancies are avoided, and the work of lorry drivers and dock workers is safeguarded."

When asked to respond, I explained that the union's proposal was not sensible. Our forecasts showed that future shipments would be sufficient to keep all fork-lift drivers at work, we needed to minimise costs for our customers, and it was impractical to give indefinite employment guarantees.

I then surprised the convener by continuing: "Because there's no desire to displace drivers, we're prepared to bring in additional work to the CMA if the fork-lift operators will start packing containers. Both the Dagenham engine plant and the Langley truck plant will move their overseas parts shipments to the CMA for consolidation if containers are used."

I then quantified the volumes and showed how no fork-lift driver should expect to be displaced in the foreseeable future.

"Sounds good to me," was the national official's response. "Does anyone disagree?"

He looked at his colleagues, but no-one spoke up in opposition. The convener appeared at a loss for words, so the matter was settled. The national official asked for the changeover to be made during the August shutdown, when workers would be least affected, and said he would take care of the lorry drivers and dock workers. I shook hands with a tight-lipped and sullen convener, my director complimented me on resolving the issue and the company's senior negotiator praised the solution. My only disappointment was that I would not be in the KD plant to witness the introduction of the new shipping process.

I was proud of the settlement since it balanced productivity with job security. The original idea for the solution had come from the shipping manager, but I had made it work. That evening I explained the details to Jean-Louise, who thought I had been patient and creative. She wondered if the increased level of cooperation from the trade union was as a result of its collaborations with the government.

* * *

Slowly I grew to respect Walt and, despite his idiosyncrasies, he offered me alternative perspectives on personnel practices as part of my coaching. He talked about the crazy British trade unions, the absurdity of West Germany granting holidays nearly three times as long as those in America, the high automatic cost-of-living increases given in Belgium, the expensive benefits offered in France and the strangeness of Dutch businesses paying union dues on behalf of their workers. These practices were unfamiliar to me, but I began to appreciate how local cultures and traditions affect community expectations, and how there often is no right or wrong answer. Usually there are several ways to accomplish something, although Walt always argued that there was only one correct way and that was the American approach. As long as I was willing to work hard and was determined to be successful, nothing else mattered to him.

He was proud of his New Jersey heritage, and even once talked to me about his birdwatching pursuits when he was growing up. He did not know much about British birds, but he reminisced over watching golden eagles and bald eagles in the New Jersey countryside; these were species I had never seen, although I had tried to see a golden eagle during my holiday in Scotland. Walt had great respect for his home state and admired the eagle and what it represented. He was probably prouder of having identified a golden eagle, a rare visitor to his state, than his sightings of the more common bald eagle, and his ability to talk about personal accomplishments that I was unable to match was part of his supremacy over me.

Slowly, I grew comfortable with my foreign duties. They included evaluating Ford's management positions across Western European countries, administering the parent company's expatriate programme throughout Europe and reviewing and notifying Dearborn of changes in staff employment conditions in each of Ford of Europe's subsidiaries.

* * *

It was a Friday afternoon during August when I received an unusual telephone call from Jean-Louise that led to reconnecting with my father. The opportunity was totally unexpected. She called to remind me to bring home a bottle of St Julien Bordeaux from the off-licence across the road, as she had promised to take it to a friend's home for dinner the following evening. The event was important because Jean-Louise wanted to start developing our daughter's social skills by introducing her to her friend's one-year-old. Once I confirmed that the wine was safely in the boot of my car, she switched topics and said, "Do you know anyone in Wolverhampton?"

It was an out-of-the-ordinary question. "Why do you ask?" I replied.

"Well, a letter has arrived postmarked Wolverhampton. It's addressed to you and appears very official."

I told her I did not know anyone in Wolverhampton and would look at the letter when I returned home.

That evening, I found out that the letter came from a solicitor who was asking me to travel to Wolverhampton to meet with him and discuss a matter that he said was personal and confidential.

After I had shared its contents with Jean-Louise, she commented: "It seems rather strange and intimidating. Maybe you should call on Monday to see if it's serious or not."

Early Monday, I called the telephone number shown on the letterhead. A woman with a strong Midlands accent answered and transferred me to a Mr Graham, who she said was handling the matter. I was taken completely by surprise with what followed.

"I don't wish to alarm you," said Mr Graham, "but I want to talk to you about your father, your biological father. He was a close friend of mine and died a few days ago. One of his last wishes was that I meet with you to explain who he was and why he never made contact with you. He always regretted that he never talked to you, but he feared that your mother would tell his wife of your existence if that happened. If you visit me, I'll tell you more."

I was in shock. Why would my father act in this manner? Was the solicitor being honest, or were there other motives? My mother had always kept my background secret, and maybe there were good reasons, yet I felt a surge of curiosity that was difficult to suppress.

I think the solicitor sensed my conflict, as he continued: "Think about it and keep an open mind; call me in a couple of days. I understand your doubts."

That evening, I discussed the conversation with Jean-Louise.

"It's supposed to be about the person who sent us the mysterious wedding gift, my real father," I told her. "Apparently he's dead and the solicitor wants to talk to me about him."

Thoughtfully, she responded: "If it's your biological father, and you don't go, you'll never find out anything about him. It's your decision, but I'd go if I were you. We can decide later what you do with the information."

The following day, I called the solicitor and arranged to meet in his office. It was a long journey, and I kept wondering if I had made the right decision. Then I would recall Jean-Louise's advice and continue driving. On arrival, I was ushered into the solicitor's office where he sat with a folder and a wooden box on the desk in front of him. After a few pleasantries, he began.

"Your father knew of your existence but never had the confidence to contact you. He was angry that your mother sued him for child support, and he refused to answer any of her letters. His own marriage collapsed, and afterwards most of his time was spent travelling around Europe with his violin, visiting music academies. Sometimes he even played on the streets to earn money."

This totally confused me as I recalled my mother's letter.

"But he can't be my father," I said. "My father was an engineer."

"That's true, but not after he went bankrupt," was the solicitor's reply. "He was a successful civil engineer until he overreached himself financially and his company fell into receivership. Then he went missing for several years until his parents found him and moved him in to live with them. Afterwards, he started his tours of Europe. He may have been uncaring towards you when you were young, but he had a difficult life himself."

"And how do you know he's dead?" I asked.

"He died of a blockage in his pulmonary artery while travelling across Europe. It wasn't expected and his body was returned to his ex-wife who had him cremated."

I was not sure I wanted to know any more details. I did not feel bitter or angry about what I had been told, but I needed more time to reflect on its meaning. How could my father choose to communicate in this way after treating me and my mother so poorly?

"So, what do you want me to do?" I asked.

"There's nothing for you to do. I've fulfilled my promise, and you can contact me if you have questions in the future, but before you leave, there's a final matter. Your father wanted me to give you this."

With that, he handed me the wooden box. It was made of polished walnut, about twelve inches long by six inches wide and two inches high, and it contained a set of mathematical instruments resting on top of a royal-blue satin material. Each instrument was meticulously polished, with working parts made of metal and handles made of carved bone. It reminded me of the KD gift, but it was of a higher quality and more expensive-looking.

"These were your father's drafting instruments. He wanted you to have them."

I think I muttered "thank you" but had nothing further to say. I stood up, announced that I needed to be on the road and thanked him for his time.

During the journey home, I constantly replayed what I had been told, but I could not reach any firm conclusions. There seemed to be no point in dwelling on what I had learned, and I did not want the incident to interfere with my future. I had been brought up by a loving mother, I was making good progress with my career and was happily married with a family. I did not need any posthumous well-wisher at this stage of my life.

I told Jean-Louise what I had discovered, and I think she was as amazed as I. We agreed there was nothing that would change our situation and that keeping the matter to ourselves was probably the best option, rather than risk harming any relationships that I already had. It was a difficult decision to make, but protecting the dignity of my mother was my primary concern.

* * *

A few days later, there was an unexpected commotion at the house next door. It had been vacant ever since we had moved into our new home, but on this particular morning there was a huge lorry outside, with German lettering on its sides. That evening, we met our new neighbours, a husband and wife who came from Cologne with their two children, a son aged five and a baby a few months older than our daughter. The husband worked for Ford and had been assigned from Ford of Germany to Ford of Europe's Dunton Technical Centre. Their belongings included approximately 1,500 bottles of Moselle wine that they carefully stored in the garage, and we quickly formed a close friendship!

At the start of September 1974, I took my first business trip to Spain. I went to bed early the night before, to be certain that I would be in Stansted in time to catch the morning Ford flight. I ought to have felt guilt at leaving Jean-Louise behind, but the excitement of travelling as a specialist in international matters blotted out any other worries. Ford of Spain would shortly launch the company's new small car (the Fiesta) in Europe, and my role was to prepare job grades and install employment conditions to enable the company to attract the best talent in Spain.

At about the same time, I took delivery of my new, top-of-the-line Ford Granada Ghia, trimmed in Sahara beige, with a tobacco-coloured vinyl roof. The model had been launched two years earlier, but the Ghia edition had only recently become available. James came over to prepare Jean-Louise's mini-van for sale and I think he was envious of my new vehicle. It was not easy for Jean-Louise to give up her mini-van, but she agreed that it was impractical for transporting our daughter.

Our daughter attended her first motor car races at Brands Hatch, the Castrol British Saloon Car Championships, during the late August Bank Holiday. We had thought about attending the British Grand Prix a month earlier, but we decided that the noise and crowds would be too much for her. Even so, she disliked the earmuffs that we made her wear for protection, and she was frightened by the noise and the large crowds of people.

Our German neighbours soon replaced Chris and Angela as our closest friends and, when they wanted to go out in the evening, Jean-Louise babysat for them while I looked after our daughter. Our usual reward was to share a bottle of wine.

Nationally, the government was renegotiating the terms of Britain's membership in the Common Market, and the Social Contract seemed to have established relative calm, despite the occurrence of some very large wage increases. Inflation continued to be high but the effects of Common Market membership on consumer prices appeared to have settled down. Most important to me was that I now had time to spend with my daughter without feeling guilty about neglecting work. Fortunately, Walt was not typically American in one respect: He arrived at work on time and usually left punctually at 5pm. This allowed me to get away early and spend the evenings with my daughter.

(Jean-Louise, September 1974) "It's been a quiet time, spending summer at home and making sure my father has enough sugar for his tea. It's amazing the crises bureaucrats can create. Our daughter is crawling, and I often take her up the hill in her push-chair to the High Street shops. She attracts a lot of attention and I'm meeting more people in the neighbourhood. I have volunteered to work for one day a week at school, starting in the autumn term, as long as I'm given adequate warning and can arrange care for my daughter.

"John's job is off to a good start, and he's started travelling to the continent. I've not previously experienced being left on my own overnight, with the exception of the sewing machinists' dispute. I'm adjusting by trying to wake up earlier than my daughter to take care of her, and I'm spending more time with friends to prevent boredom. The most significant event was John's discovery about his father. It's shocking and unbelievable, but there's nothing we can do, so getting on with his life and ignoring what he's learned is probably the best approach.

"Our new neighbours are fun, and I like their Moselle wine. The wife doesn't work so we often chat over the garden fence. Since her English is limited, I'm helping translate the words she hears but doesn't understand. It's good that I studied German at school.

"There's still talk about coming out of the Common Market, and with increases in food prices and the recent shortage of sugar, it might be a good idea.

"I'll miss my mini-van. The Cortina is fine, but I'm looking forward to the smaller Escort. My father is well, we rarely hear

from John's mother, and Chris is now living in Nottingham. I would like to ask John's new boss to dinner, but John says it's not worthwhile because he'll decline. He doesn't socialise with Europeans in case it compromises his work.

"Finally, I'm pleased that we stayed at home for this year's holiday. In mid-August, the holiday tour company, the Court Line, went bankrupt, stranding around 100,000 travellers. We easily could have been among those unlucky tourists."

Golden eagle: this is regarded as the world's largest, fastest and most nimble bird of prey (length 75-88 cm/ 30-35 inches). Adults are dark brown, with lighter golden-brown plumage on the back of the head and neck, a yellow beak and brown eyes. They also have long, broad wings with a span of approximately 215cm/ 85 inches, a longish, wedge-shaped tail, and a powerful beak and talons. Approximately 500 pairs breed in Scotland, but currently there are none in England or Wales.

The golden eagle is the most widely distributed species of eagle in North America, with the majority in the west, ranging from Alaska down into Mexico. Southern populations of birds are mainly sedentary but those breeding in the north usually fly south for the winter. It is estimated that there are around 20,000 to 30,000 golden eagles in North America.

The bald eagle is the national bird of the United States, with an estimated population of around 30,000 in Alaska and a similar number in the 48 contiguous states. It is a fish-eating species.

34

Divers, Loons And The Kaakkuri

OUR DAUGHTER HAD learned to crawl by autumn 1974, and was experimenting with squatting and pulling herself up onto her feet before stumbling around the home, holding onto furniture. For protection, her mother sometimes confined her to the red rubber-and-mesh playpen, despite the child's loud objections. When I left for work, my daughter was usually asleep, and in the evenings on my return she was being fed. She and I had enjoyed the warm, dry summer evenings when we sat outside on the garden sun lounger; she would perch on my stomach or climb over my back under the watchful eyes of her mother.

At weekends, the three of us shopped until our daughter became tired and morngy (grumpy), signalling that it was time to return home. It was a quiet time, free from discomfort and inconvenience, at least for a few weeks, despite the fact that the country's economic condition was worsening. Annual inflation was now over 17 percent, a 34-year high for Britain, and higher oil prices, large wage settlements and British industry selfishly investing offshore rather than at home were blamed for the rise.

We showed off our two luxury cars by parking them in the driveway, and we continued to set aside money for baby things by staying out of London. I had been brought up not to borrow money (except for a home mortgage) and neither of us possessed a credit card, so personal funds had to be available to support whatever we purchased. The credit card "ACCESS" (via the Midland Bank) had only just been introduced, and while the BARCLAYCARD was a little bit older, many retailers had not adjusted to accepting this type of payment. Worries were it would cause consumers to spend money they did not have and its availability was considered an "undesirable American influence".

More time was spent in front of the television during the evening in order to avoid paying for a babysitter. We upgraded to a colour TV, which was rented since this arrangement was more economic than buying at the time. Rumbelows, the High Street electronics retailer, charged a modest monthly fee and repaired our set free of charge whenever it broke down. Memories of my trip to Wolverhampton faded, the box of drafting equipment was put away in a drawer. Sugar was now provided by our neighbours who received their supply from friends visiting them from West Germany.

Signs indicated that the trade unions were continuing to cooperate with the government to minimise disruption in the workplace, and the powers-that-be were accepting settlements that were probably higher than they wished. The Labour government fulfilled its promise to protect trade unions by passing the Trade Union and Labour Relations Act, 1974 (TULRA), that reaffirmed their right to exist, confirmed that labour contracts were not legally binding and that unions and members were exempt from legal damages caused by industrial action. At the same time, the former Conservative government's Industrial Relations Act was repealed.

Despite this ethos of national cooperation, certain groups of workers regarded themselves as special cases and thought that the Social Contract did not apply to them. One of the earliest groups was the manual workers at Ford of Britain who, on 10th September 1974, stopped work in Dagenham and Halewood to demand a new pay raise, even though it was only seven months since their last one-year wage settlement had been implemented. They dismissed the Social Contract as voluntary and some members cynically regarded it as no more than a political invention; vehicle production stopped and tens of thousands of workers were laid-off.

Government help for the company became unavailable when, on 18th September, the Prime Minister announced a second general election for 1974, to be held on 10th October, and dissolved Parliament. The purpose was to transform his minority government into one with a workable majority. Ford of Britain had no choice but to negotiate alone, and in late September conceded a two-year settlement, effective 1st October, with pay raises of 38 percent, including an immediate award of 17 percent. The men were back at work before the general election took place, and the standard practice of Ford of Britain to extend the same increases to its salaried staff continued.

Ford workers were not the only ones to receive large settlements. There was a 28 percent award for TV workers, and 30 percent was given to nurses. During the election campaign, the Labour party was predicted to win, and on 10th October it was re-elected with a slight overall majority. It confirmed its commitment to the Social Contract and said it would continue a voluntary approach to pay and price controls.

Walt thought the Ford of Britain settlement was absurd. "They're no more than a bunch of Communists," he said disgustedly. "It's amazing what they get away with. Don't they understand they're destroying their jobs and the livelihoods of their families?"

Simultaneously, he was appalled when he heard of gangs of Ford's Dagenham workers refusing to go home after being laid off; instead they were blockading production and destroying property and equipment. These actions were especially disruptive when they occurred early during the nightshift because the workers were angry that they were being laid off late at night.

My European colleagues agreed with Walt and boasted about the reliability of their own country's workforce. I stayed silent, although I was disquieted that British workers appeared to be so militant and disruptive compared with employees elsewhere. Privately, it appeared to me that the centre of trade union power in Britain had shifted from the national structure to shop-floor representatives who more effectively persuaded workers to go on strike and paid little attention to government authority.

* * *

The sugar shortage became more severe during November 1974 when, for three weeks, a blockade stopped deliveries from the largest sugar refinery in London. It was rumoured that the government intended to reduce sugar subsidies, which would cause prices to go up and make it more difficult for management to afford pay raises. Sugar disappeared from the shelves in some grocery shops for up to six weeks. We chose to avoid foodstuffs requiring sugar as much as possible, and we resigned ourselves to having a Christmas cake (rich fruit cake, oven baked and infused with brandy) that would not include the traditional outer layers of marzipan and white royal icing; it was impossible to buy the icing sugar.

By the end of 1974, annual inflation had climbed to 20

percent and ever larger wage demands were being submitted. During December 1974, 33,000 members of the national bakers union went on strike in support of a 66 percent wage claim. The union called for a ban on Sunday working and overtime, but its members took unofficial action to stop work altogether. I was lucky to find close to my office a small, family-run bakery that stayed open, and where I could purchase loaves of bread early in the morning. Additionally, we switched to crispbread and fed our daughter rusks (a light, dry biscuit prepared for use as baby food) to conserve supplies.

The year-end holiday was spent at home. Our daughter celebrated her first birthday wearing a pink and green party dress, and she was helped to open her gifts by her mother. She insisted on opening the largest parcels first, and was rewarded with wooden building blocks, a music box, several board books, clothes, a Fisher Price walking toy and a red and white pram for her doll. Jean-Louise's father watched in awe as we wished our daughter merry Christmas and a happy first birthday.

* * *

A few days into the New Year, we called in to see our neighbours. The purpose was for me to ask them about Cologne because I was about to visit Ford of Germany as part of my research into a proposed European company statute called *Societas Europaea*. The regulation permitted the establishment of European companies, and Ford of Europe wanted to know if it should incorporate under this regulation if it passed (it did not). I hoped my neighbours could tell me what to do during the evening, because the trip involved an overnight stay. After talking about Cologne jazz clubs, the conversation switched to some photographs that our hosts had on the table and shared with us. They said they were taken during a holiday in Ibiza, Spain the previous year. It was their regular holiday location and, several years earlier, they had bought a two-bedroom apartment in a building near a resort called San Antonio.

"Why don't you stay there next year?" our hosts suggested. "We only rent to people we know, and it's easy to get to. It has its own swimming pool, and the beach is close by."

It sounded like a good idea. We had never been to Ibiza.

"Can we take friends?" I asked, thinking of Chris and Angela.

"Yes, of course."

The following day, Jean-Louise called Angela, and they decided we should go on holiday together during the forthcoming summer. At Easter, we visited Chris and Angela in Nottingham to finalise arrangements and to introduce our daughters to each other, as Angela's baby had been born earlier. We then drove over to Manchester to spend time with Jean-Louise's father. He was talking about moving to a smaller house, and repeated his intention of not living with us.

We discussed the miners' second annual wage award of 35 percent that had just been approved during February 1975, and the negotiations with the railway workers which we hoped would end without industrial action (a 27.5 percent award was eventually accepted the following month). Annual inflation continued upwards and reached 25 percent, the highest it had been in Britain since 1800. We were glad we could manage financially, largely due to my general salary increases that were the same as those negotiated by the unions for Ford of Britain's manual workers.

A few weeks before, the government had announced the outcome of its negotiations with the European Economic Community and declared that a national referendum would be held on 5th June 1975 to determine if Britain should remain a member. The new terms included a regional development policy that should help certain communities in Britain, a correction mechanism to adjust Britain's budget contribution and broadened access to New Zealand's dairy products. The terms were endorsed by Parliament and the Referendum Bill was passed to allow the ballot to take place.

Polls before the announcement had indicated that the electorate was lukewarm about membership in Europe, although the government's February 1975 White Paper argued in favour of staying in. Both the Labour government and the Conservatives backed the new terms. Jean-Louise remained sceptical and received reassurance when the Labour Party held a one-day meeting in late April 1975 and voted 2 to 1 to exit the Common Market.

* * *

My work with Walt broadened into assisting some of the European sales company's update their remuneration programmes, and I also helped with the coordination of the Ford of Europe Senior Salary Survey. The latter study involved collecting market data on salaries for positions comparable to executive jobs in Ford of Europe. My role was to prepare the job descriptions, create organisation charts and liaise with the consulting firm as it gathered the market data. Walt took a close interest since the results would affect the pay of his seniors, and if not carried out to their satisfaction, might affect his reputation and accelerate his repatriation.

During the next few weeks, my travels expanded to include Ford of Europe's sales companies based in Copenhagen, Helsinki and Amsterdam. These were mostly one-day trips, but in Helsinki I was asked to help the company carry out its own salary survey, necessitating a weekend stay. I chose not to go sight-seeing in the city, but instead I went birdwatching with the help of a local Ford of Finland employee. One of the species I wanted to see close-up was the red-throated diver. Many times I had observed these birds migrating over the North Sea past Spurn Point. They flew low and fast over the water, usually in small flocks (and sometimes individually), in single file, with their necks extended forward and their feet stretched out behind. Other than for the breeding season, these birds generally live out at sea.

Luckily, there was an opportunity to see them in their nesting habitat. In Finland, red-throated divers arrive during April to breed on the many marshy ponds close to lakes where fish can be caught. We drove a few miles north of Helsinki, and for several hours I enjoyed watching these shy and vigilant birds. They swim gracefully, sometimes in pairs, with their neck erect, bill tipped upwards and body low in the water. Occasionally, they disappear under water, looking for food, and I listened to the males' plaintive love cries (low pitched moans), the warning croaks when they sensed my presence and their meowing musical calls.

This was the first time I had formally extended my bird watching internationally and I found it stimulating and fascinating. I hoped that in the future I could expand the hobby beyond spotting species that appeared in Britain to varieties that were no more than vagrants back home, and maybe even exotic kinds that were usually seen only in zoos.

* * *

Jean-Louise celebrated her thirtieth birthday by telling me that she was once more pregnant and that the baby was due in November. We were delighted, although we realised that raising two children would be much more challenging than one. Jean-Louise had returned to teaching for one day a week, but we decided that this should end following the summer school break. Curiously, James was now at the same school as Jean-Louise and had supported her transition back into teaching, and he was disappointed that he would lose his professional contact with a person he considered to be his best friend at school. We decided not to tell our daughter that another baby was on the way, although she seemed to sense what was going on and became clingy and demanding of her mother.

* * *

A short time later, on 5th June 1975, the European Communities referendum took place. We were bombarded with newspaper and television advertising, arguing from both sides and eventually voted "yes". For Jean-Louise, it was a borderline decision because of her worry that Britain would lose its sovereignty—an outcome predicted by the "vote no" advocates. The counter argument was that Britain needed to be a member of the largest concentration of trading power in the world, and that the opponents' arguments were speculative and unreliable. The election turnout was 64 percent, and two out of three participants voted to remain.

* * *

Early July had us preparing for our holiday with Chris and Angela. My office was quiet with Walt on home leave in America. The main surprise in Britain was that the trade unions had agreed to a formal one-year limit on pay increases as part of the government's latest "attack on inflation". The following month, a White Paper came through our letter box explaining that, effective from August 1975, the government would limit pay increases to once every 12 months and that awards should not exceed £6 a week (approximately 10 percent). The two exceptions were prior commitments (which allowed Ford to implement its increases through September 1976), and adjusting women's pay to be equal with that of men by the end of 1975.

The announced acceptance by the trade unions of an incomes

policy gave us hope that the future would be more orderly and predictable, and that inflation would fall. Financially, I was well looked after; I received a further merit adjustment and was told that the bonus for my first six months with Walt was being paid into my bank account in accordance with the company's Supplemental Compensation Plan. The amount (approximately two-thirds of my monthly salary) was not a fortune, but the fact of it being given was what was important, as it meant that I was meeting the requirements of my position and had successfully acclimatised to working in international personnel management. There were concerns, communicated by Walt, that Ford's corporate profits might not fund the Plan in future years, and studies were underway to examine changes that would strengthen the incentive aspects of the bonus arrangements.

In the interim, I completed preparations for our holiday in Spain with Chris and family, hoping that soon there would be more time for international birdwatching. I looked forward to relaxing and enjoying the Spanish sunshine, sea, sand and sangria.

(Jean-Louise, July 1975) "It's been a memorable year and probably the best one in my life. I have a beautiful daughter who's now walking and can say a few words, John's relaxed at work and is usually home on time, and he places his family ahead of everything. He likes international work, and I've adjusted to his travels overseas. He still struggles with time for birdwatching but his trip to Helsinki sounds as if it was an exception. I hope he will stay working in headquarters and never return to industrial relations in Dagenham.

"I'm pregnant once more and excited to be having a second baby. I'm used to running the household and taking care of

the family, although I feel a little sad that my teaching career has ended—at least for now. James says he will miss me; he has been an important provider of encouragement during my eight years in the profession. However, I don't think I can teach and look after two young children at the same time.

"Now I'm pregnant, my doctor has warned that his union has begun industrial action against the government because of its intension to require doctors in public service to abandon private practice. It's all about socialising the National Health Service. The dispute involves non-cooperation rather than a strike, so I hope it won't interfere with the birth of our second child.

"At least we have a clear decision on the Common Market. We're staying in, and I think that's right. Mr Callaghan was responsible for leading the negotiations with the Europeans and seems to have been very successful. There's also a school of thought that he might one day replace Prime Minister Wilson. There's still no end to high inflation and we'll see if the latest agreement between the government and unions helps. The supply of sugar was a mess, and I have our neighbours to thank for our deliveries from Cologne.

"I'm very much looking forward to the holiday in Spain with Chris and Angela, and we're going to share babysitting in the evenings so that each couple can take turns to go out on their own. Then I'll get ready for the birth of my second child and become a stay-at-home mum."

Red-throated diver: This is a slender, graceful, migratory bird, with a slightly up-tilted bill. It is a medium-sized seabird and the smallest member of the diver family at about 55 cm/22 in. long. It breeds across Scandinavia, northern Russia and Iceland as well as in northern Scotland, Orkney and the Shetlands. During the breeding season, it has blackish-brown plumage on its back, neck and head, greyish-white underparts, a red throat and a black tail. In winter, the red on its throat disappears and its face and throat become pure white, while the upper parts of its body are brown and finely speckled with white. It swims with its body low in the water and its legs extended laterally, like oars, rather than being held below the body. It usually jumps before diving, it can stay under water for up to a minute and a half, and its large wingspan allows the bird to take off from water very quickly. About 1,300 pairs breed in Britain, and during winter this number rises to around 17,000 birds, mostly along the east coast, and patches along the west. It is estimated that 92,000 pairs breed throughout Europe. In Finnish, it is called "Kaakkuri" based on the sound it makes.

Its European relative, known as the great-northern diver, is the most widespread diver in North America and is known as the common loon. The red-throated loon breeds in Alaska and can be seen along American coasts during winter.

35

The Song Thrush

We were on our way to Spain to rent the holiday home of our kindest neighbours and to gadabout with our closest friends. I had hoped to do some birdwatching during our visit but was cautioned by Jean-Louise that I needed to help her look after our daughter and not to ignore Chris and his family. She reminded me it was our first long holiday together as parents. Nevertheless, I did see the elegant and rare Andouin's gull, with its red beak, and also the more common larger, yellow-legged gulls that were flying close to where we stayed in Ibiza.

I was now at ease with foreign travel, thanks to my time with Walt, and I no longer viewed Europeans as strange, having worked alongside them in Ford of Europe. Prices were lower in Spain, restaurant menus used pictures rather than words to guide tourists on what to eat and banks changed into pesetas our sterling Travellers' Cheques (a cheque for a fixed amount that could be cashed after the holder endorsed it). Back then, foreign was foreign, with no contact back home and nothing in English on television.

We left Luton airport with Chris and his family early in the morning. I found seats in the smoking section at the rear of the aircraft because my wife wanted to smoke, while Chris checked his wife and daughter into the non-smoking area at the front of the cabin. Jean-Louise took care of our child while I occupied the window seat. I gazed out at the billowing white clouds and started to daydream. My mind drifted to my childhood days when holidays were spent in dreary caravans, rented bungalows and youth hostels, usually close to the cold and windswept shoreline of the Yorkshire coast. Money back then was in short supply and I was typically left on my own to do what I chose. Here I was, sitting in a comfortable aeroplane, with a stunning family, flying towards the Mediterranean's rich blue waters and a sunny, warm island of red earth, pine-covered hills and pink and red bougainvillea, and with enough pesetas in my pocket not to worry about how much we would spend.

Jean-Louise sat beside me, attractive as ever, and still using the *Tweed* perfume that I sometimes purchased from duty-free shops during the return journeys after my overseas business trips. Her outfits had changed over time to floral-patterned dresses, Mothercare maternity apparel and more formal blazers with skirts. Her hair was shorter, cut to just below her ears in a page-boy style, and she had replaced her spectacles with contact lenses.

My outward appearance had altered thanks to the more stylish clothing that Jean-Louise insisted that I wear. Physically, I wore eyeglasses to correct my short-sightedness, and the battle with my hair had been won as it now lay flat across my scalp and covered my ears. My teeth remained crooked, my body still turned lobster-pink under the sun, I still looked younger than my age and I showed no signs of putting on weight.

I reflected silently on my progress to date. There had been no plan; I had simply taken advantage of whatever opportunities had come my way, knowing that I was responsible for my own destiny. I had never felt desperate about what was happening, although I was occasionally very anxious about work. At the start, my career decisions were self-centred, but slowly I learned to balance work with my family life. In many ways my achievements had been built on serendipities, ranging from free higher education, hearing about the "milk round", the "cup of tea" incident with Mr Welsh and my impulsive acceptance of the Ford traineeship, to stumbling into Personnel Management (now Human Resources)—a function about which I had known nothing—and most recently into international personnel work. I also had the advantage of employment at a company that was very successful, despite its awful industrial relations record, and that generously extended to its staff the same general increases that it negotiated for its manual workers. My times in Dagenham were nightmares, but I had seen them through and was now working in a building close to home in a function that was increasingly important to multi-national firms.

It was satisfying to think that I had made something of myself, although I felt that there was still more to come, and I appreciated all the help I had received. There had been no single component in my existence that had opened the doors to success; it was a combination of circumstances and grasping hold of what was presented in my efforts to do better.

Managing our household budget, I realised that my employer had increased my salary five-fold since I was hired in August 1966, whereas prices had risen by only 150 percent during the same period, despite the intuition that everything always cost more.

During our eight years of marriage, the savings we had accumulated were fairly modest, but we did own a fully-furnished home, the value of which was increasing in giant strides (around 40 percent during our first year of ownership because of housing shortages, wage inflation and the availability of mortgages), and our debts were no greater than a manageable mortgage and a small loan that was still owed on the dining room table and chairs. Thanks to the government's education policy at the time we attended university, neither of us had any student debt to worry about and, compared to pensioners and people who had lost their jobs for whatever reason, we were well off. I wondered what might have happened if I had become a hospital porter or a farm hand.

My wife had also played a critical role in my advancement, including suffering the consequences of my impulsive job decisions. Admittedly, there was help from other people along the road, but none did more to guide me than Jean-Louise. Despite our different backgrounds, opposing political beliefs and her questions over Ford's treatment of women, she looked after me from the day I left university, and she did for me what my mother had done until I started in higher education. She had put up with my decision that left her to go to Reading University on her own and forgiven my one-night flirtation with Vanessa. She even encouraged my birdwatching, and in return I put up with James. We had both learned to be tolerant.

These thoughts abruptly ended when my daughter clambered onto my knee, wanting to look out of the window, and carrying the Spanish doll that I had bought during one of my visits to Ford of Spain in Valencia. A little while later, we were told to fasten our seat belts and prepare for the descent into Ibiza airport.

* * *

After 30 miles (50 km) of driving from the airport, our neighbours' flat appeared in the distance. It was situated in a white-washed block of homes that stood amid a field of rubble, none of which we had seen in the photographs our German neighbours had shown us. For security, a twelve-foot-high wall surrounded the structure, with access on one side, and we were relieved to see that inside the wall the place was much more attractive.

The flat itself was decorated with off-white walls and glazed, dark-red terracotta floor-tiles; the lounge furniture was bold and chunky, made of dark wood and chestnut-brown leather, and accented with bright yellow and cobalt-blue cushions. Complimentary wine was waiting for us in the kitchen refrigerator, and the property was scented with a potpourri of cinnamon pieces and dried oranges. The staircase up to the bedrooms was adorned with blue and white floral mosaic tiles, and beyond the landing were a master bedroom and a much smaller guest bedroom. There was a solid wooden double-bed in each room, with a matching wardrobe and side-table, and several pieces of wall-mounted iron sculpture. We tossed a coin, and our friends won the master suite.

Several chairs and a table stood in a small area at the front of the flat, and around the corner was the complex's swimming pool. Along the near-side of the pool, a row of geraniums showed off their attractive salmon pink and red flowers, and across the water, pink bougainvillea climbed the white-washed walls. The weather was perfect, sunny and warm, and our first exploration was a walk across the rock-strewn field to the nearby beach. Chris and I wheeled the babies' pushchairs, and on the way back we stopped to buy groceries.

The beach was golden sand that crunched under foot, and it ran in both directions well into the distance. The turquoise-coloured sea formed ripple marks at the edge of the beach, and the flower-scented air was carried by soft, light breezes over a landscape of mottled browns, rich creams, pale greens and blues. It was extraordinarily peaceful, as there was only a handful of beachgoers present, the birds were enjoying a siesta and high-rise hotels had not yet arrived in the area.

During the daytime we shared stories and caught up with each other's news. Chris told me how he had discovered that his father's firm depended on one very large customer only, and he had been busy diversifying the company to include long-distance transportation now that Britain was in the Common Market. It had been important to him a few weeks earlier that the results of the referendum kept Britain as a member of the European Economic Community. He asked about Ford and my plans to stay with the firm. I told him I had no intention of leaving, despite vehicle sales having fallen to their lowest level in ten years. I thought Ford was in a far better shape than British Leyland which, as a result of the Ryder Report published earlier in the year, was in the process of being placed under government control and would receive over £1 billion to fend off bankruptcy. Chrysler UK and Vauxhall (a subsidiary of General Motors) were launching new models to better compete with Ford of Britain.

"What about Walt?" Chris asked. "Do you enjoy working for an American?"

I told him that I was treated well, although Walt was sometimes critical of my work, and his decisions could be irritating. He expected a great deal from his people but I had learned a lot. I shared with Chris the story of how he was in an uproar when Ford of Italy implemented salary increases without his approval. The company had been ordered by the Italian courts to pay staff no less than the firm's published grade minimums, and these retroactive adjustments were implemented before Ford of Europe was notified. Walt was livid and asked me to check with Ford of Europe's General Counsel to be sure the increases were legally required. Once confirmed, I was instructed to send a warning letter to Italian management, reminding them that Walt needed to approve all salary increases, legally required or otherwise, "before" they were granted.

Meanwhile, Angela and Jean-Louise had shifted their conversation to family matters.

"What'll you do once the second baby arrives?" Angela asked Jean-Louise. "Will you try to teach?"

"Not for at least a couple of years; I've resigned from the school, but they say they will take me back when I'm ready."

"Does John help you at home and with your daughter?" was Angela's next question.

"Now he's back at headquarters, yes, regularly," Jean-Louise smiled.

"And what about his birds?" Angela was recalling my birdwatching on Strangford Lough.

"Not as much as before. He doesn't have time because of work, and the weekends he spends with us. He's done some birdwatching overseas, but most of his travel is to large cities and therefore there's no opportunity to see anything."

I nodded in agreement.

Chris and I recalled our early days in Ford. We talked about David, wondered about the whereabouts of Chris's first girlfriend who had arranged the "Vanessa" party, and debated the careers of some of the senior staff we knew at Ford on the basis of "where are they now?" I admitted that long ago I had lost contact with my university friends, although Chris mentioned that he continued his friendship with Richard, my fellow lodger during the third year at Hull.

"At least I now understand what you're saying," Chris declared with a grin. "Back then, it was difficult to interpret your Yorkshire accent."

I joked that my accent was no worse than his wife's strong Irish brogue.

"Do you still go to Brands Hatch?" Chris sounded a little jealous. "That's something I miss living in Nottingham."

"Not anymore," I told him. "We've taken our daughter once, but she didn't like it and the doctor warned us that loud noises might cause her permanent hearing damage."

During the holidays our infant was the happiest we had ever seen. She delighted in excavating the sand, paddling along the edge of the sea and floating in the complex's swimming pool on her water-wings. She especially loved the white bonnet and lime-green swimming suit decorated with white polka dots that she wore every day. She ran straight into the water whenever we let her, and she tried to pet every dog we met on our walks. She liked looking after Chris and Angela's daughter, and told Angela that she was going to have a baby of her own. We enjoyed the holiday so much that we decided to go together to Albufeira a year later.

* * *

Back in the office, not a lot was happening. Walt returned from his home leave predicting serious problems for the company. Apparently the United States car market was suffering a serious slump in sales, and large inventories of unsold vehicles had accumulated. He had heard that it was unlikely the Supplemental Compensation Plan would fund or be able to pay out bonuses for 1975 due to low global profitability.

Meanwhile, Britain remained in a double-dip recession. The economy was chaotic, with companies like the motorcycle manufacturer Norton-Villiers-Triumph going into receivership, and others like the specialist car builder Jensen Motors dramatically reducing its workforce. Latest reports indicated that about 1.25 million people were unemployed, which was a relatively low percentage at 4.5, but double the rate of a few years earlier. By October 1975, the country's annual inflation rate had touched 26 percent, and although Jean-Louise and I worried about what might happen next, I thought myself fortunate to have found a reasonably secure position. Since most of my duties involved countries outside Britain, I believed I was fairly well protected from redundancy.

We showed off our Granada Ghia to relatives by attending a family christening in Manchester, and at a wedding of my cousin in a village outside York. Socially, our lives were focused on friends and family, and we eliminated most outside leisure activities in order to conserve our earnings and get ready for our second child.

It was appropriate to stay out of central London because the Irish Republican Army had resumed its bombing campaign. On 5th September 1975 there was an explosion at the London Hilton hotel that killed two people and injured 63, and on 9th October a bombing outside a tube station killed one person and injured another 20.

* * *

At the start of November 1975, I proposed to Jean-Louise that we should take our daughter to the local Guy Fawkes bonfire on Wednesday, the 5th of the month. It would be 10 years since we first met, thanks to Anton, and I wondered about his whereabouts. I assumed he must still be living in Hull, although I later learned that he had moved overseas shortly after obtaining his doctorate, which probably explained why we lost contact with one another. Over dinner one evening, I announced: "On Wednesday, it's 10 years since we first met. I'll be home early, and I think we should take our daughter to the bonfire to celebrate."

Jean-Louise welcomed the suggestion and asked if James

and his family could be invited as she had not seen him since she had finished teaching. I thought it was a good idea, and at about 4.30pm on 5th November, we set off on foot to the bonfire that was being held in a field about a quarter of a mile away from where we lived. The evening was dry and mild.

We packed a shoulder bag with snacks, nappies, two packs of twenty-inch sparklers, matches and a change of clothing for our daughter. We also had a flask of tomato soup, several sausage rolls, some lemonade and a pack of biscuits. I pushed Louisa in her green-and-white-striped collapsible pushchair and Jean-Louise ambled alongside me. Our daughter occasionally escaped and scampered along the pavement, pointing to various objects and babbling the words she had mastered. Once tired, she returned to the comfort of her buggy.

James and family met us at the corner of the High Street and Sun Street, and we walked across the road together. There was already a large gathering, and the bonfire had just been lit. Jean-Louise and James' wife took care of the three children while James and I chatted.

There were lots to talk about; three days earlier an art student had firebombed the Royal Pavilion in Brighton for no other reason than he felt anti-social, and recently the Queen and Prime Minister Wilson had inaugurated the first pumping of oil from the North Sea. We speculated about the London Spaghetti House siege when eight staff members of the restaurant had been taken hostage and held for five days, and we wondered if the incident had been an attempted robbery or a political statement by the Black Liberation Army against discrimination, as the attackers had claimed. Rhodesia's peace talks had failed and the civil war between Ian Smith's white government and the African nationalists continued; General Franco's 36-year rule of Spain had come to an end because of illness (he died a few days later); and Iceland had extended its territorial fishing limits from 50 miles (80 km) to 200 miles (320 km). In the United States, the Vietnam War was over, and the United States Supreme Court had ruled that states could support teachers who spanked misbehaving pupils, as long as the students had ignored suitable warnings.

Our conversation then turned to personal matters. James told me he had been appointed the head of his department, and he was thinking of creating his own company to offer vocational training to sixth form students. He talked nostalgically about working with Jean-Louise and was saddened by the expectation that she would not return to teaching because of my success at Ford and her need to care for two children. He was still a union representative and believed that the Social Contract would eventually work to solve Britain's economic problems. More of his East Ham friends were now unemployed, and they had either moved away to find new jobs on the docks, or were putting up with whatever they could find locally.

I told him it was unlikely that I would move from my current job for at least another year because I thoroughly enjoyed overseas work and it was more secure than domestic responsibilities. I was fortunate that Ford of Britain continued to prosper despite what was happening elsewhere in British motor industry. His chirpiness returned as he changed the subject and asked, "What about birdwatching? Is that something you still do, or does helping Jean-Louise take up all your time?"

I returned his smile. "I have time for both, but helping Jean-Louise comes first."

I told him that there were very few species of bird that I could now see in Essex that were new to me (except the odd vagrant), and therefore I spent much less time on spotting birds. During my travels to other countries I tried to do some birding, and I also hoped that one day soon I could return to Spurn Point Bird Observatory for a few days, as birdwatching was still my chosen hobby. I reminisced that it seemed like an eternity since my childhood days when I raided the nests of lapwings and moorhens (the common gallinule in North America) and took their eggs to eat for breakfast. If the moorhen's egg did not float and the lapwing's eggs were not pointed inwards, these were signs that the egg-laying was incomplete and therefore the eggs had not yet addled. I added that my major difficulty with birdwatching was that Jean-Louise found the hobby cold and boring, and she preferred not to accompany me with our daughter. However, I said I would always be grateful for the activity because of the skills it had provided me that were important to me to be successful during my adult life.

James gave me a strange look saying: "I'm not sure I understand."

I tried to explain how the expertise I had developed as a birdwatcher helped me both in my career as well as in my social development.

"I'm still not sure what you're talking about," persisted James. "It seems that all you do with birdwatching is stand and wait for the bird to fly by. I don't see how that helps with life."

"But it's what it teaches you," I replied. "It helped me develop skills that I could use as an adult. For example, it taught me to be patient, it made me think analytically, it showed me the importance of clear communications, and it assisted me to become well-organised and aware of the time, otherwise I would never have been birdwatching when birds were most likely to be present."

I then talked about my first visit to the Spurn Point Bird Observatory and my discovery that birds have feelings and personalities like humans. I had watched two partridges fly over the Warren Cottage on the evening of my arrival and saw the female fly into some electric wires where she was beheaded.

The male landed and remained on the ground for at least 30 minutes, calling out for her. It was an upsetting experience but it made me realise that birds are intelligent and care for each other, just like humans.

I admitted to James that, in my early days, I never thought about how birds felt when I stole their eggs, and I remembered collecting and trading the bright blue eggs with dark speckles of a song thrush. These eggs were more attractive than a blackbird's eggs, which were about the same size, but a dull, bluish green with reddish-brown blotches. The prettier the egg, the better exchange I could negotiate at school. The problem was finding a sufficiently large supply. Both species nested in the same habitat and, from the outside, built similar looking nests that were difficult to see inside. I solved the problem by learning that, if I reached into a nest and could feel its interior was lined with mud, it belonged to a song thrush, whereas the blackbird's nest was always lined with grass. It never occurred to me to wonder why the adult song thrush hung around the nest for a day or so after I took its eggs.

James thanked me for the explanation, but I am not sure he was convinced by my story. It did not matter; it was what I was thankful for.

As the bonfire burned, the two families separated. We drank our soup, ate the sausage rolls and chased our almost-two-year-old, who kept trying to toddle off into the dark. The event was much better organised than 10 years earlier. There were no bangers thrown, the display was organised by professionals, only adults were allowed close to the bonfire and earlier there had been strict rules controlling the sale of fireworks. We lit our sparklers and watched as streams of sparks cascade down their stems. When our daughter fell asleep and the air turned chilly, we started our trek back home. On the way, I mentioned to Jean-Louise that I might start to investigate my father's family now that I had more time. She said it was not a good idea and I would probably upset my mother.

As we neared home, our German neighbours came out to greet us and asked if they could follow us into our house, carrying several bottles of wine. In return for sharing their Moselle, they asked me to explain the purpose of Bonfire Night and who was this person called Guy Fawkes? After a few minutes, I began the story about the person I considered as my hero when I was a child, with my wife beside me, Treacle lying in front of us on the carpet, our daughter asleep upstairs and me thankful for the kindness of life.

(Jean-Louise, late November 1975) "I'm home from the hospital where the doctor took good care of me despite the private-sector dispute with the government, and John and I now have a healthy baby son. So far, our daughter has been curious rather than jealous, and she tries to stroke and kiss her sibling whenever I'm nursing him. John takes care of her when he's home and I've tried to reassure her that she's important to us and we love her. My father looks on from his chair and smiles at her antics. I often think of my mother and how proud she would be of her granddaughter and grandson. John's mother is visiting next month, on her way to join another cruise.

"Finally, things are happening in Britain that will help women. This year's Sex Discrimination Act came into force a few days ago. It may be too late for me, but it's supposed to stop discrimination against women at work, in housing, and who require education and training, although there is nothing that protects us against maternity and work-life conflicts. However,

at least it's a step in the right direction, and complements the Equal Pay Act that comes into force at the end of next month. Not all employers are happy; there's speculation that some firms are avoiding the Equal Pay regulations by employing women in roles where there are no male equivalents.

"John and I thrive on each other's company, and I don't think either of us is dissatisfied with the relationship. Life with two children will bring new responsibilities, but we'll make allowances for each other, not take disagreements too seriously and be trusting of one another. Occasionally he becomes obsessive over something unimportant and stubbornly ignores my input. I've learned to take no notice and not to argue because that only makes matters worse. If I'm respectful and patient, we usually reach an agreement a couple of days later, often by one of us poking fun at the other.

"Now I'm not working I need to watch my weight, and I'm thinking of taking up tennis; John says he might return to playing cricket, and our neighbours keep popping over; so far, they haven't run out of German wine. I think playing cricket will get in the way of John's birdwatching, but it's up to him to decide his priorities.

"My circle of friends keeps growing. I've met several mothers with children the same age as mine, and I'm in close contact with the neighbours on both sides of the house. I see James less frequently now that I'm not working, but I enjoyed our get-together at the recent Guy Fawkes bonfire. I've lost contact with the people I knew in Hull and Reading, but I'm still in touch with my two bridesmaids and their families. My physics teacher friend and her family are moving to the other side of London because her husband has found a job with an office equipment firm.

"It was fun being on holiday with Angela and Chris, and I'm

excited about going away again next year. I keep reminding John to organise the holiday, but his excuse is that Portugal is still in turmoil. Apparently, the Communists are trying to take over the newly appointed democratic government.

"All in all, though, life is good, and I'm thankful."

Song thrush: This well-known songbird is mainly resident and widespread in Britain, where there are approximately one million breeding pairs. Numbers declined by more than half after the 1970s, possibly due to loss of feeding and nesting habitats, but have recently shown signs of increasing. It is a medium-sized bird, 23 cm/ 9 in. long, and readily recognised by its brown back and the black, drop-shaped spots on its buff-white underparts. The bird's beautiful, loud and distinctive call is usually delivered by a solitary individual perched atop a lofty branch or other elevated location; it is a bold, bell-like song that permeates the countryside with notes or phrases repeated three or four times. The nest is built by the female, takes up to three weeks to construct and is usually situated low down, deep in a hedge or bush, where it can readily be raided by cats, jays, magpies and foxes, and this may also have contributed to the decline in numbers referred to above.

The species is only seen as a vagrant in North America, where its closest looking relative is the smaller Swainson's thrush.

36

California Dreaming

(Jean-Louise, late October 1979) "I'm near Lake Tahoe in Nevada at the Ponderosa Ranch. My five-year-old daughter and three-year-old son are with me, as well as my husband, and we're visiting a theme park based on the western television series 'Bonanza'. It was a programme John and I watched on television at home during the early 1970s. The family has just had its picture taken with us wearing old fashioned western outfits. We came to live in California two months ago.

"Travelling by car is quite different over here, and it's a little unpredictable at the moment because of the oil crisis. The Iranian Revolution has affected oil supplies and there's been panic buying. It's not really a petrol shortage; they call it 'odd-and-even rationing' because we can buy petrol only on evenly numbered days that coincide with our licence-plate number. The car is a large Oldsmobile Cutlass that's daunting to drive after my Ford Fiesta, Ford's smallest European car. The Iranian crisis has worsened because the Shah was recently given access to the United States for medical treatment, and maybe because John has just hired someone who used to work at the Tehran American School!

"It's a long story, but we're living close to San Francisco because of John's work. We transferred here during late August, and I'm still in the process of discovery and adjustment. There are many more opportunities for women in the United States but, unfortunately, I'm classified as an 'alien' and not permitted to work. I'm not sure I want to be here; it's a little intimidating and far from my father and family, and I worry about earthquakes. There was a major one in southern California a few days ago that added to my worries. I left my father behind, although he says he'll visit us early in the New Year, and it'll be only the second foreign country he has seen.

"John has become very successful in international remuneration and foreign service programmes, and has been posted here by the bank he joined in London 18 months ago. Now he is responsible for pay and benefit programmes in every country worldwide in which his employer operates, except for the United States. We have leased our house in Essex, and Treacle has been adopted by a friend of John's mother. So far, John's done nothing about investigating his father's family, and it's unlikely he'll do anything while we're over here.

"In a month's time, we're invited to dinner with some English people for what's called 'Thanksgiving'. It's apparently to celebrate the arrival of the pilgrims in America. John says it's like a British harvest festival, except that it takes place in homes rather than at churches. I plan to make a trifle for the sweet.

"Our son was born in good health two weeks after the 1975 bonfire night, and I stayed away from teaching to look after our two children. According to James, I missed out on a special salary adjustment averaging close to 30 percent that teachers received as a result of a government study. Contact with our German neighbours in Essex has been lost, and I've not heard from James lately. Occasionally I receive letters from Angela,

who says they'll visit us soon, and my friend the physics teacher writes to me. Both my bridesmaids are still in contact and have said they'll arrange a holiday over here; as has John's mother.

"John stayed with Walt for a further two years after our son's birth, but he was increasingly frustrated. His boss had little empathy for the Old World, and the decline in Ford's worldwide profits limited what was possible in Europe. At the beginning of 1978, John was head-hunted to work for an American bank in London. They wanted to use his international personnel experience in their Europe, Middle East and Africa operations, giving him the chance to broaden his country knowledge beyond Western Europe. He never expected that international work would be his passport out of Ford, always expecting at some point to return to industrial relations. After accepting the bank's offer, and before we came here, he spent 18 months commuting by train from Essex to central London, except when he was travelling overseas.

"Throughout his career, John has been very fortunate with the help he has received from other people and has been very opportunistic with his decisions. Although he gives credit to the basic skills he learned during birdwatching, I believe that serendipity played an important part in his success; also, he listened and acted on the advice given by others. It was not practical to plan a career around an emerging global business world. Yet in recent times, more and more companies have integrated their people, products and affiliates worldwide and have encouraged national governments to deregulate and dismantle trade barriers. John's work on introducing containerisation in the Case Marshalling Area was one example of the growing importance of international trade, and the need for it to become more efficient and cheaper for transporting goods around the world.

* * *

"Industrial relations stayed chaotic prior to us leaving Britain, both at Ford and across the country, in part because annual inflation continued to run at around 25 percent. The government had given up on voluntary wage controls and introduced a statutory pay limit during the second half of 1975 of approximately 10 percent for one year which the trade unions accepted. In August 1976, a second 12-month phase was implemented that lowered the limit to around 8 percent; again, the unions supported the government, but less enthusiastically. In July 1977, the government announced that the second-phase restrictions would continue for a further 12 months, which the unions disliked, but accepted after prolonged negotiations and assurances that the government would not interfere in pay negotiations. At least the wage controls helped to reduce annual inflation to around 16 percent during 1976 and 1977, and down to 8 percent in 1978.

"During July 1978, the government announced a new 12-month incomes restriction of 5 percent beginning 1st August 1978, whereas the trade unions had hoped for a return to free collective bargaining. There was a strong negative reaction from workers. One of the first confrontations was with hourly-paid employees at John's former employer, Ford of Britain. During autumn 1978, the company offered its unions the statutory 5 percent and an invitation to productivity talks. The response was immediate: 15,000 workers walked off the job, and their colleagues followed as the transport workers union declared the strike official. Nine weeks later, the company conceded a 17 percent pay award and weekly productivity payments of £4, much to the anger of the government. It responded by threatening business sanctions against Ford (and other companies that breached the 5 percent limit) that

provoked strong criticism from the opposition Conservative Party led by Margaret Thatcher.

"The settlement became the forerunner of *'The Winter of Discontent' and the major disruptions that affected our home lives. First, the petrol-tanker drivers went on strike during January 1979 for a 60 percent wage increase, causing petrol shortages, long waits at the petrol pumps and motorists fighting among themselves to get to the front of the queue. This was followed by the railway workers staging one-day strikes that disrupted the daily commute to London. Then the other lorry drivers, who delivered everything except petrol, stopped work in support of a 40 percent wage claim. Supermarkets were quickly emptied of bread, sugar, butter, flour, salt, cereals, biscuits and toilet paper, and panic buying and hording returned. People spent much more time in the home. Tomatoes and fruit were left rotting on the docks, butchers complained of no meat deliveries, and farmers claimed that their pigs were starving because animal food deliveries had been blocked.*

"Finally, it was the turn of the public sector, whose employees kicked-off with a 'day of action' during January 1979 and continued their campaign with a succession of stoppages. Affected were hospital workers, dustbin men, librarians, school caretakers, grave diggers, public lavatory attendants, water and sewage workers, road gritters and airport staff. The country was in turmoil. Libraries closed, hospitals accepted urgent cases only, and if you happened to die, you had to wait for a grave to be dug. I soon found myself storing piles of rubbish in black bags at the front of the house, hoping they would be collected one day by the dustbin men. Meanwhile, John was away visiting places like Cairo, Karachi, Madrid, Manama, Paris and Frankfurt. He was happy to be travelling, and at least he could bring home food

supplies that were difficult to find in Britain as well as toys for the children.

"The effects of the chaos caused two significant events. First, the James Callaghan government (Harold Wilson resigned as Prime Minister in April 1976) failed to win a vote of confidence, and a general election took place on 3rd May 1979. It was won by Margaret Thatcher (who had taken over leadership of the Conservative Party from former Prime Minister Edward Heath in February 1975). The Conservative Party promised to better balance the interests of the British people with the rights of trade unions. The second event was our family decision to join the 'brain drain', at least temporarily. John's employer wanted him in its California headquarters to manage employee remuneration worldwide. Thereafter, they promised to either return him home to London or send him somewhere else. Consequently, in late August 1979 we left Heathrow on a Pan Am flight for San Francisco. For me and the children, this was our first visit to America.

"So far, it's been tolerable here. We've rented a modern-designed, single-family home, with floor-to-ceiling picture windows, wood panelling and gabled ceilings, and the furniture is also rented. Some of the words people use here are strange, and my daughter's school-teachers appear to be more interested in playing games than educating her. Taking up tennis after I stopped work has turned out to be a benefit, and I've already found a group of women tennis players who welcomed me. John's using public transport to get to work; not surprisingly, he catches the first bus out of the valley and the last bus home, but at least his hours are predictable, and he doesn't work at weekends.

"He's explained to me that we will have to spend Christmas in Canada. Apparently the bank obtained the wrong work visa for him and we are being thrown out of the country by

the immigration people to collect the correct paperwork in Vancouver. For me and the children, it's exciting; we can visit the zoo and go sightseeing, while John has to queue outside the United States Consulate.

"For the time being, his birdwatching is limited, although he's purchased 'An Audubon Handbook of Western Birds'. He was shocked that it shows over 460 species in the western United States, as this is almost double the number currently on his Life List. He's also confused because Americans call some species by names that are different from those he is used to in Europe. For example, there are murres not guillemots, loons in place of divers, linnets known here as house finches and tits called either titmice or chickadees. He's proud of spotting several new species, such as the highly vocal scrub-jay, the perching and swooping western bluebird, the green blur of Anna's hummingbird as it flies by in search of food, and the inconspicuous but large sparrow known as the California towhee.

"I've no idea what will happen to us in the future, assuming we are let out of Vancouver, but I sense there are many changes ahead of us. I have already visited someone's home and was introduced to a videocassette recorder (VCR), and there's talk about everyone owning a personal computer. Apple is talking about replacing its current model with something cheaper and easier to operate (what was to become the Macintosh), and IBM hopes to launch a competing product with what it calls a "DOS" in a few months' time. I've also been told to buy my children an Atari Video Computer System (VCS).

"For the time being, I'm resting at home and enjoying the sunshine."

Acknowledgements

THIS NOVEL WOULD not have been possible without access to multiple documents that were available on the internet. Additionally, I was helped by the many records that I personally accumulated, and which survived the years when I was moving between jobs, employers and countries. I am especially grateful to the Ford Motor Company Limited of Britain for the memories it left me with and to the UK Institute of Personnel and Development (currently the CIPD) that gave me the education in personnel management necessary for my career.

I must also acknowledge Henry Friedman and Sander Meredeen (both of whom I was acquainted with at Ford) for their memory joggers and the details they provide in their book *The Dynamics of Industrial Conflict.* Statistical information on Ford of Britain vehicles at the time of my narrative are contained in Martin Rawbone's publication, *Ford in Britain.*

For the text of the story, I give special thanks to my development editor,—Mary Rakow of San Francisco,—who improved the narrative and, more importantly, urged my creativity. I am also indebted to Liz York in London who spent many hours proof reading the work, and also Kelley Way of Walnut Creek, California who provided thoughtful legal advice.

In addition, I owe thanks to Sarah Spencer of Gatekeeper

Press who guided the book's cover design and assisted with some of the bird illustrations. More importantly, I have "Nik" of Book Beaver in Britain to thank for many of the illustrations. I must also recognise the Royal Society for the Protection of Birds (RSPB) that nurtured my birdwatching skills through my early years, ably assisted thereafter by the National Audubon Society in the United States. I will never forget the Warden and my friends at Spurn Point Bird Observatory during the 1960's.

Special recognition goes to members of the Larkspur Boys' Book Club (Bill, Bruce, Dave, Jack, Richard and Terry) for their encouragement and advice, the Bay Area Independent Publishers' Association (and especially Ruth, Becky, John and Val) for their author guidance, the Marin County Lucas Valley Poker Group (Chuck, Dave, John, Mike, Rick and Tom) for their recommendations on the book's cover design and Book Passage (Corte Madera, California) for its input to the novel's storyline. My thanks are also due to Nancy Reich, who gave me infinite encouragement and advice, and my son and daughter (Robert and Louisa) for their support at all stages. I particularly want to thank the people who took time to review early drafts, including Chris and Angela in Nottingham; Jane in York; Damien in London; Donna and Steve in New York; Audrey and Tony in Salt Lake City; and Richard Owens in Mill Valley, California.

My deepest gratitude goes to my departed wife, Mary Lynne, on whom so much of Jean-Louise is based, and who acted as the motivation behind this book. Last of all, my thanks go to you, the reader.

Birdwatcher Appendix

THE FOLLOWING FEW pages provide an extract from my Birder Notebook that I composed as a teenager; the example I give was written during April 1961 when I visited Spurn Point Bird Observatory, probably for the first time. I share it to illustrate the life-long passion I have for birdwatching and to give encouragement to those of you who might desire to embrace the hobby, even if it is no more than sitting on a chair in your garden, armed with binoculars, a telephoto camera and an appropriate Bird Identification Field Guide.

Along with the Notes taken during my visits to other birding sites, these data form the basis of my life list of species I have seen. The drawings I made back in 1961 were to remind me of what I observed and to help me justify to my peers the identification of certain species.

Bird watching today is much easier thanks to the proliferation of birding organisations; for example, the ones I am familiar with include the American Birding Association, the Cornell Laboratory of Ornithology, the Audubon Society, the Royal Society for the Protection of Birds and the British Trust for Ornithology. There are also multiple local birding clubs, as well as the organisations committed to conservation such as the Nature Conservancy, the World Wildlife Fund and the Sierra Club. At least, with this novel, I hope to have sparked your curiosity.

The hobby is recorded as the second most popular outdoor activity in the United States after gardening, and in the United Kingdom the pastime is more popular than fishing.

And do not be confused with what people call you—"bird watcher" is fine. The term "birder" can be used but may be confused with wildfowl shooters or males who chase after girls. "Ornithologist" suggests an expertise of a scientific nature and "lister" or "ticker" indicates someone whose main purpose is to add to their bird list. And finally there is "twitcher", those bird watchers who drop everything to frantically chase after rare birds to add to their life tally.

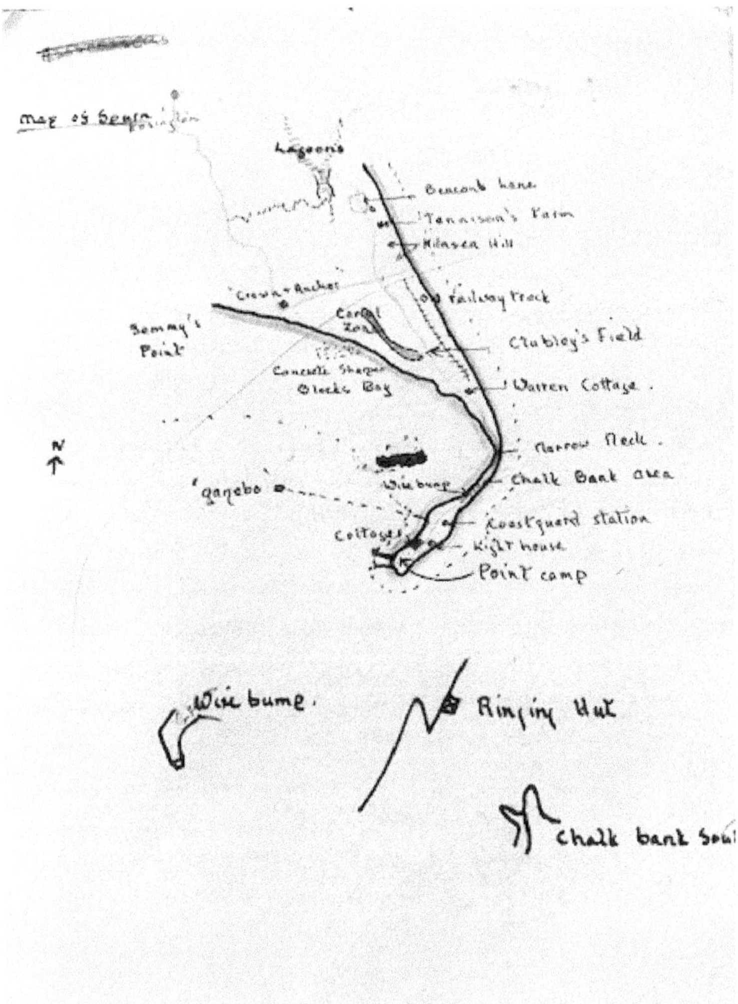
Lagoons
Beacon Lane
Tennison's Farm
Kilnsea Hill
Crown + Anchor
Railway Track
Clubley's Field
Warren Cottage
Narrow Neck
Chalk Bank area
Gazebo
Cottages
Coastguard station
Light house
Point camp
N
Wireburne.
Ringing Hut
Chalk bank

SPURN **APRIL 10th – 13th (inc) 1961**

Spurn is the most South Easterly extent of Yorkshire, and has been formed by the deposition of sediment brought from the North, when the sea current is arrested by the emerging Humber current. However, the coast is under constant threat of erosion by the sea, especially at the narrow Neck. The sand is held together largely by buckthorn and coarse grass. The area is littered with the remnants of the 2nd World War such as pill boxes and huts, some of which have been converted into habitable huts. At the point are the cottages, the lighthouse, the coast guard and lifeboat station, and the remnants of what was the centre of activity in the last war.

The observatory has been established for many years, and bird ringing is a prominent feature using numerous traps. Many migratory birds come down here especially in bad weather but many other fly over. Last Autumn a Pallas's Leaf Warbler was seen which led to the inauguration of a "Lifer-Tin" which is a tin to which you pay a 1d or 3d, for each new species you see according to its rarity. All birds ringed, seen, and retrapped are stored down in separate registers.

Willow Warbler
Black Redstart
♂
Reed Bunting
♂

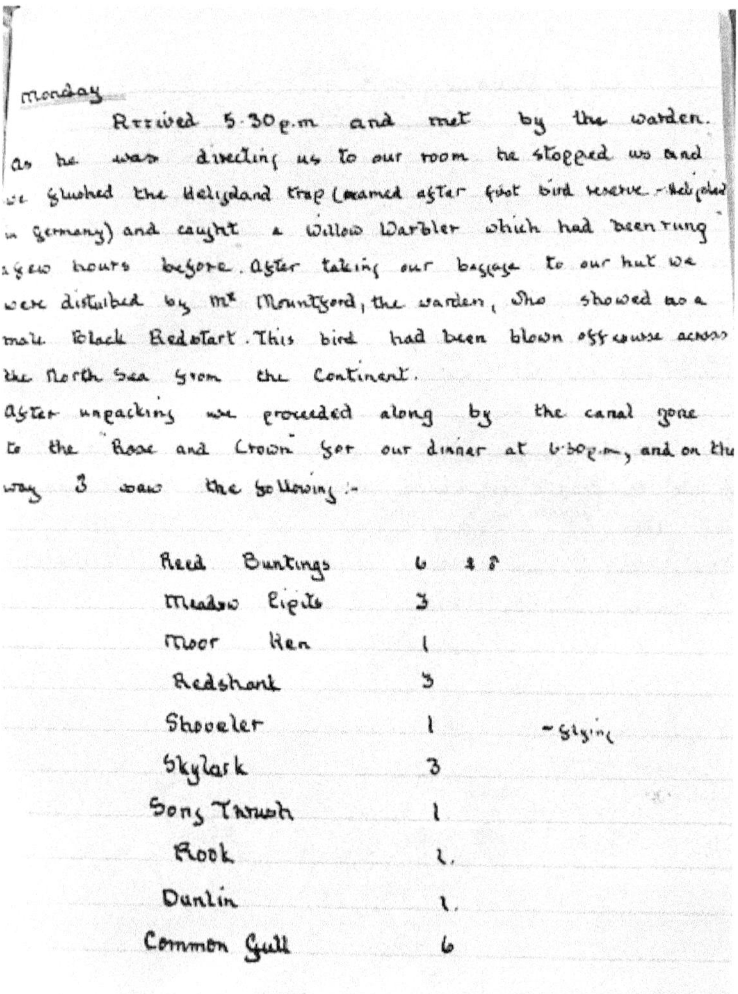

Monday

Arrived 5.30p.m and met by the warden. As he was directing us to our room he stopped us and we flushed the Heligoland trap (named after first bird reserve - Heligoland in Germany) and caught a Willow Warbler which had been rung a few hours before. After taking our baggage to our hut we were disturbed by Mr Mountford, the warden, who showed us a male Black Redstart. This bird had been blown off course across the North Sea from the Continent.

After unpacking we proceeded along by the canal gone to the "Rose and Crown" for our dinner at 6.30p.m, and on the way I saw the following:-

Reed Buntings	6 & 8	
Meadow Pipits	3	
Moor Hen	1	
Redshank	3	
Shoveler	1	- flying
Skylark	3	
Song Thrush	1	
Rook	2.	
Dunlin	2.	
Common Gull	6	

Whinchat
♂
Ringed Plover
Greenfinch
♂

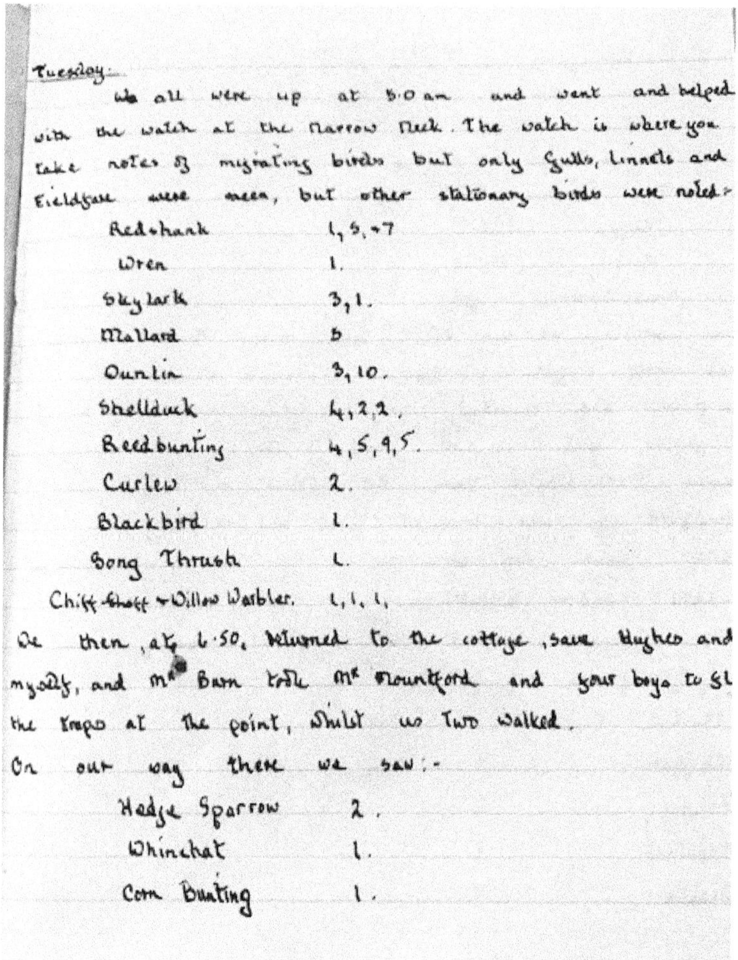

Tuesday:

We all were up at 5.0 am and went and helped with the watch at the narrow neck. The watch is where you take notes of migrating birds but only Gulls, Linnets and Fieldfare were seen, but other stationary birds were noted:-

Redshank	1, 5, +7
Wren	1.
Skylark	3, 1.
Mallard	5
Dunlin	3, 10.
Shellduck	4, 2, 2.
Reedbunting	4, 5, 9, 5.
Curlew	2.
Blackbird	1.
Song Thrush	1.
Chiff ~~Chaff~~ + Willow Warbler.	1, 1, 1,

We then, at 6.50, returned to the cottage, save Hughes and myself, and Mr Barn took Mr Mountford and four boys to see the traps at the point, whilst us two walked.

On our way there we saw:-

Hedge Sparrow	2.
Whinchat	1.
Corn Bunting	1.

Scaup
♂
Redwing
Dunlin
Summer.

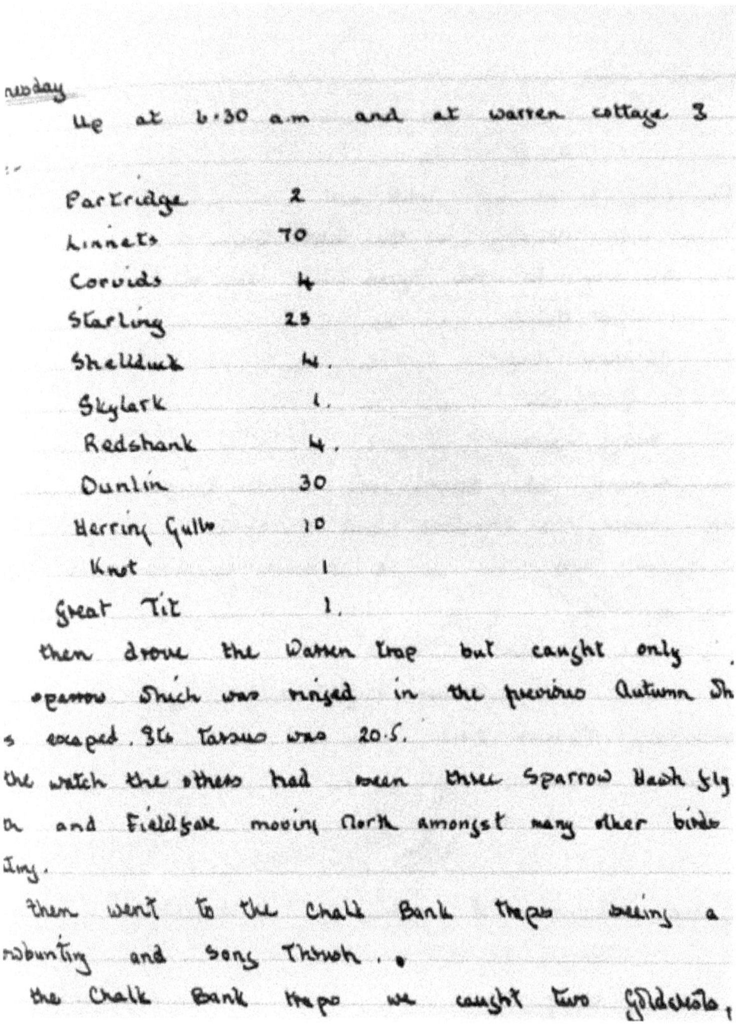

nesday

Up at 6.30 a.m and at warren cottage 3

:-

Partridge	2
Linnets	70
Corvids	4
Starling	25
Shellduck	4.
Skylark	1.
Redshank	4.
Dunlin	30
Herring Gulls	10
Knot	1
Great Tit	1.

then drove the Warren trap but caught only .
sparrow which was ringed in the previous Autumn Sh
s escaped. Its Tarsus was 20.5.
the watch the others had seen three Sparrow Hawk fly
n and Fieldfare moving North amongst many other birds
ing.

then went to the Chalk Bank traps seeing a
nbunting and Song Thrush. .

the Chalk Bank traps we caught two Goldcrests,

Wheatear !

& returned at 7.15 to the cottage and helped clean the rooms. At 9.0 a m we went for our breakfast, on way seeing two golden Plover.

At 10.20 am caught bus to Hull whilst Mr Burn took our baggage.

Birds Rung at Spurn Jan 1st – March 21st.

Partridge	5	Hedge Sparrow	18*
...inged Plover	1	Starling	26
Dunlin	11	Greenfinch	450
...kylark	17	Linnet	15
...melark	5	Chaffinch	16
...ng-tailed tit	5	Brambling	2
Wren	3	Yellowhammer	3
...ng thrush	21	Reed Bunting	7
...ackbird	40	Snow Bunting	15
Robin	1	House Sparrow	18*
...iffchaff	1	Tree Sparrow	3
...ldcrest	5	Total	1180

* Including re-ringed

Lightning Source UK Ltd.
Milton Keynes UK
UKHW020635290621
386339UK00009B/443

9 780999 855553